Hand of the Morningstar

Confession

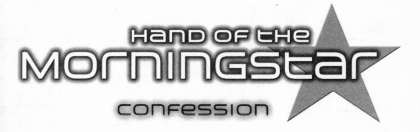

ZONDERVAN®

Confession
Copyright © 2008 by Lamp Post, Inc.

Requests for information should be addressed to:
Zondervan, *Grand Rapids, Michigan 49530*

Library of Congress Cataloging-in-Publication Data
Miller, Mike S.
 Confession / written by Mike Miller and Brett Burner ; illustrated by Eric Ninaltowski.
   p. cm. -- (Hand of the morningstar ; v. 3)
 ISBN-13: 978-0-310-71371-5 (softcover)
 ISBN-10: 0-310-71371-4 (softcover)
1. Graphic novels. I. Burner, Brett A., 1969- II. Ninaltowski, Eric. III. Title.
 PN6727.M555C66 2007
 741.5'973--dc22

                        2007030933

All Scripture quotations, unless otherwise indicated, are taken from the *Holy Bible: New International Version*®. NIV®. Copyright © 1973, 1978, 1984 by International Bible Society. Used by permission of Zondervan. All rights reserved.

All rights reserved. No part of this publication may be reproduced, stored in a retrieval system, or transmitted in any form or by any means — electronic, mechanical, photocopy, recording, or any other — except for brief quotations in printed reviews, without the prior permission of the publisher.

This book published in conjunction with Lamp Post, Inc.; 8367 Lemon Avenue, La Mesa, CA 91941

Series Editor: Bud Rogers
Managing Editor: Bruce Nuffer
Managing Art Director: Sarah Molegraaf

Printed in the United States of America

---

08 09 10 11 12 • 8 7 6 5 4 3 2 1

HAND OF THE MORNINGStar
CONFESSION

> HE WILL BRING TO LIGHT WHAT IS HIDDEN IN
> THE DARKNESS AND WILL EXPOSE THE
> MOTIVES OF MEN'S HEARTS.
> —1 CORINTHIANS 4:5

SERIES EDITOR: BUD ROGERS
STORY BY BRETT BURNER AND MIKE MILLER
ART BY ERIC NINALTOWSKI
TONES BY DIEGO CANDIA
CREATED BY BRETT BURNER

ZONDERVAN®

ZONDERVAN.com/
AUTHORTRACKER
follow your favorite authors

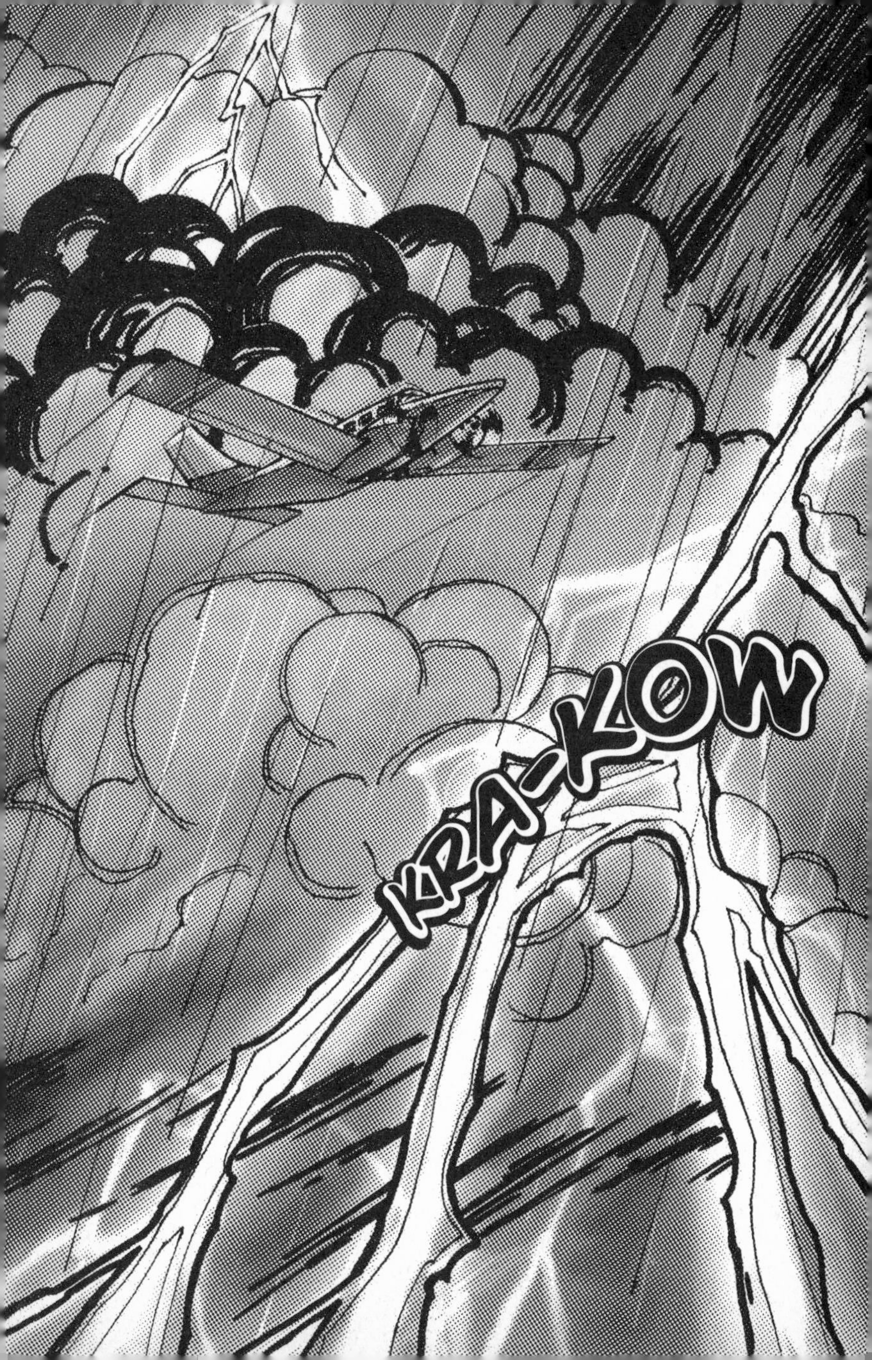
KRA-KOW

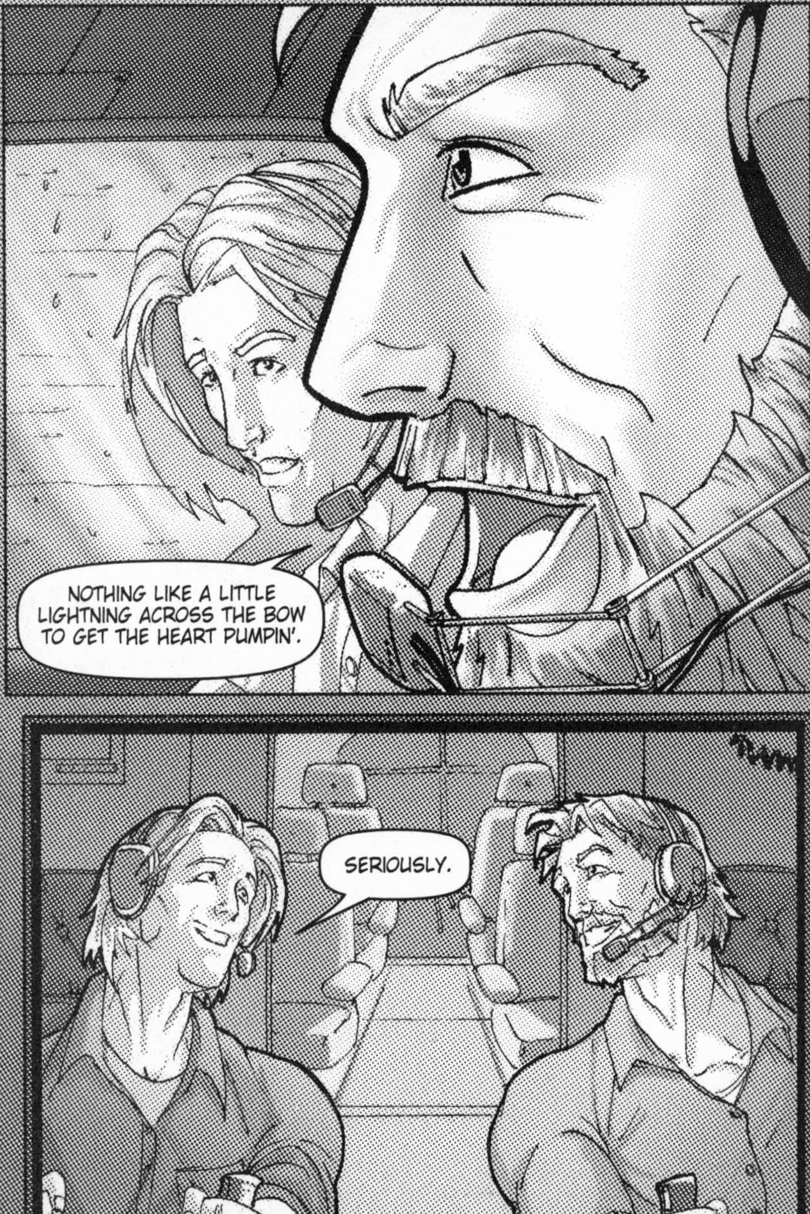
NOTHING LIKE A LITTLE LIGHTNING ACROSS THE BOW TO GET THE HEART PUMPIN'.
SERIOUSLY.

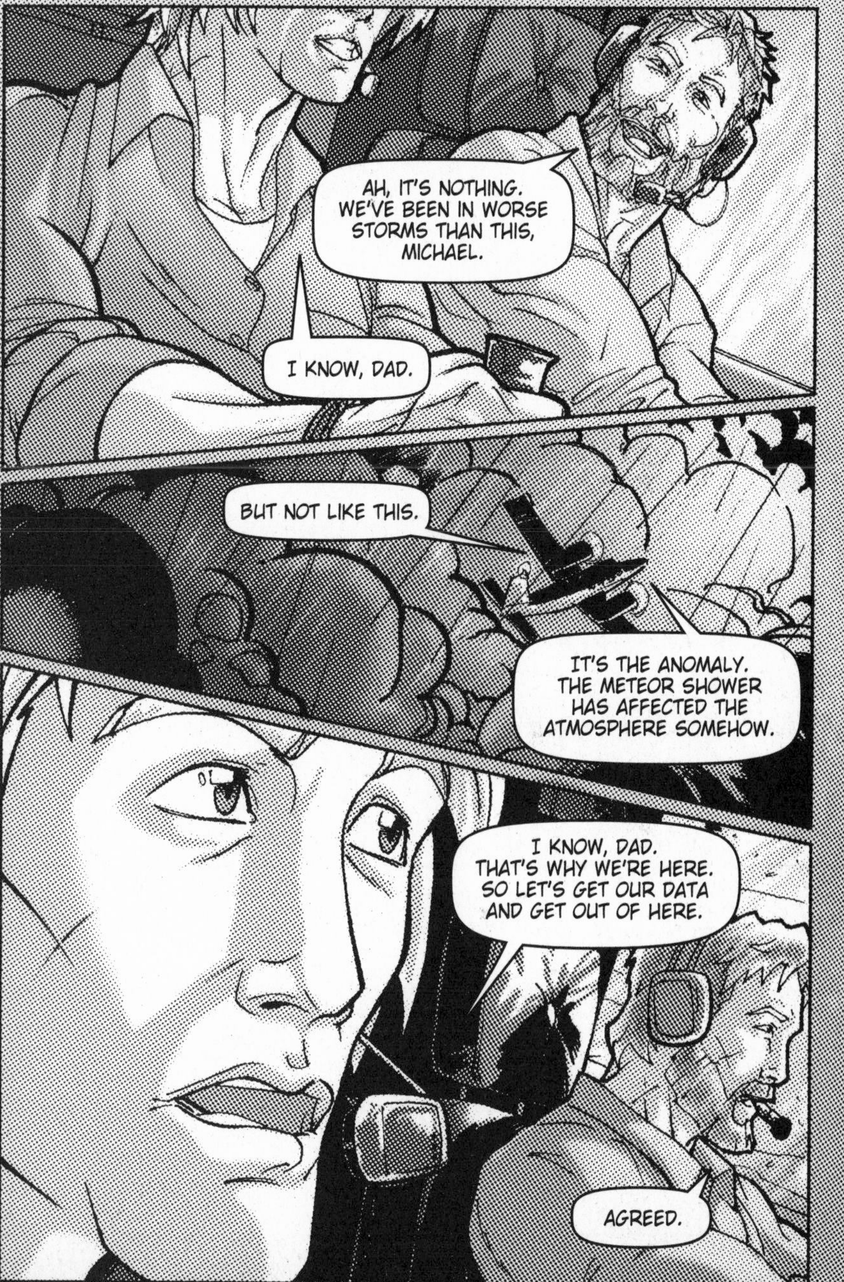
AH, IT'S NOTHING. WE'VE BEEN IN WORSE STORMS THAN THIS, MICHAEL.
I KNOW, DAD.
BUT NOT LIKE THIS.
IT'S THE ANOMALY. THE METEOR SHOWER HAS AFFECTED THE ATMOSPHERE SOMEHOW.
I KNOW, DAD. THAT'S WHY WE'RE HERE. SO LET'S GET OUR DATA AND GET OUT OF HERE.
AGREED.

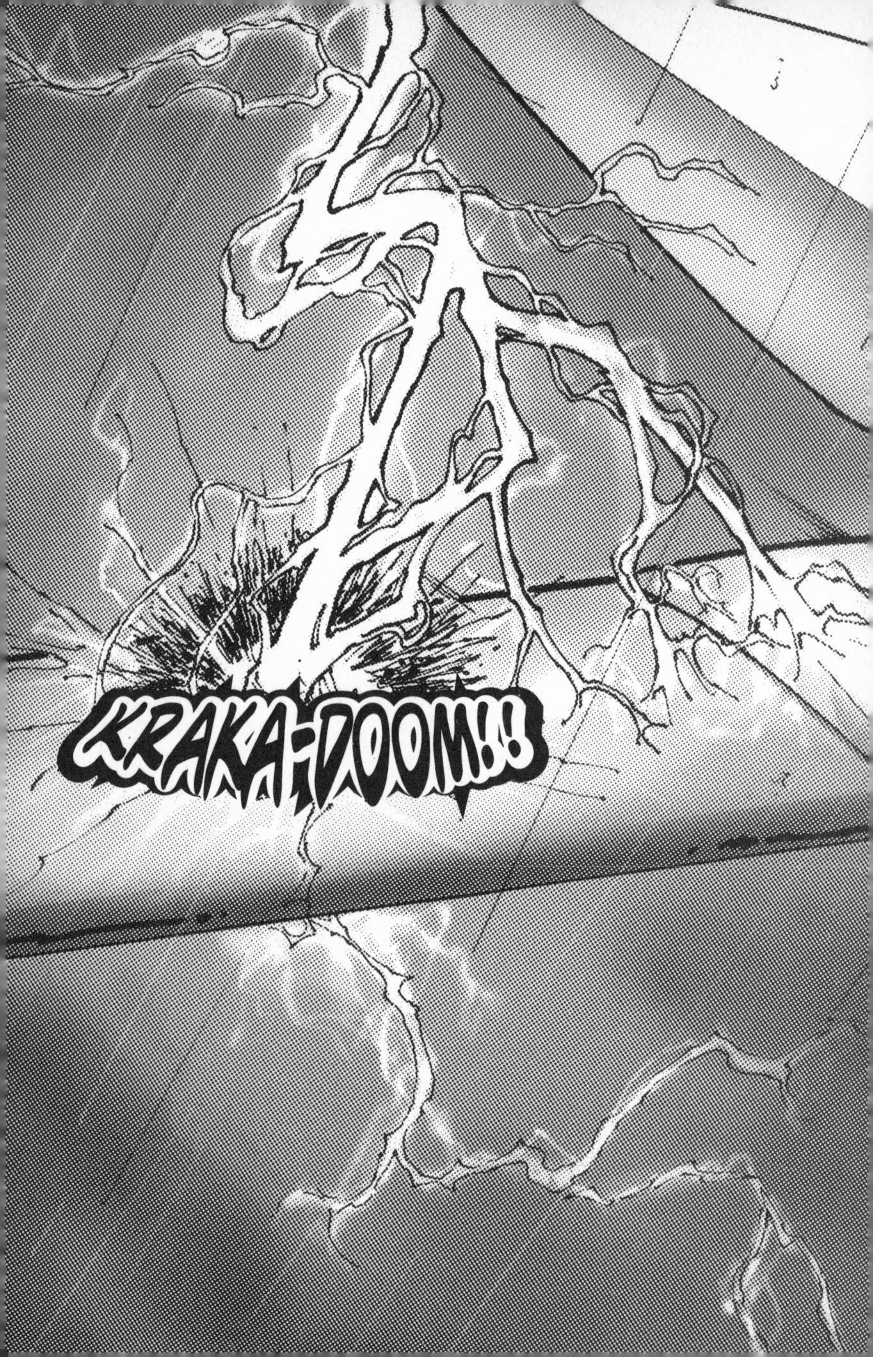
KRAKA-DOOM!!

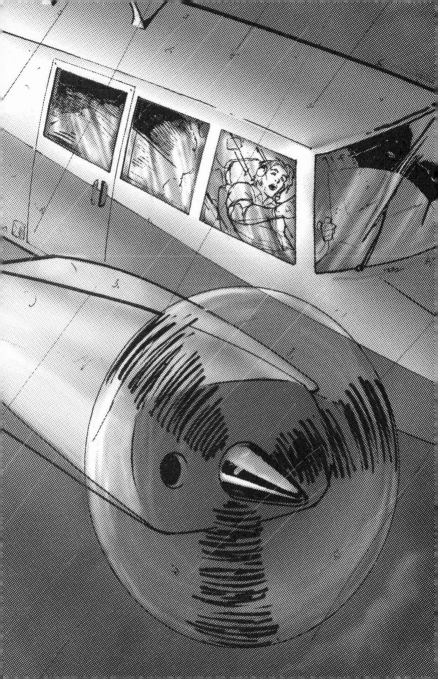

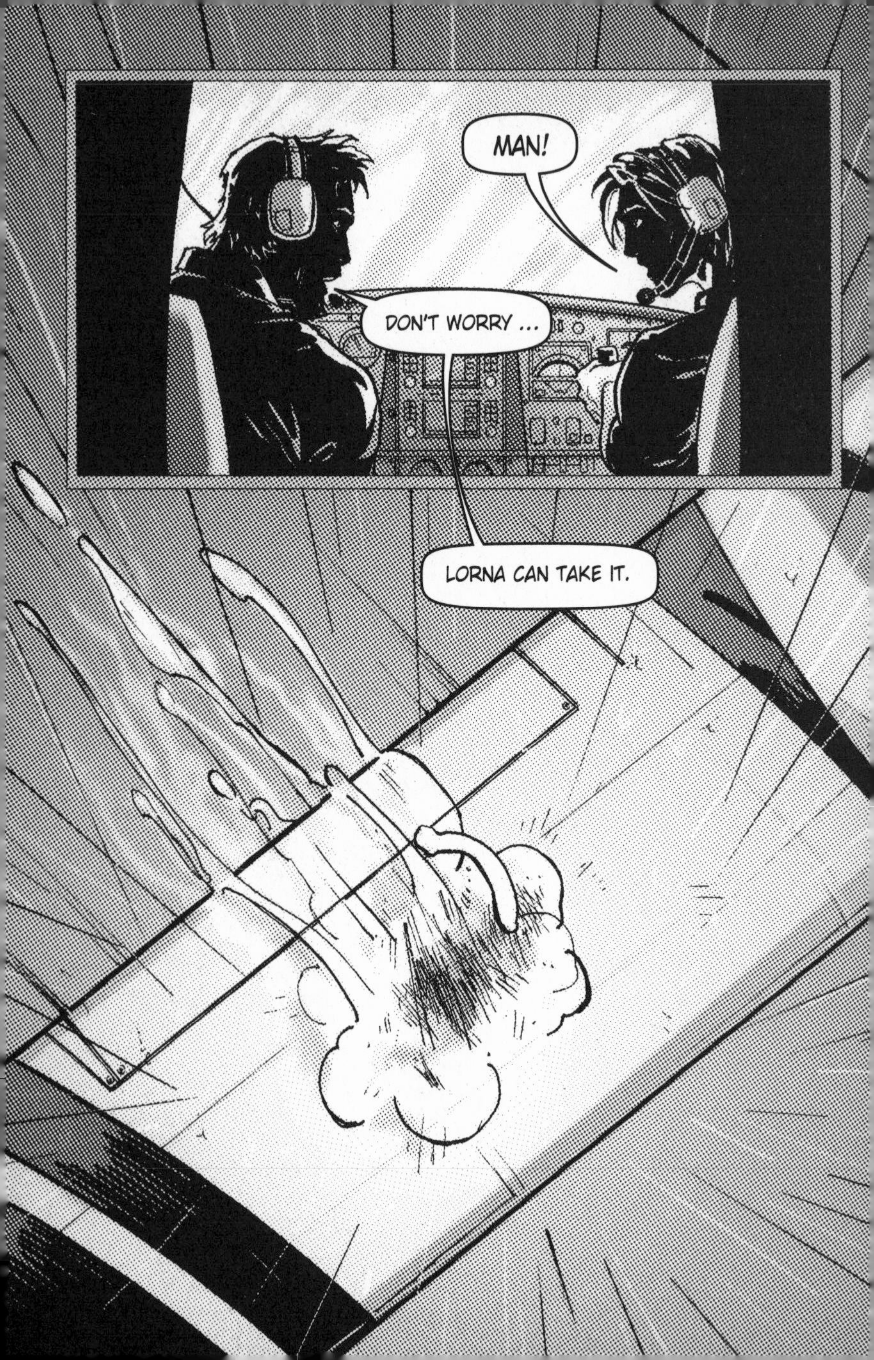
MAN!
DON'T WORRY ...
LORNA CAN TAKE IT.

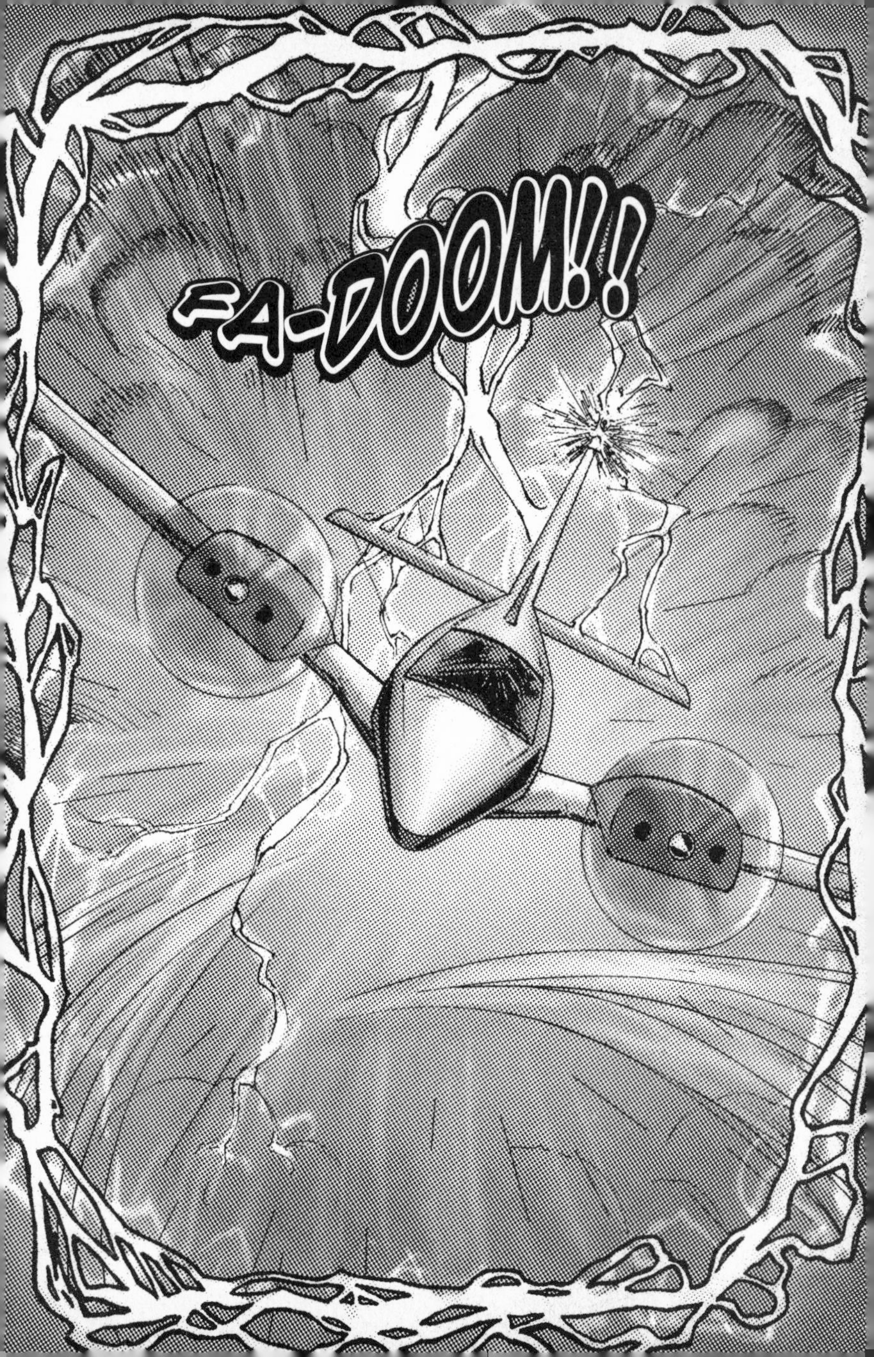
KA-DOOM!!

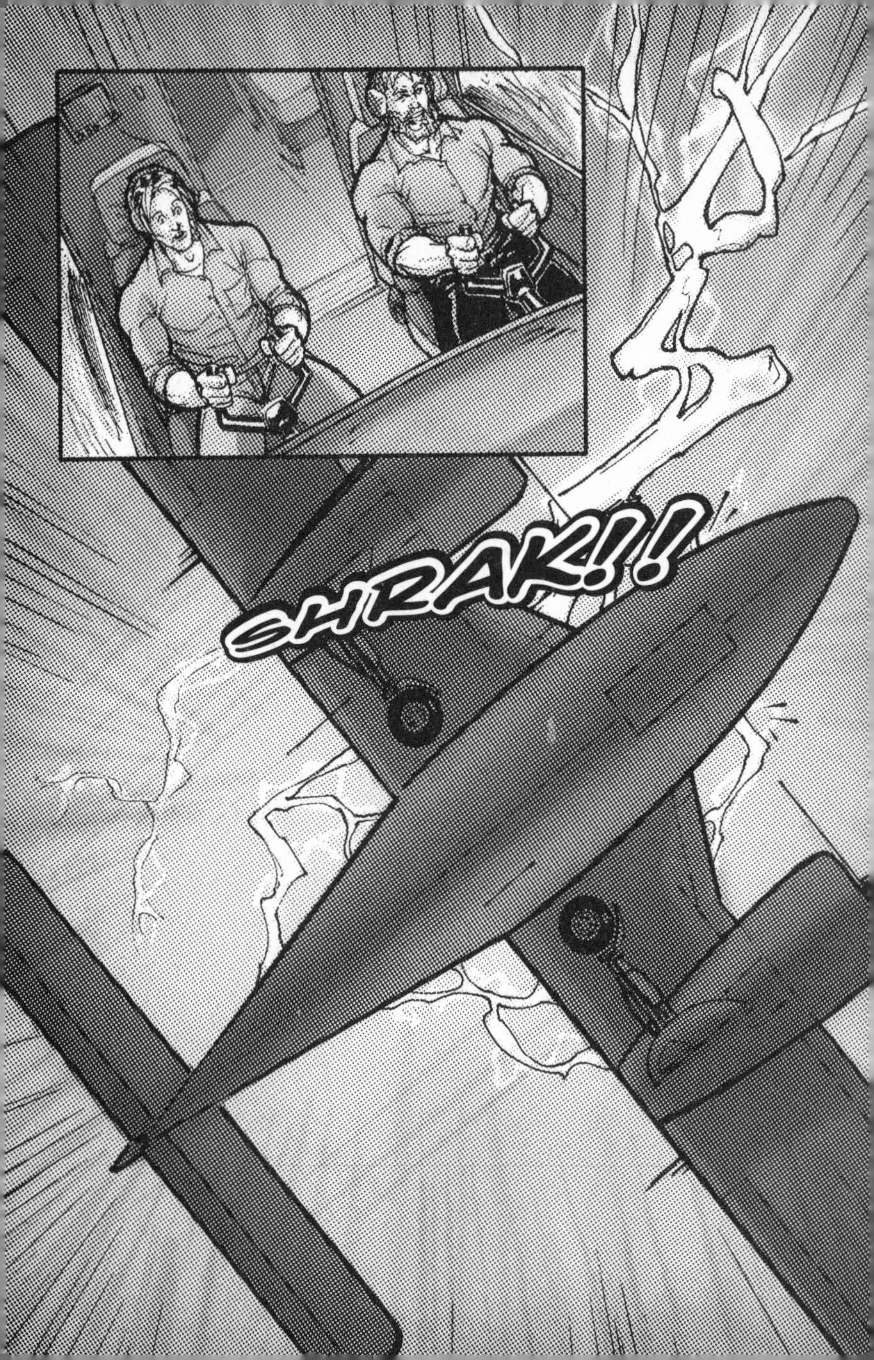
SHRAK!!

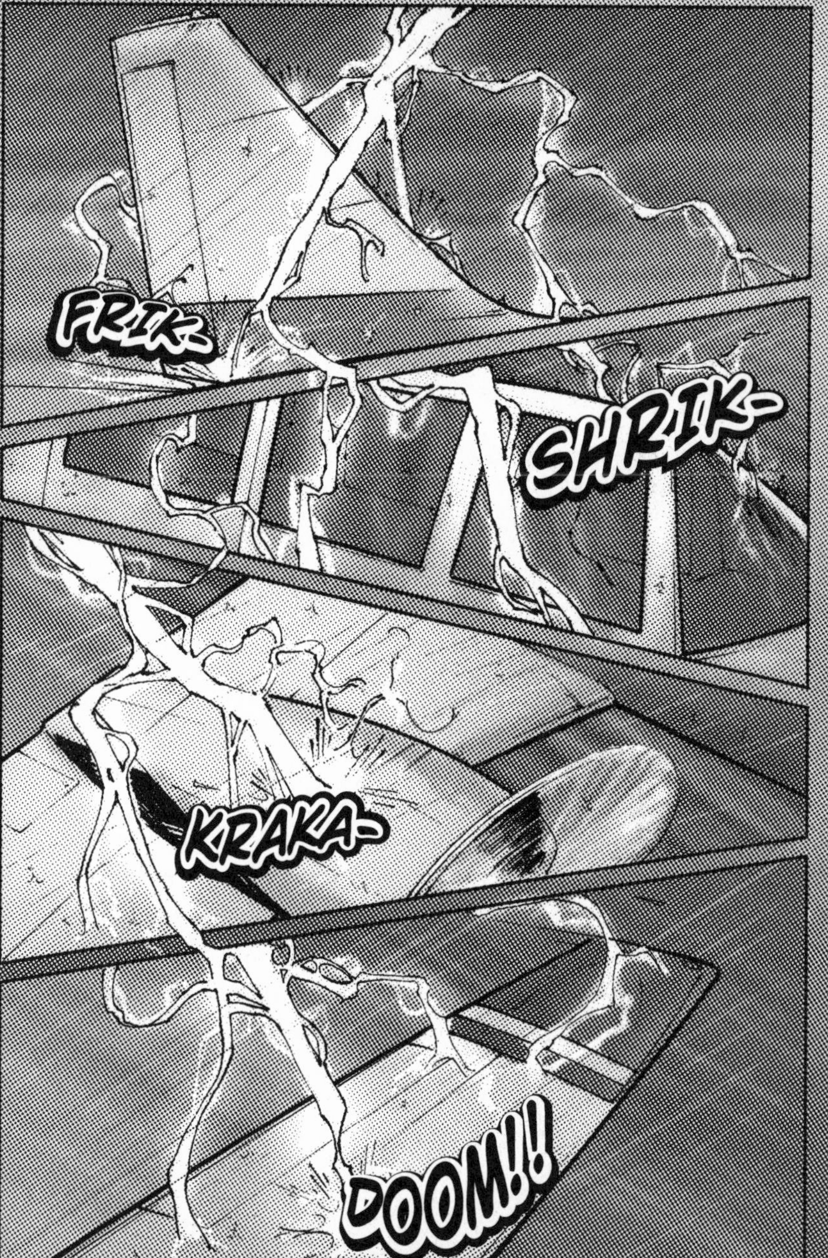
FRIK-
SHRIK-
KRAKA-
DOOM!!

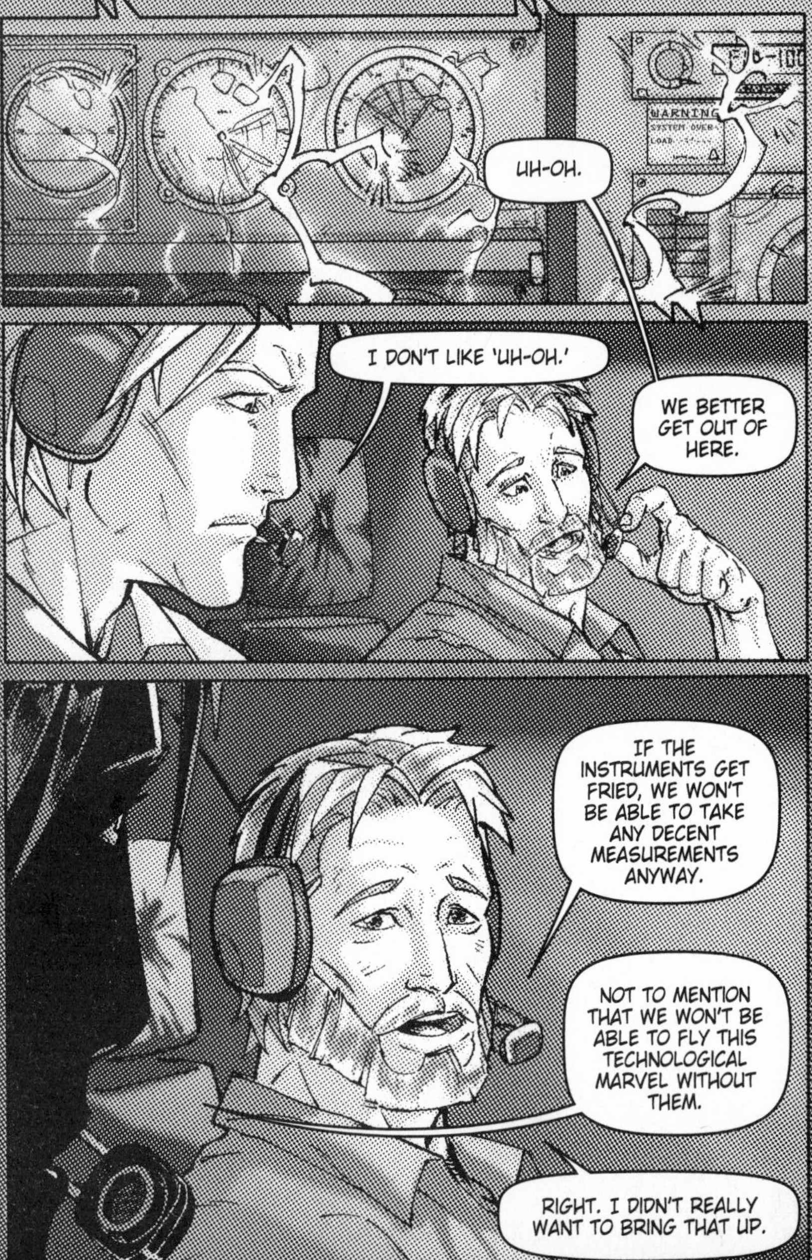
WARNING
SYSTEM OVER-
LOAD
UH-OH.
I DON'T LIKE 'UH-OH.'
WE BETTER GET OUT OF HERE.
IF THE INSTRUMENTS GET FRIED, WE WON'T BE ABLE TO TAKE ANY DECENT MEASUREMENTS ANYWAY.
NOT TO MENTION THAT WE WON'T BE ABLE TO FLY THIS TECHNOLOGICAL MARVEL WITHOUT THEM.
RIGHT. I DIDN'T REALLY WANT TO BRING THAT UP.

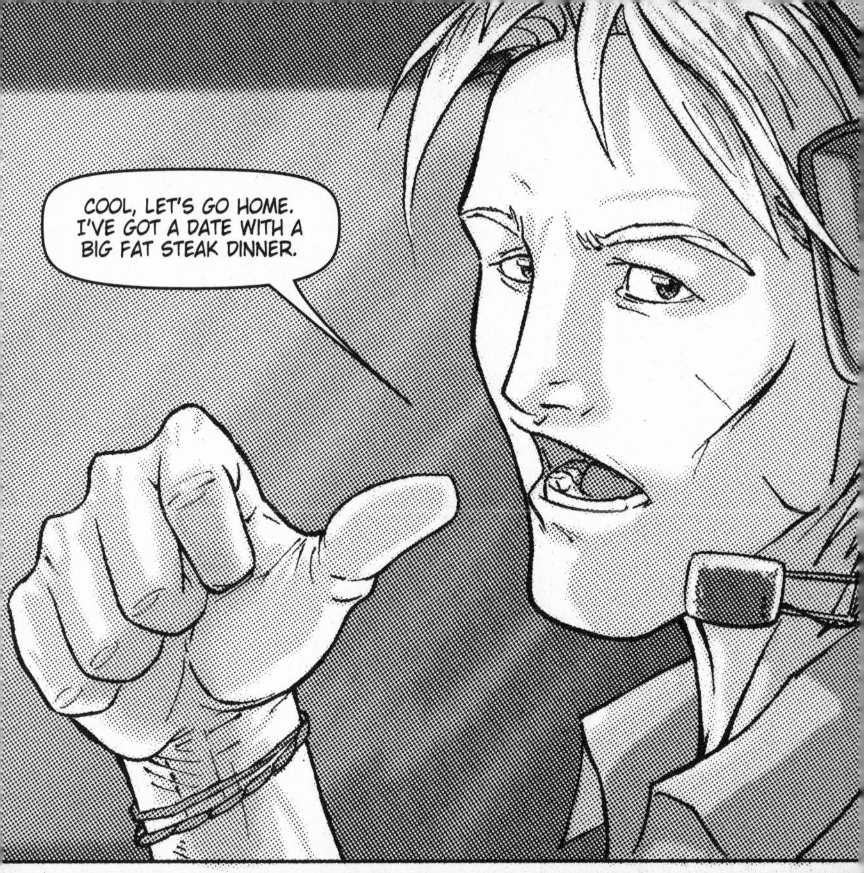
COOL, LET'S GO HOME. I'VE GOT A DATE WITH A BIG FAT STEAK DINNER.

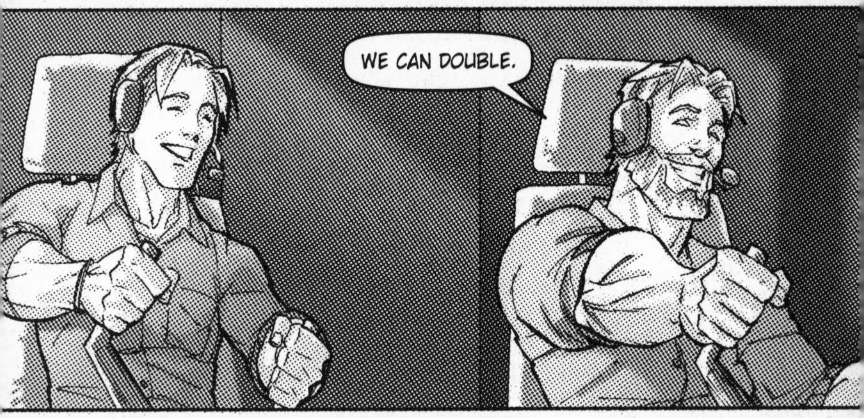
WE CAN DOUBLE.

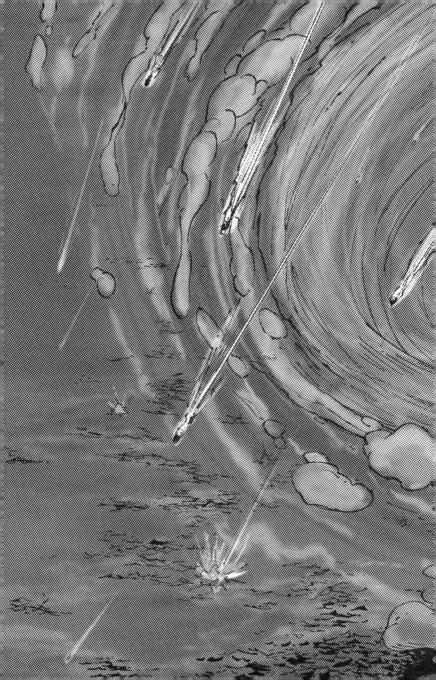

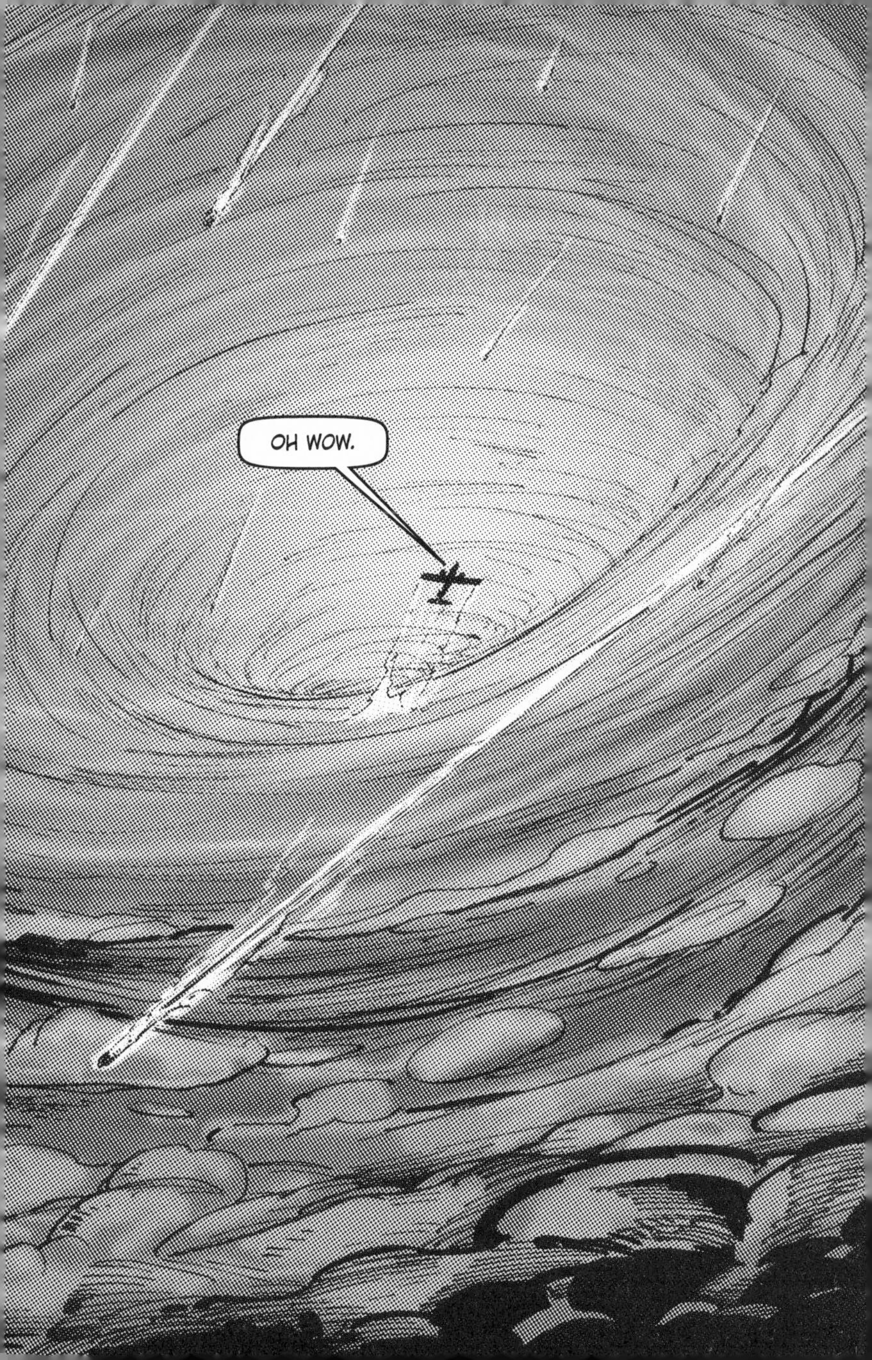
OH WOW.

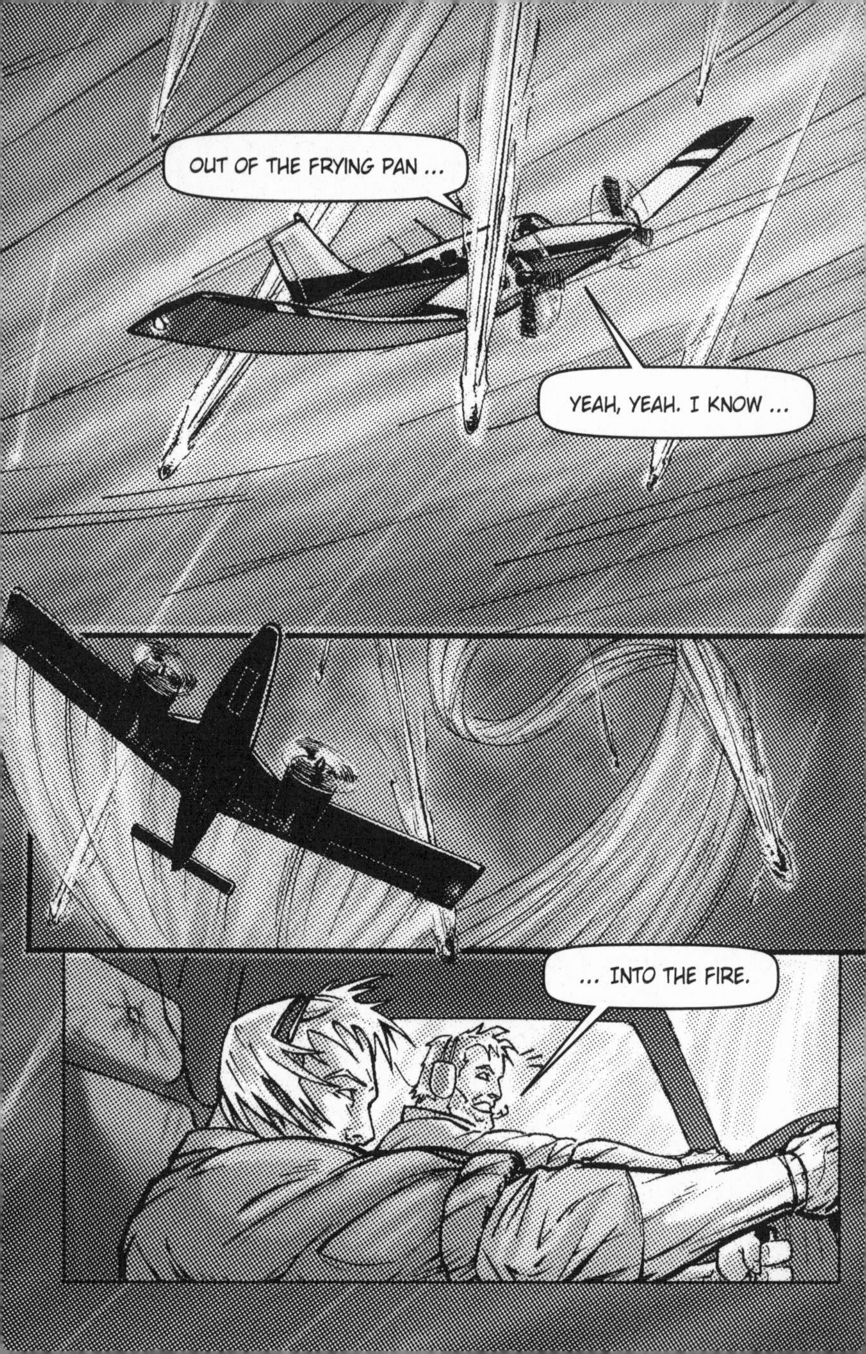
OUT OF THE FRYING PAN ...
YEAH, YEAH. I KNOW ...
... INTO THE FIRE.

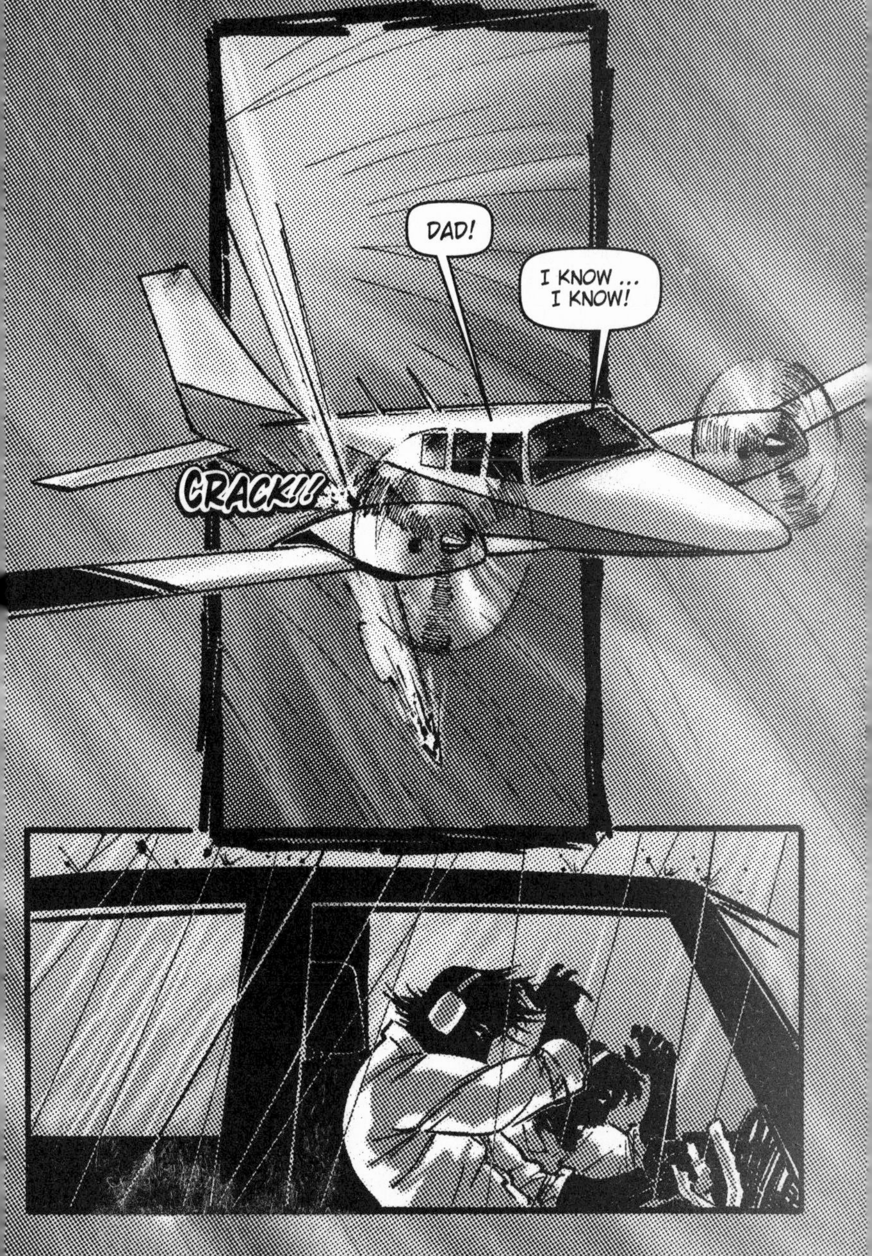
DAD!
I KNOW ... I KNOW!
CRACK!!

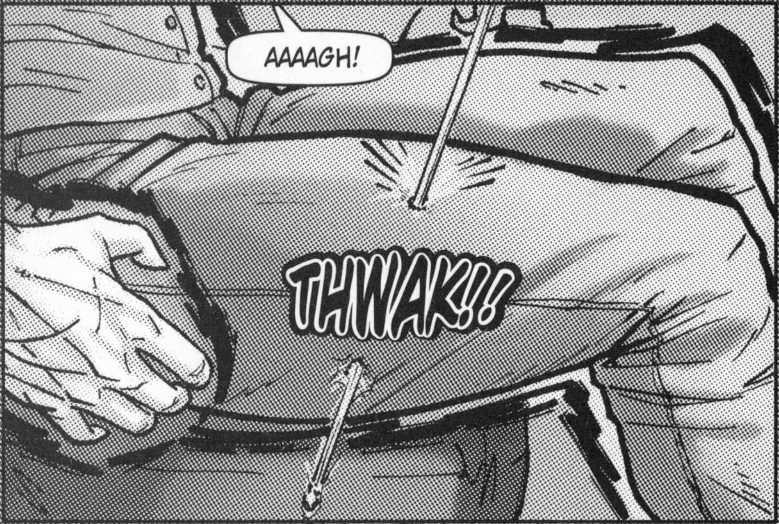
AAAAGH!
THWAK!!!
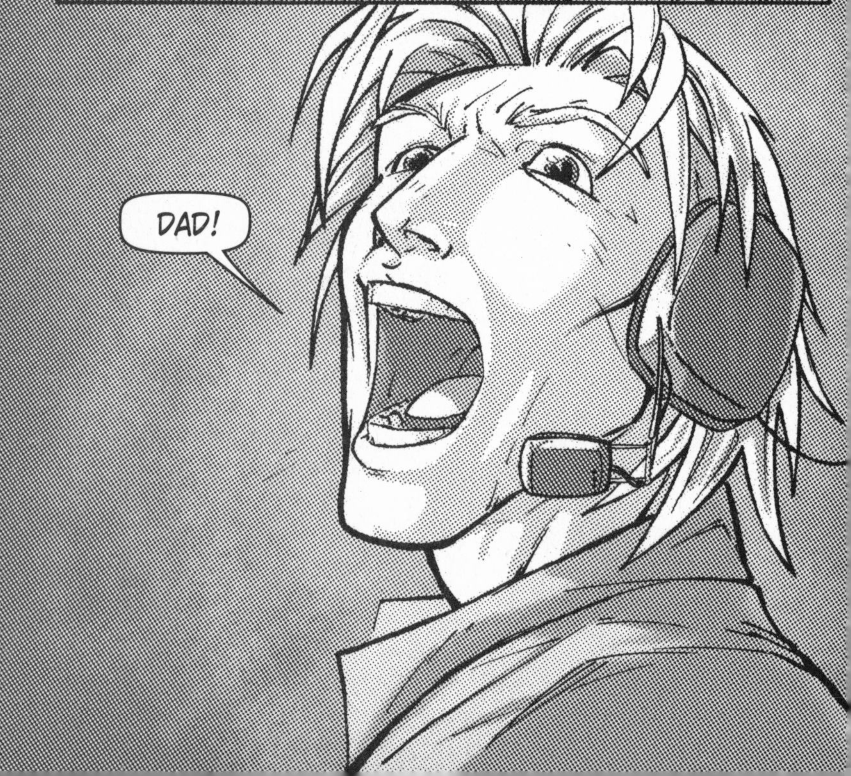
DAD!

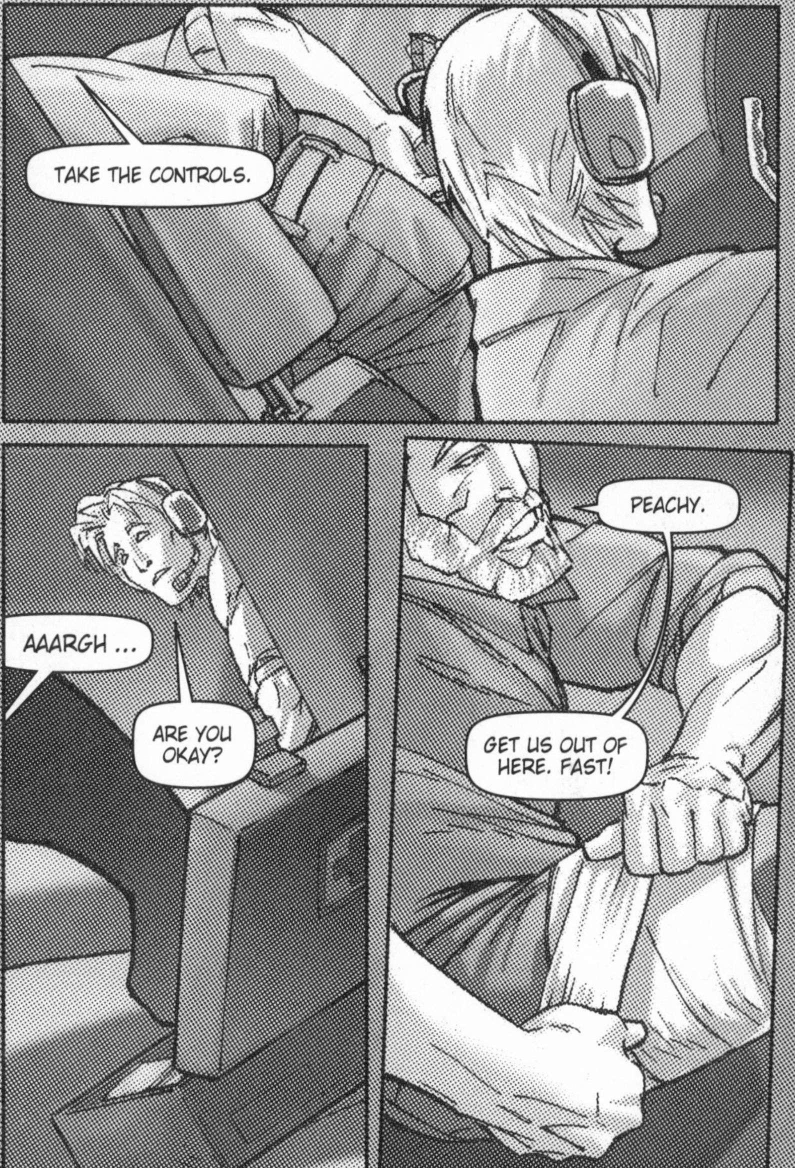
TAKE THE CONTROLS.
AAARGH ...
ARE YOU OKAY?
PEACHY.
GET US OUT OF HERE. FAST!

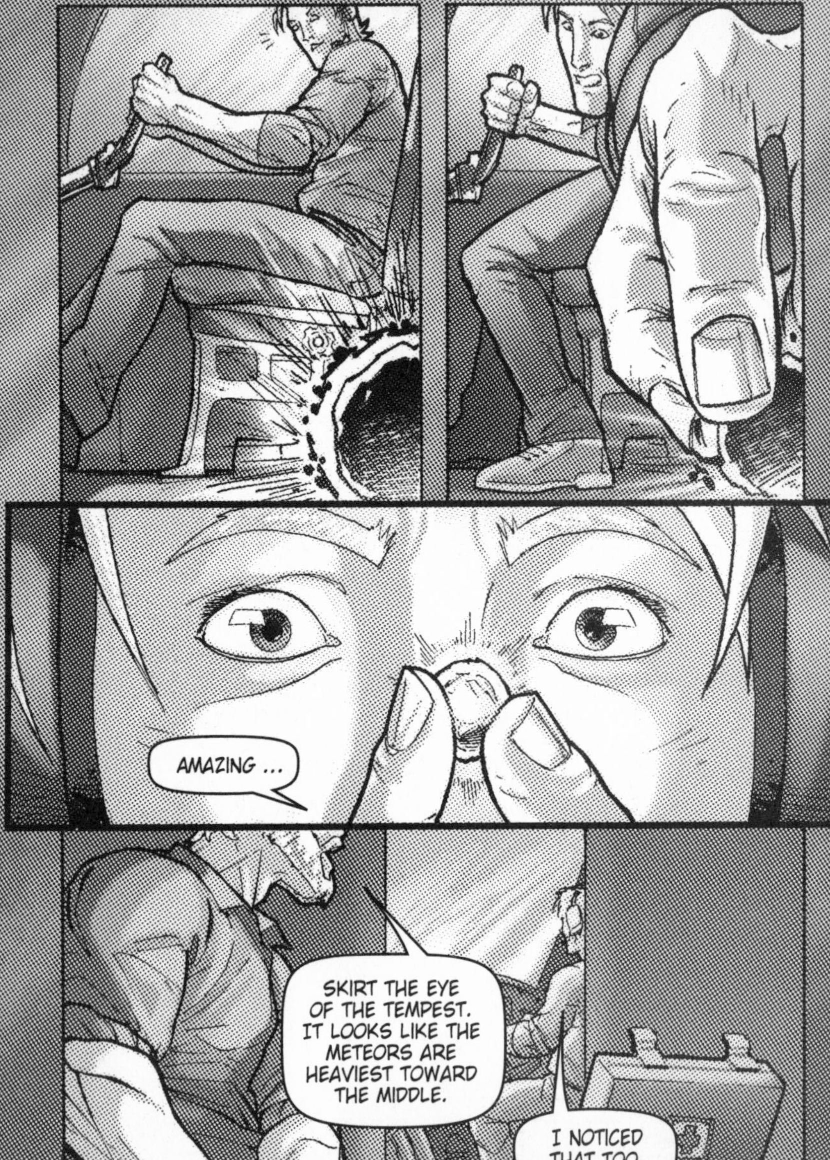
AMAZING ...
SKIRT THE EYE OF THE TEMPEST. IT LOOKS LIKE THE METEORS ARE HEAVIEST TOWARD THE MIDDLE.
I NOTICED THAT TOO.

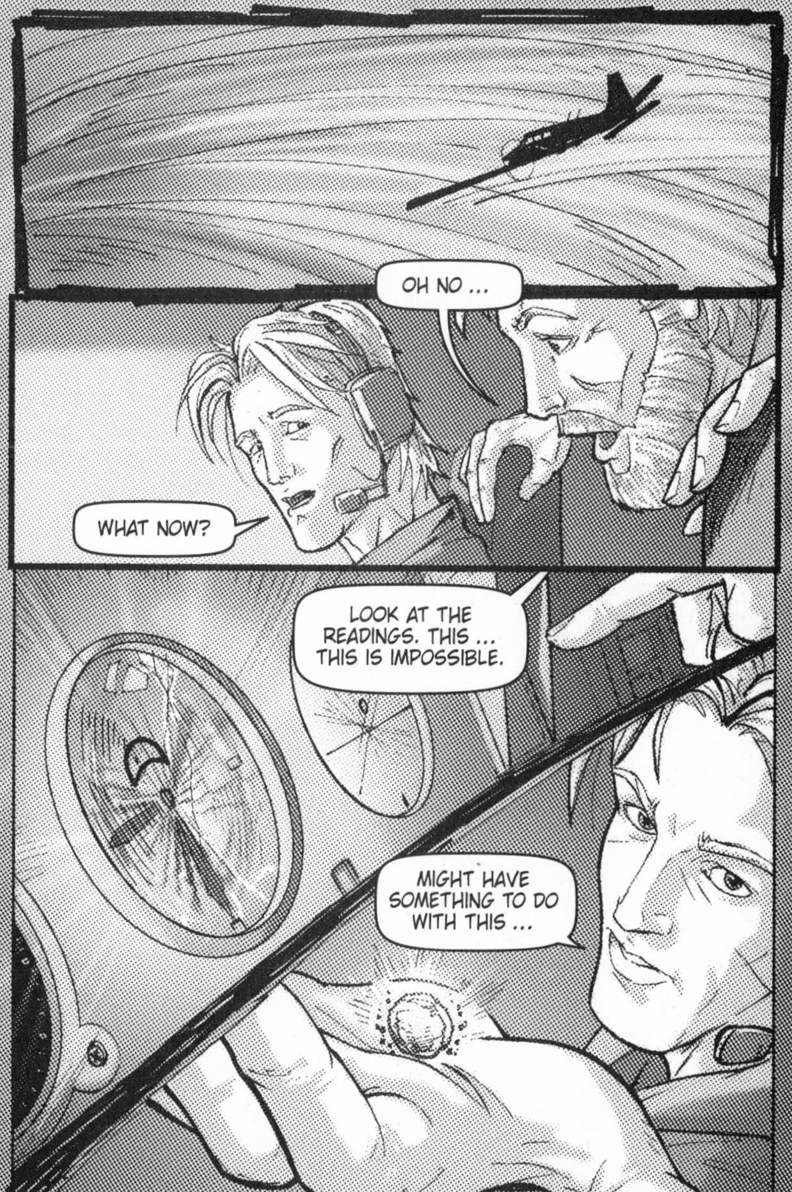
OH NO ...
WHAT NOW?
LOOK AT THE READINGS. THIS ... THIS IS IMPOSSIBLE.
MIGHT HAVE SOMETHING TO DO WITH THIS ...

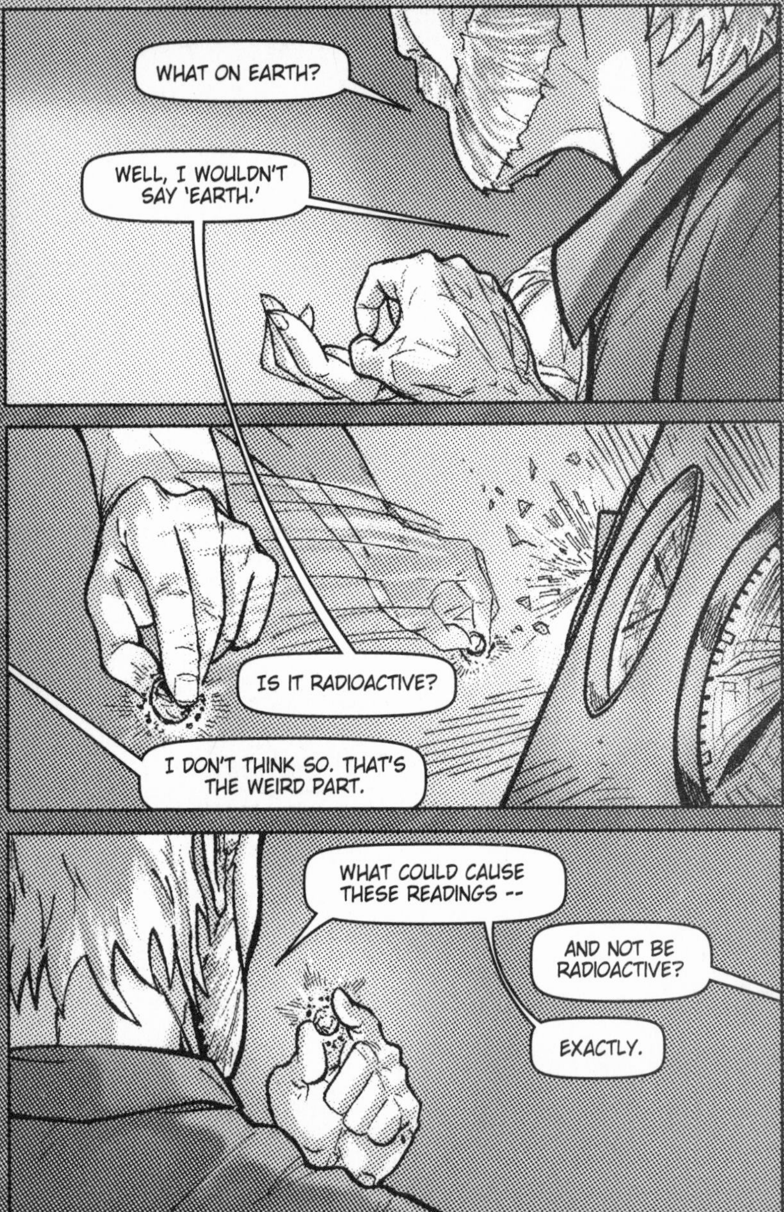
WHAT ON EARTH?
WELL, I WOULDN'T SAY 'EARTH.'
IS IT RADIOACTIVE?
I DON'T THINK SO. THAT'S THE WEIRD PART.
WHAT COULD CAUSE THESE READINGS --
AND NOT BE RADIOACTIVE?
EXACTLY.

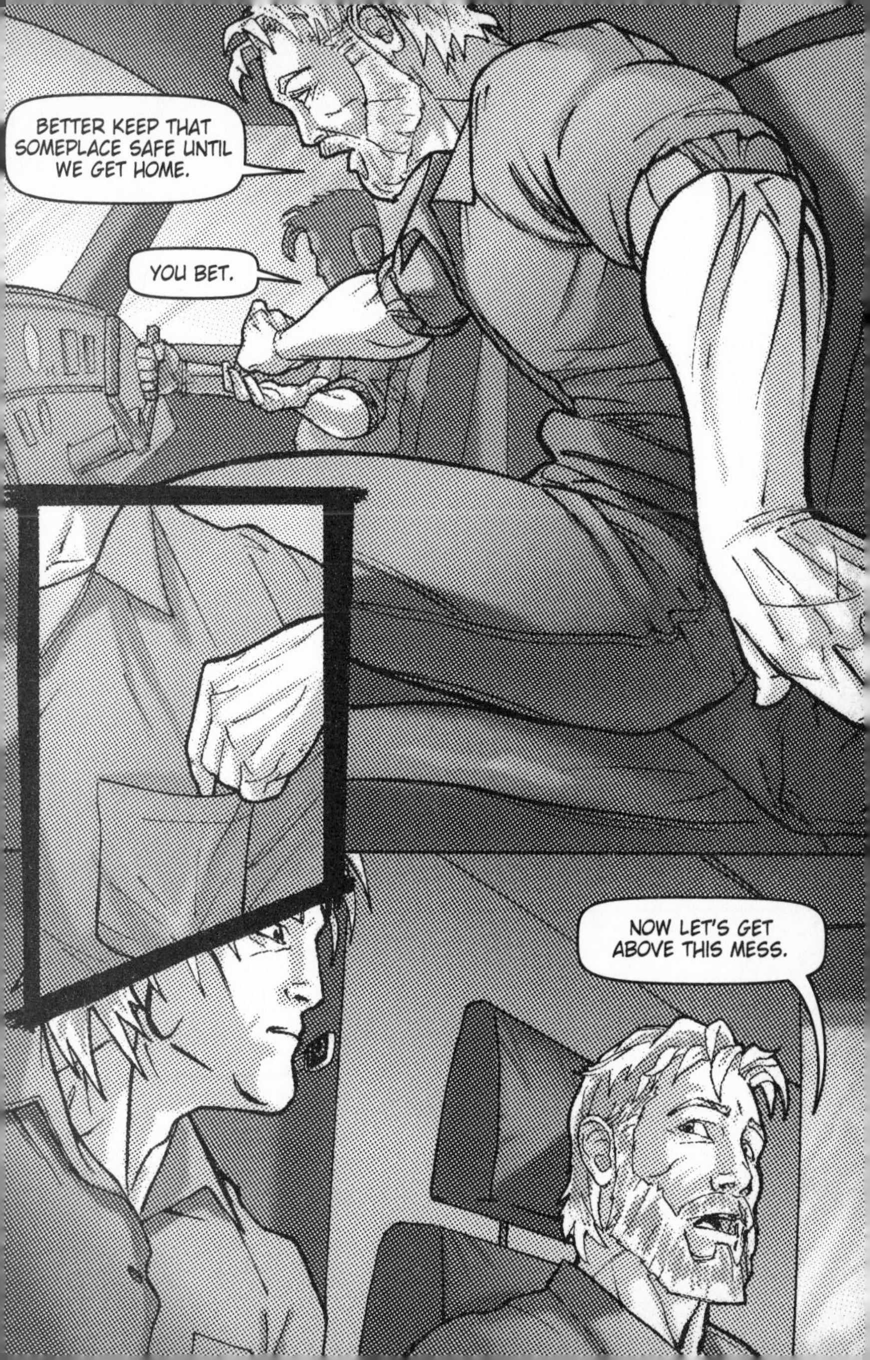
BETTER KEEP THAT SOMEPLACE SAFE UNTIL WE GET HOME.
YOU BET.
NOW LET'S GET ABOVE THIS MESS.

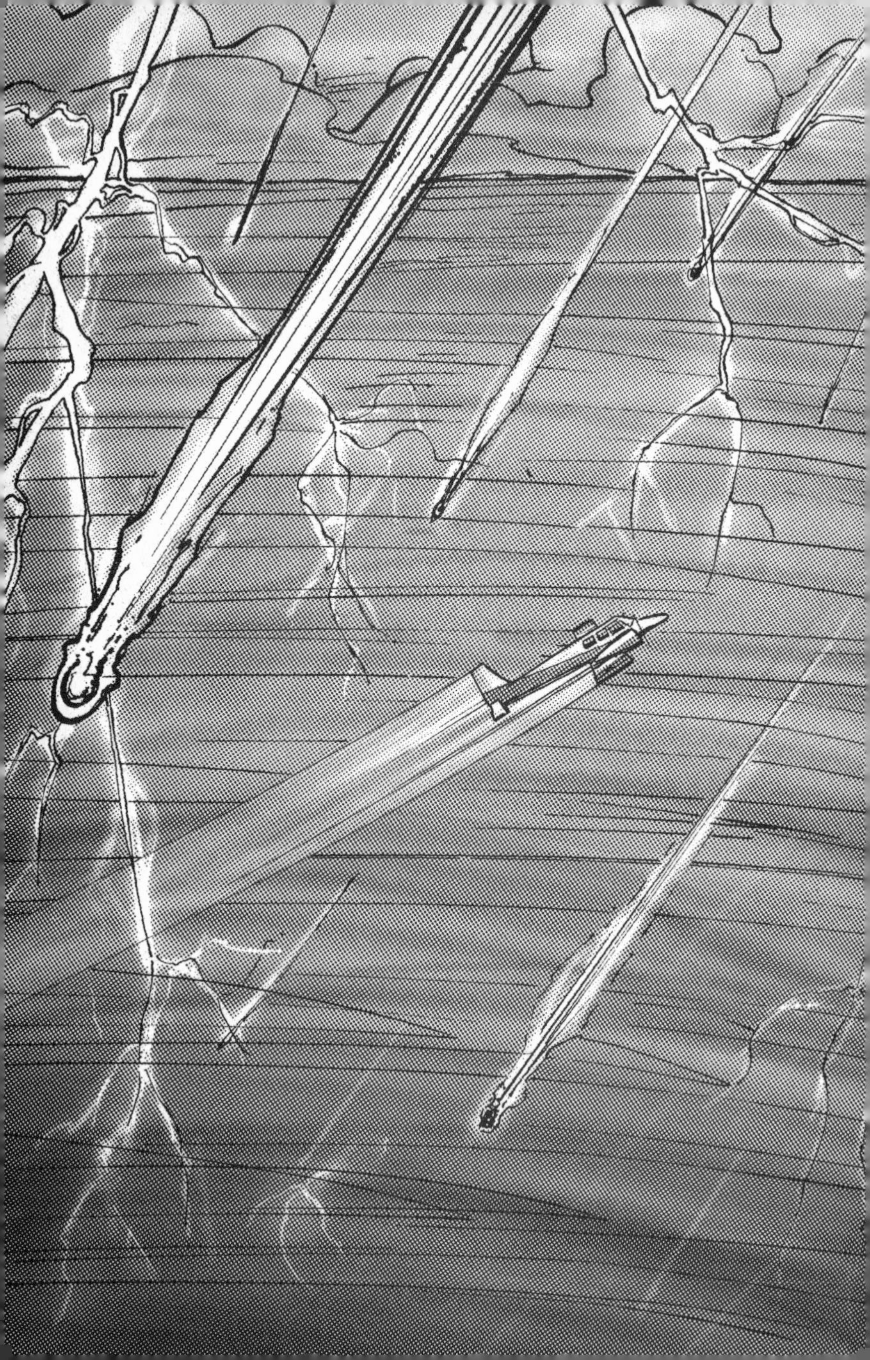

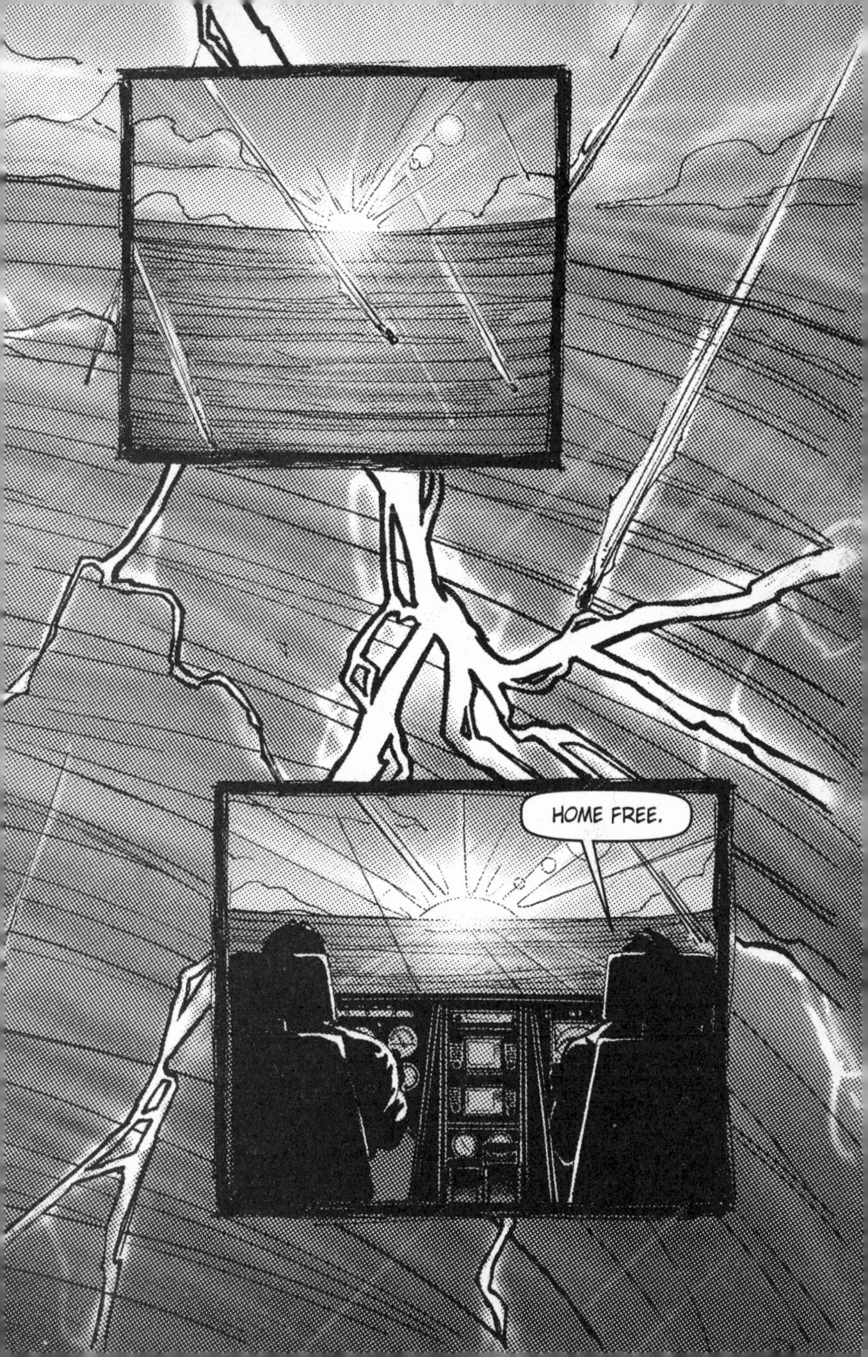
HOME FREE.

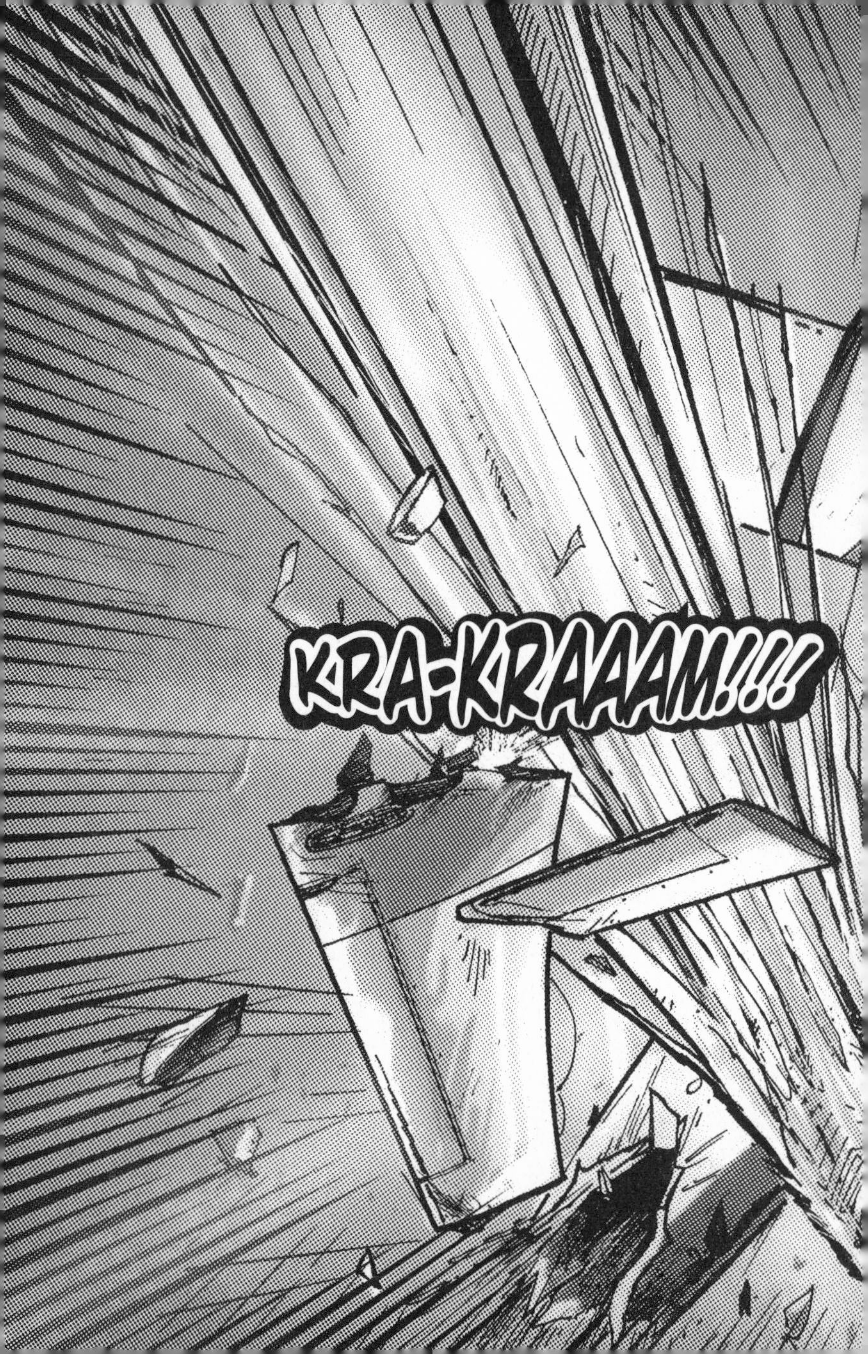
KRA-KRAAAM!!!

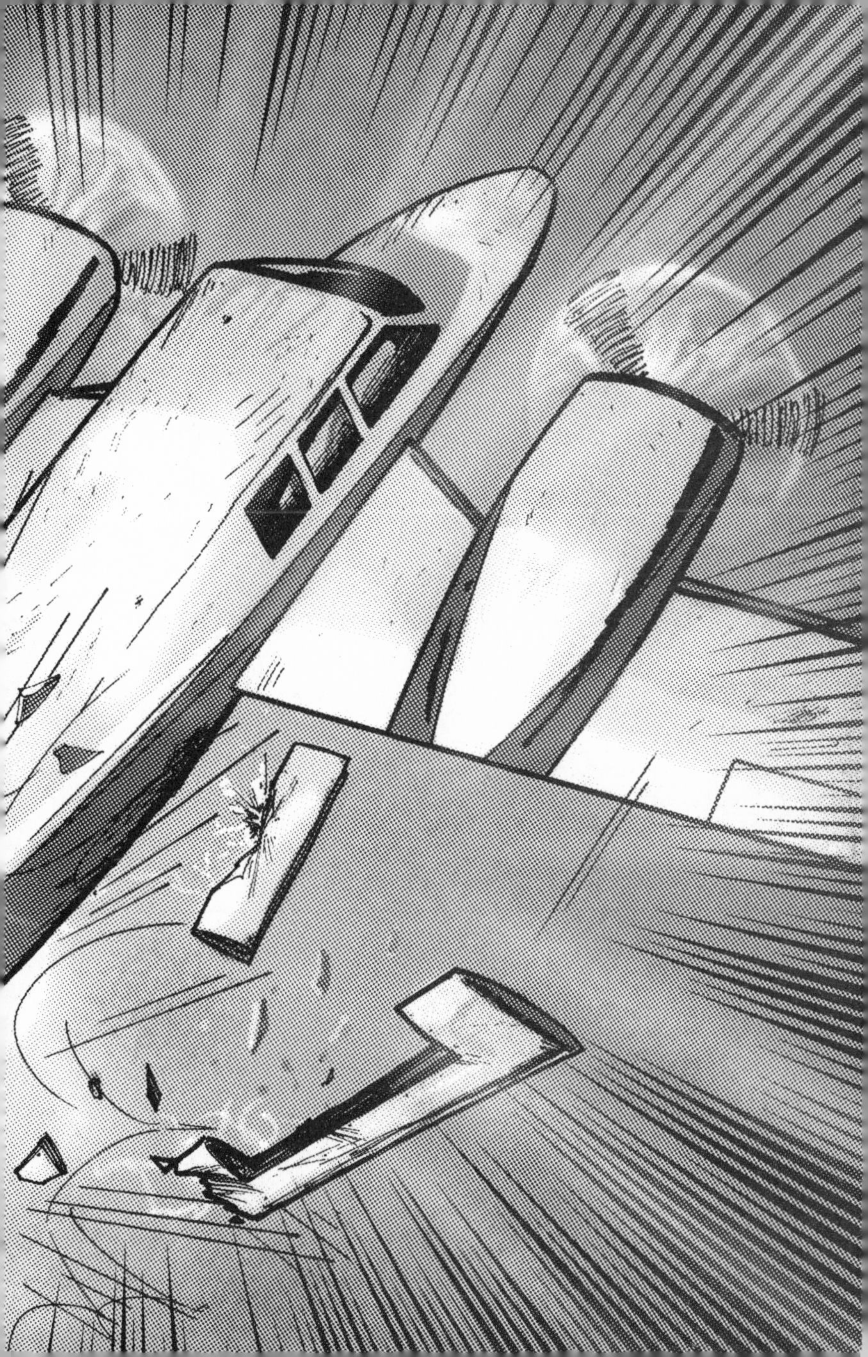

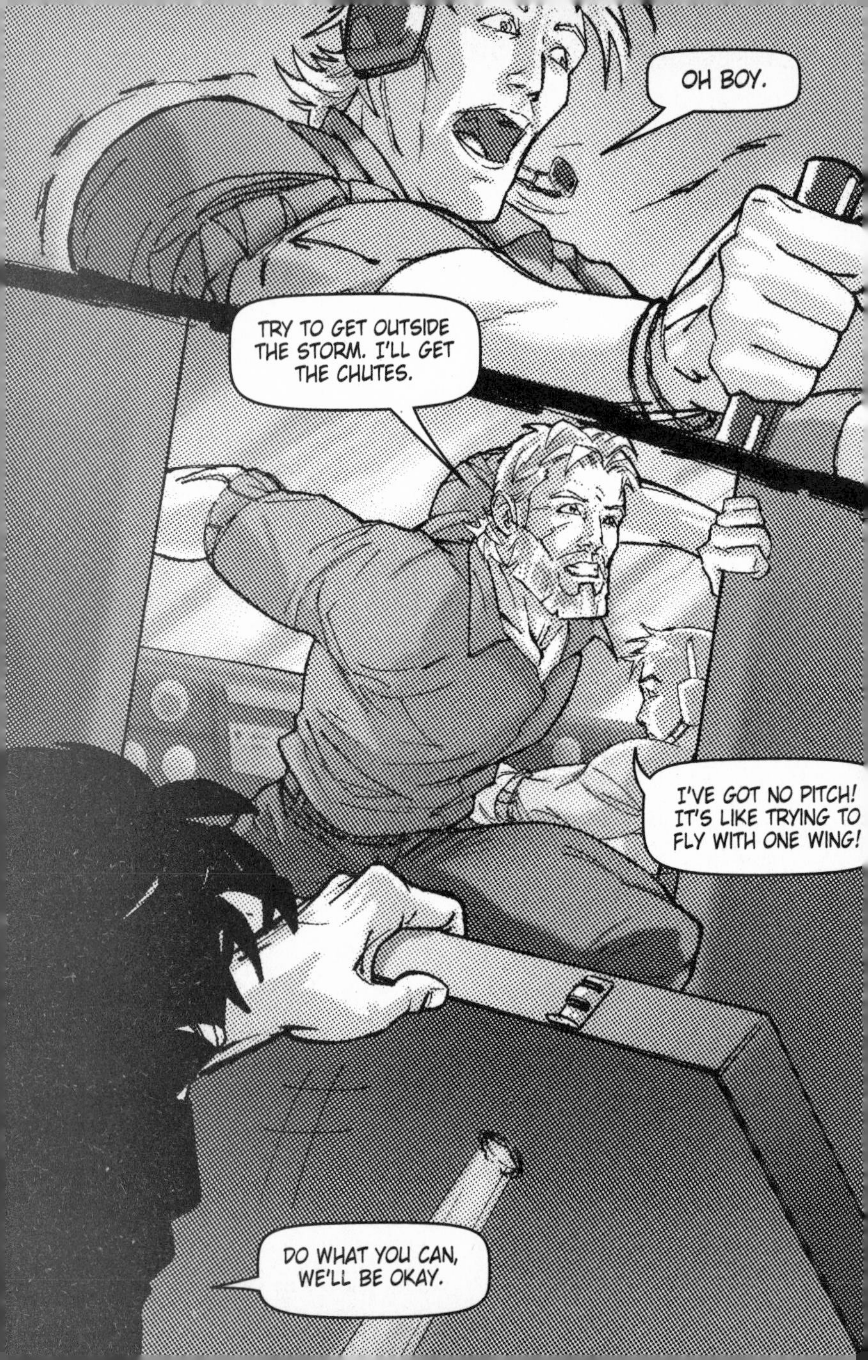
OH BOY.
TRY TO GET OUTSIDE THE STORM. I'LL GET THE CHUTES.
I'VE GOT NO PITCH! IT'S LIKE TRYING TO FLY WITH ONE WING!
DO WHAT YOU CAN, WE'LL BE OKAY.

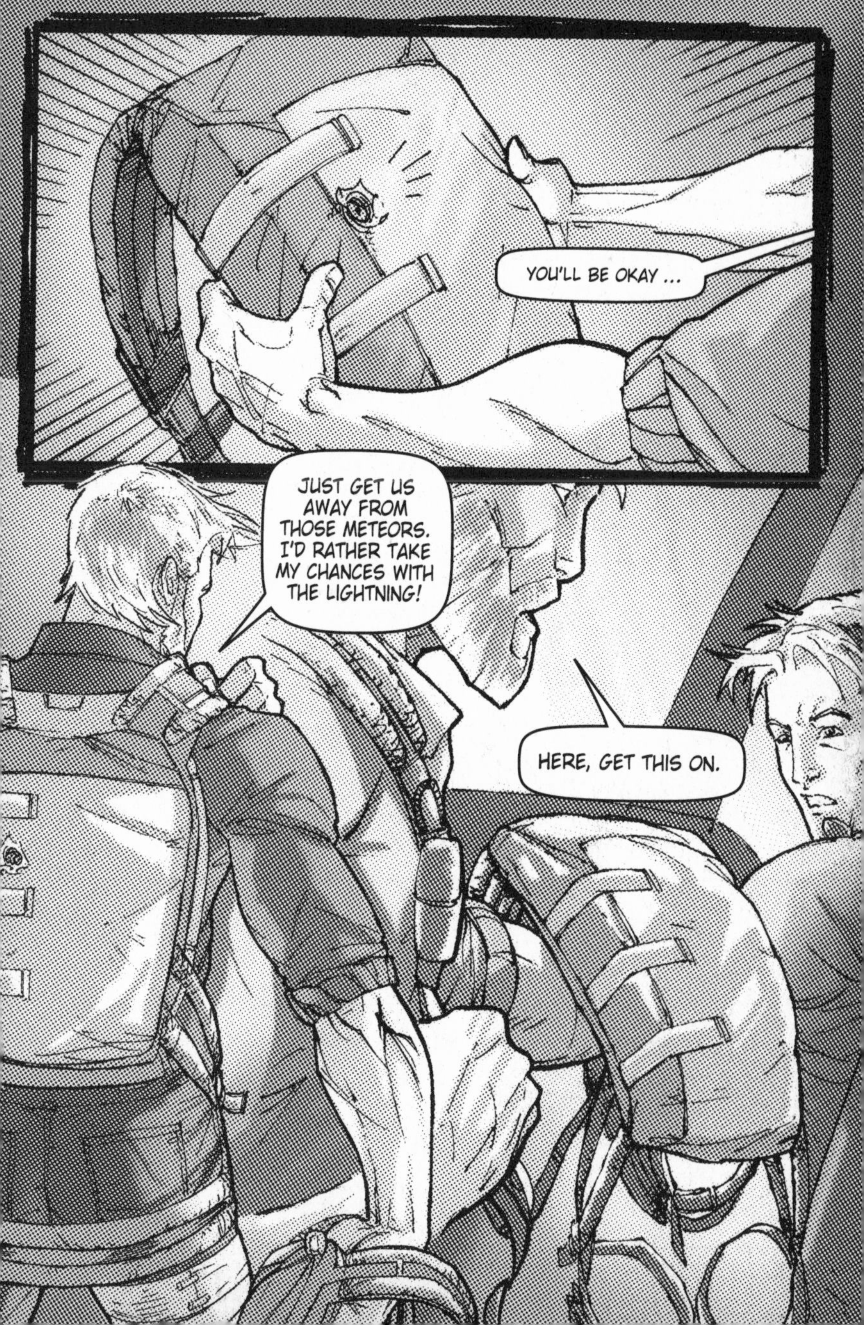
YOU'LL BE OKAY ...
JUST GET US AWAY FROM THOSE METEORS. I'D RATHER TAKE MY CHANCES WITH THE LIGHTNING!
HERE, GET THIS ON.

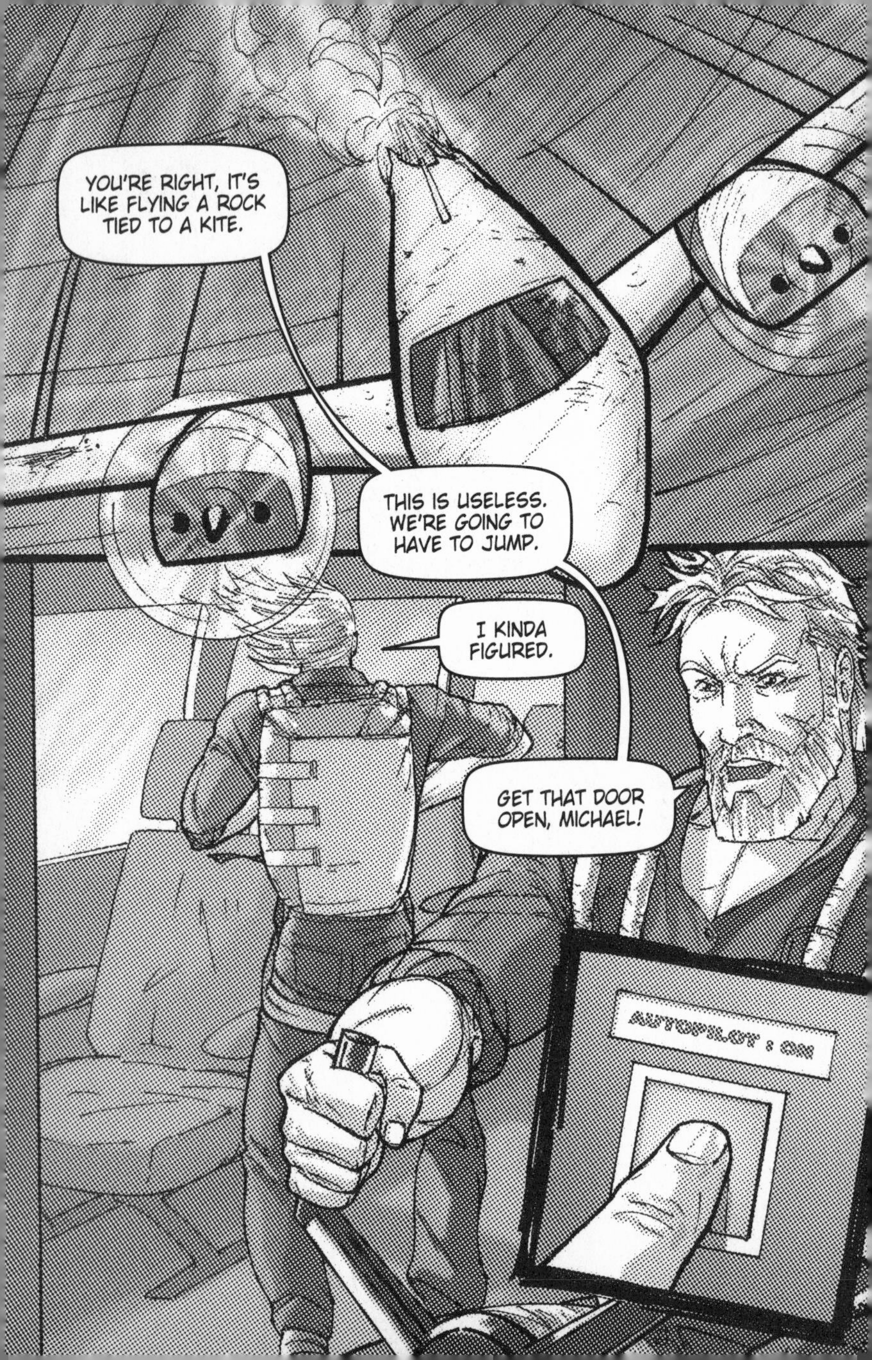
YOU'RE RIGHT, IT'S LIKE FLYING A ROCK TIED TO A KITE.
THIS IS USELESS. WE'RE GOING TO HAVE TO JUMP.
I KINDA FIGURED.
GET THAT DOOR OPEN, MICHAEL!
AUTOPILOT : ON

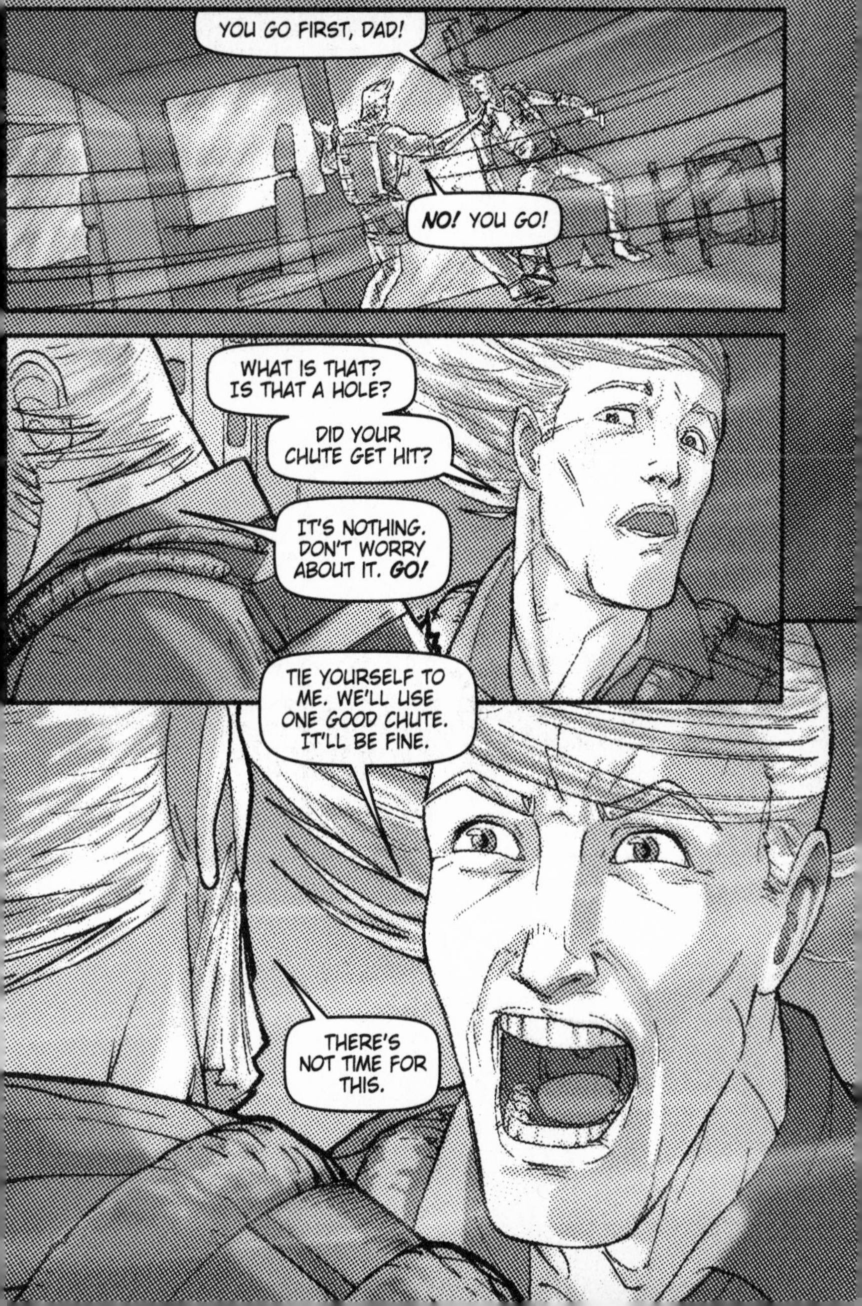
YOU GO FIRST, DAD!
NO! YOU GO!
WHAT IS THAT? IS THAT A HOLE?
DID YOUR CHUTE GET HIT?
IT'S NOTHING. DON'T WORRY ABOUT IT. GO!
TIE YOURSELF TO ME. WE'LL USE ONE GOOD CHUTE. IT'LL BE FINE.
THERE'S NOT TIME FOR THIS.

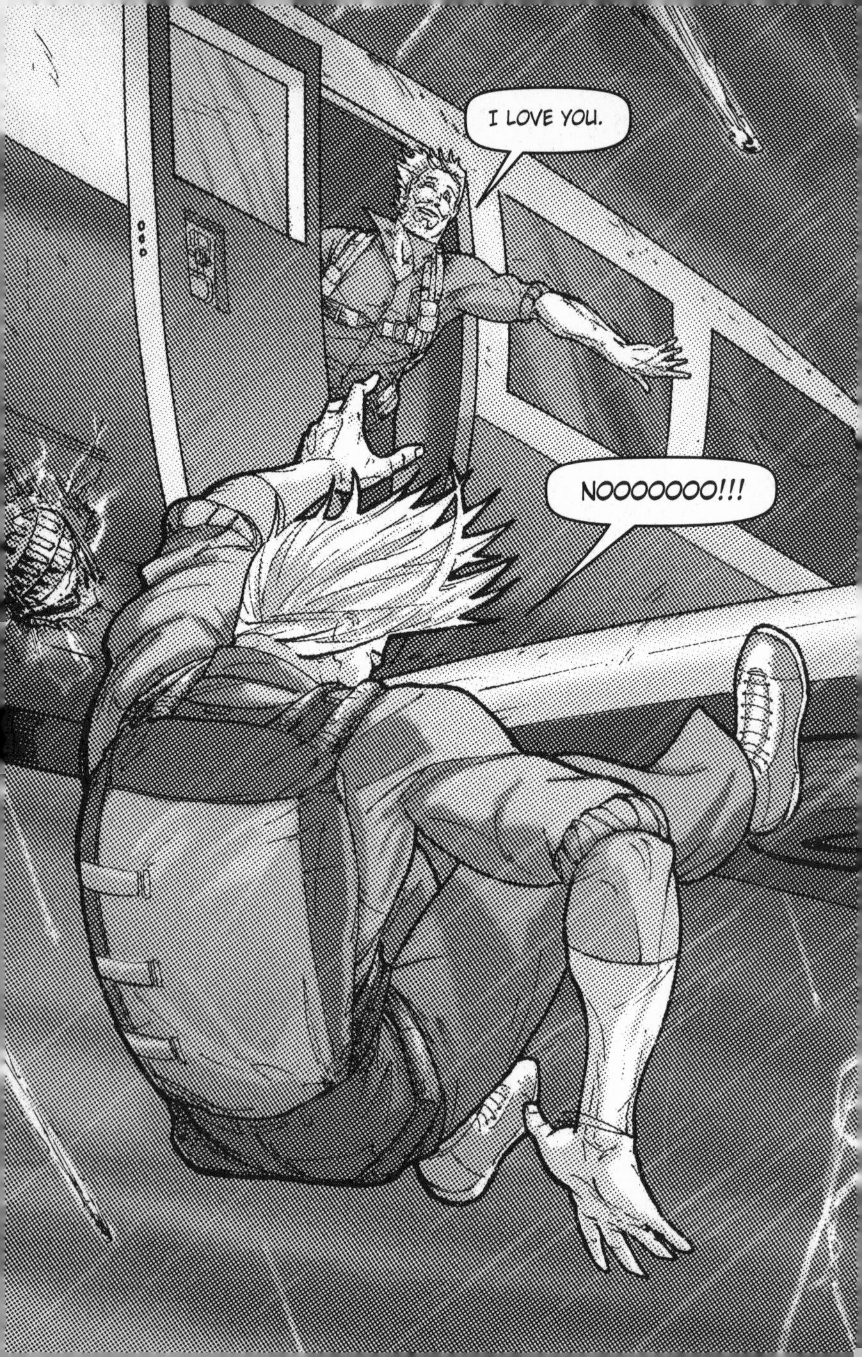
I LOVE YOU.
NOOOOOOO!!!

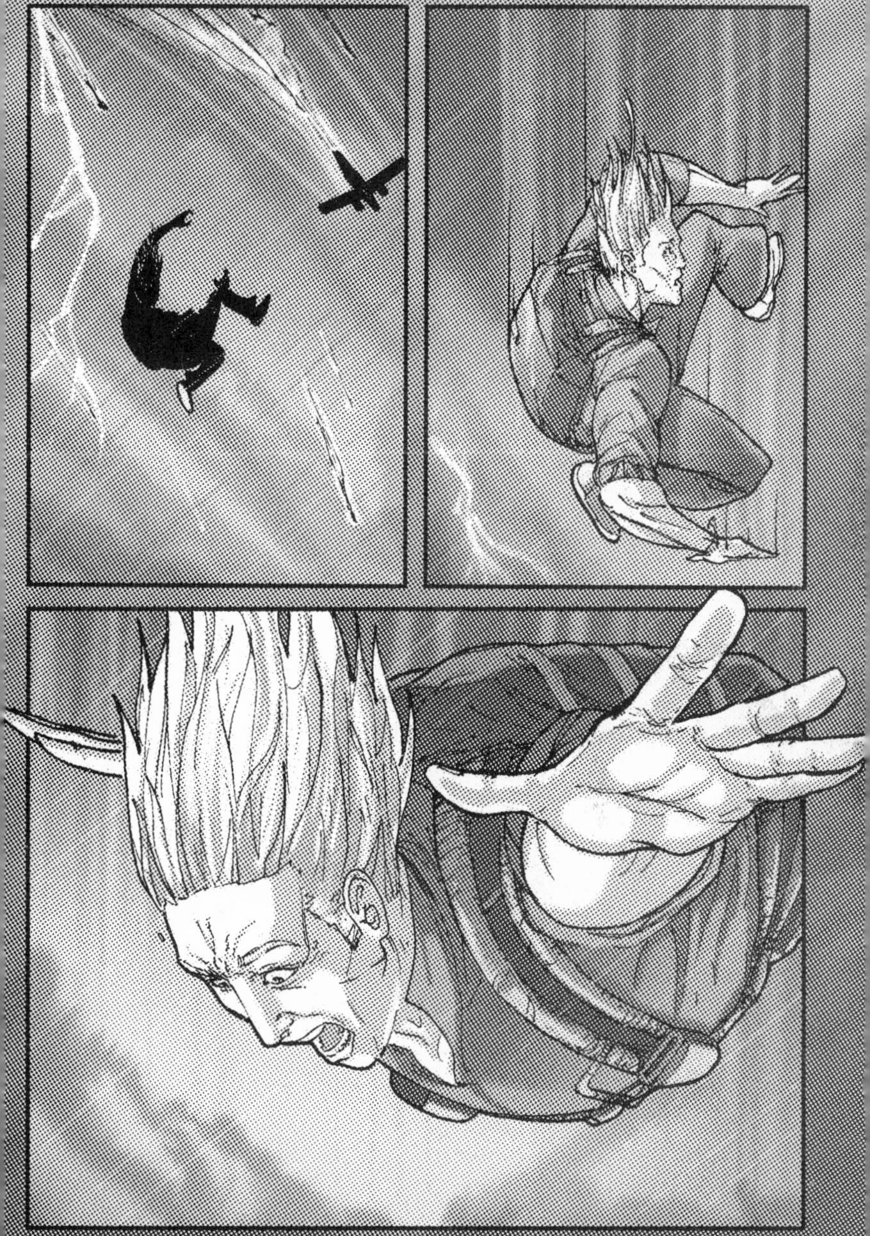

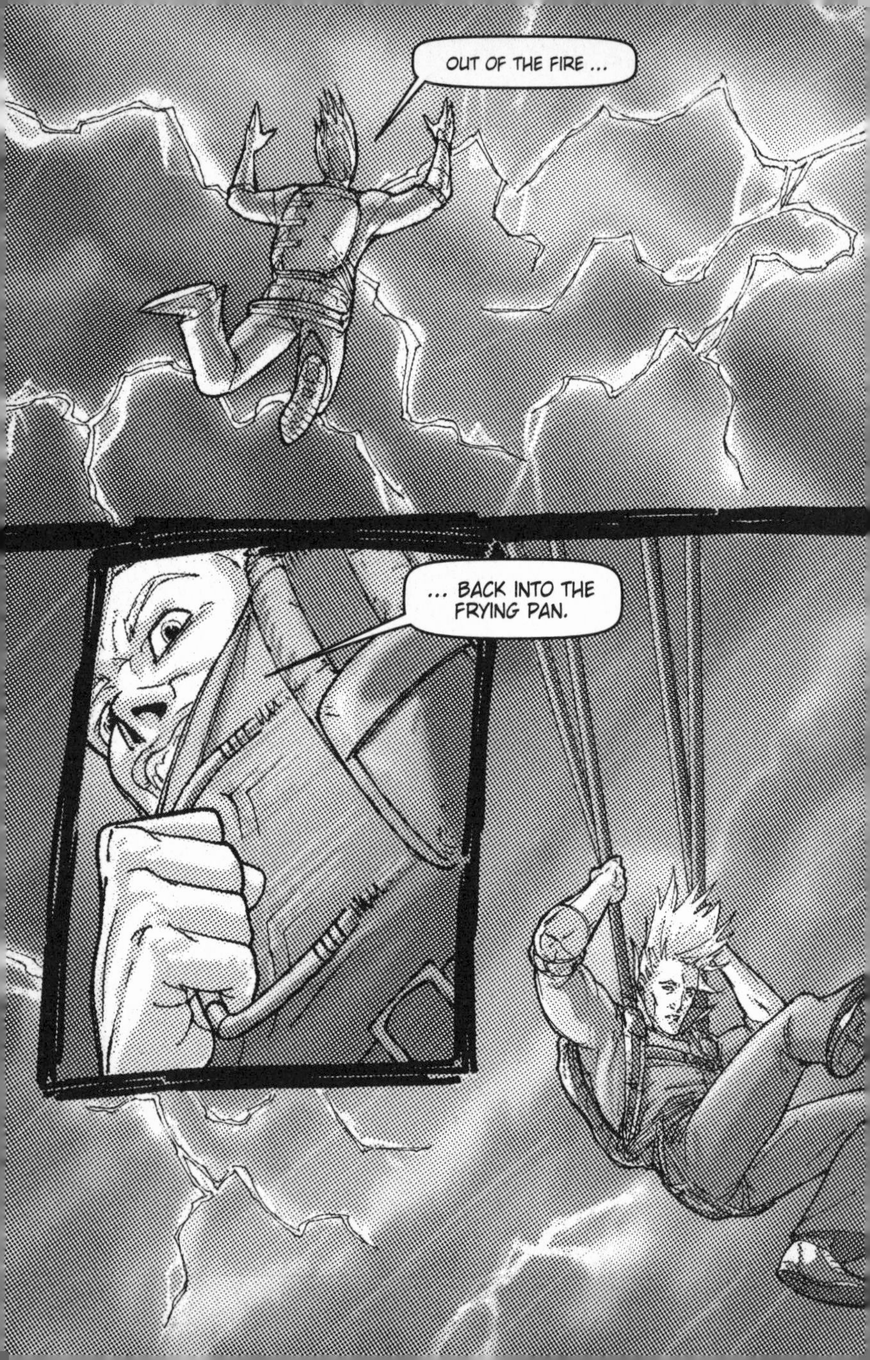
OUT OF THE FIRE ...
... BACK INTO THE FRYING PAN.

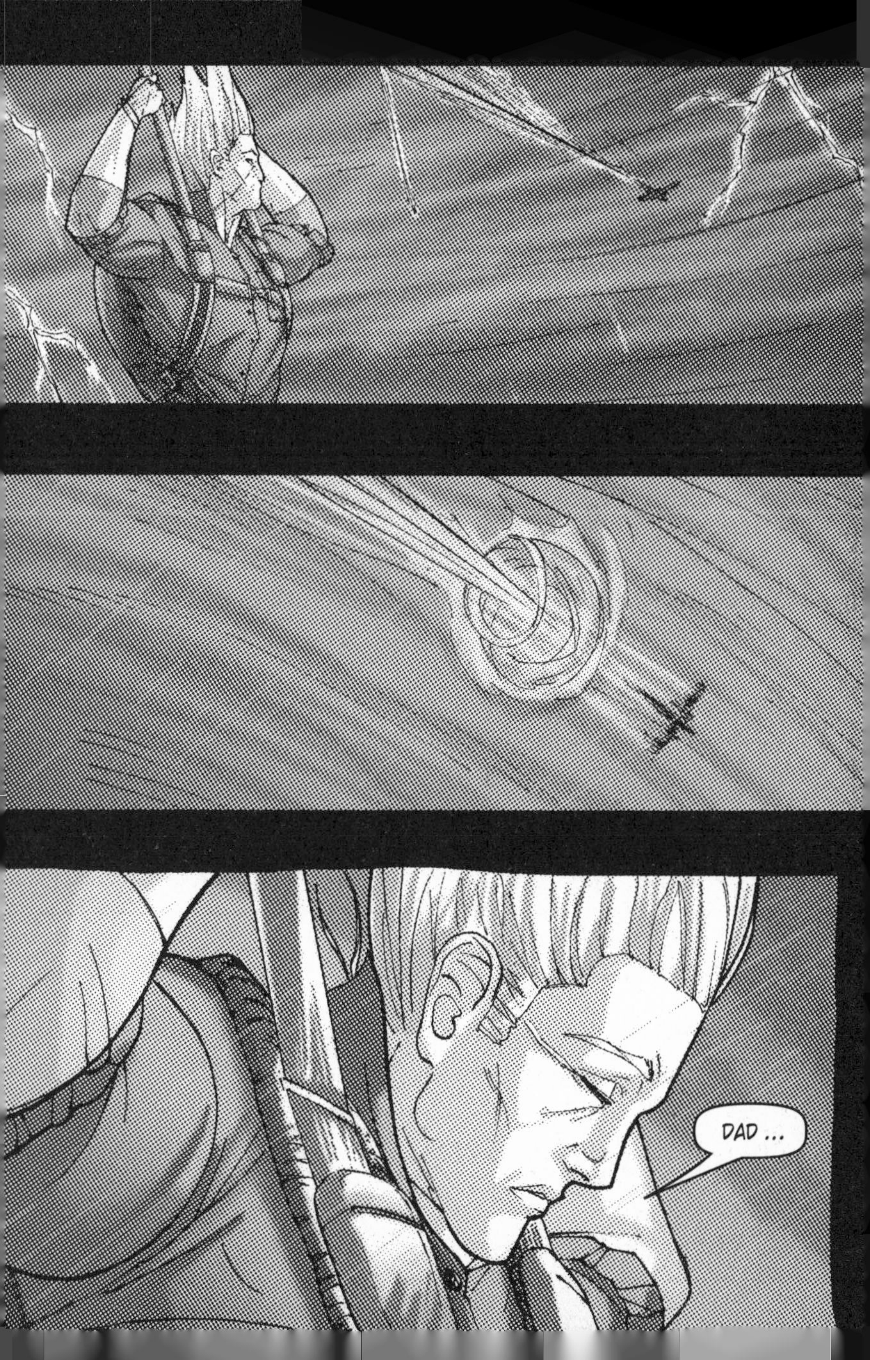
DAD ...

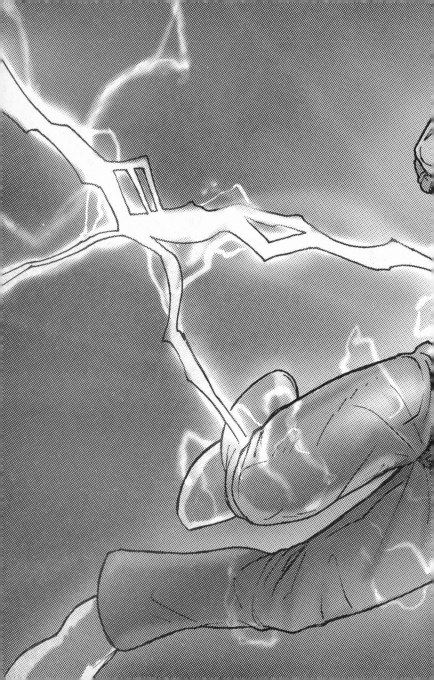

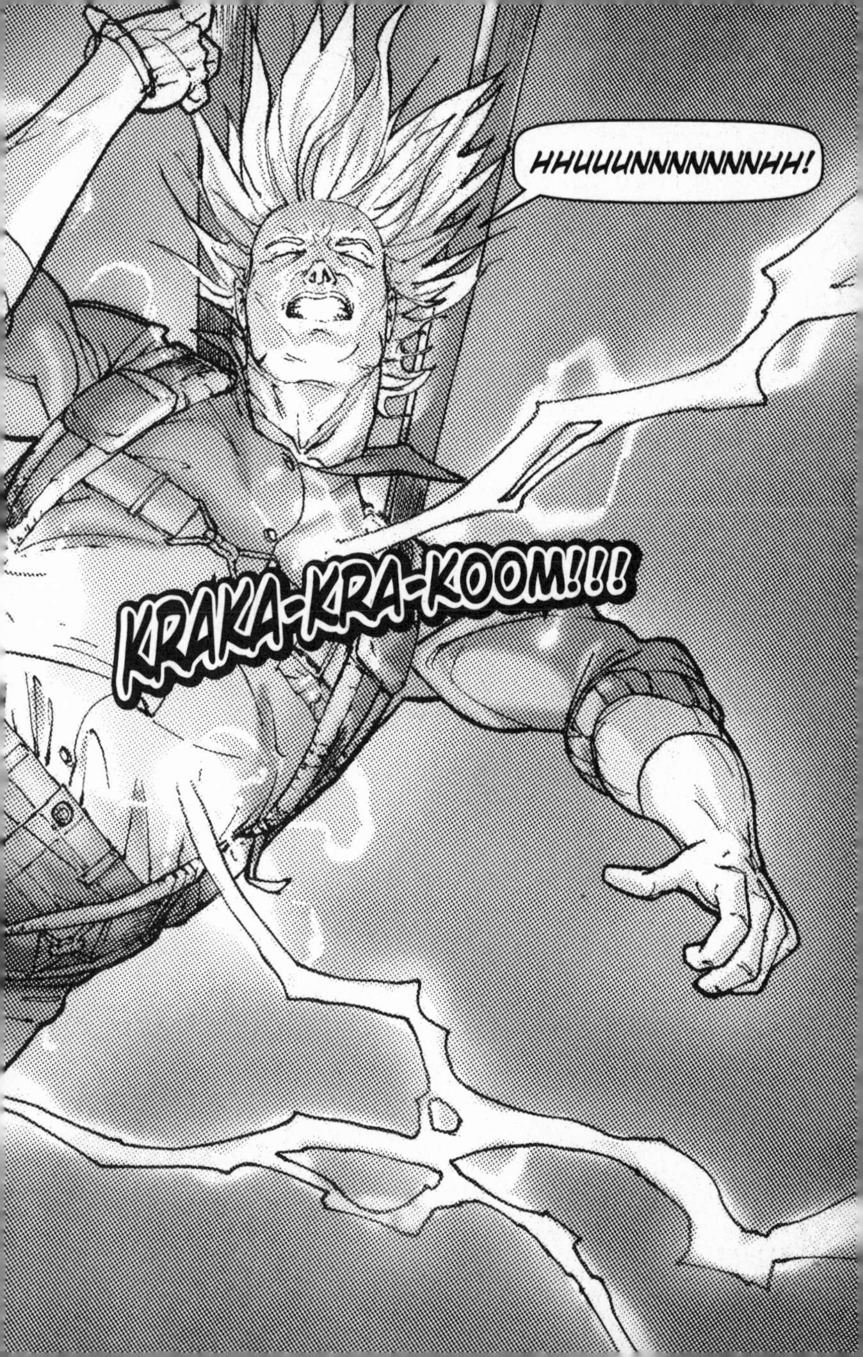
HHUUUNNNNNNNNHH!
KRAKA-KRA-KOOM!!!

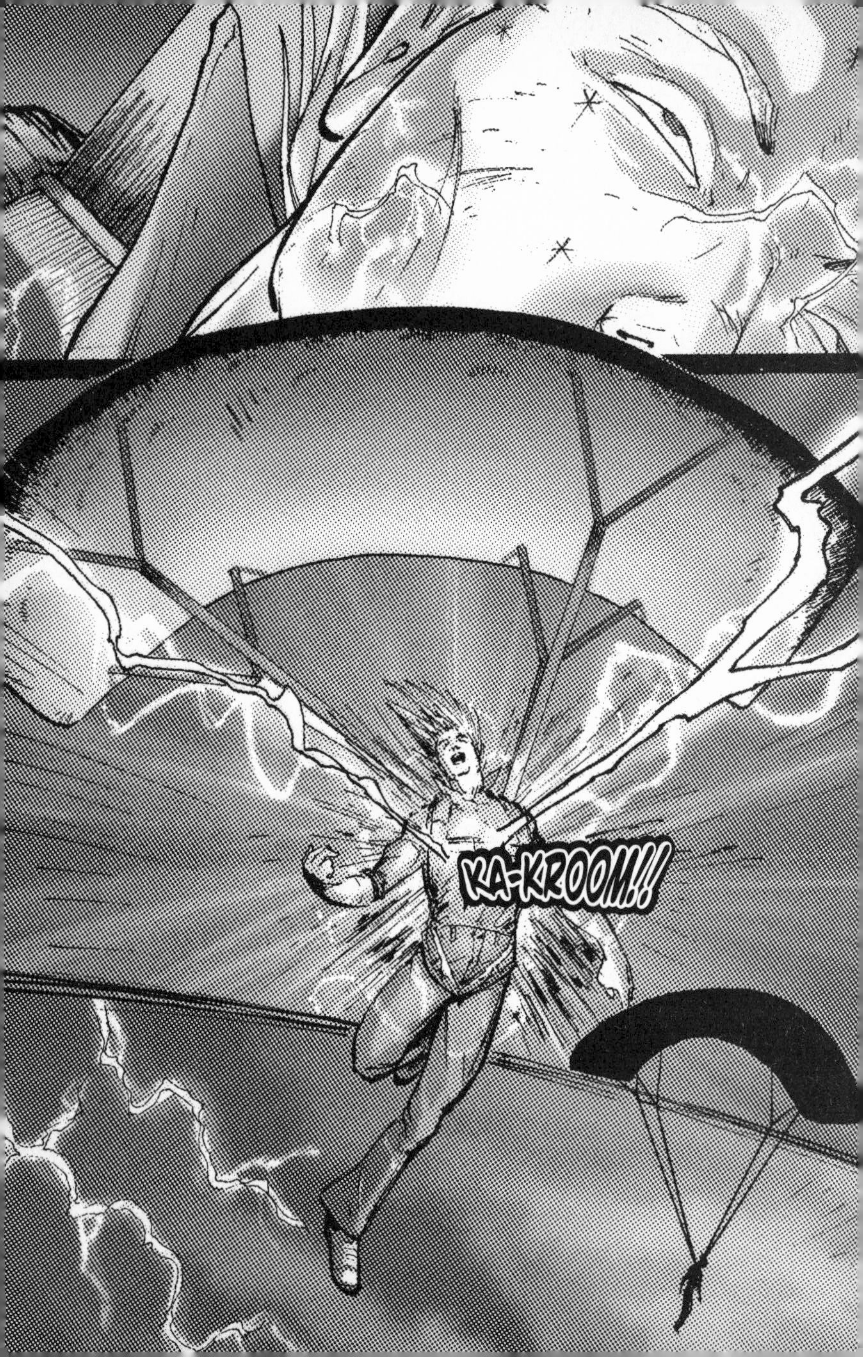
KA-KROOM!!

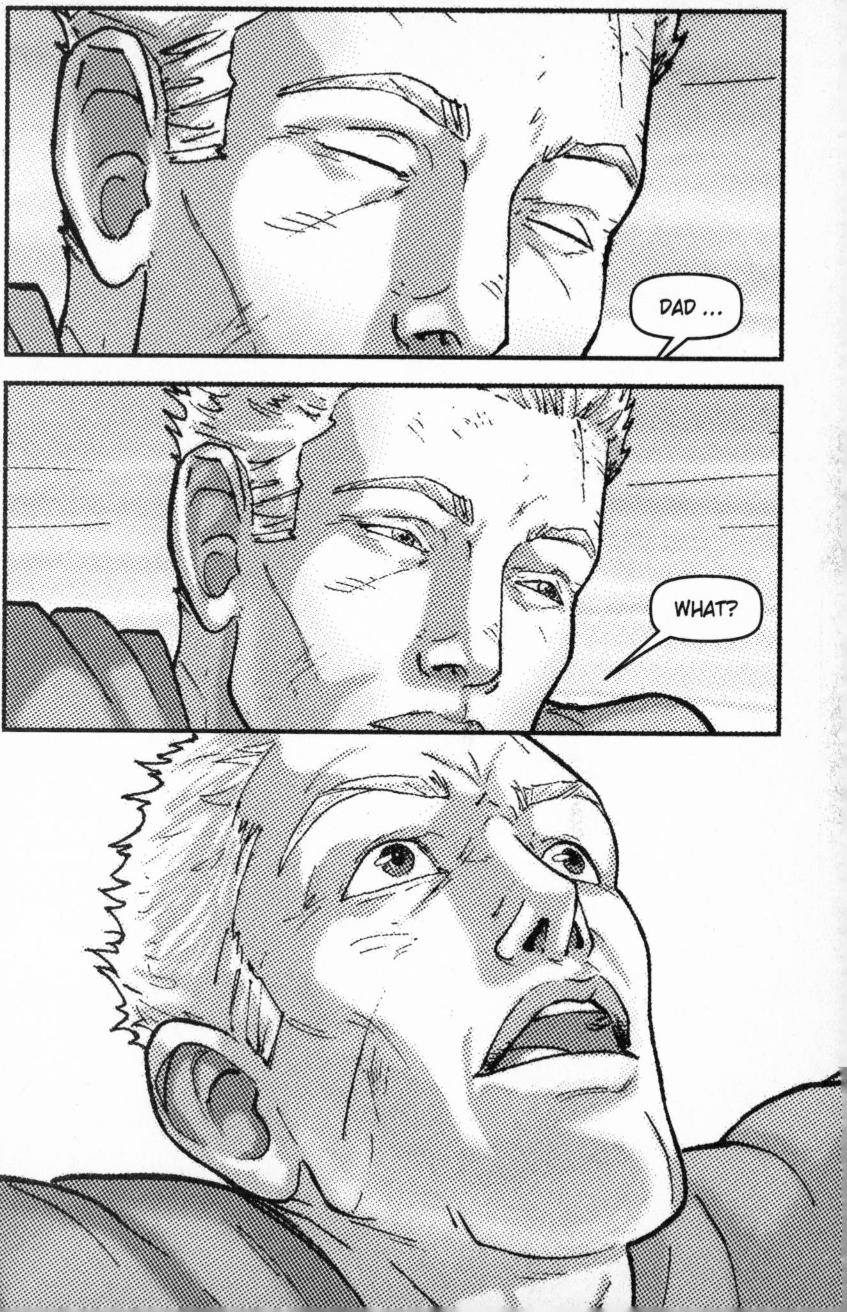
DAD ...
WHAT?

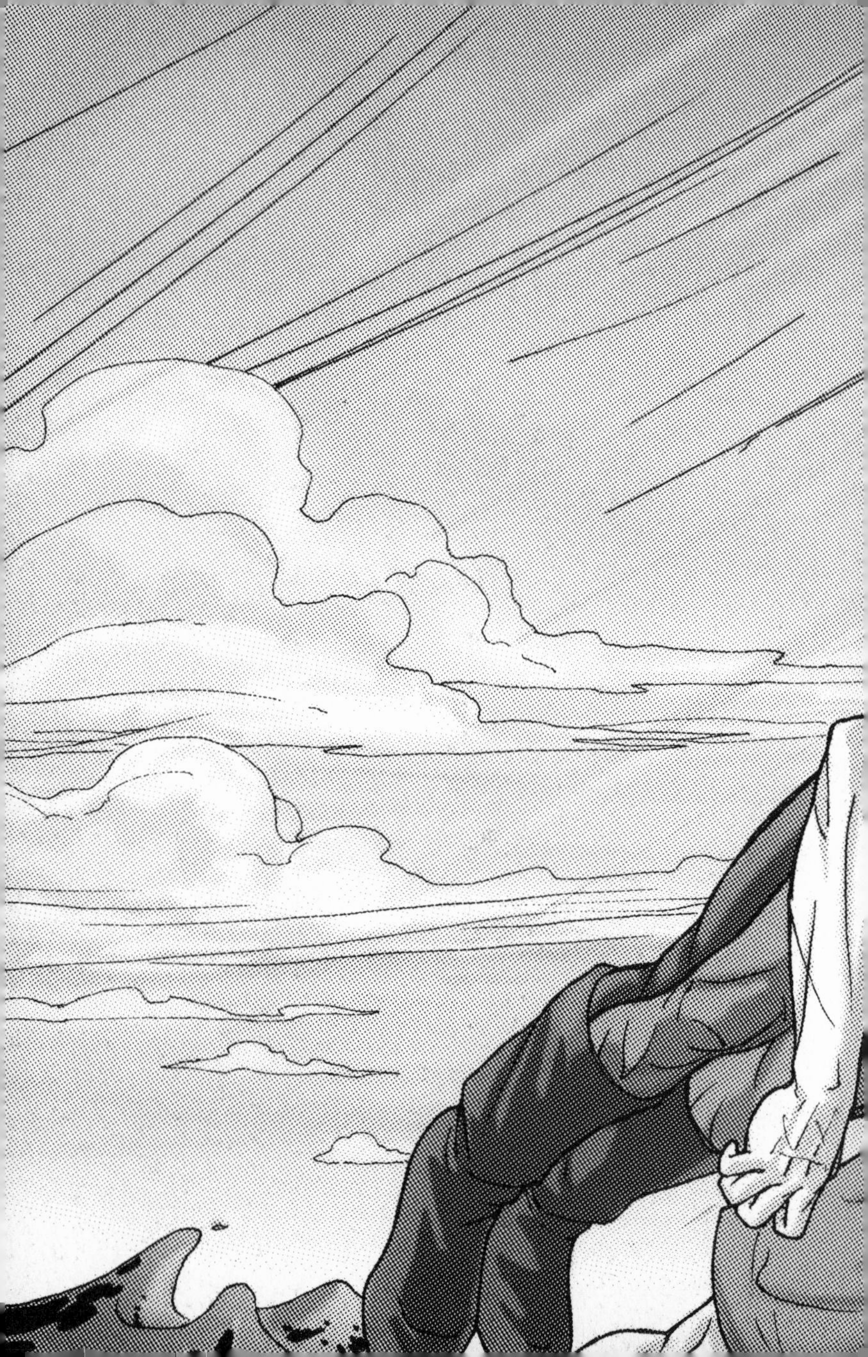

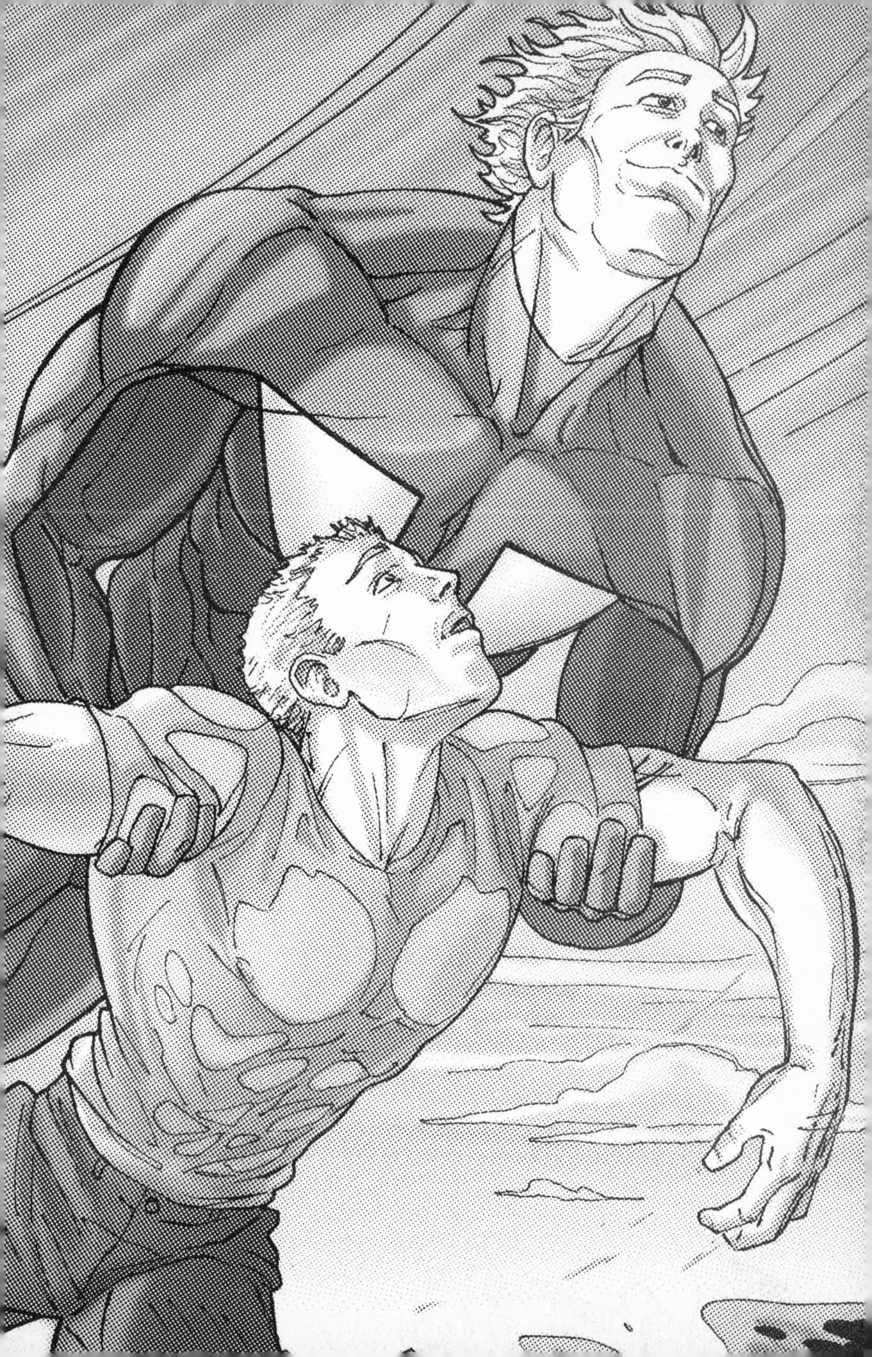

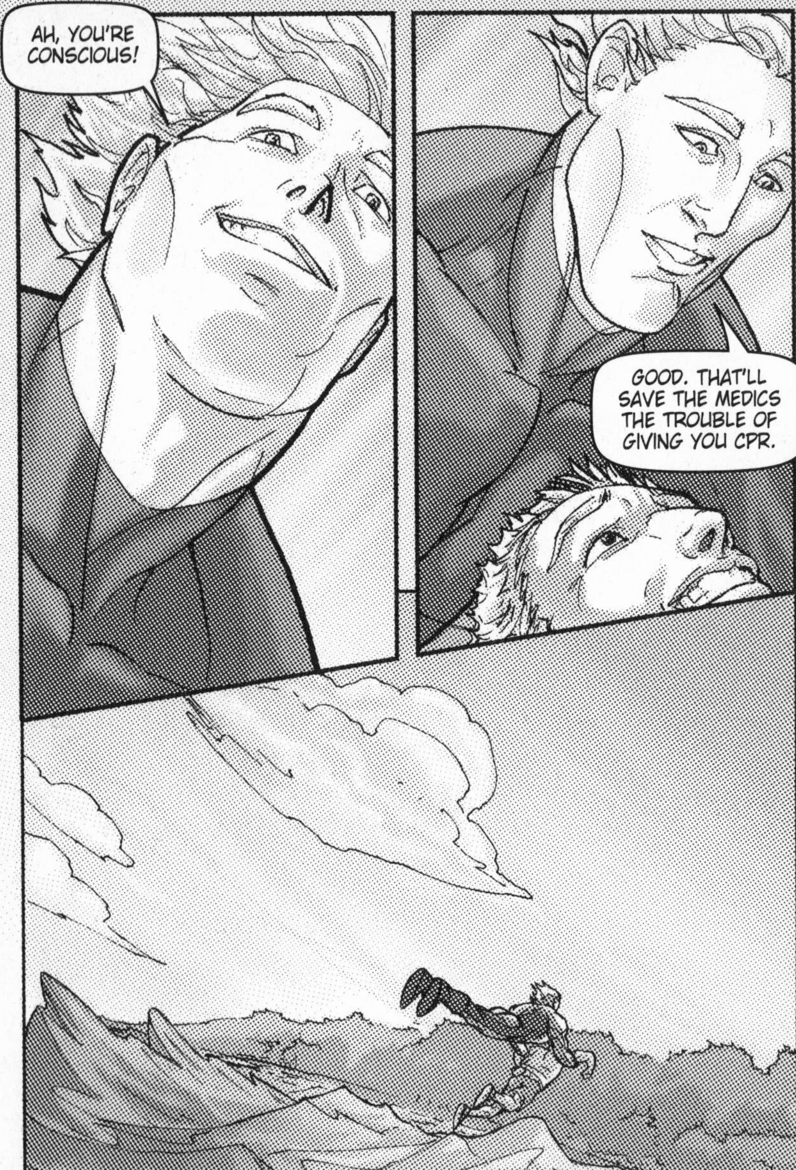
AH, YOU'RE CONSCIOUS!
GOOD. THAT'LL SAVE THE MEDICS THE TROUBLE OF GIVING YOU CPR.

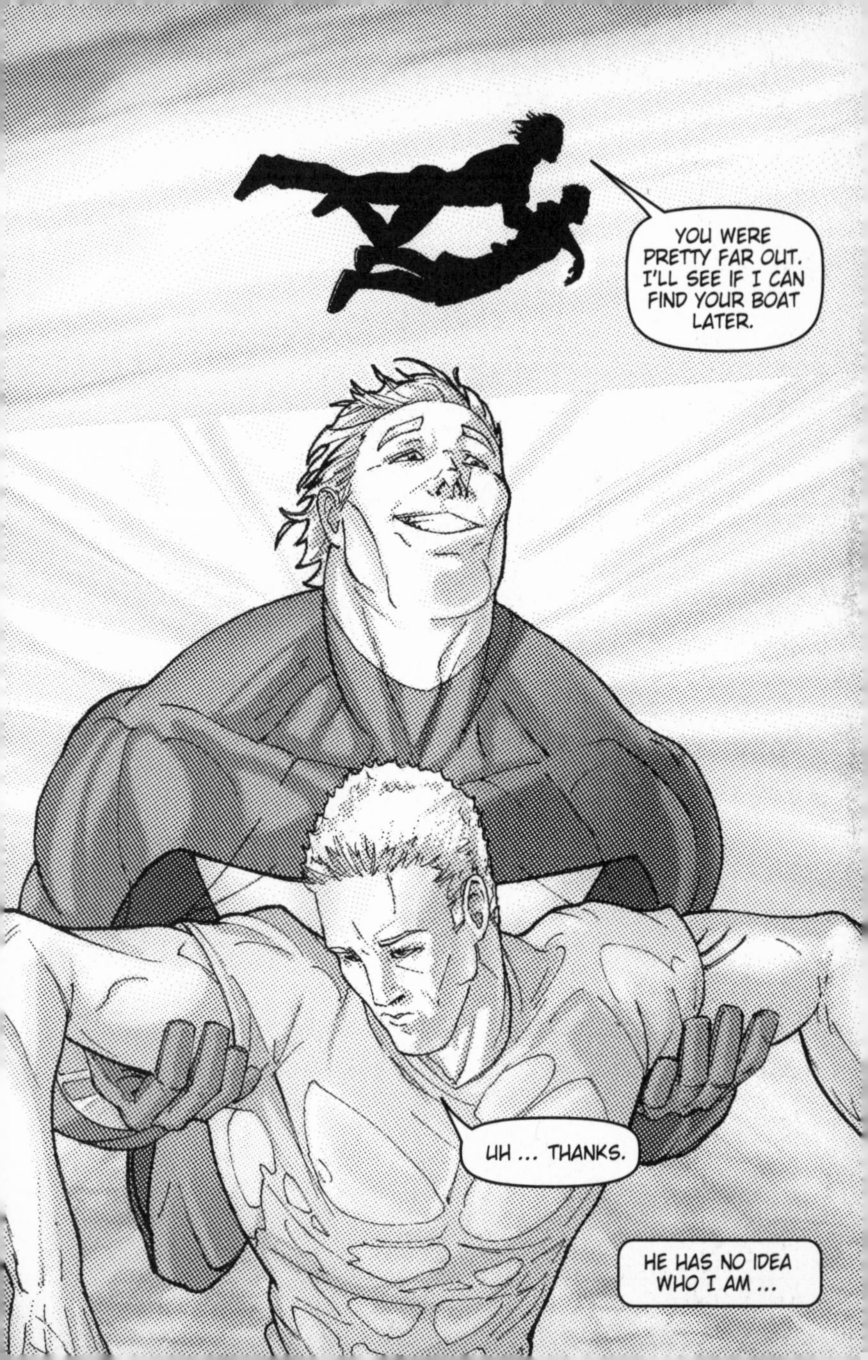
YOU WERE PRETTY FAR OUT. I'LL SEE IF I CAN FIND YOUR BOAT LATER.
UH ... THANKS.
HE HAS NO IDEA WHO I AM ...

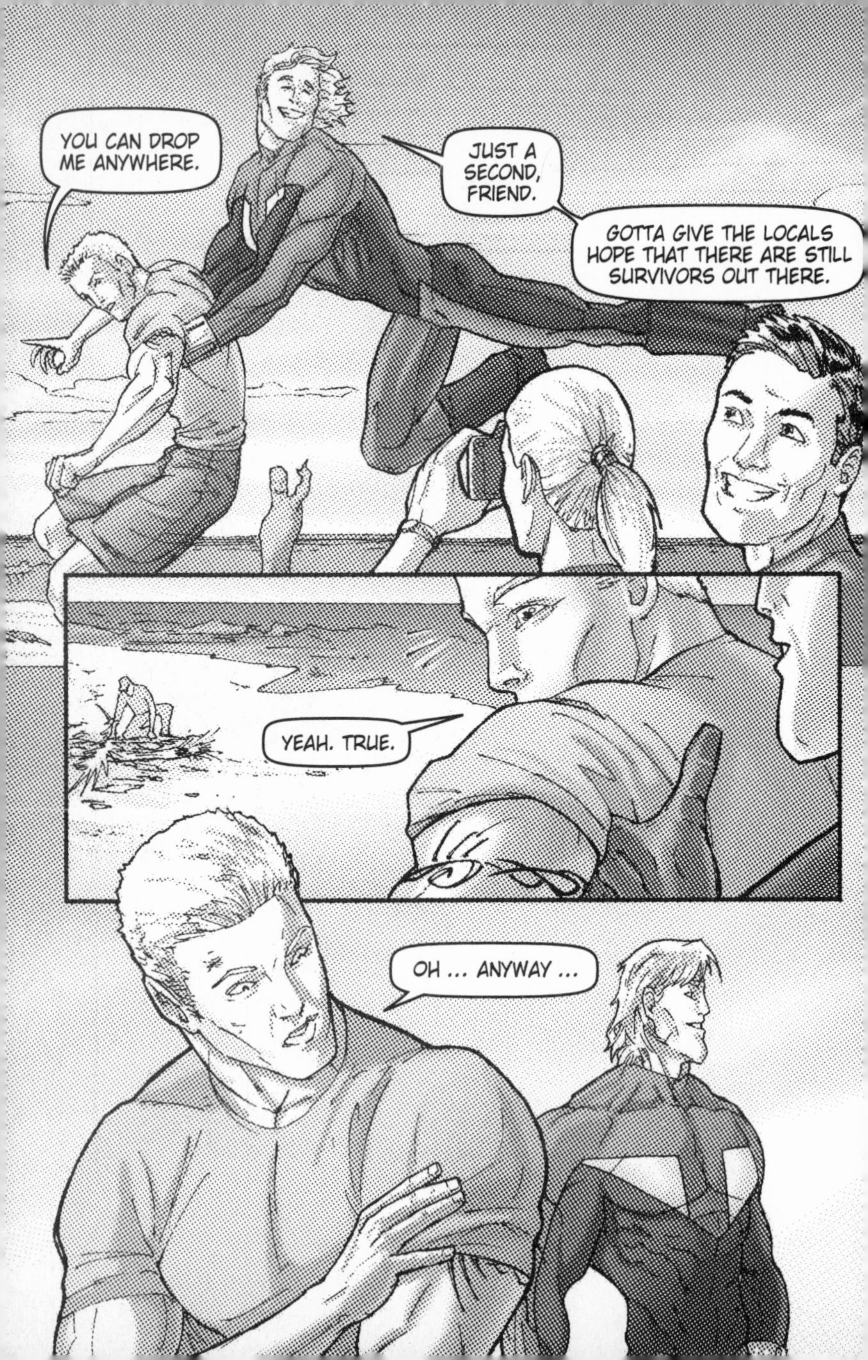
YOU CAN DROP ME ANYWHERE.
JUST A SECOND, FRIEND.
GOTTA GIVE THE LOCALS HOPE THAT THERE ARE STILL SURVIVORS OUT THERE.
YEAH. TRUE.
OH ... ANYWAY ...

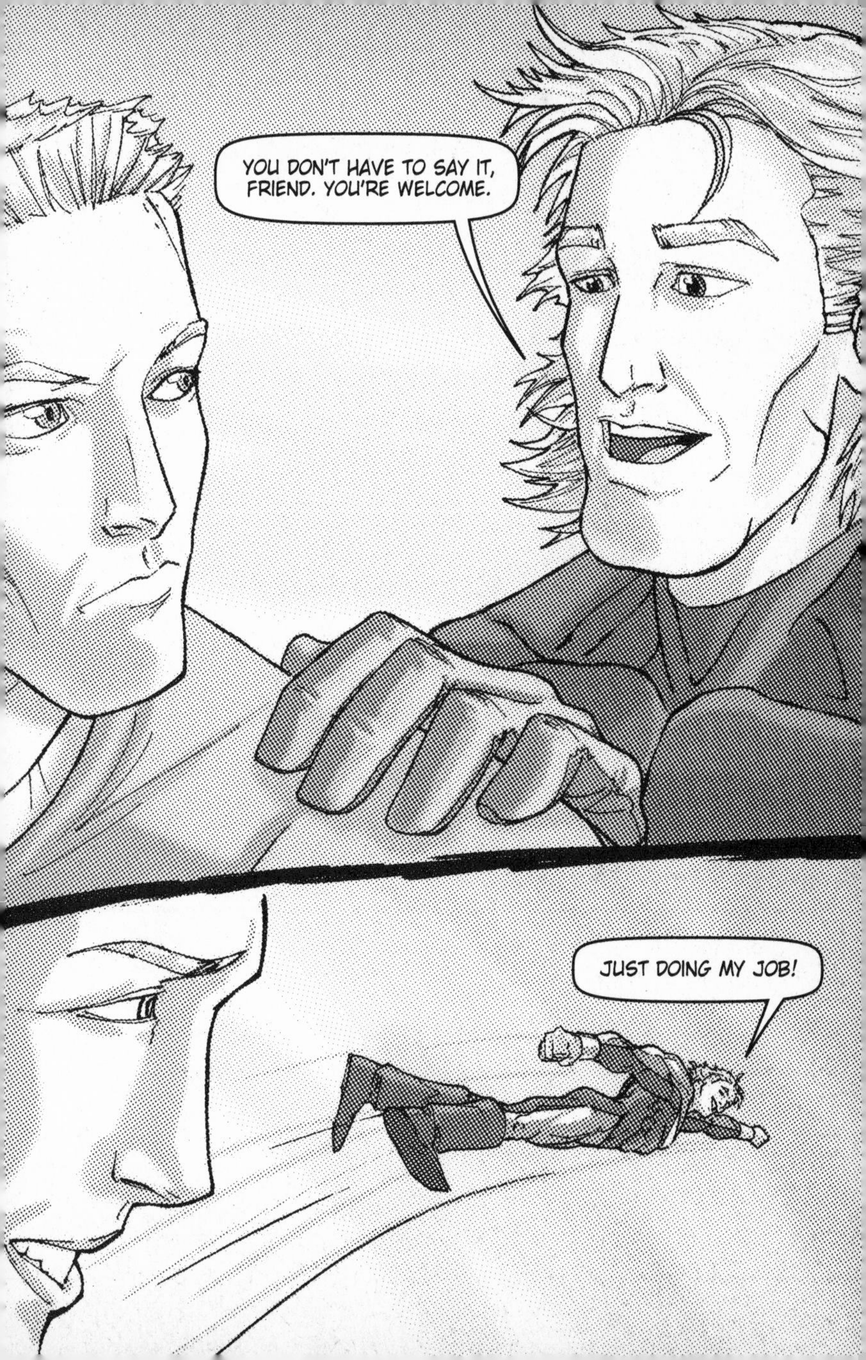
YOU DON'T HAVE TO SAY IT, FRIEND. YOU'RE WELCOME.
JUST DOING MY JOB!

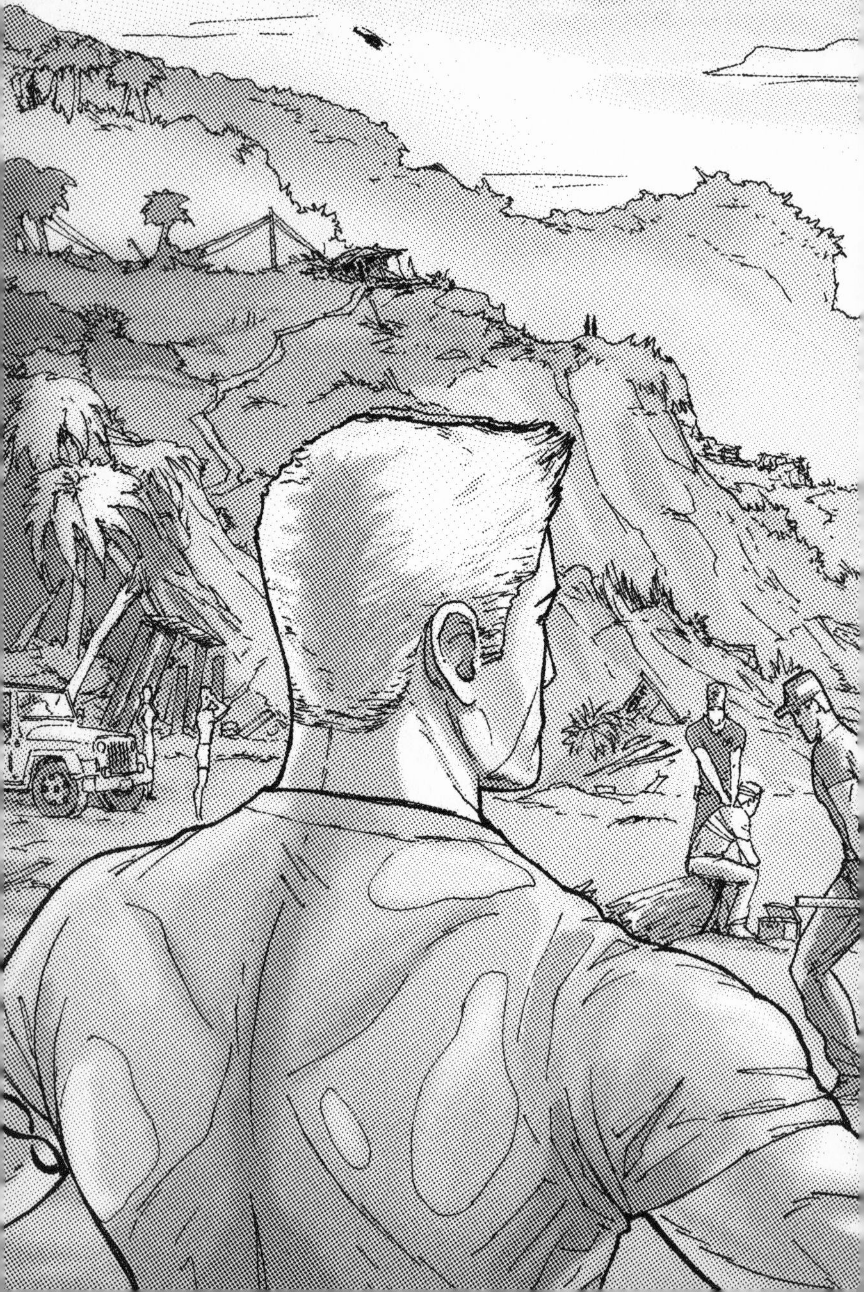

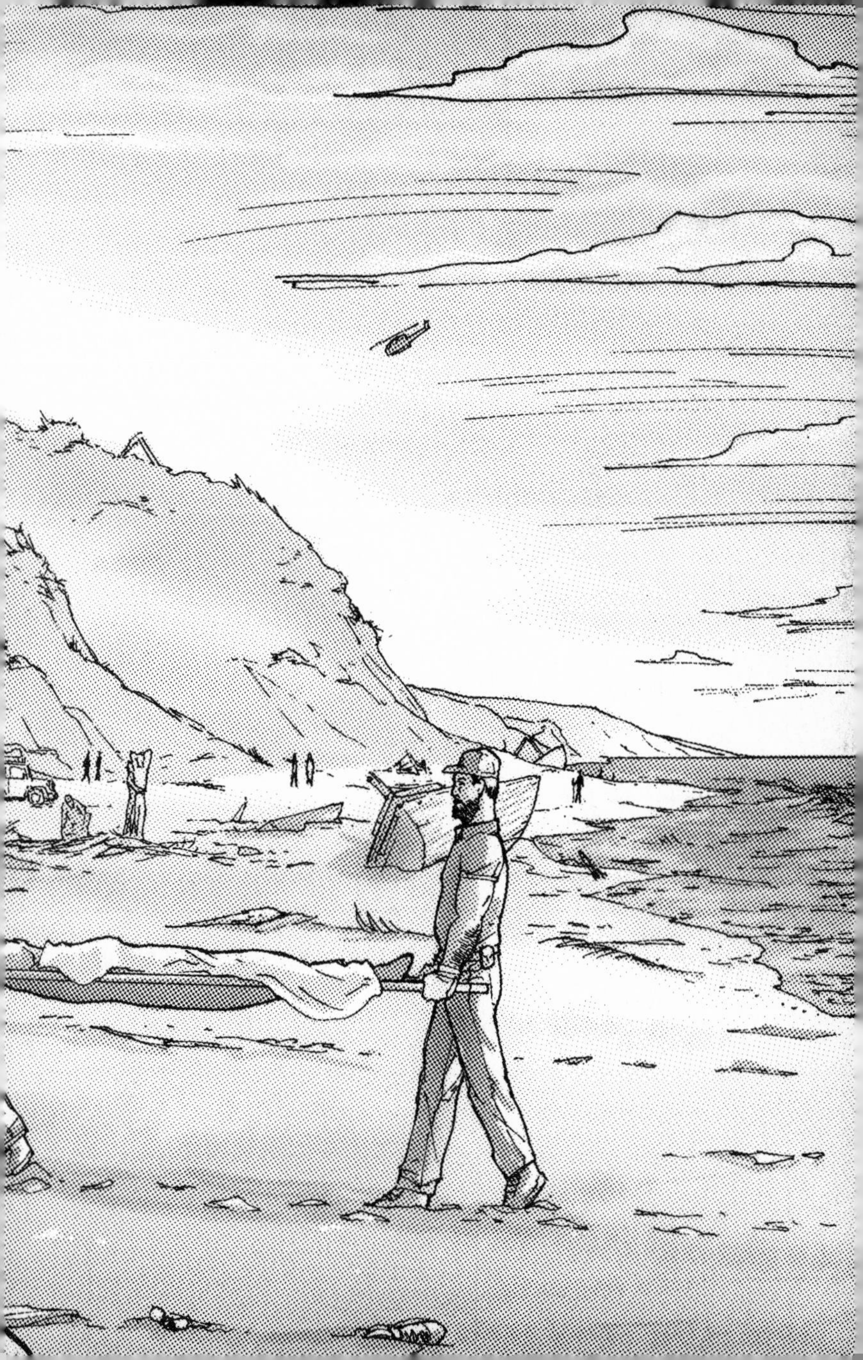

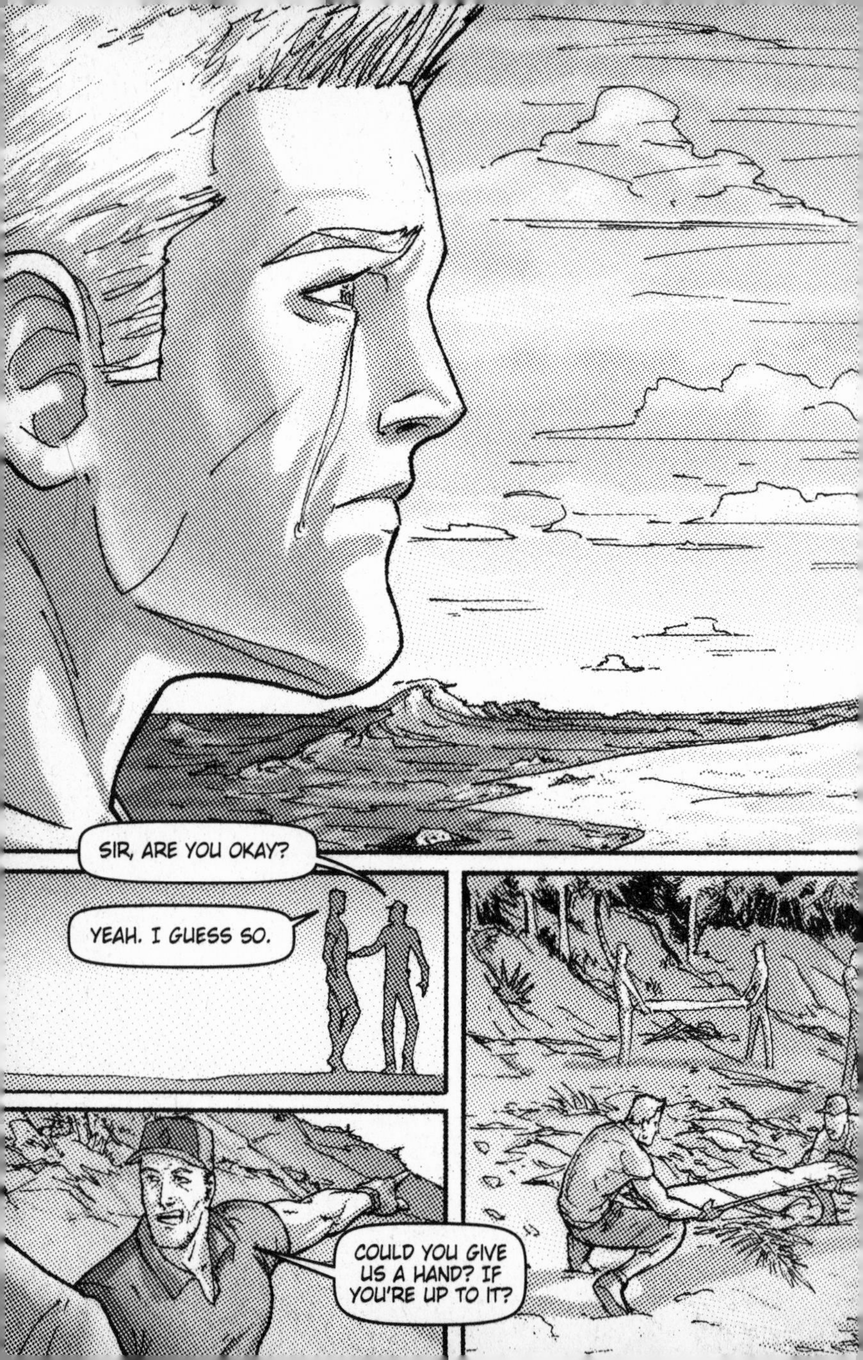
SIR, ARE YOU OKAY?
YEAH. I GUESS SO.
COULD YOU GIVE US A HAND? IF YOU'RE UP TO IT?

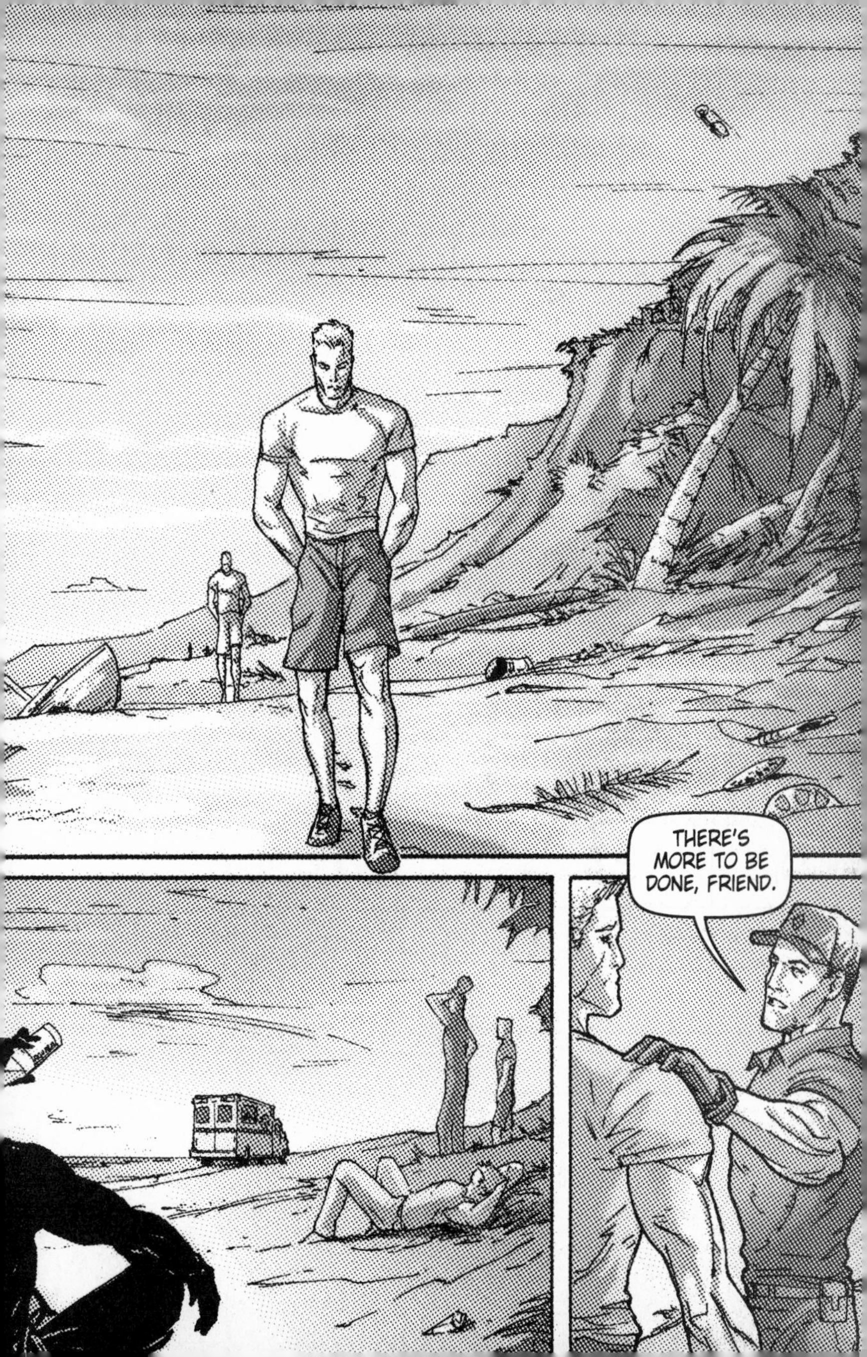
THERE'S MORE TO BE DONE, FRIEND.

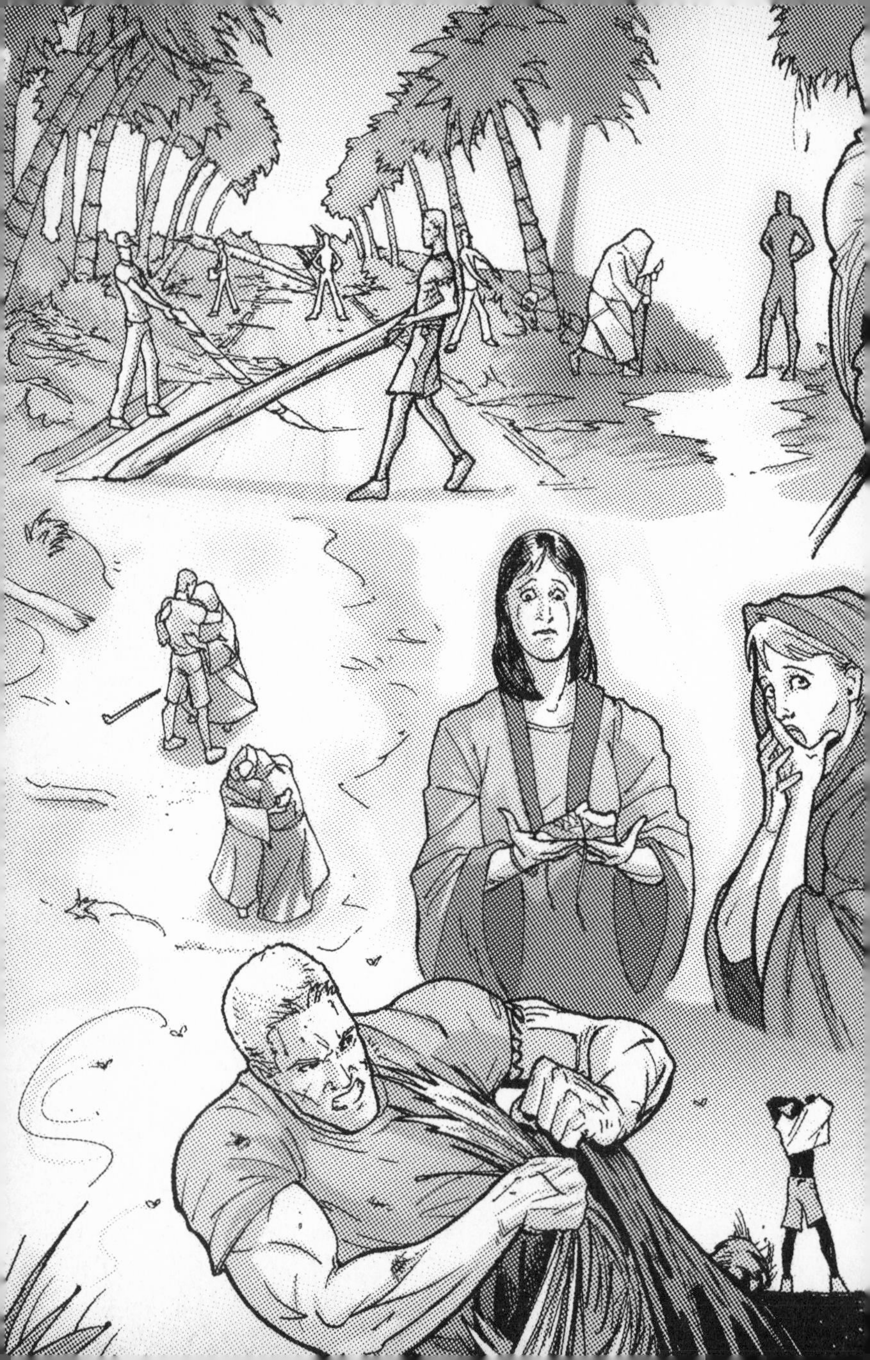

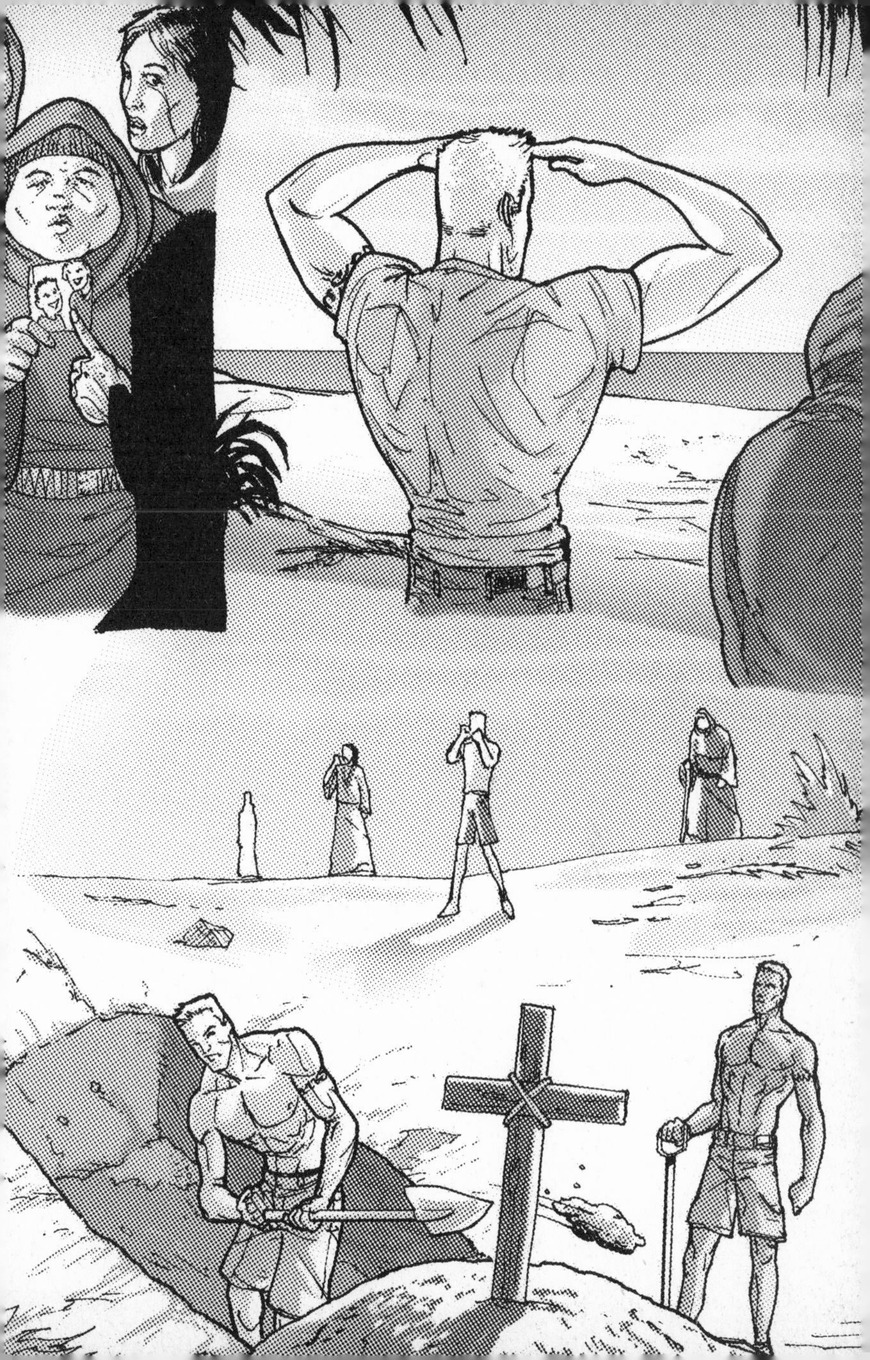

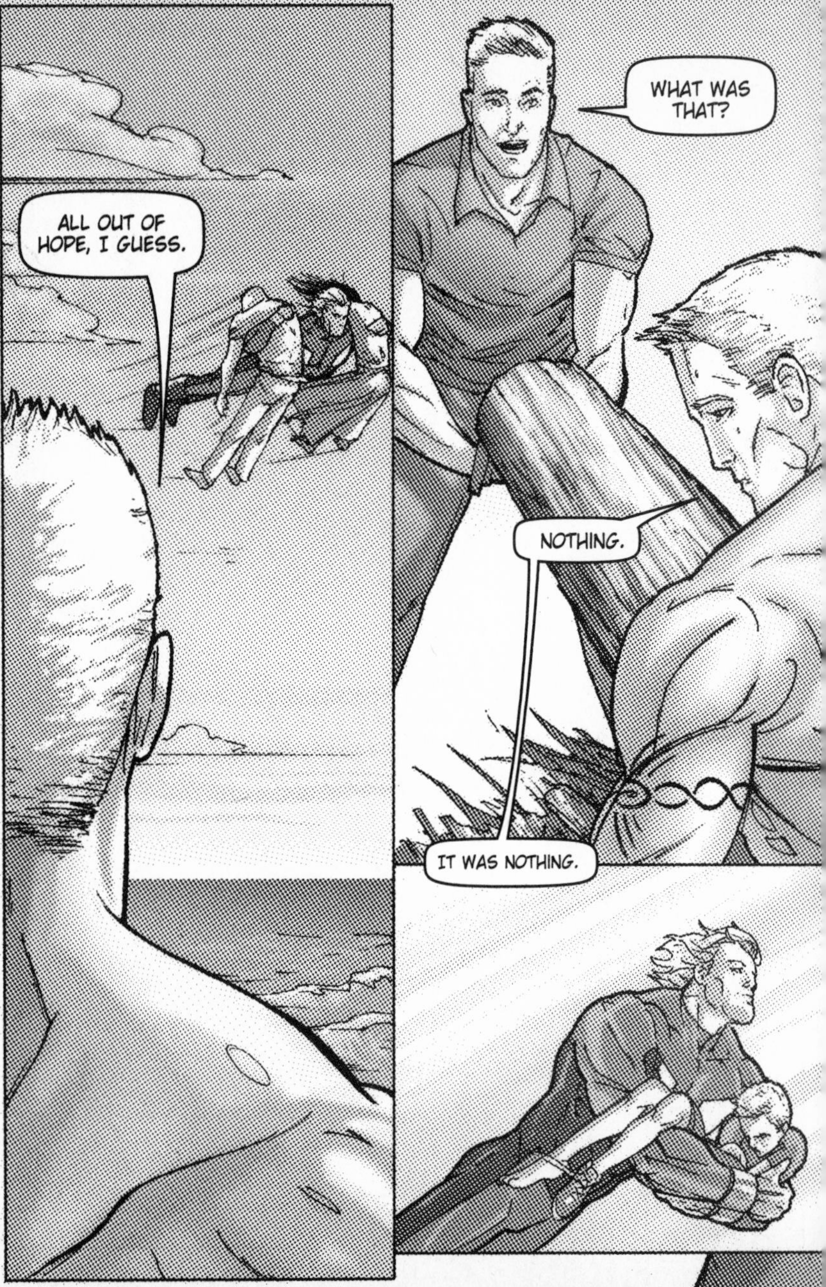
ALL OUT OF HOPE, I GUESS.
WHAT WAS THAT?
NOTHING.
IT WAS NOTHING.

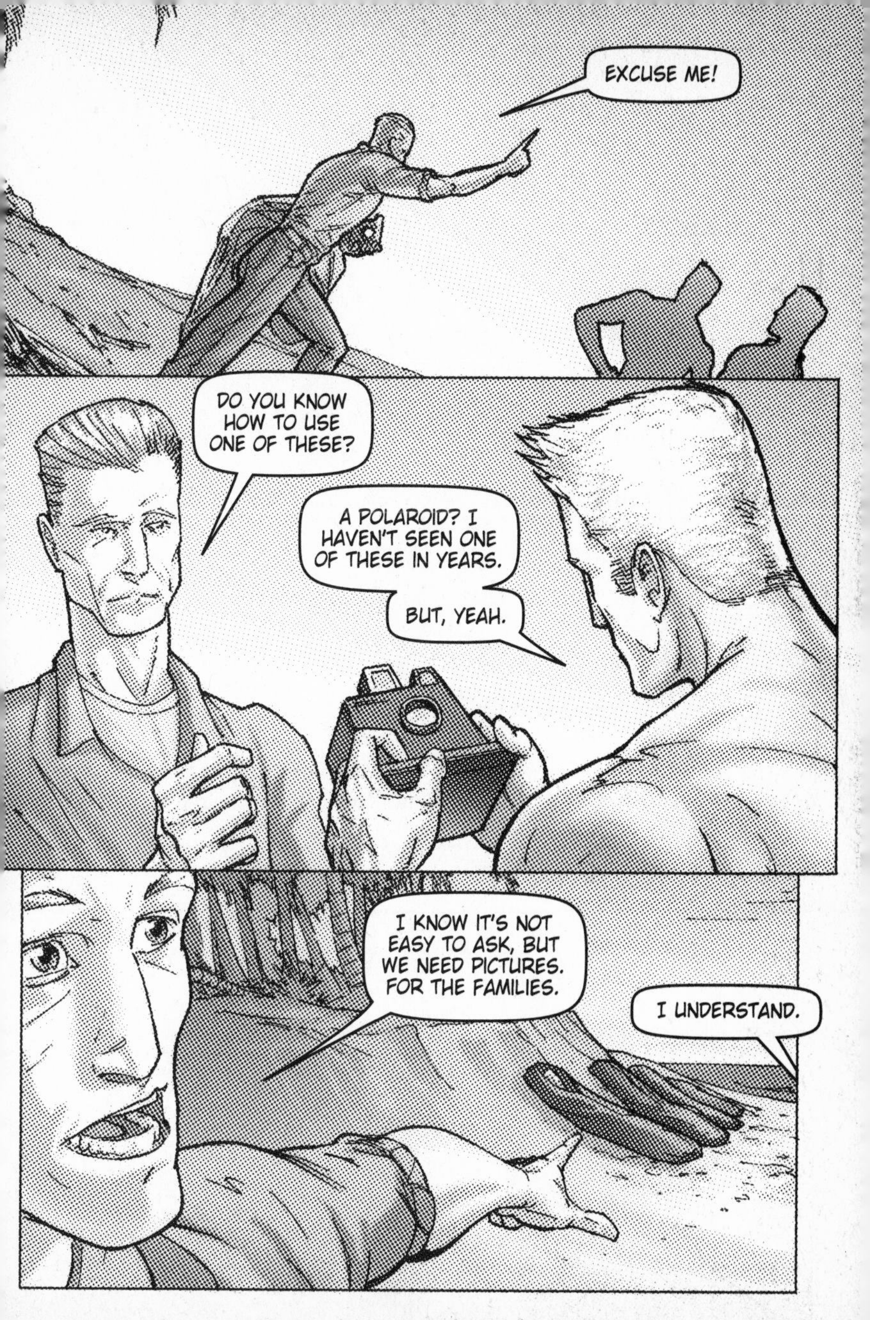
EXCUSE ME!
DO YOU KNOW HOW TO USE ONE OF THESE?
A POLAROID? I HAVEN'T SEEN ONE OF THESE IN YEARS.
BUT, YEAH.
I KNOW IT'S NOT EASY TO ASK, BUT WE NEED PICTURES. FOR THE FAMILIES.
I UNDERSTAND.

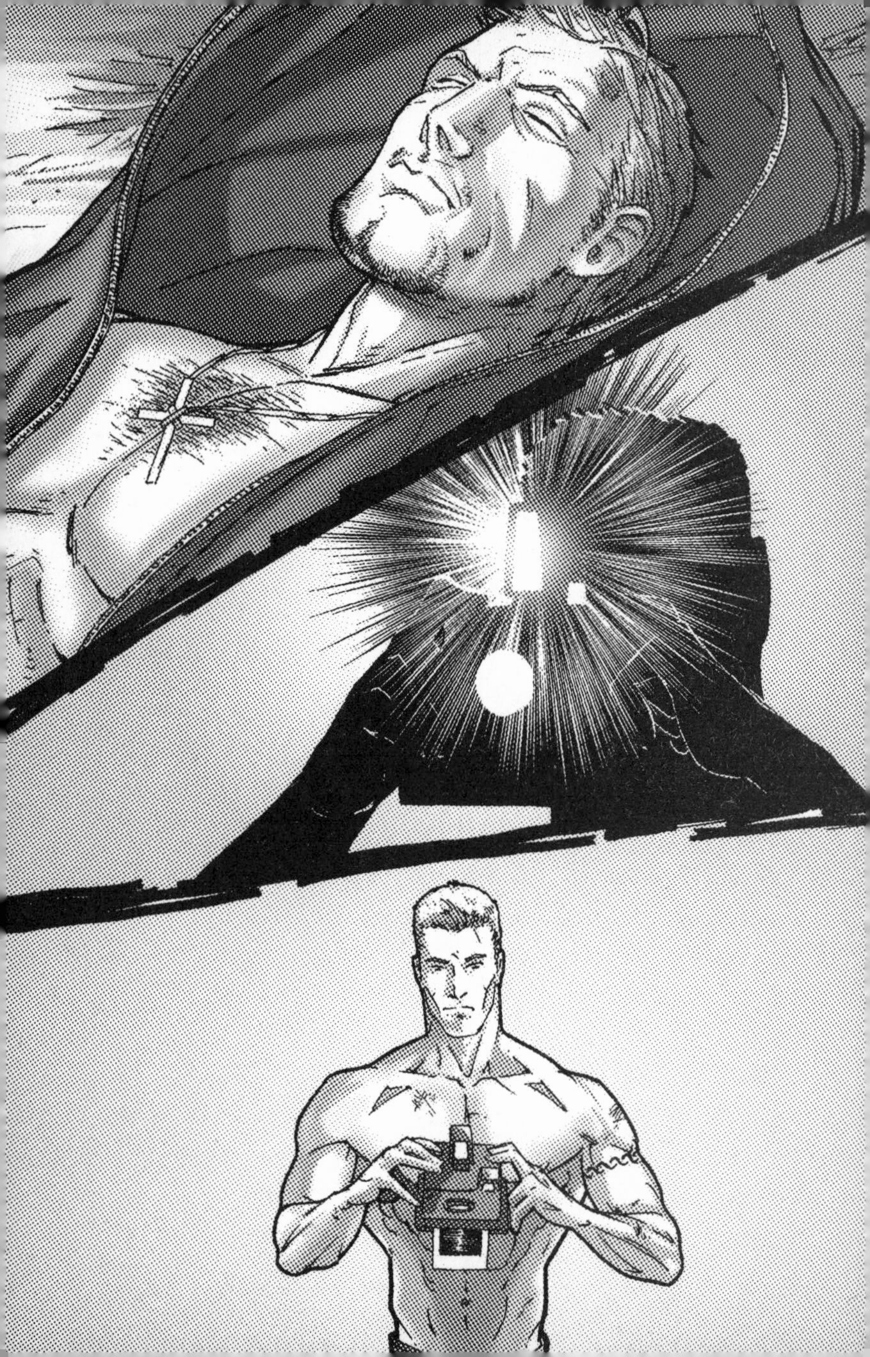

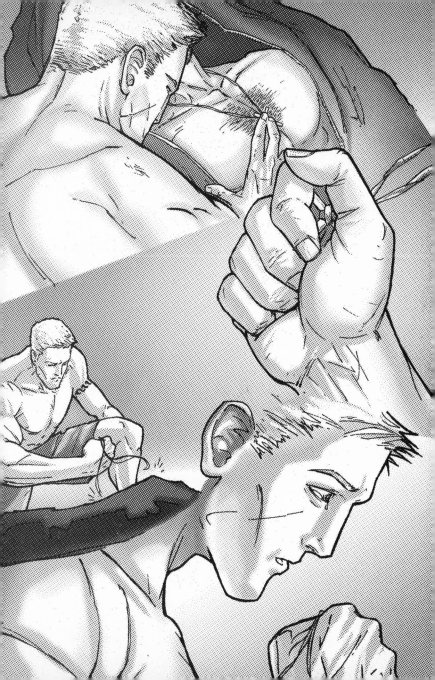

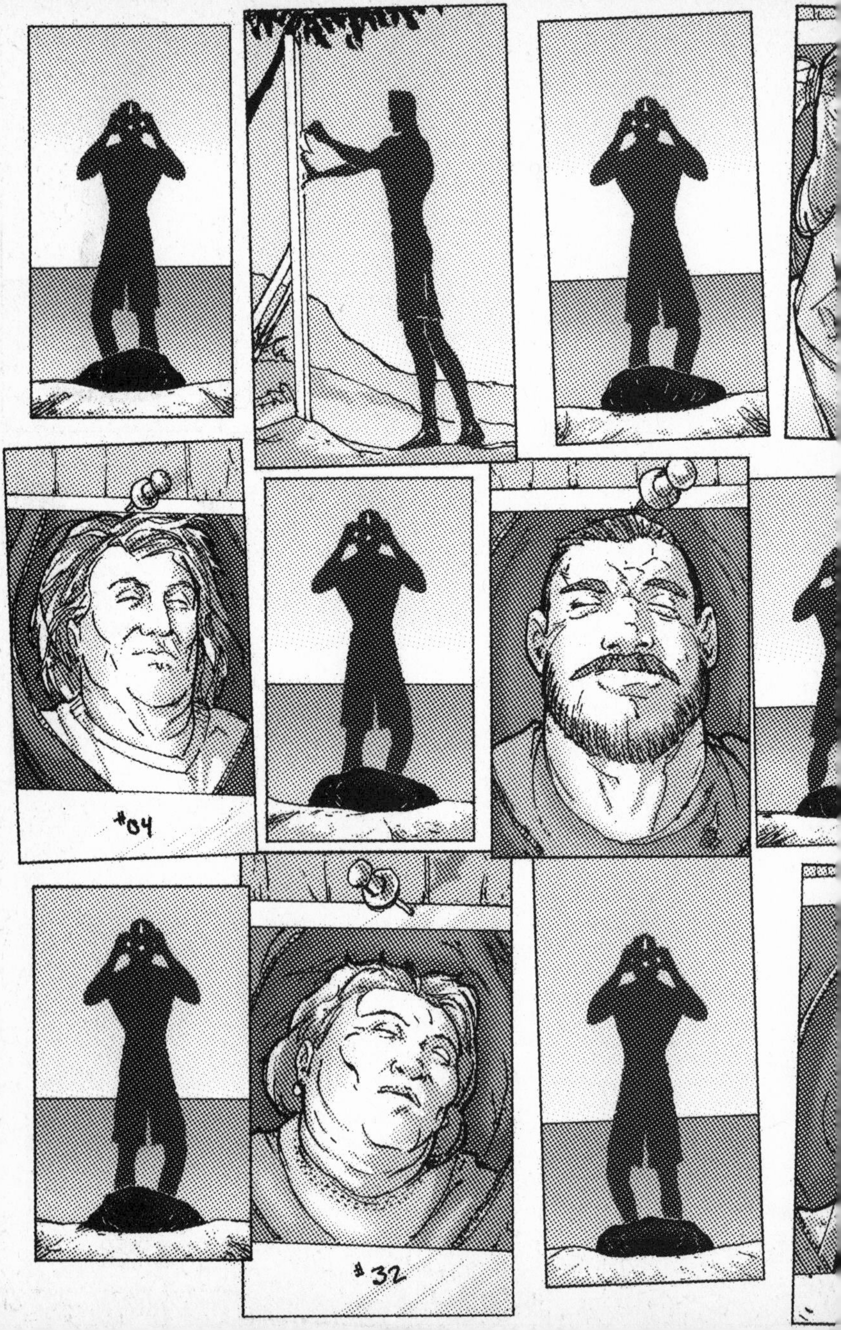
#04
#32

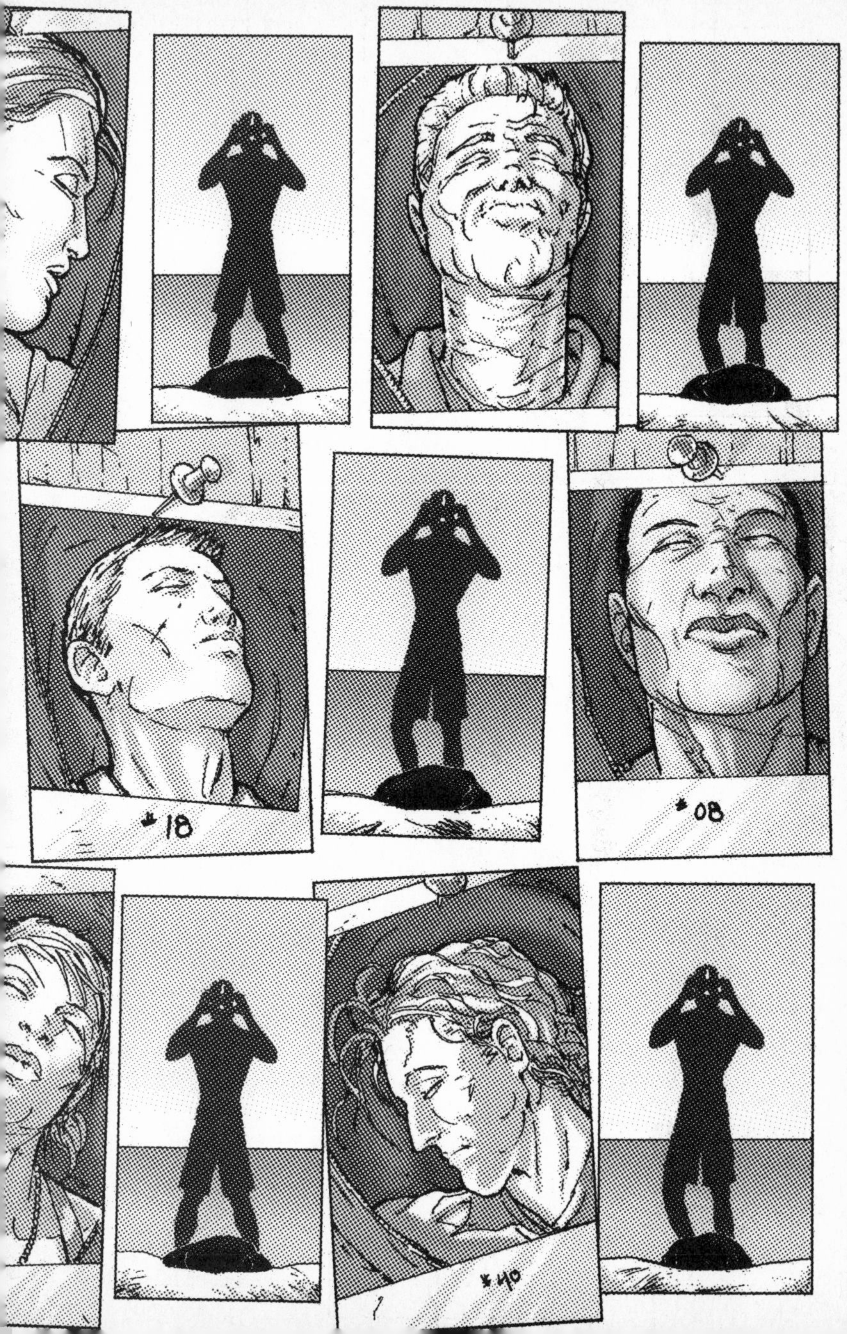

#18
#08
#40

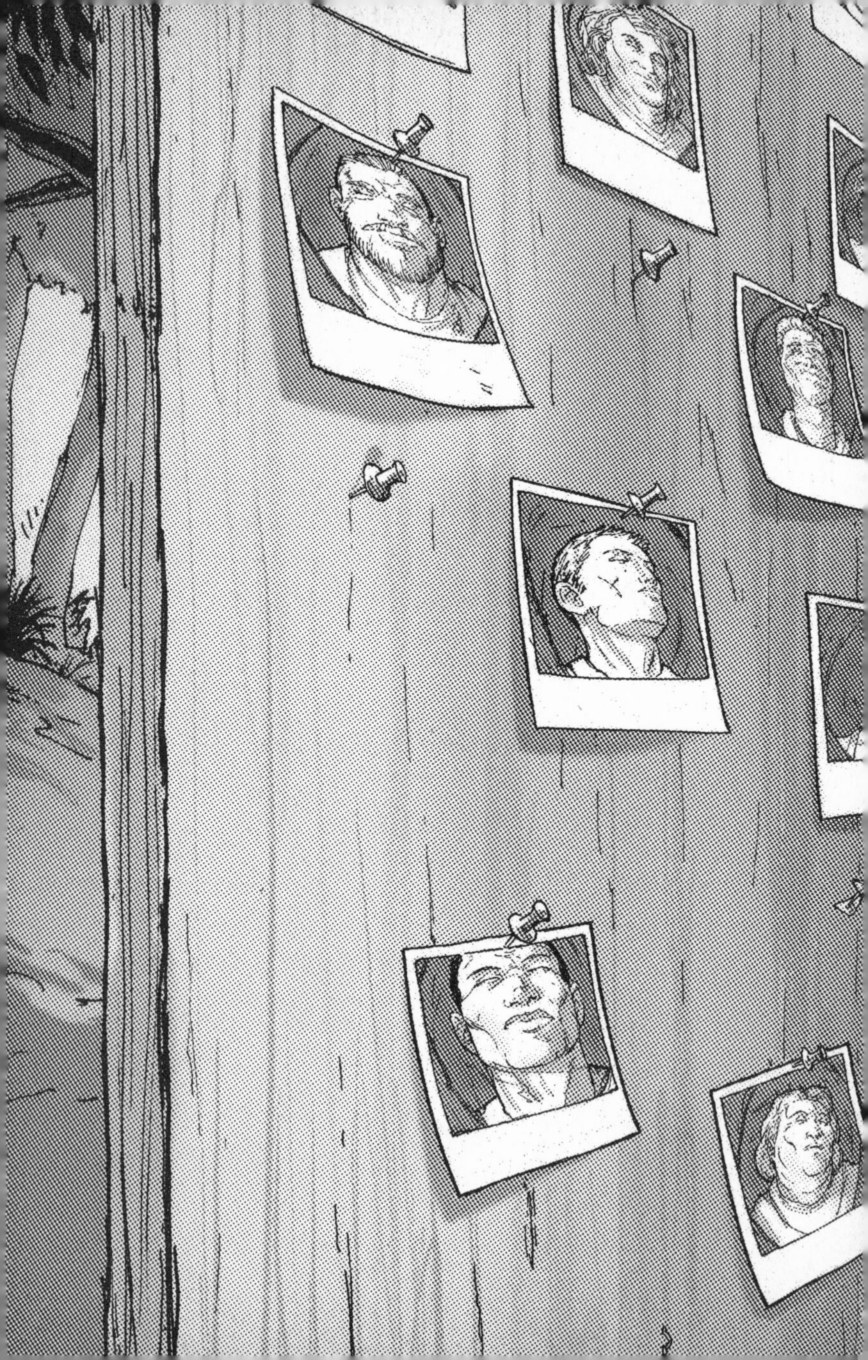

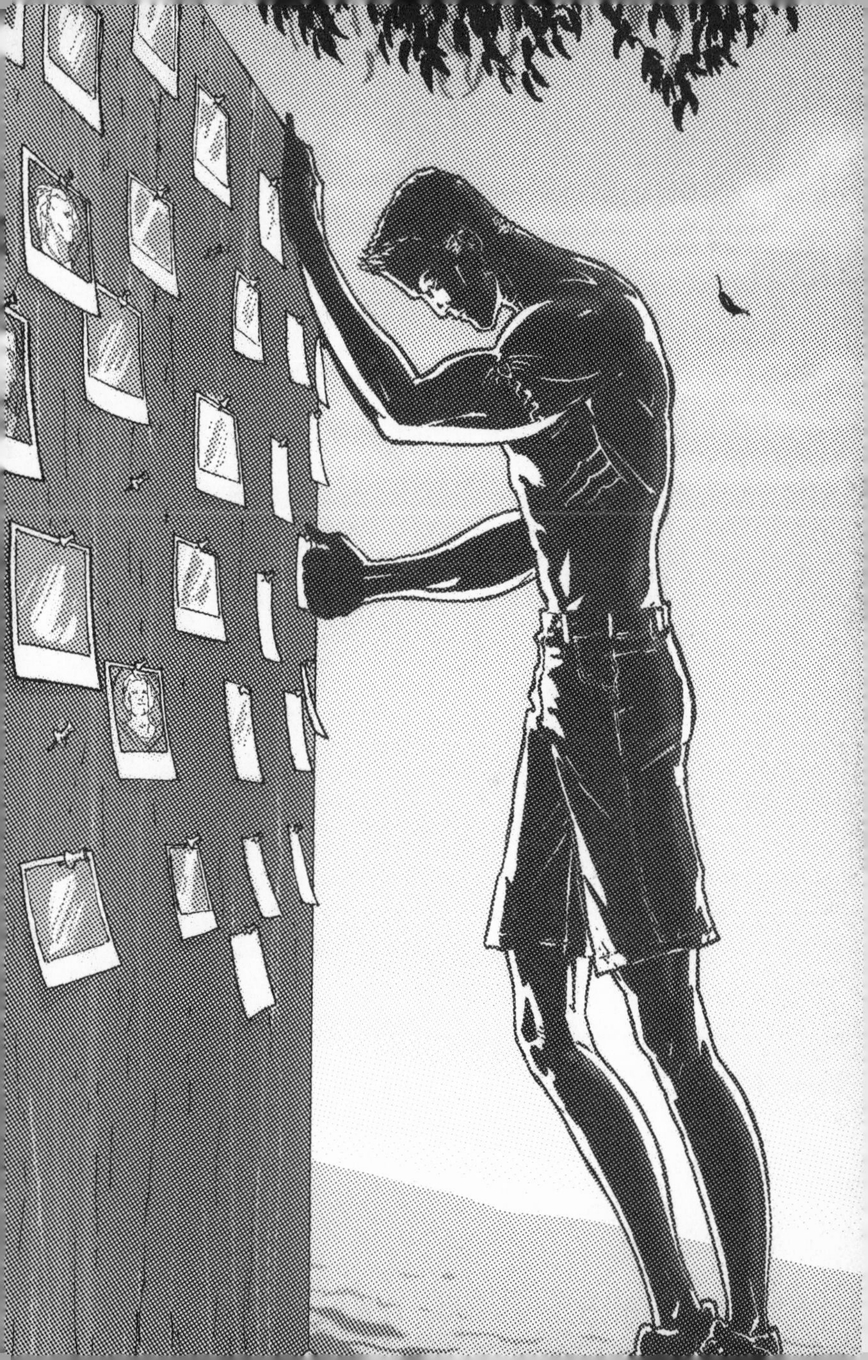

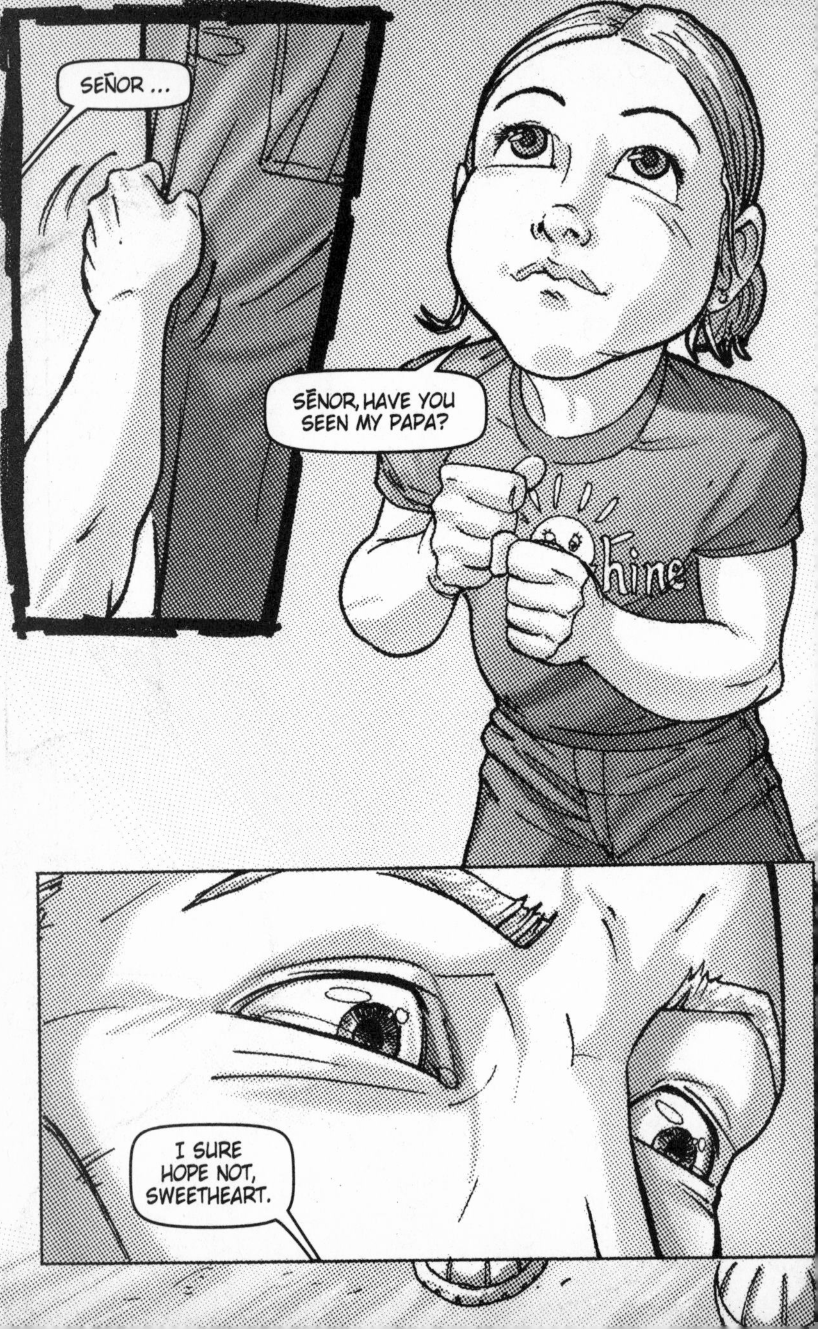
SEÑOR ...
SEÑOR, HAVE YOU SEEN MY PAPA?
I SURE HOPE NOT, SWEETHEART.

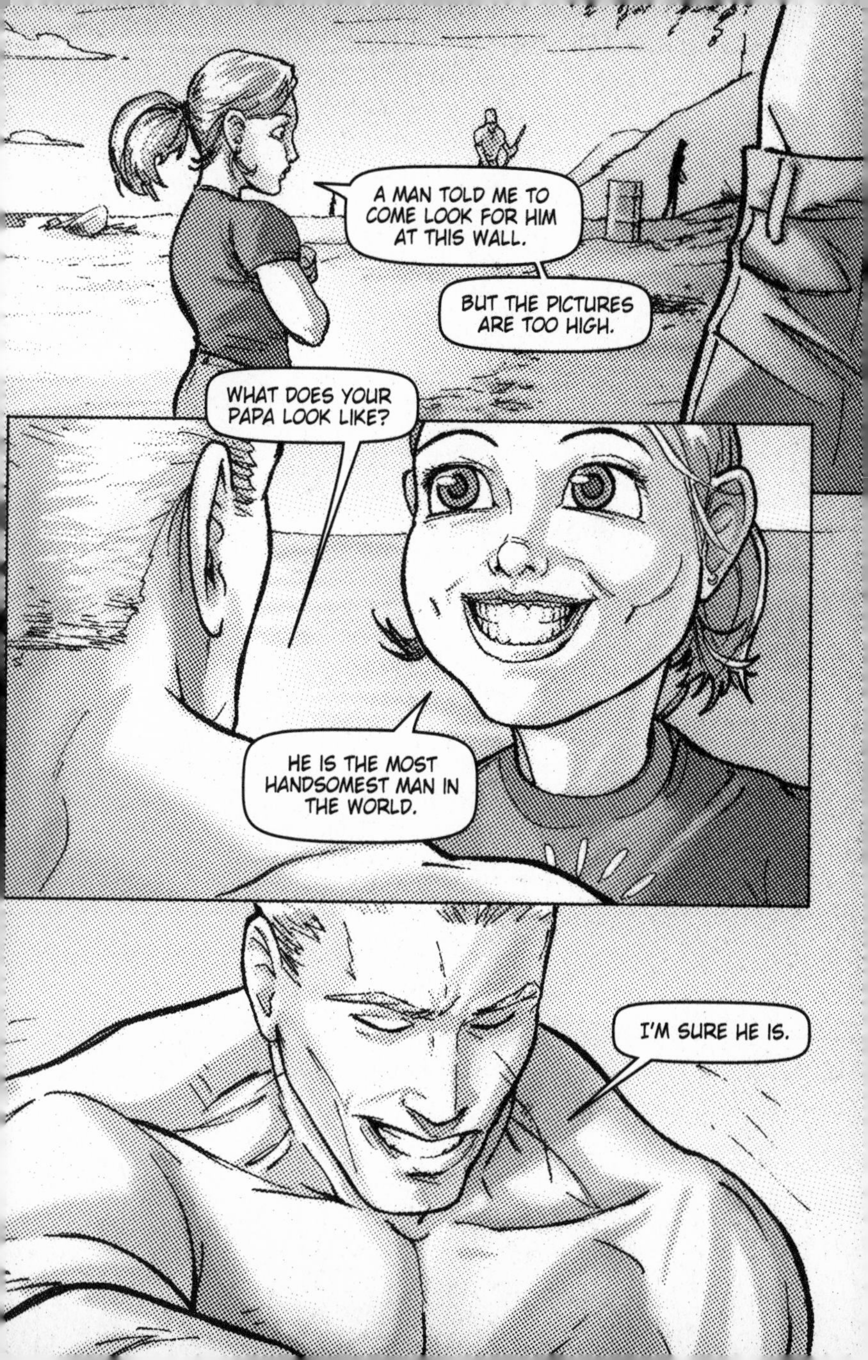
A MAN TOLD ME TO COME LOOK FOR HIM AT THIS WALL.
BUT THE PICTURES ARE TOO HIGH.
WHAT DOES YOUR PAPA LOOK LIKE?
HE IS THE MOST HANDSOMEST MAN IN THE WORLD.
I'M SURE HE IS.

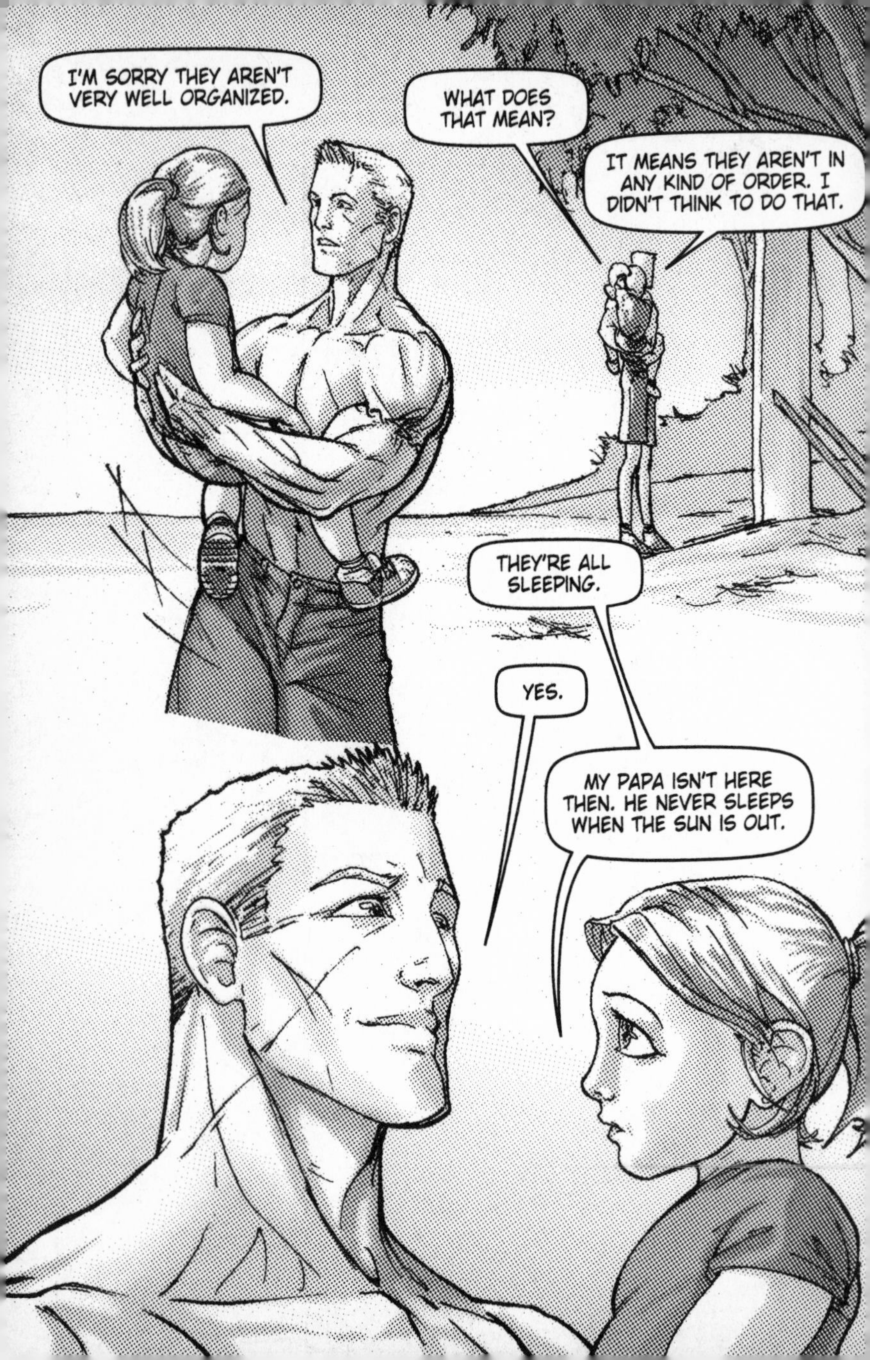
I'M SORRY THEY AREN'T VERY WELL ORGANIZED.
WHAT DOES THAT MEAN?
IT MEANS THEY AREN'T IN ANY KIND OF ORDER. I DIDN'T THINK TO DO THAT.
THEY'RE ALL SLEEPING.
YES.
MY PAPA ISN'T HERE THEN. HE NEVER SLEEPS WHEN THE SUN IS OUT.

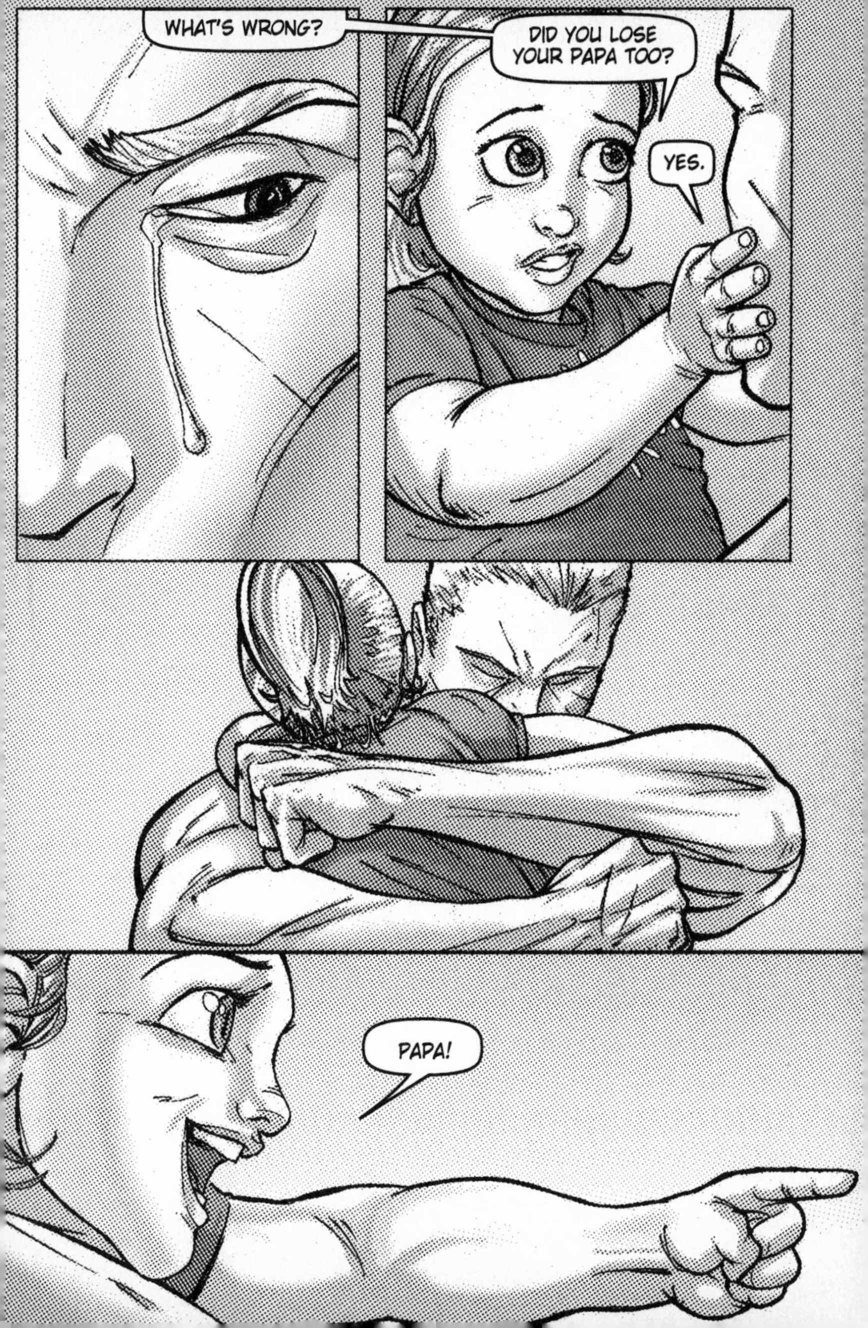
WHAT'S WRONG?
DID YOU LOSE YOUR PAPA TOO?
YES.
PAPA!

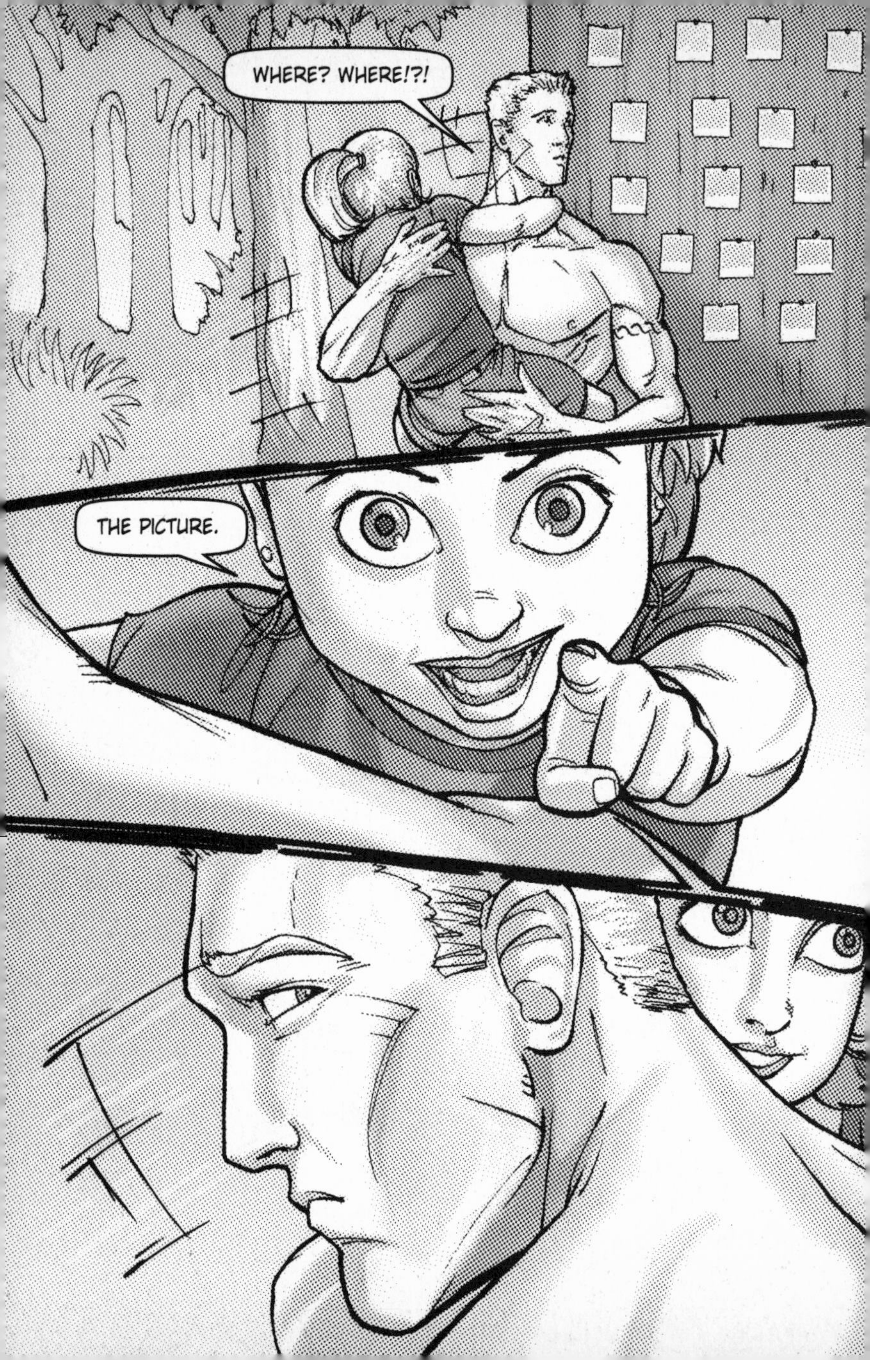
WHERE? WHERE!?!
THE PICTURE.

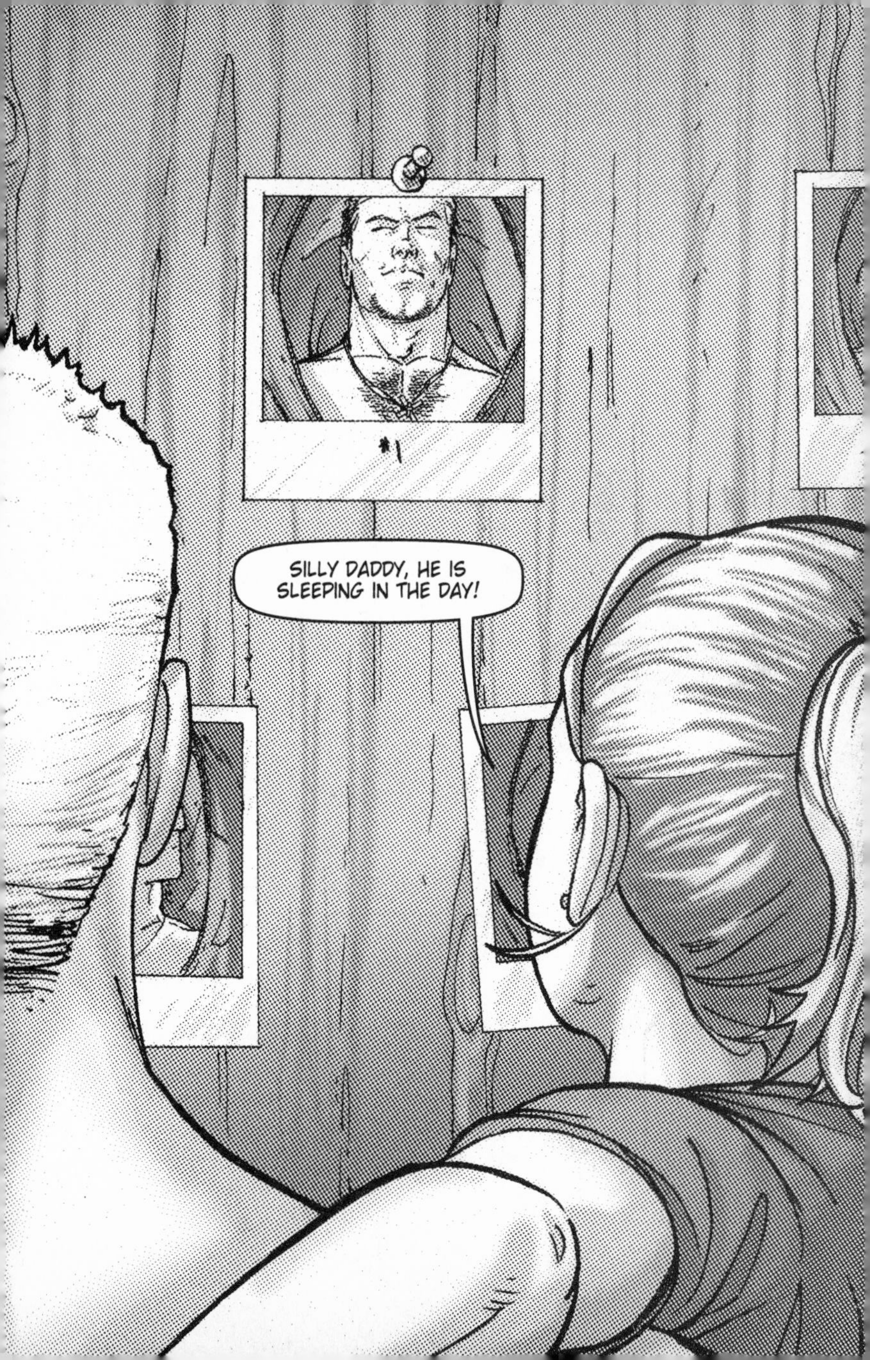
SILLY DADDY, HE IS SLEEPING IN THE DAY!

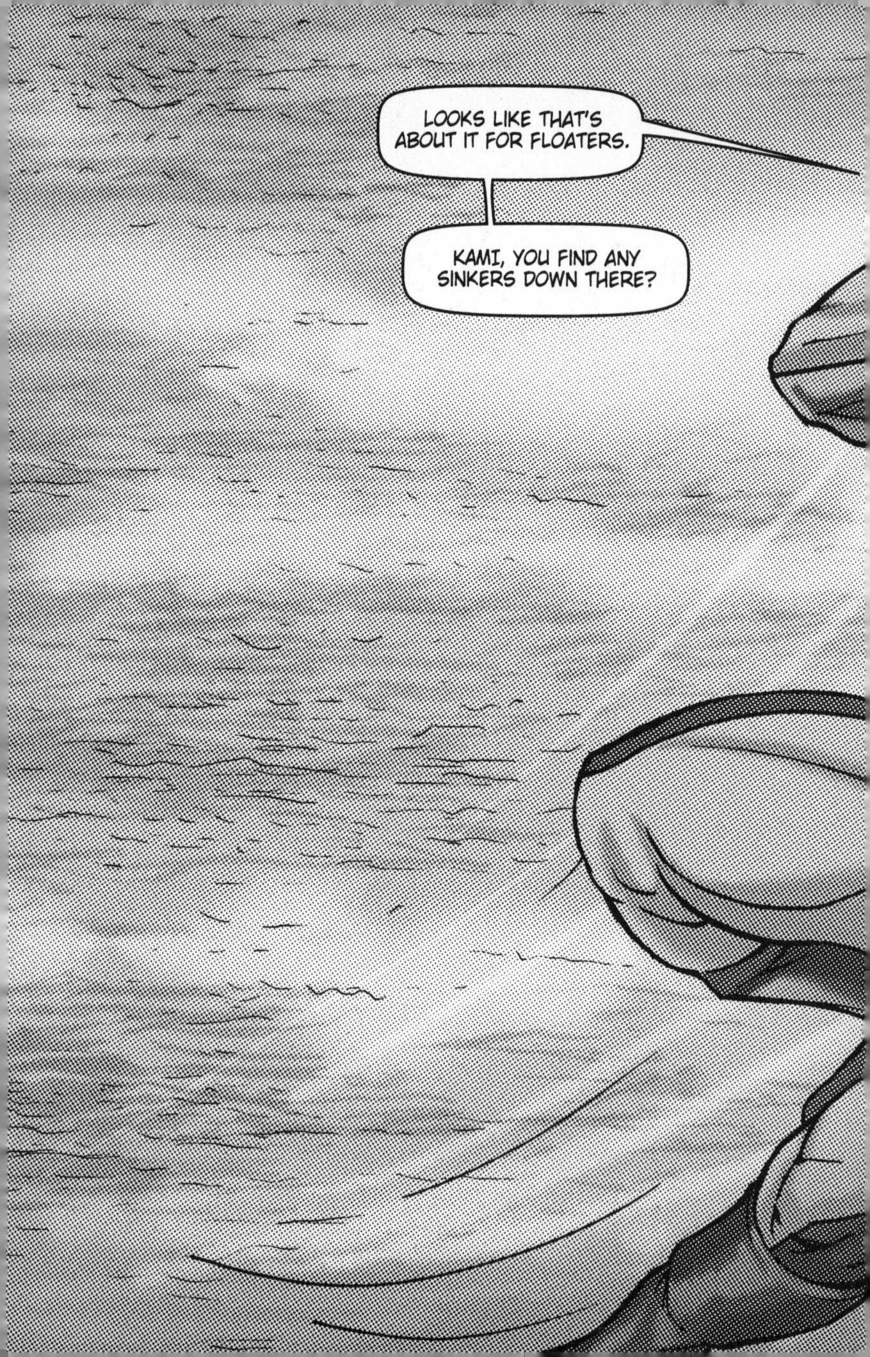
LOOKS LIKE THAT'S ABOUT IT FOR FLOATERS.
KAMI, YOU FIND ANY SINKERS DOWN THERE?

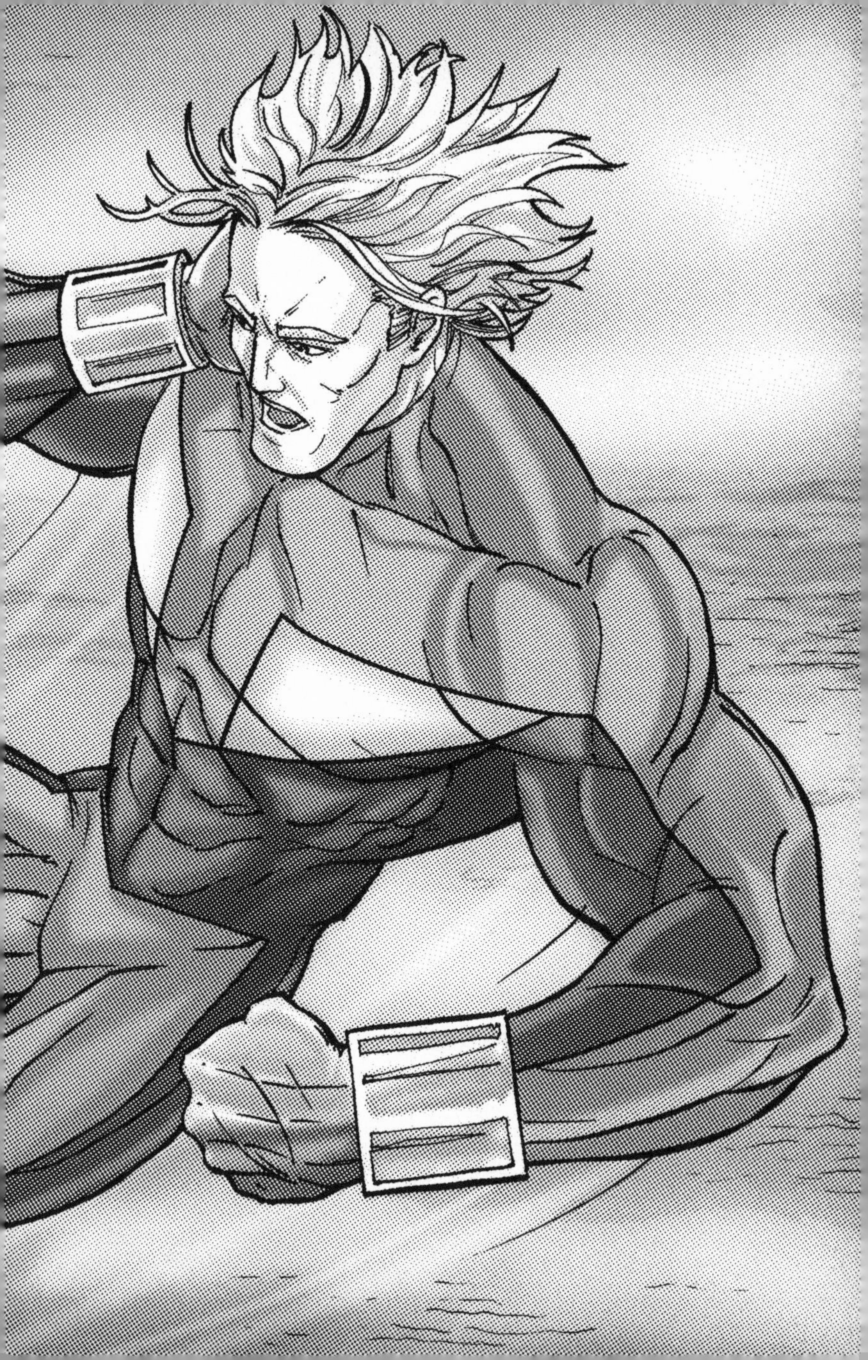

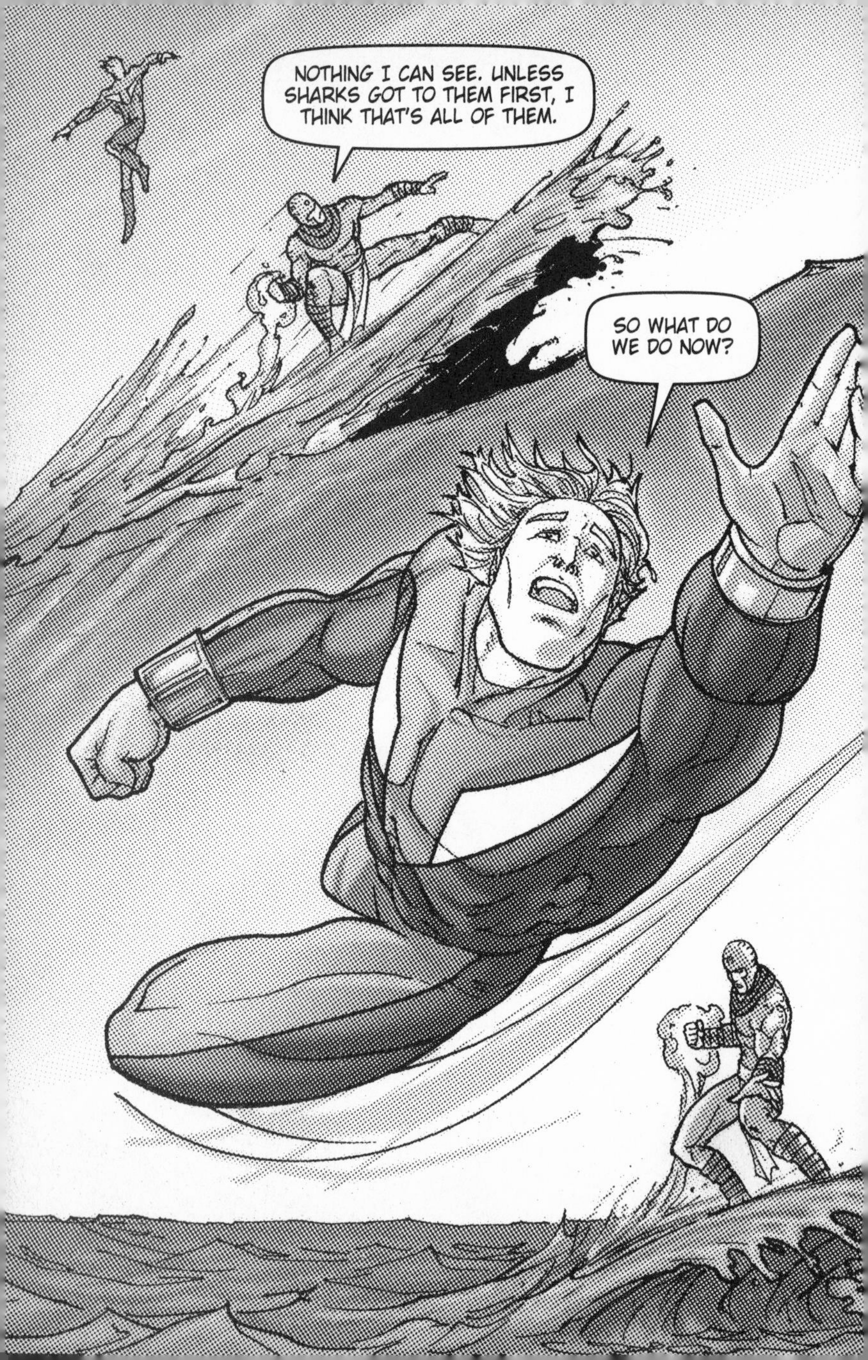
NOTHING I CAN SEE. UNLESS SHARKS GOT TO THEM FIRST, I THINK THAT'S ALL OF THEM.
SO WHAT DO WE DO NOW?

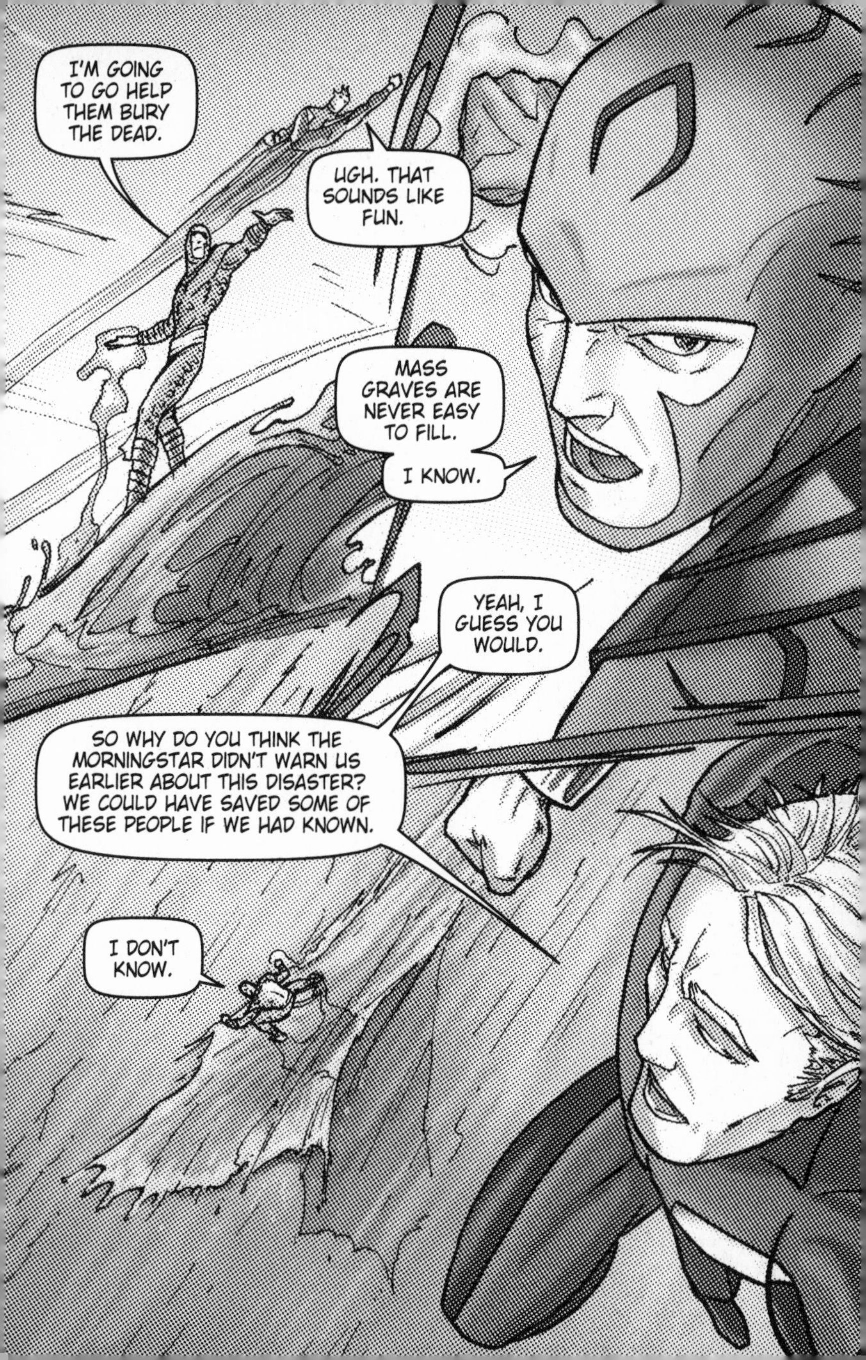
I'M GOING TO GO HELP THEM BURY THE DEAD.
UGH. THAT SOUNDS LIKE FUN.
MASS GRAVES ARE NEVER EASY TO FILL.
I KNOW.
YEAH, I GUESS YOU WOULD.
SO WHY DO YOU THINK THE MORNINGSTAR DIDN'T WARN US EARLIER ABOUT THIS DISASTER? WE COULD HAVE SAVED SOME OF THESE PEOPLE IF WE HAD KNOWN.
I DON'T KNOW.

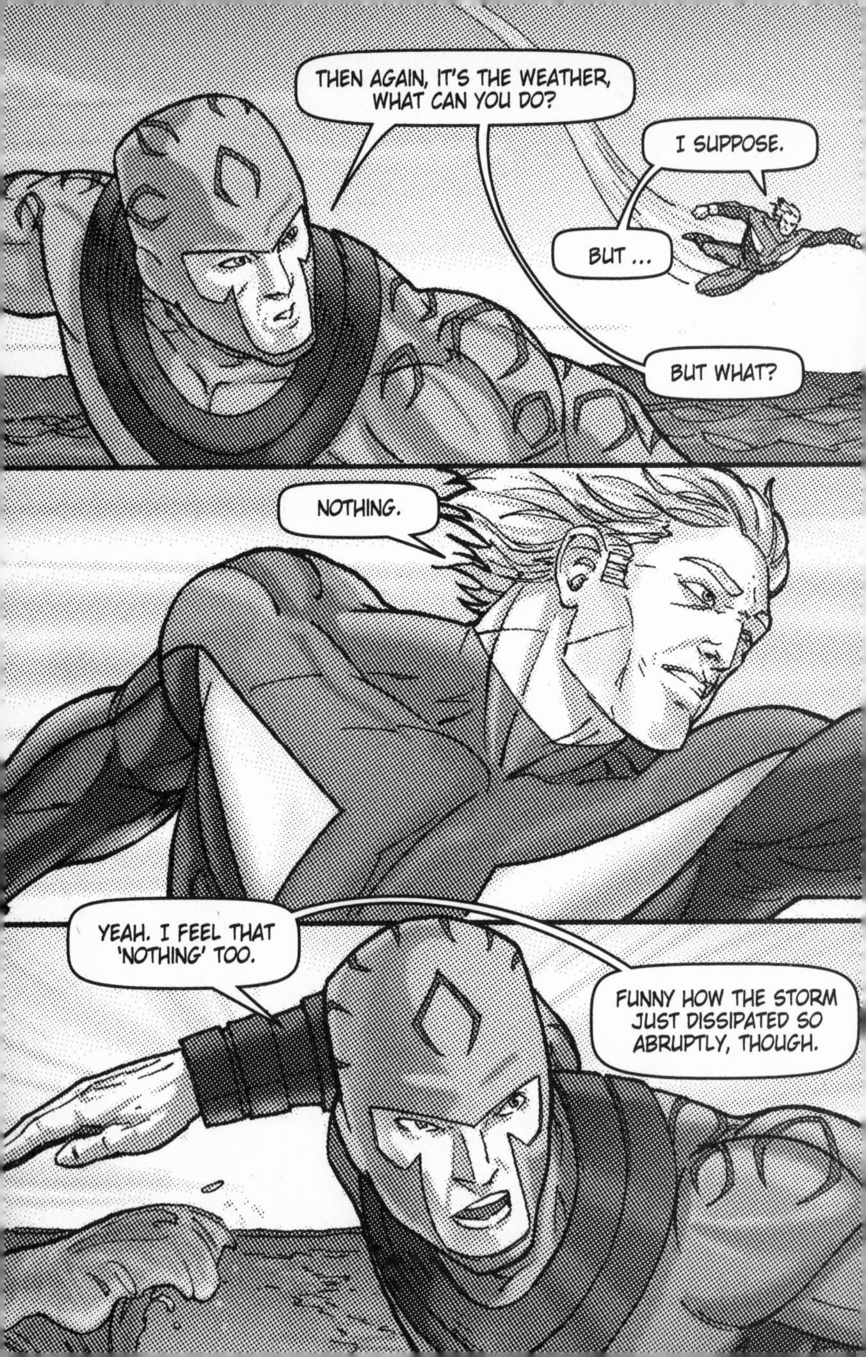
THEN AGAIN, IT'S THE WEATHER, WHAT CAN YOU DO?
I SUPPOSE.
BUT ...
BUT WHAT?
NOTHING.
YEAH. I FEEL THAT 'NOTHING' TOO.
FUNNY HOW THE STORM JUST DISSIPATED SO ABRUPTLY, THOUGH.

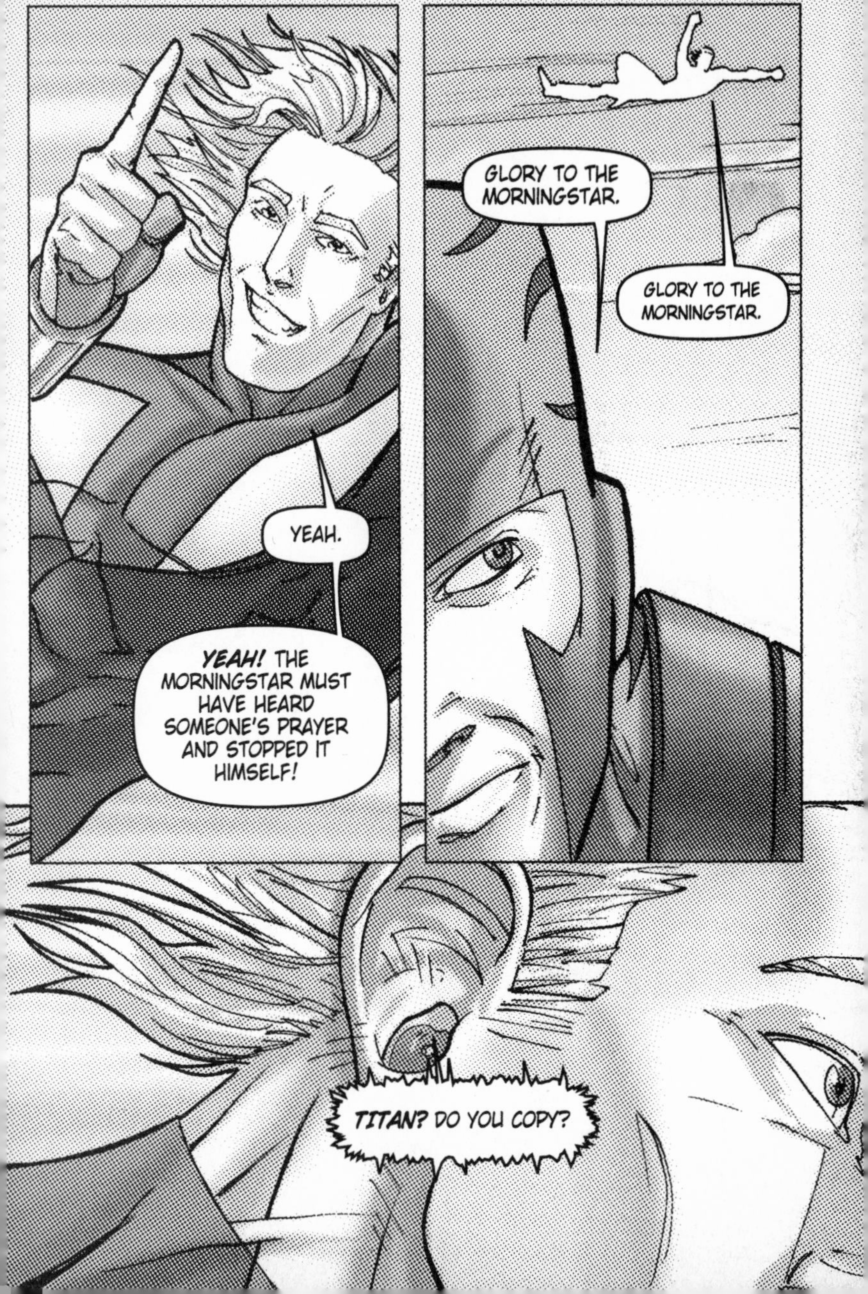
YEAH.
YEAH! THE MORNINGSTAR MUST HAVE HEARD SOMEONE'S PRAYER AND STOPPED IT HIMSELF!
GLORY TO THE MORNINGSTAR.
GLORY TO THE MORNINGSTAR.
TITAN? DO YOU COPY?

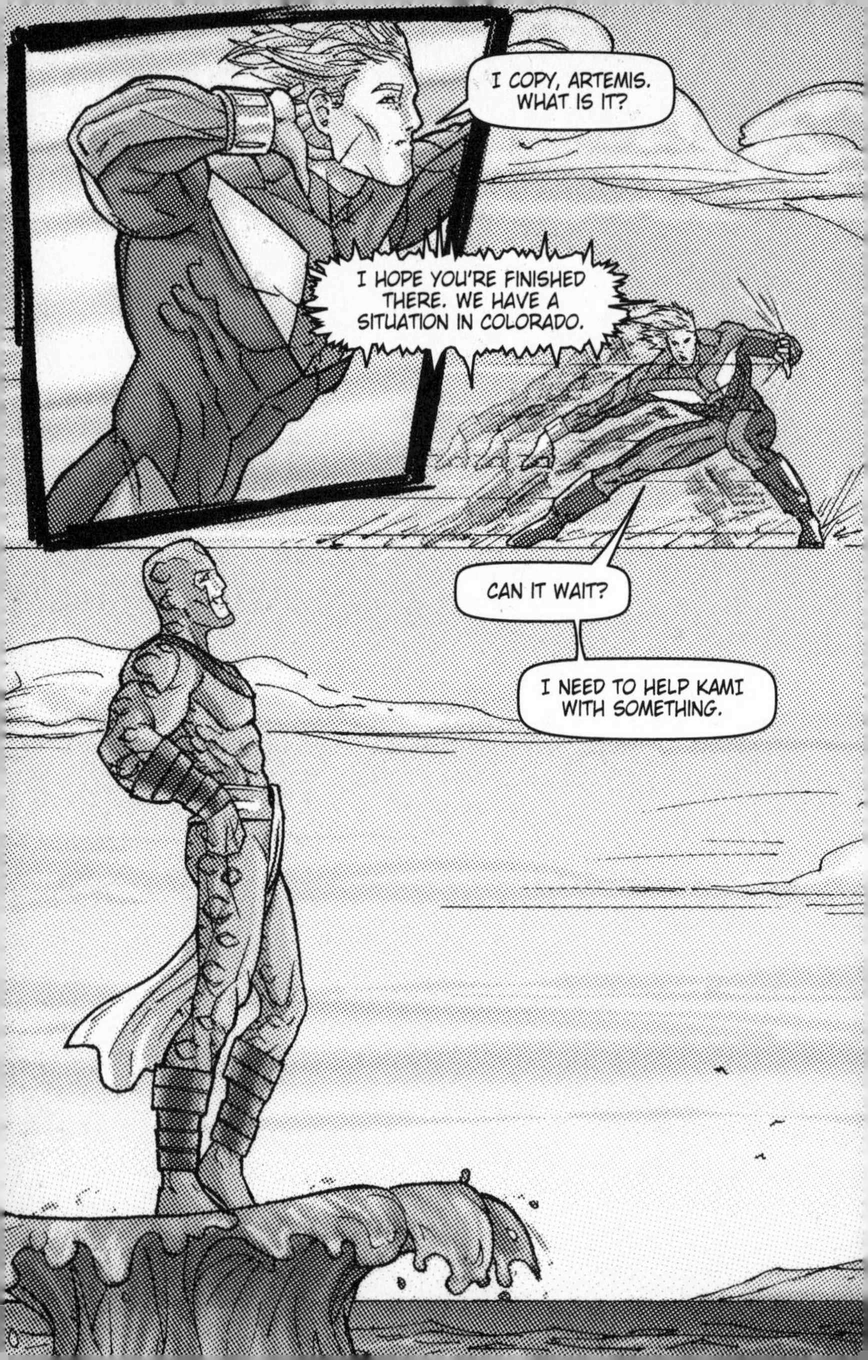
I COPY, ARTEMIS. WHAT IS IT?
I HOPE YOU'RE FINISHED THERE. WE HAVE A SITUATION IN COLORADO.
CAN IT WAIT?
I NEED TO HELP KAMI WITH SOMETHING.

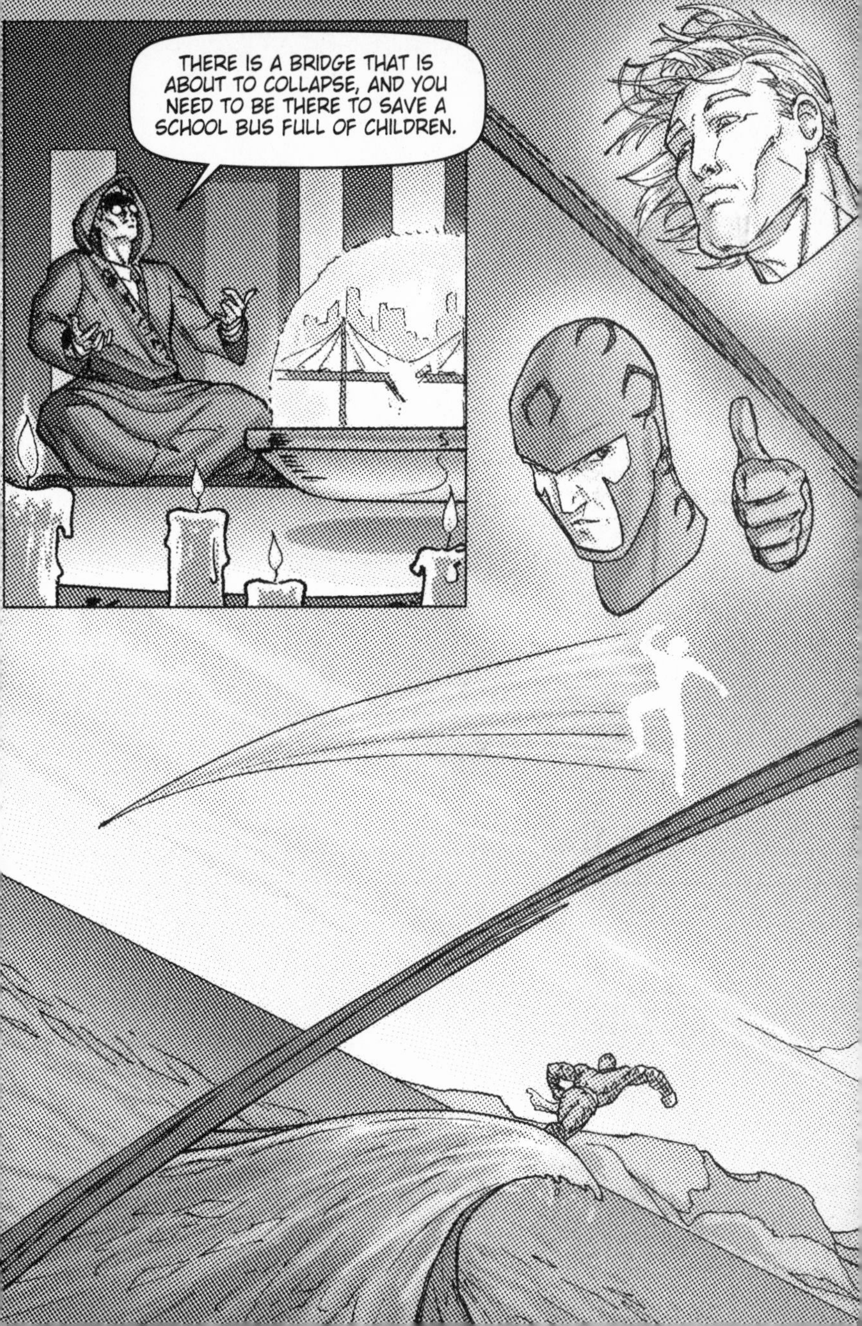
THERE IS A BRIDGE THAT IS ABOUT TO COLLAPSE, AND YOU NEED TO BE THERE TO SAVE A SCHOOL BUS FULL OF CHILDREN.

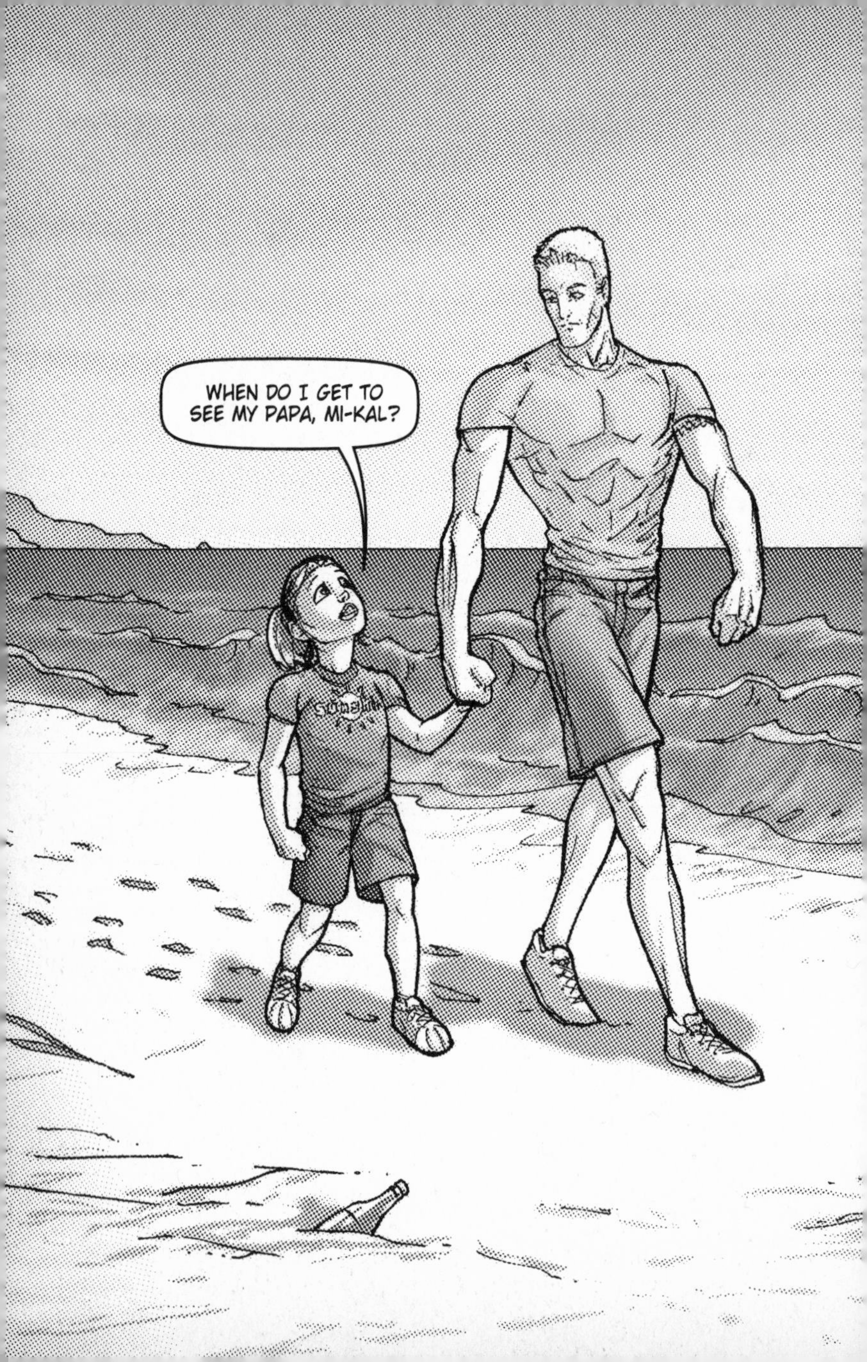
WHEN DO I GET TO SEE MY PAPA, MI-KAL?

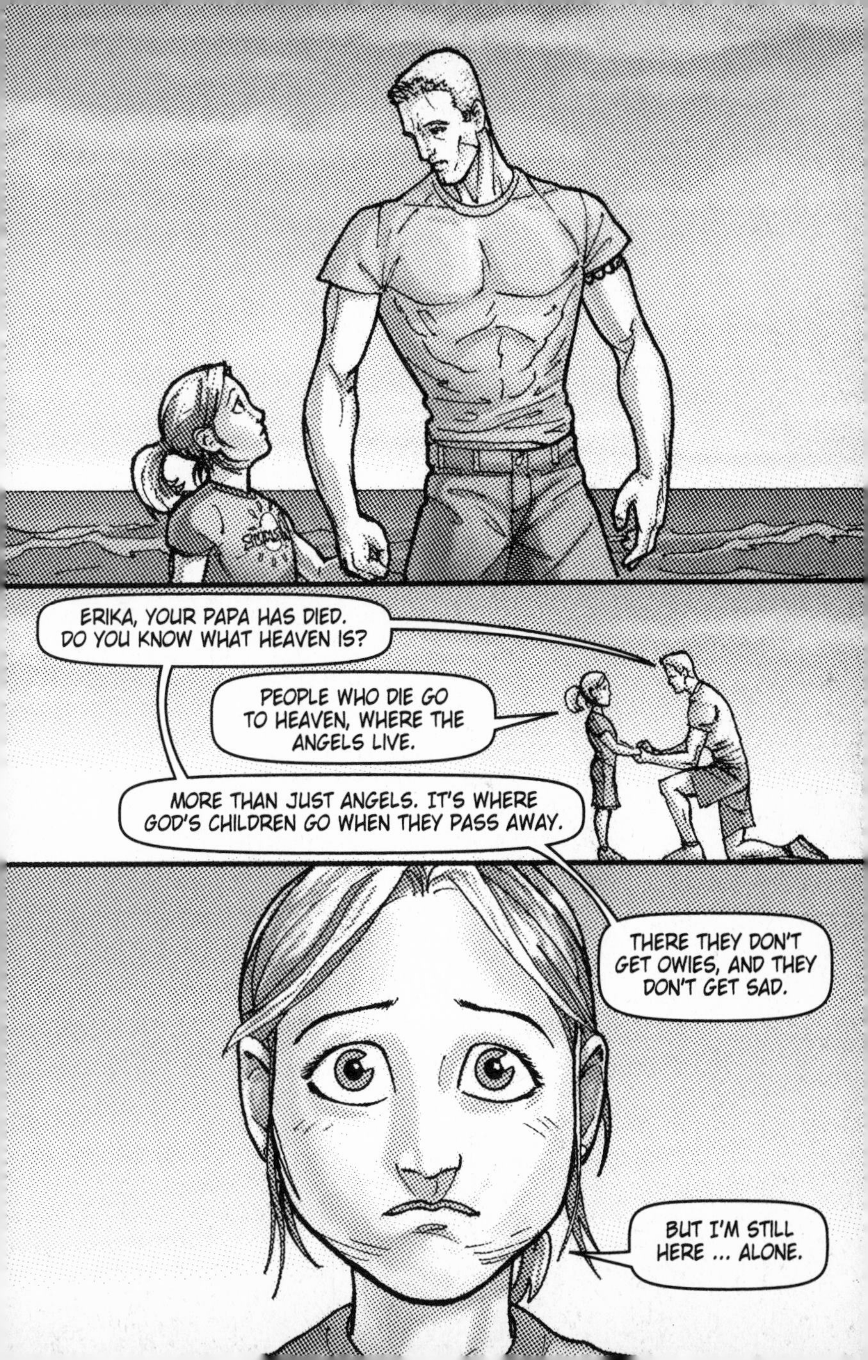
ERIKA, YOUR PAPA HAS DIED. DO YOU KNOW WHAT HEAVEN IS?
PEOPLE WHO DIE GO TO HEAVEN, WHERE THE ANGELS LIVE.
MORE THAN JUST ANGELS. IT'S WHERE GOD'S CHILDREN GO WHEN THEY PASS AWAY.
THERE THEY DON'T GET OWIES, AND THEY DON'T GET SAD.
BUT I'M STILL HERE ... ALONE.

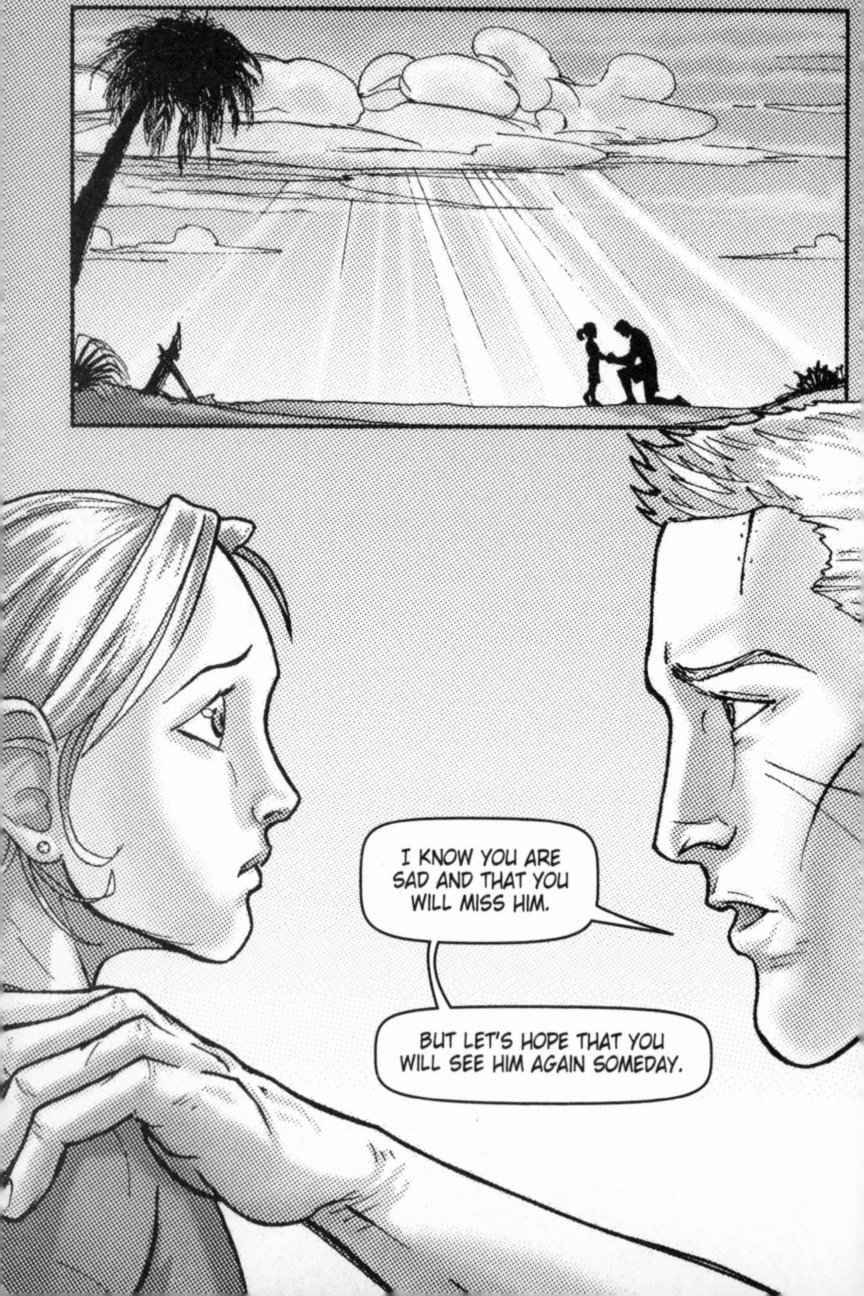
I KNOW YOU ARE SAD AND THAT YOU WILL MISS HIM.
BUT LET'S HOPE THAT YOU WILL SEE HIM AGAIN SOMEDAY.

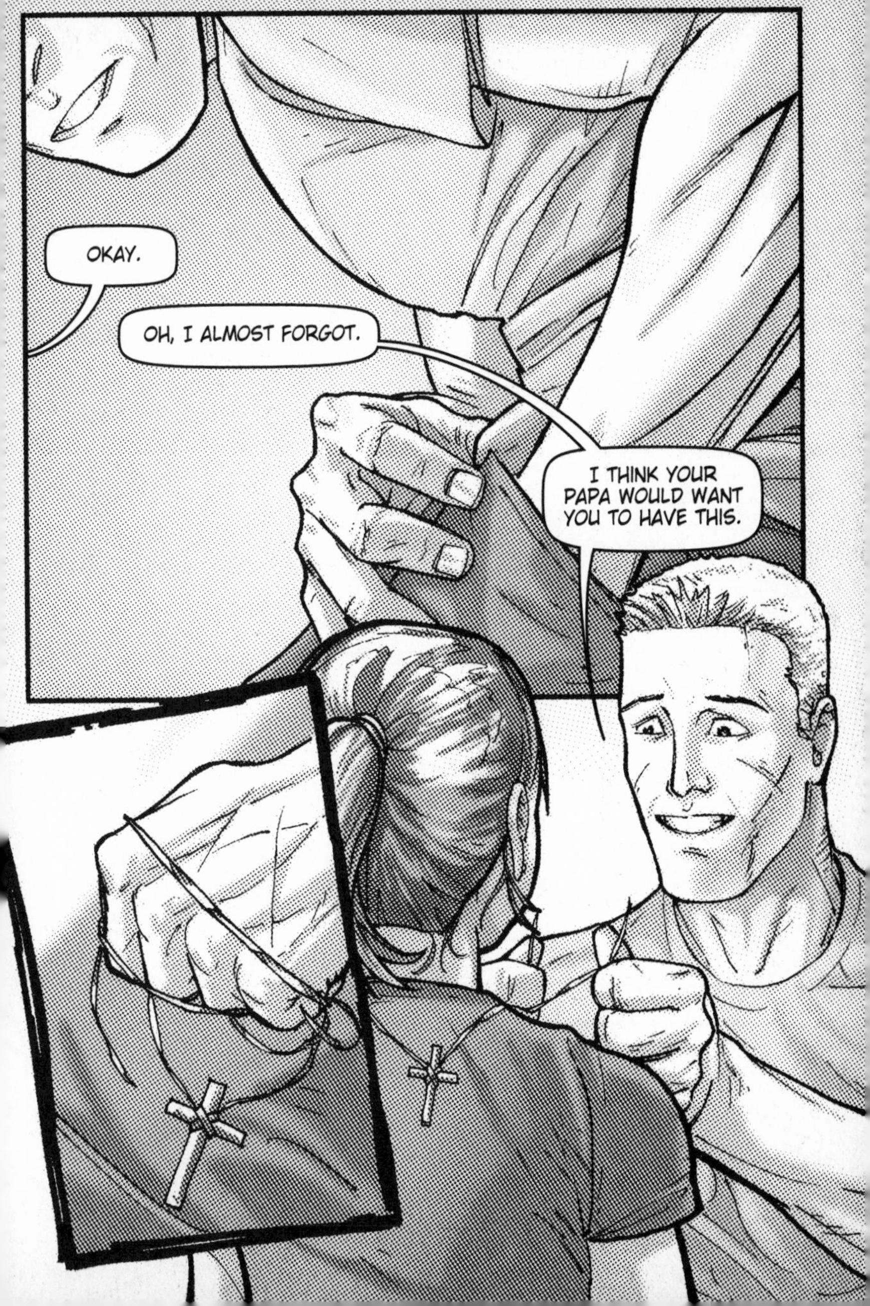
OKAY.
OH, I ALMOST FORGOT.
I THINK YOUR PAPA WOULD WANT YOU TO HAVE THIS.

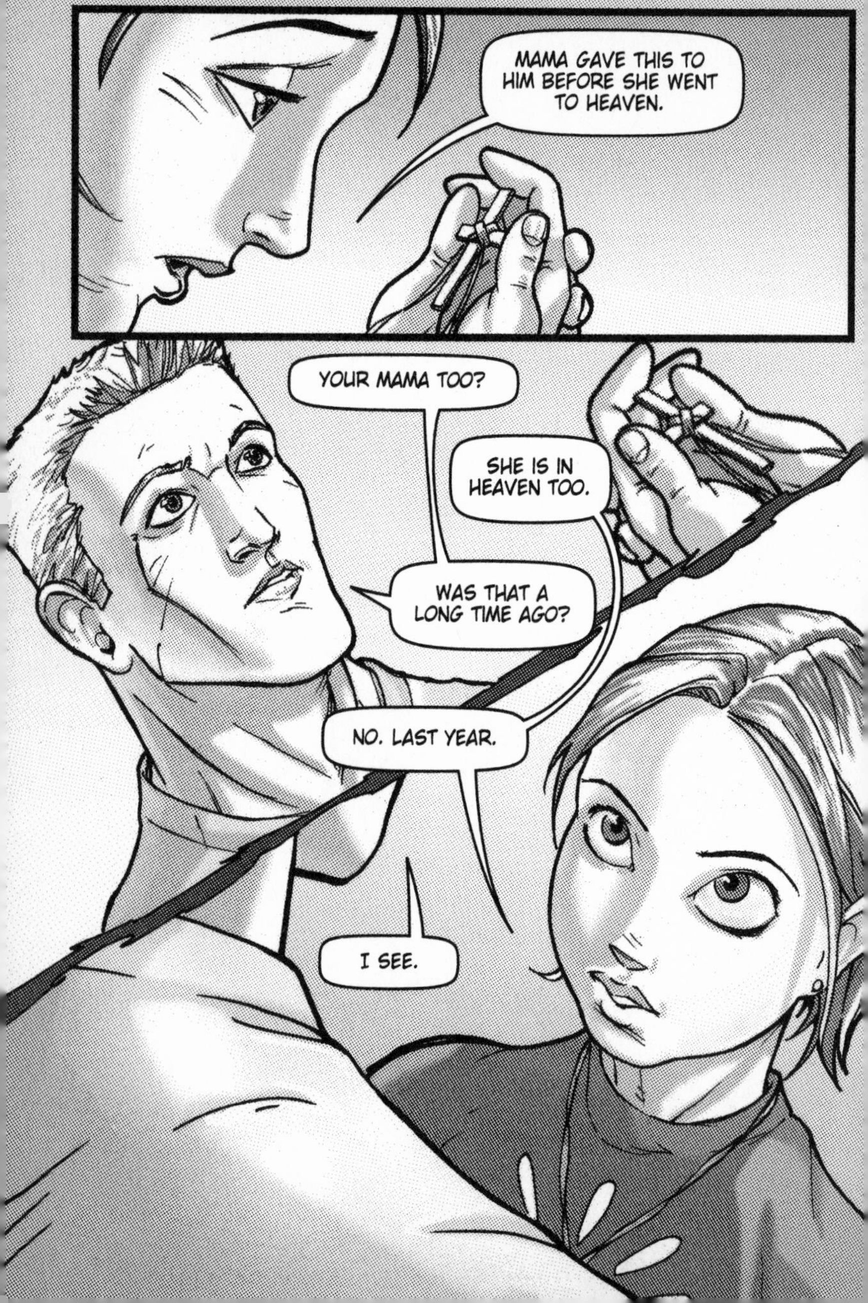
MAMA GAVE THIS TO HIM BEFORE SHE WENT TO HEAVEN.
YOUR MAMA TOO?
SHE IS IN HEAVEN TOO.
WAS THAT A LONG TIME AGO?
NO. LAST YEAR.
I SEE.

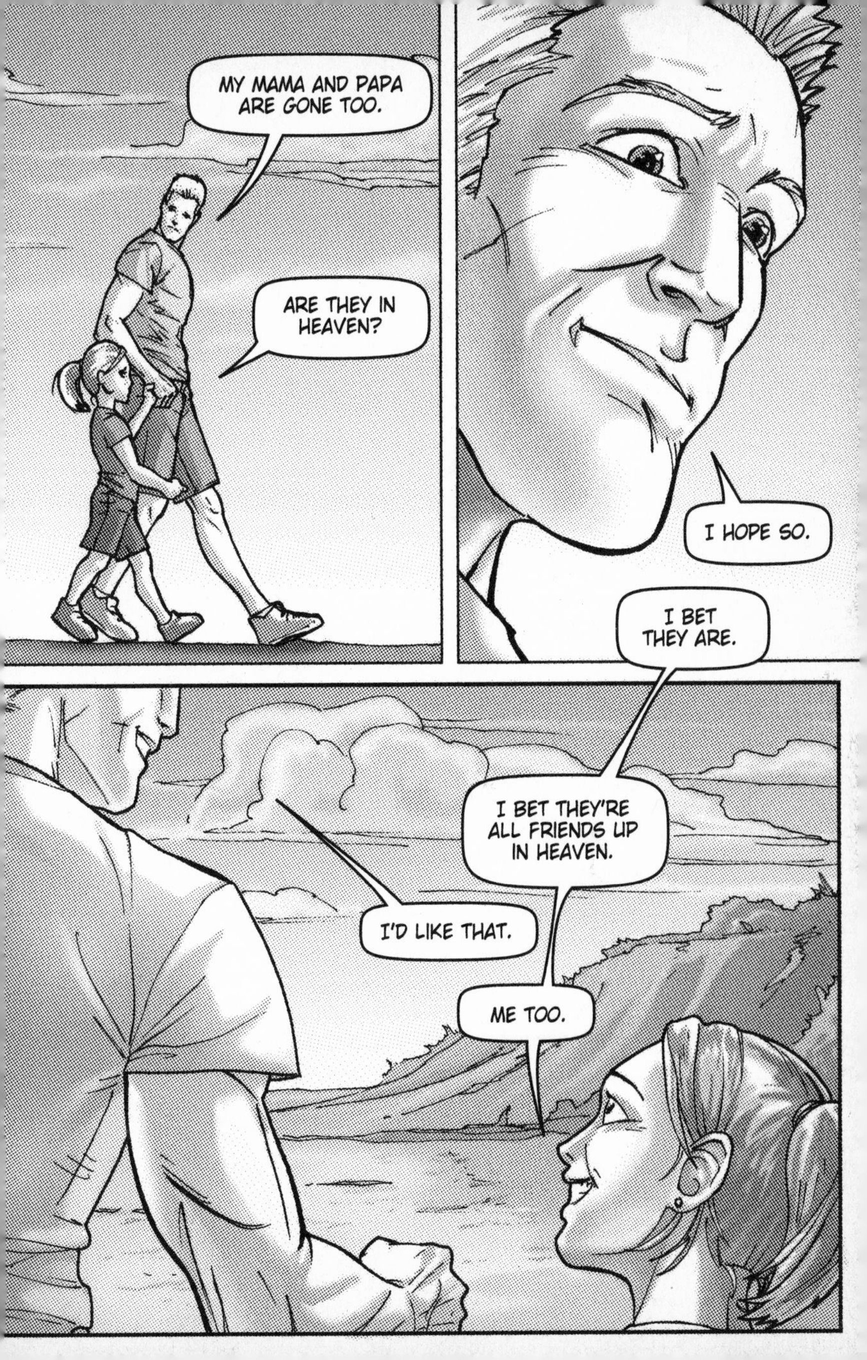
MY MAMA AND PAPA ARE GONE TOO.
ARE THEY IN HEAVEN?
I HOPE SO.
I BET THEY ARE.
I BET THEY'RE ALL FRIENDS UP IN HEAVEN.
I'D LIKE THAT.
ME TOO.

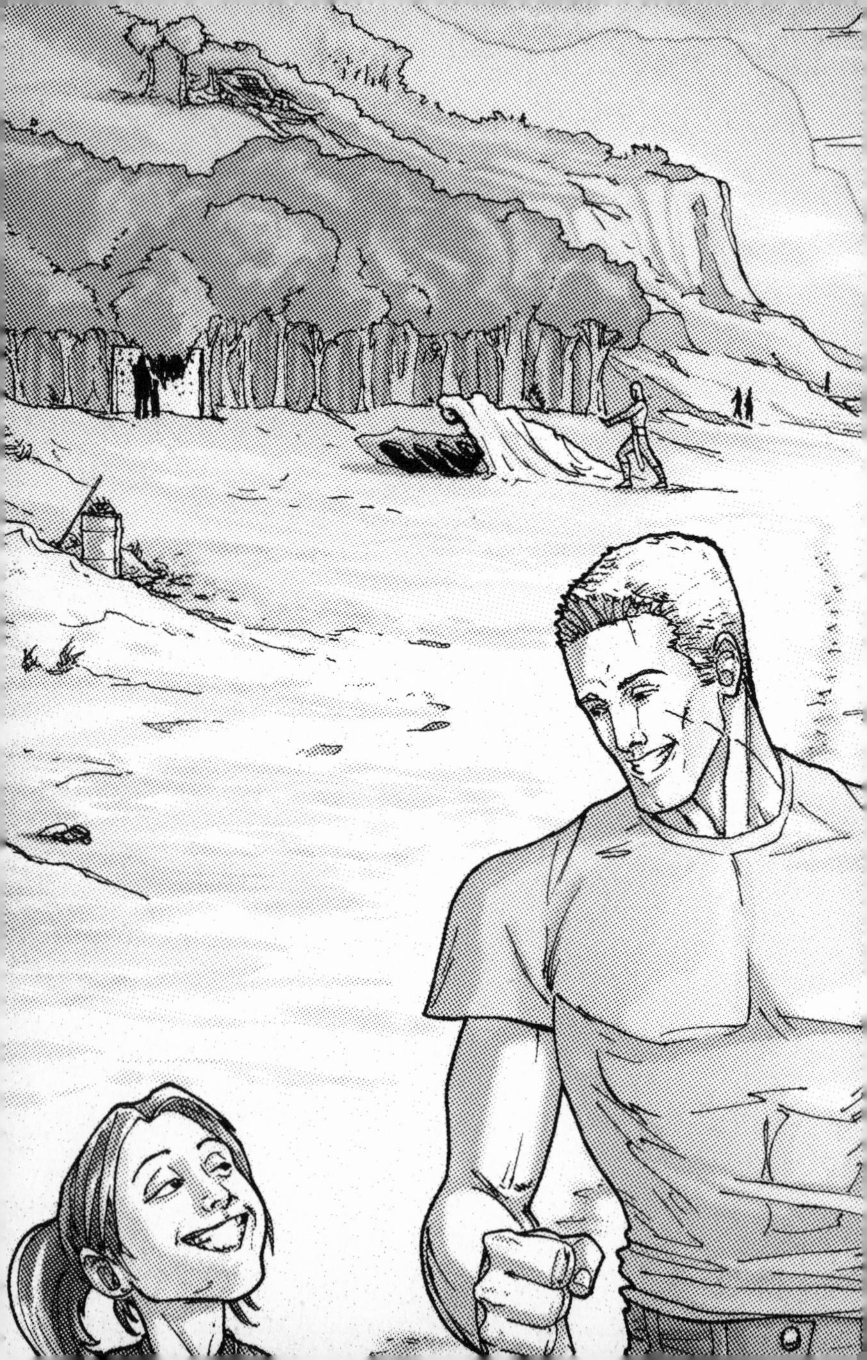

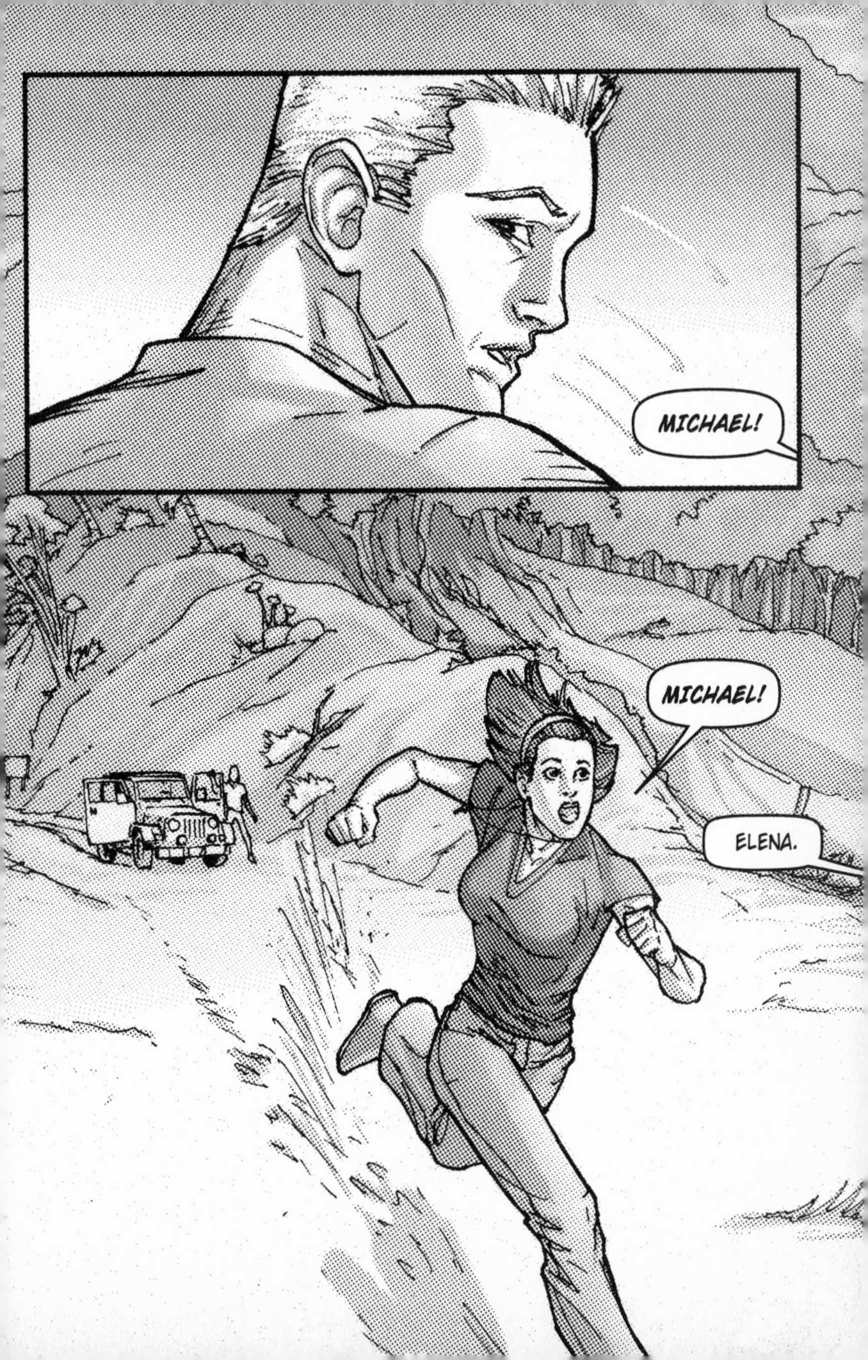
MICHAEL!
MICHAEL!
ELENA.

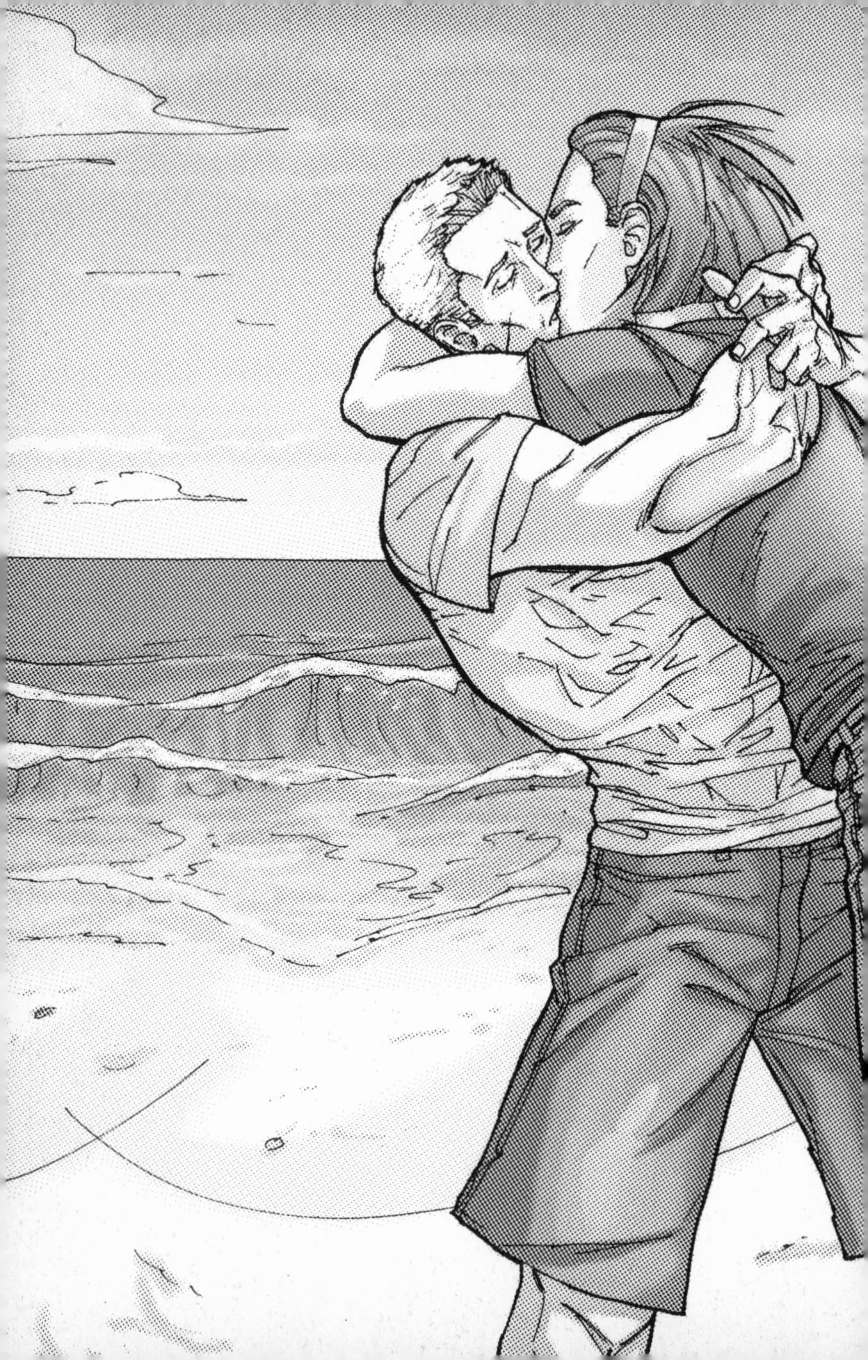

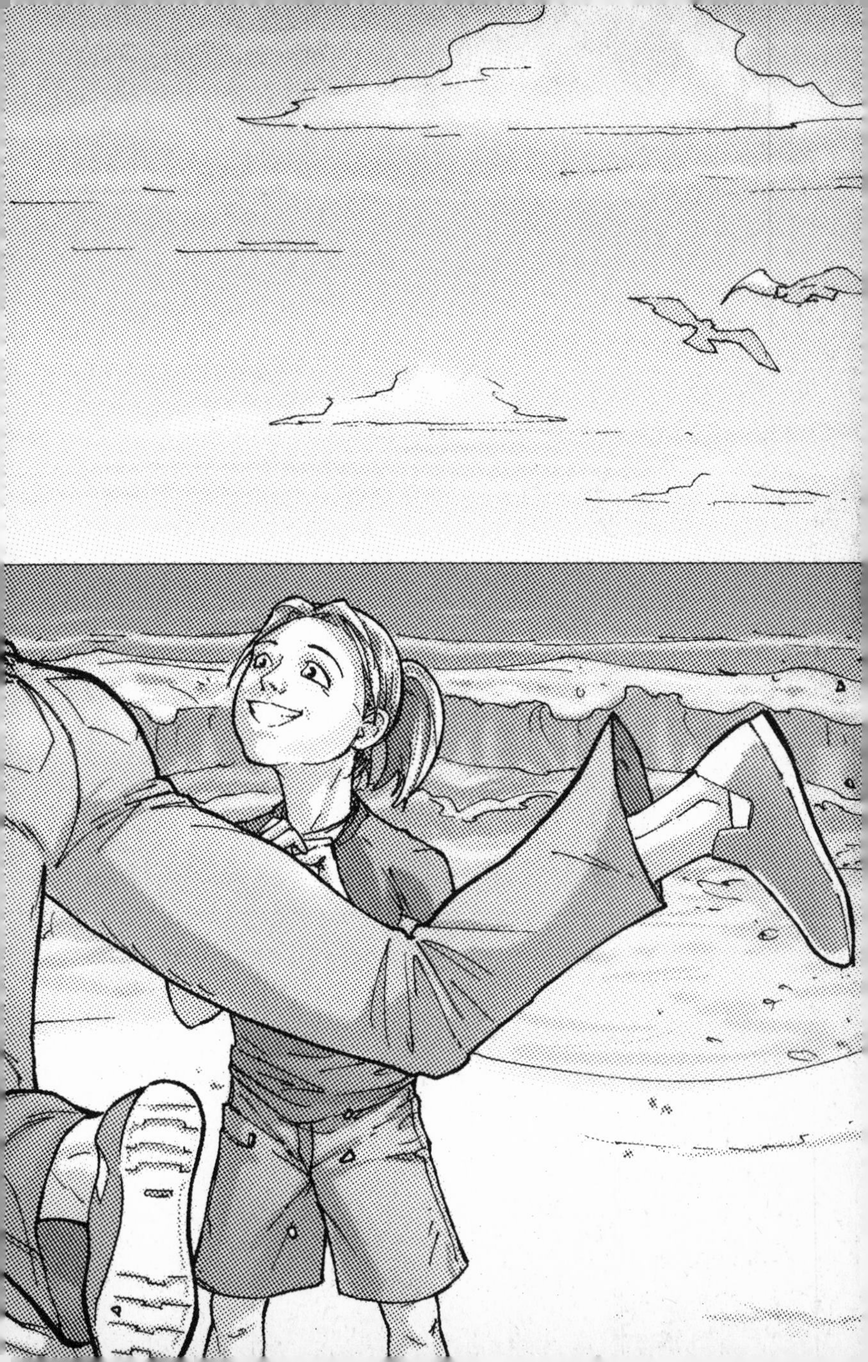

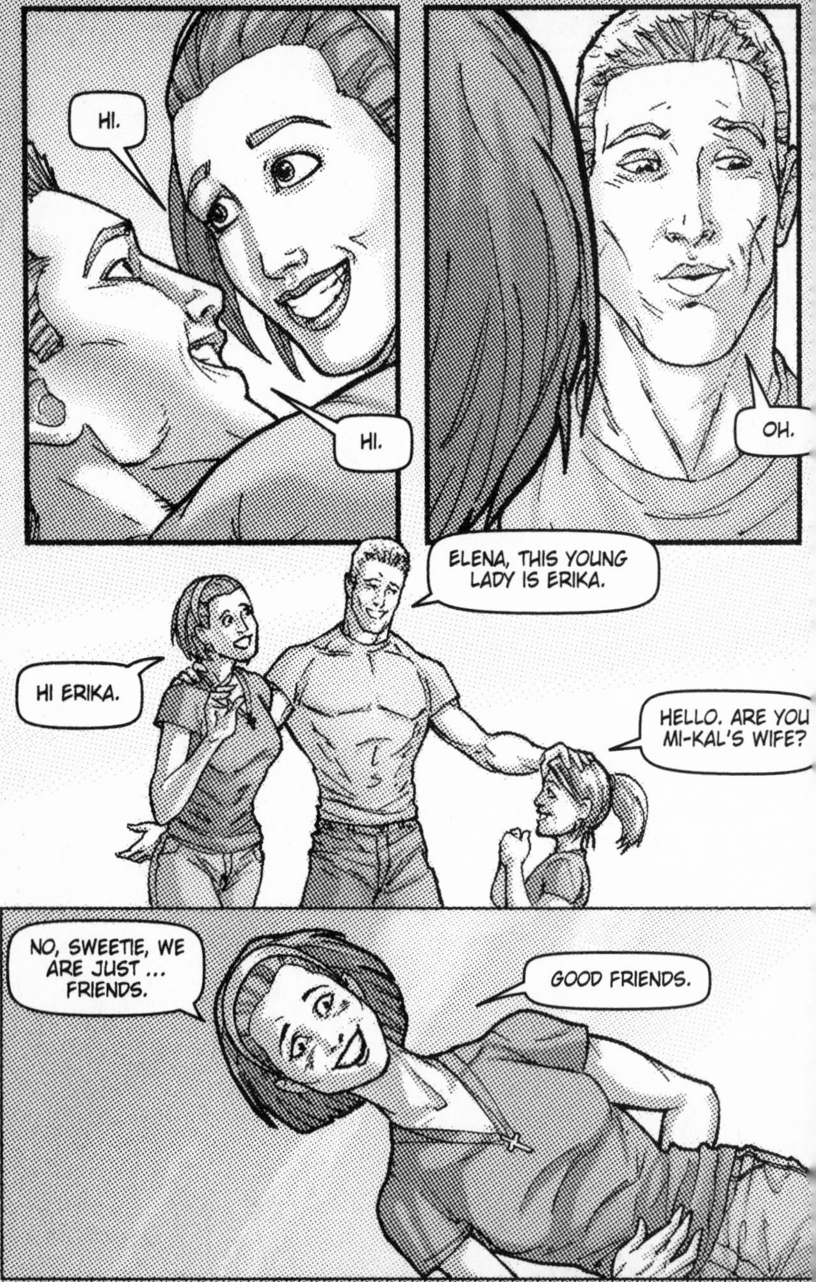
HI.
HI.
OH.
ELENA, THIS YOUNG LADY IS ERIKA.
HI ERIKA.
HELLO. ARE YOU MI-KAL'S WIFE?
NO, SWEETIE, WE ARE JUST ... FRIENDS.
GOOD FRIENDS.

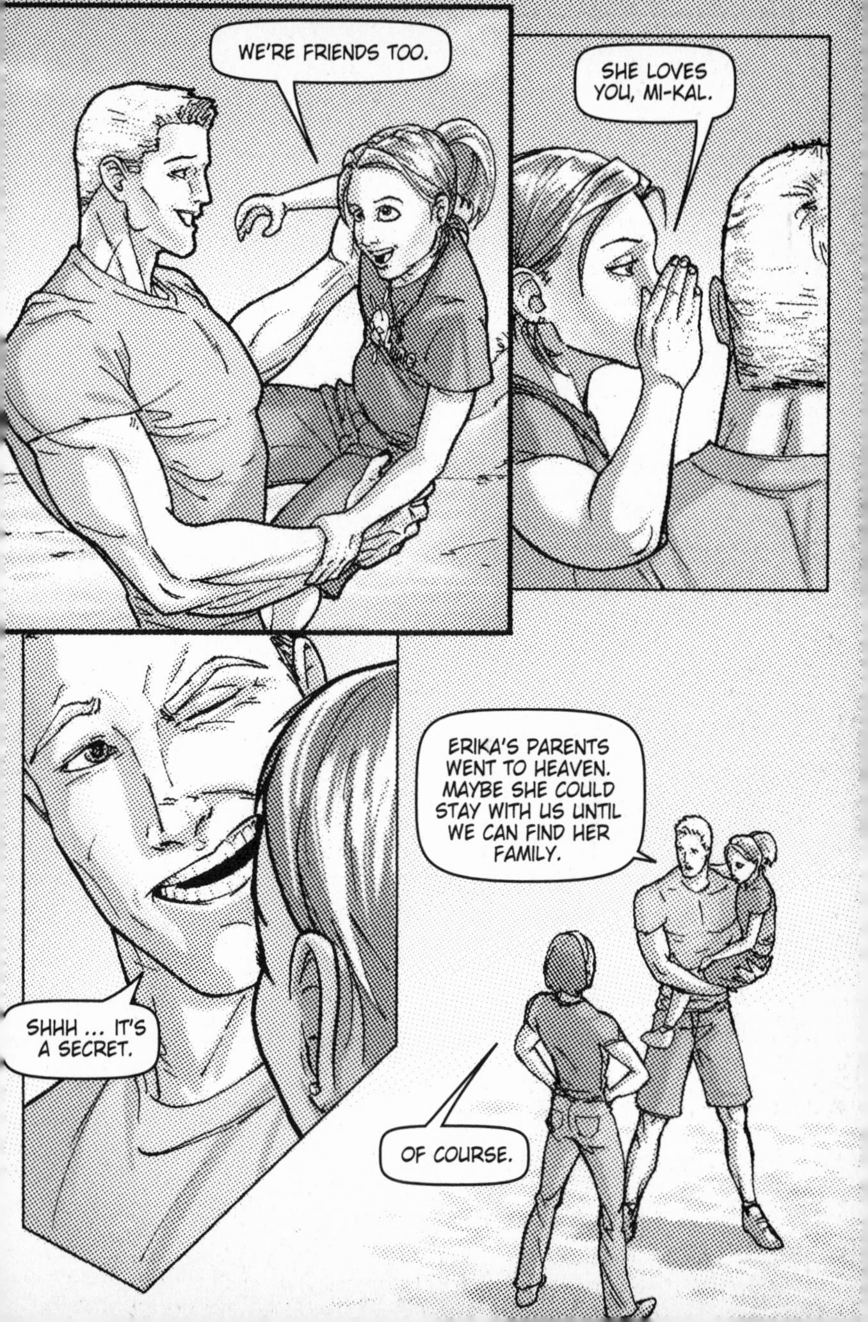
WE'RE FRIENDS TOO.
SHE LOVES YOU, MI-KAL.
SHHH ... IT'S A SECRET.
ERIKA'S PARENTS WENT TO HEAVEN. MAYBE SHE COULD STAY WITH US UNTIL WE CAN FIND HER FAMILY.
OF COURSE.

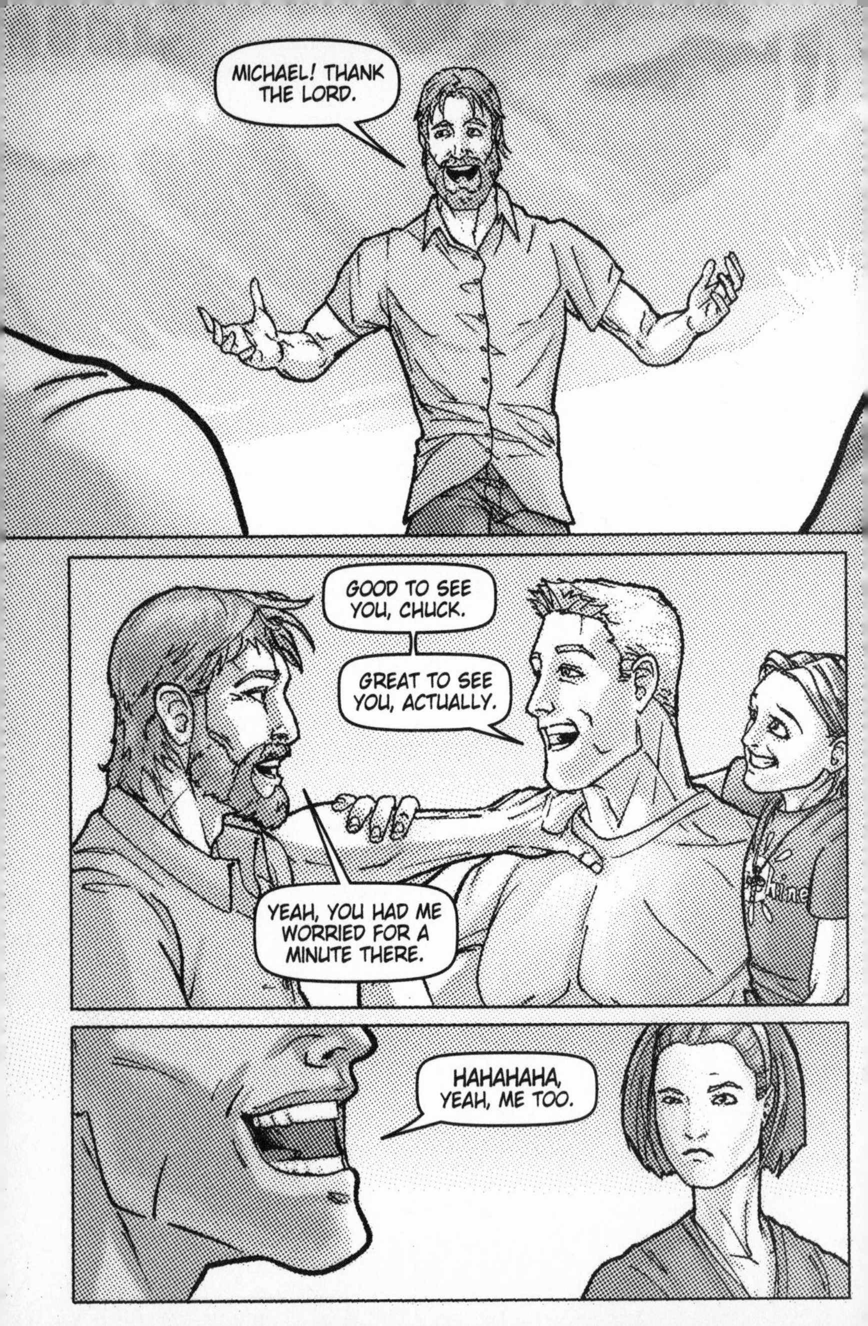
MICHAEL! THANK THE LORD.
GOOD TO SEE YOU, CHUCK.
GREAT TO SEE YOU, ACTUALLY.
YEAH, YOU HAD ME WORRIED FOR A MINUTE THERE.
HAHAHAHA, YEAH, ME TOO.

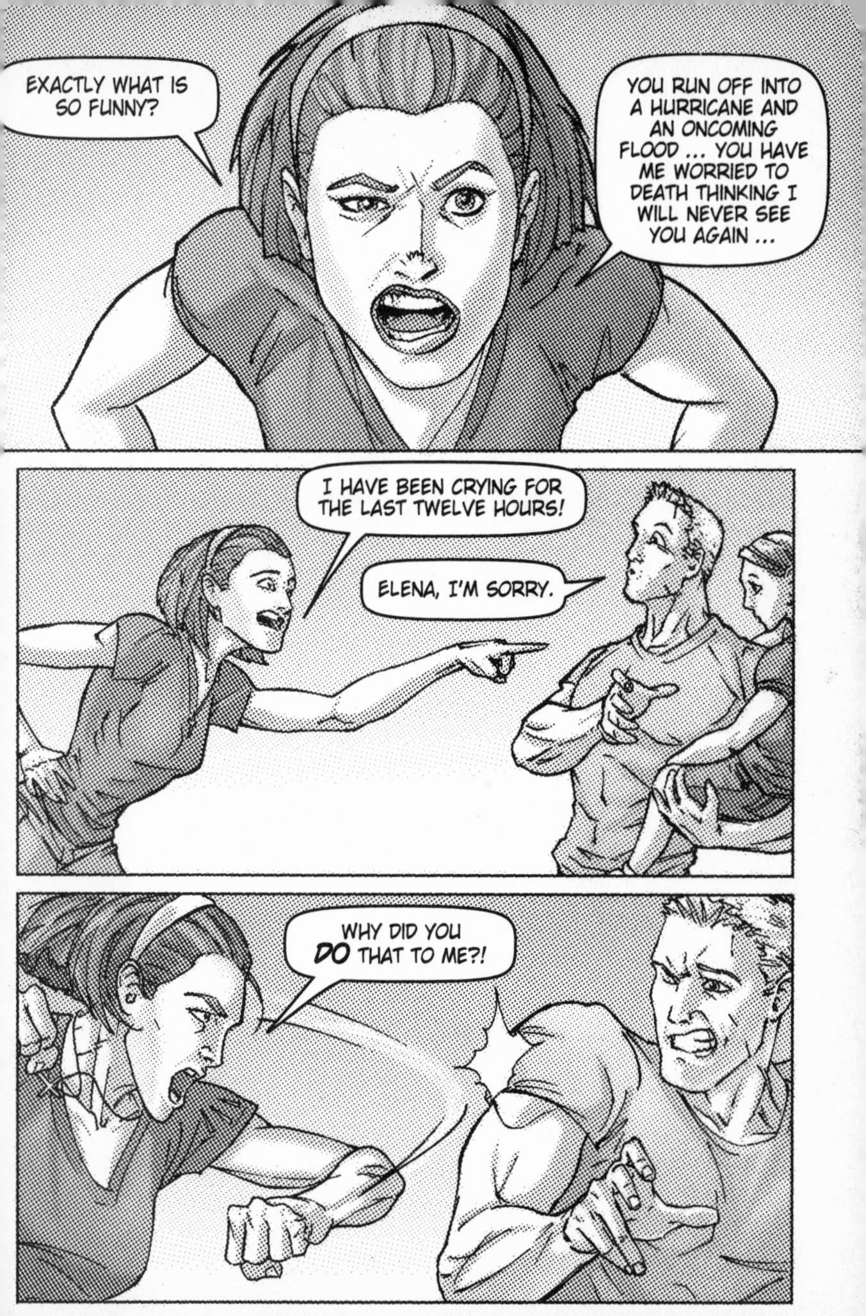
EXACTLY WHAT IS SO FUNNY?
YOU RUN OFF INTO A HURRICANE AND AN ONCOMING FLOOD ... YOU HAVE ME WORRIED TO DEATH THINKING I WILL NEVER SEE YOU AGAIN ...
I HAVE BEEN CRYING FOR THE LAST TWELVE HOURS!
ELENA, I'M SORRY.
WHY DID YOU **DO** THAT TO ME?!

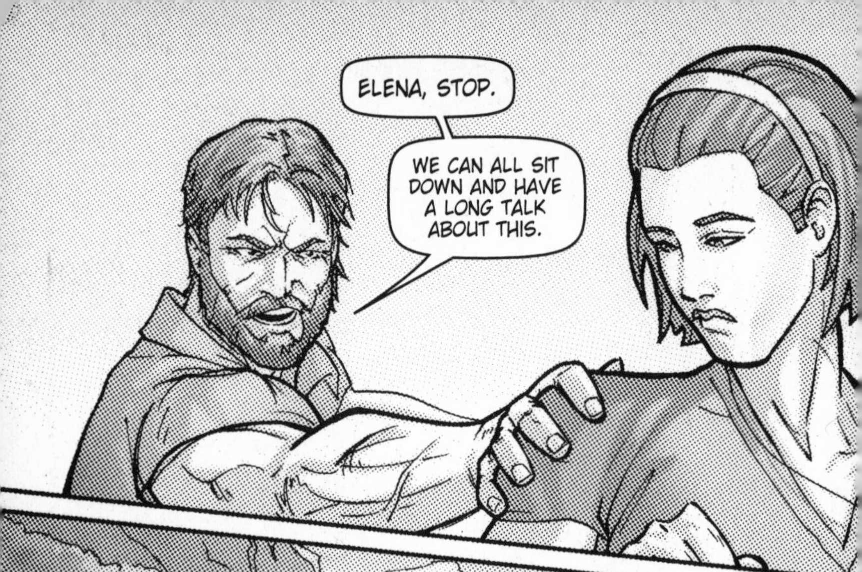
ELENA, STOP.
WE CAN ALL SIT DOWN AND HAVE A LONG TALK ABOUT THIS.
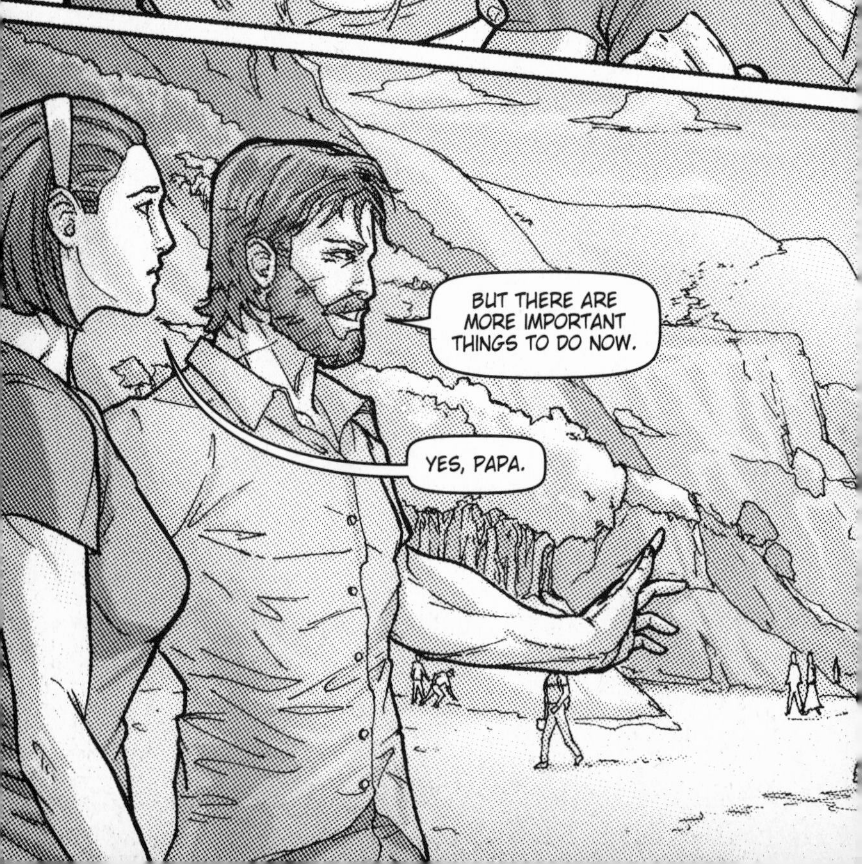
BUT THERE ARE MORE IMPORTANT THINGS TO DO NOW.
YES, PAPA.

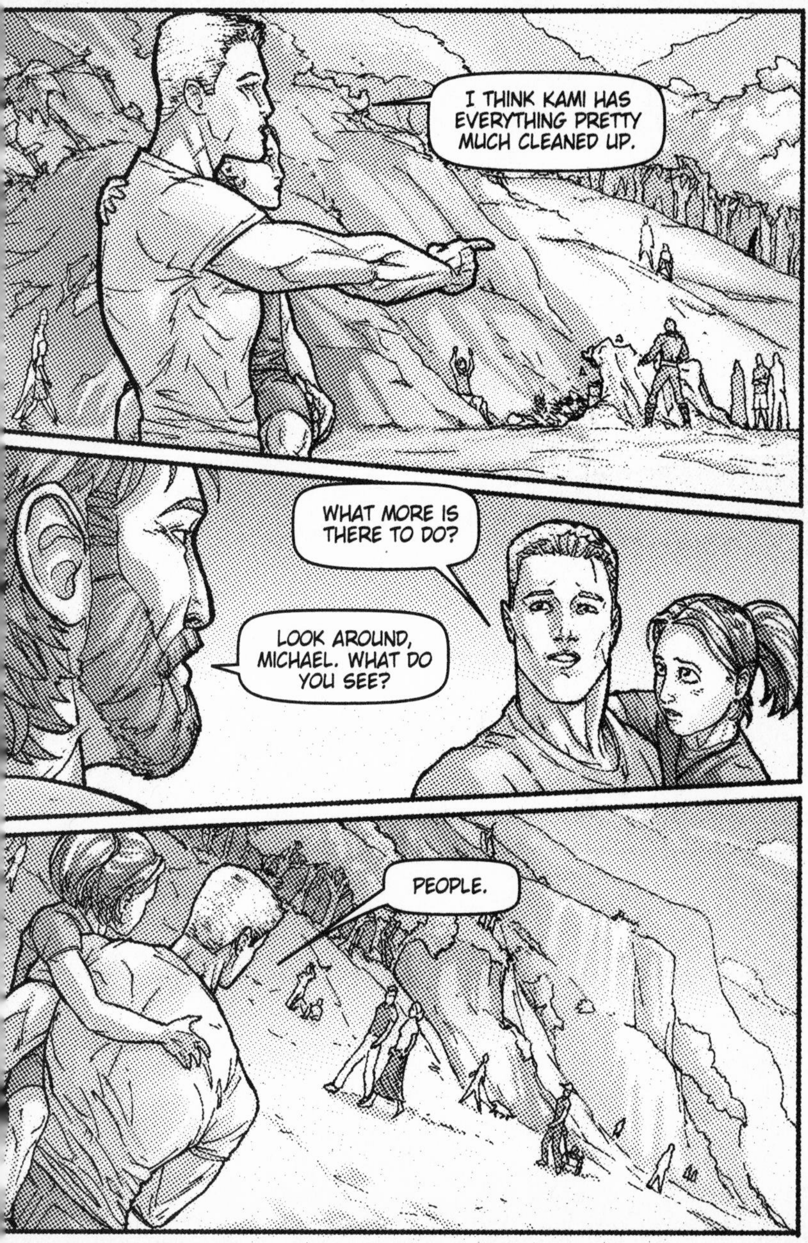
I THINK KAMI HAS EVERYTHING PRETTY MUCH CLEANED UP.
WHAT MORE IS THERE TO DO?
LOOK AROUND, MICHAEL. WHAT DO YOU SEE?
PEOPLE.

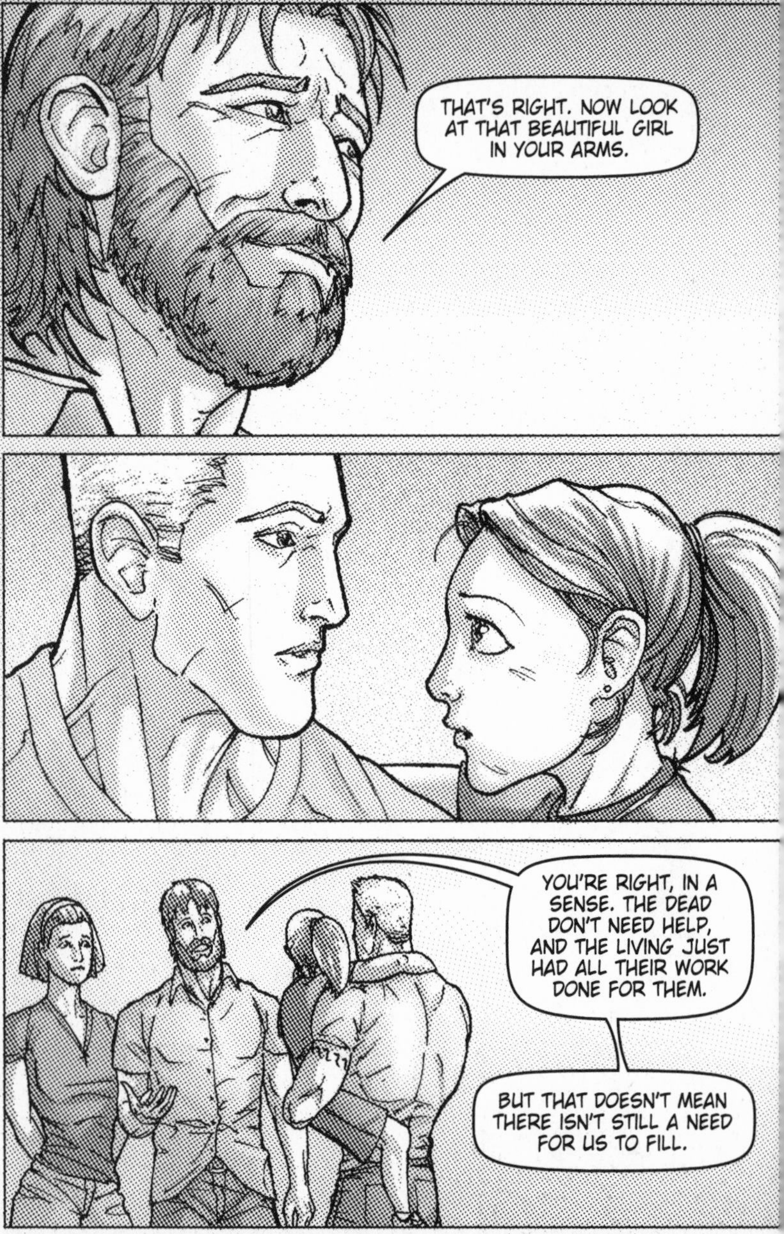
THAT'S RIGHT. NOW LOOK AT THAT BEAUTIFUL GIRL IN YOUR ARMS.
YOU'RE RIGHT, IN A SENSE. THE DEAD DON'T NEED HELP, AND THE LIVING JUST HAD ALL THEIR WORK DONE FOR THEM.
BUT THAT DOESN'T MEAN THERE ISN'T STILL A NEED FOR US TO FILL.

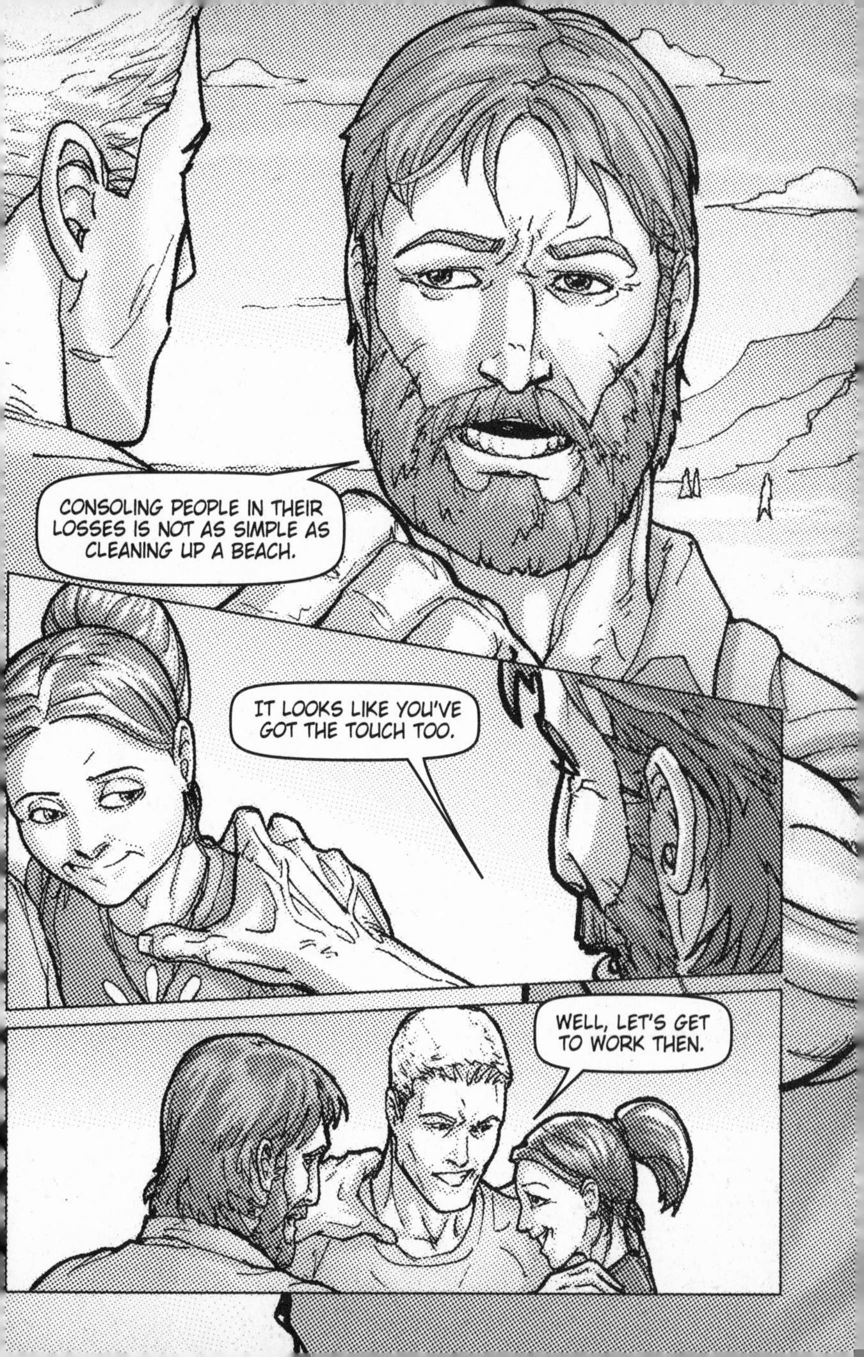
CONSOLING PEOPLE IN THEIR LOSSES IS NOT AS SIMPLE AS CLEANING UP A BEACH.
IT LOOKS LIKE YOU'VE GOT THE TOUCH TOO.
WELL, LET'S GET TO WORK THEN.

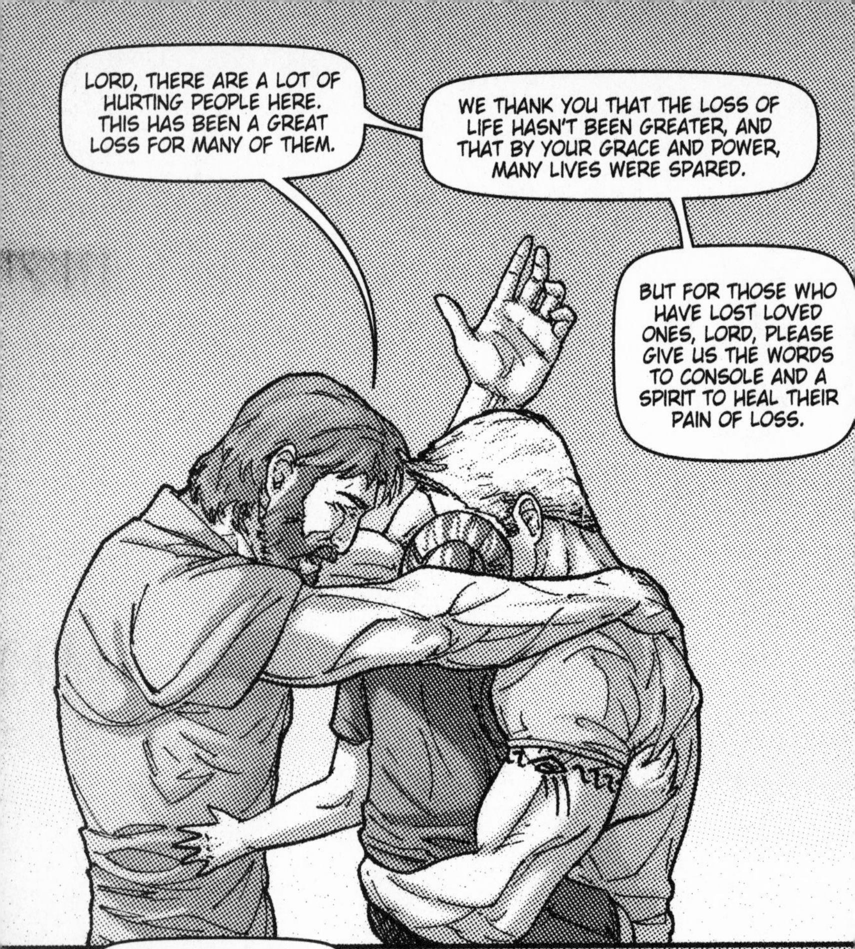
LORD, THERE ARE A LOT OF HURTING PEOPLE HERE. THIS HAS BEEN A GREAT LOSS FOR MANY OF THEM.
WE THANK YOU THAT THE LOSS OF LIFE HASN'T BEEN GREATER, AND THAT BY YOUR GRACE AND POWER, MANY LIVES WERE SPARED.
BUT FOR THOSE WHO HAVE LOST LOVED ONES, LORD, PLEASE GIVE US THE WORDS TO CONSOLE AND A SPIRIT TO HEAL THEIR PAIN OF LOSS.
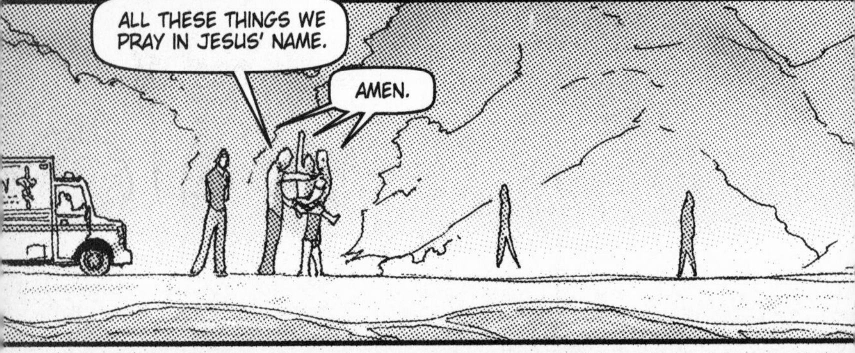
ALL THESE THINGS WE PRAY IN JESUS' NAME.
AMEN.

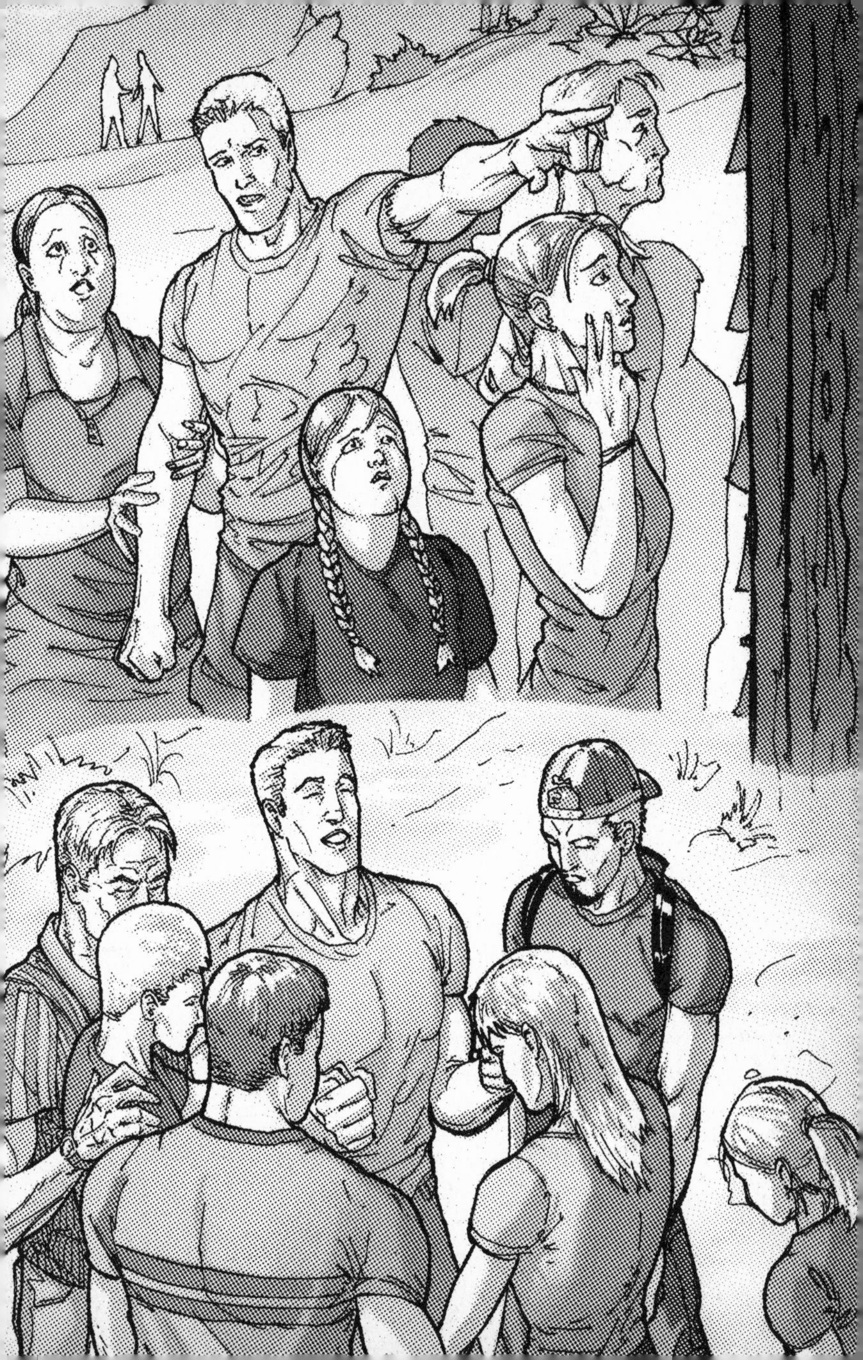

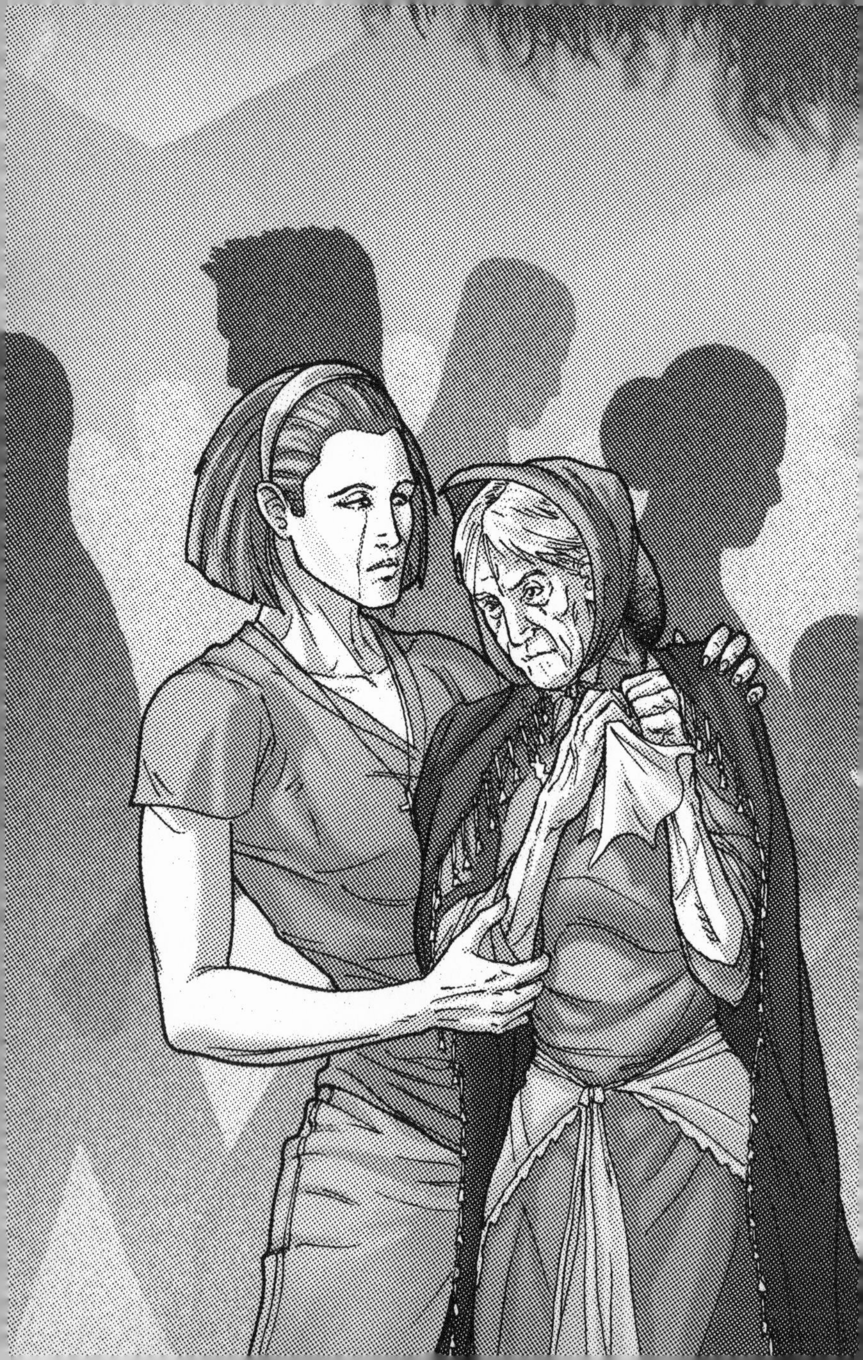

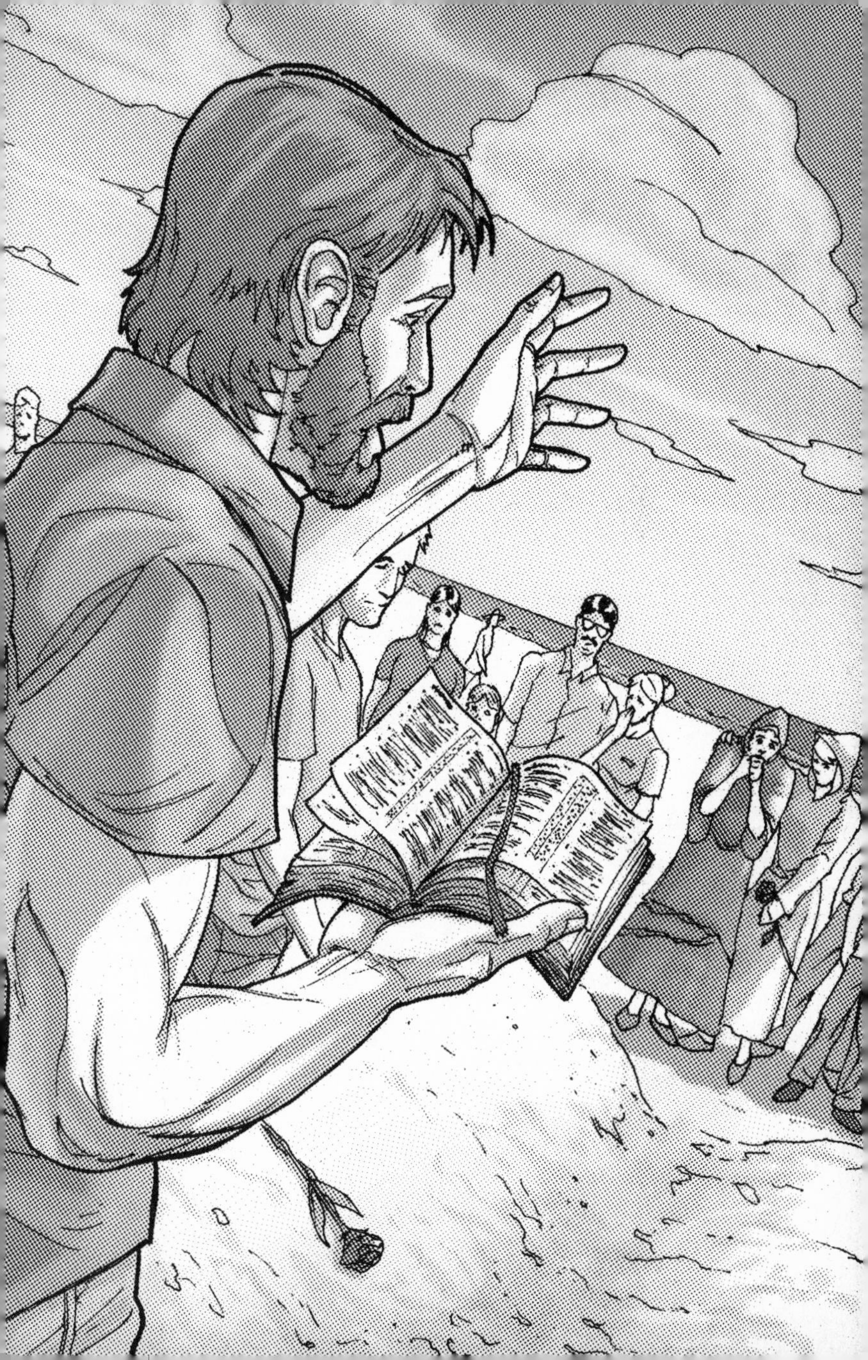

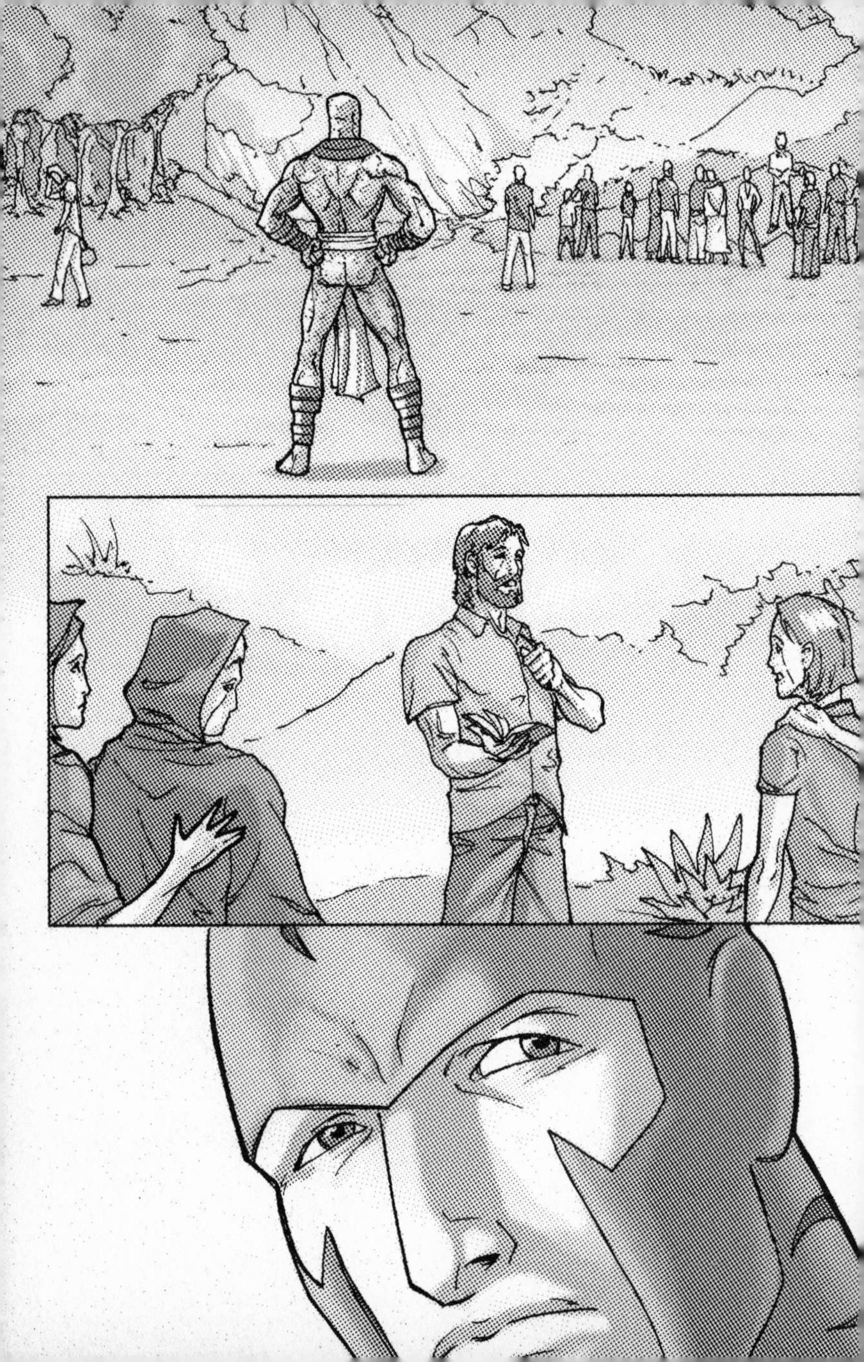

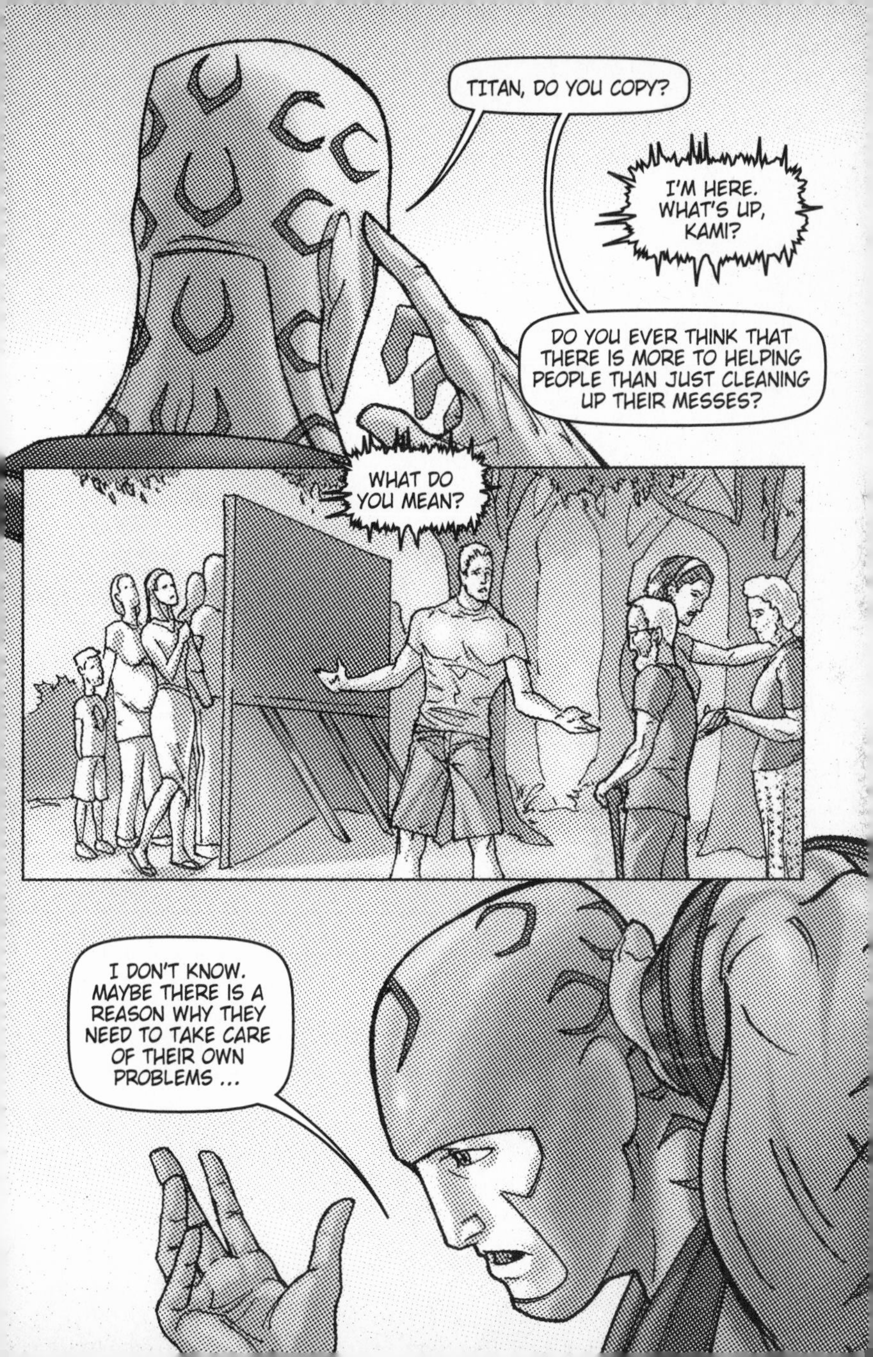
TITAN, DO YOU COPY?
I'M HERE. WHAT'S UP, KAMI?
DO YOU EVER THINK THAT THERE IS MORE TO HELPING PEOPLE THAN JUST CLEANING UP THEIR MESSES?
WHAT DO YOU MEAN?
I DON'T KNOW. MAYBE THERE IS A REASON WHY THEY NEED TO TAKE CARE OF THEIR OWN PROBLEMS ...

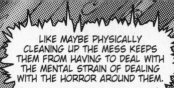

LIKE MAYBE PHYSICALLY CLEANING UP THE MESS KEEPS THEM FROM HAVING TO DEAL WITH THE MENTAL STRAIN OF DEALING WITH THE HORROR AROUND THEM.

I DON'T KNOW WHAT YOU'RE TALKING ABOUT, BRO.

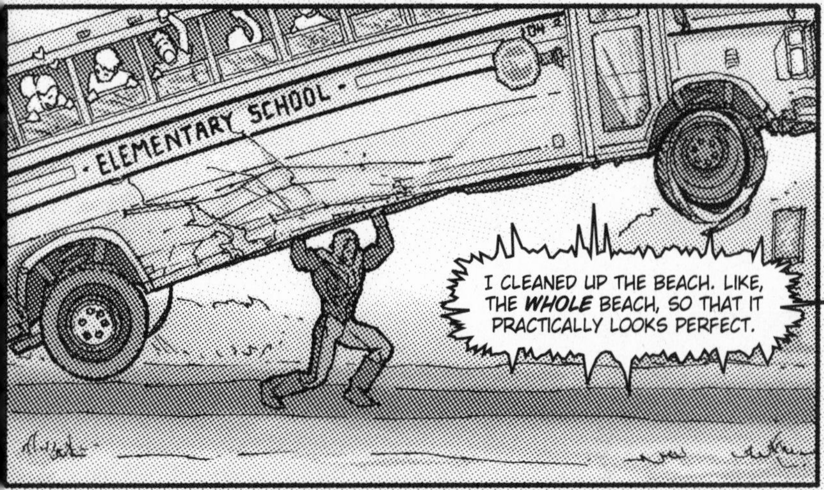
ELEMENTARY SCHOOL
I CLEANED UP THE BEACH. LIKE, THE *WHOLE* BEACH, SO THAT IT PRACTICALLY LOOKS PERFECT.

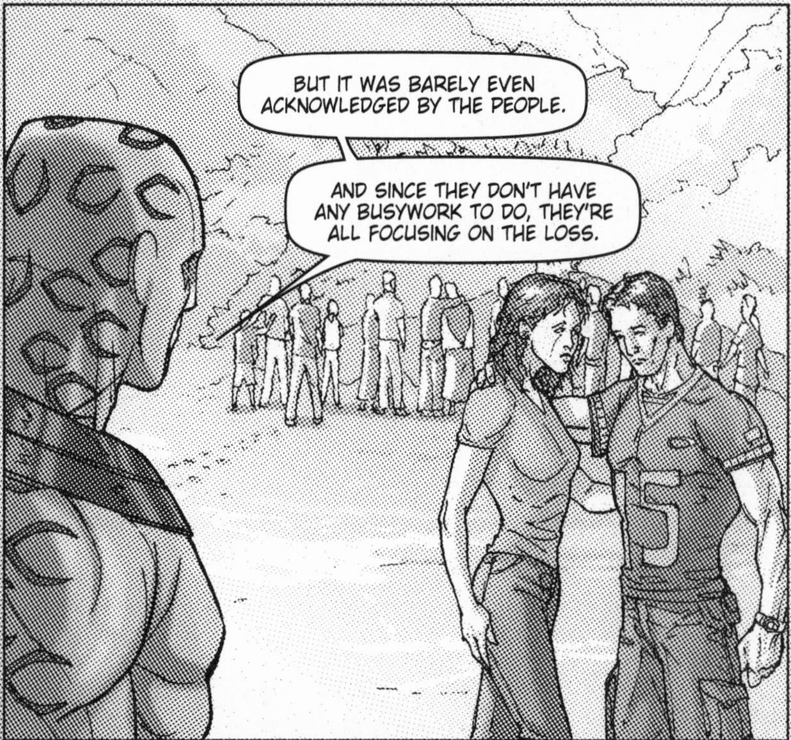
BUT IT WAS BARELY EVEN ACKNOWLEDGED BY THE PEOPLE.
AND SINCE THEY DON'T HAVE ANY BUSYWORK TO DO, THEY'RE ALL FOCUSING ON THE LOSS.

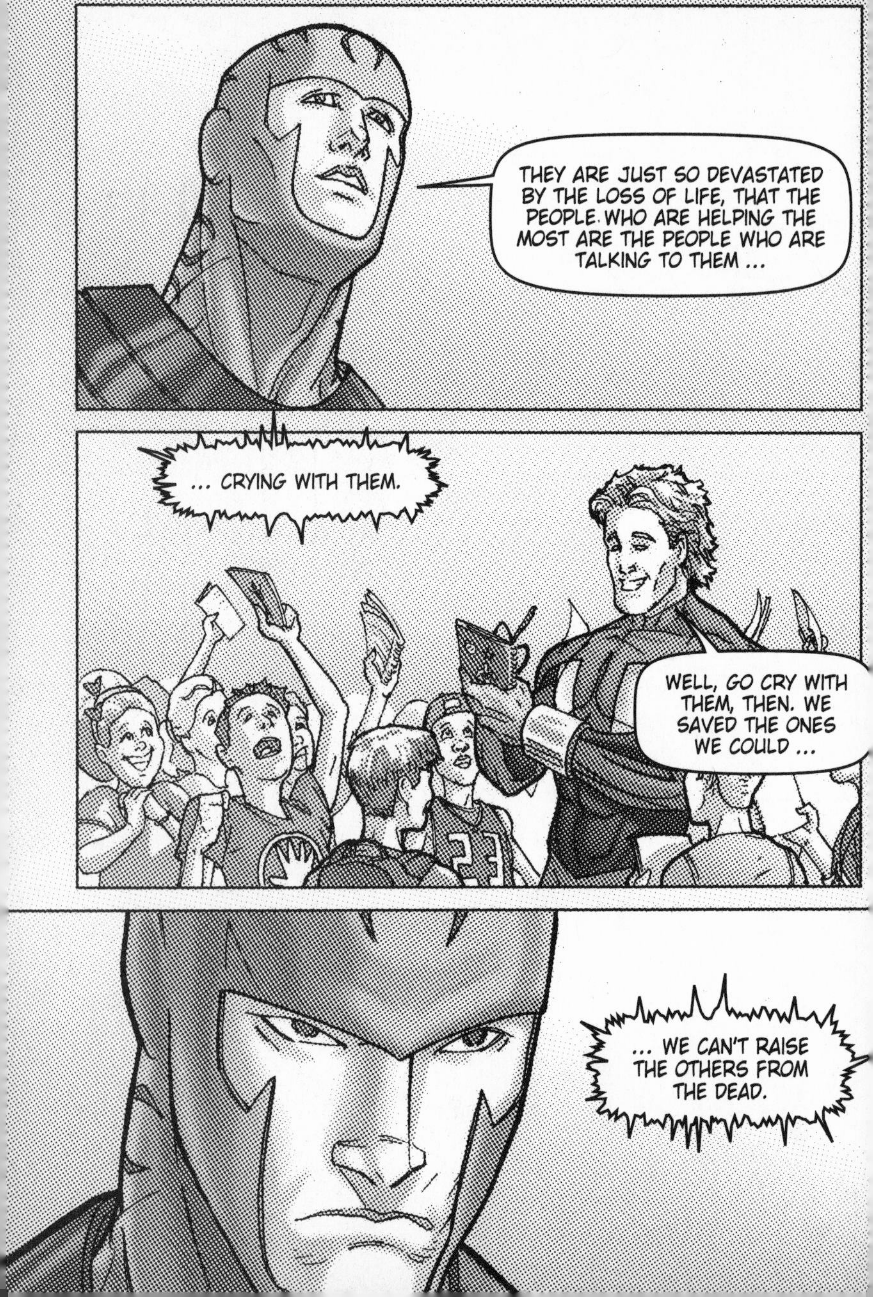
THEY ARE JUST SO DEVASTATED BY THE LOSS OF LIFE, THAT THE PEOPLE WHO ARE HELPING THE MOST ARE THE PEOPLE WHO ARE TALKING TO THEM ...
... CRYING WITH THEM.
WELL, GO CRY WITH THEM, THEN. WE SAVED THE ONES WE COULD ...
... WE CAN'T RAISE THE OTHERS FROM THE DEAD.

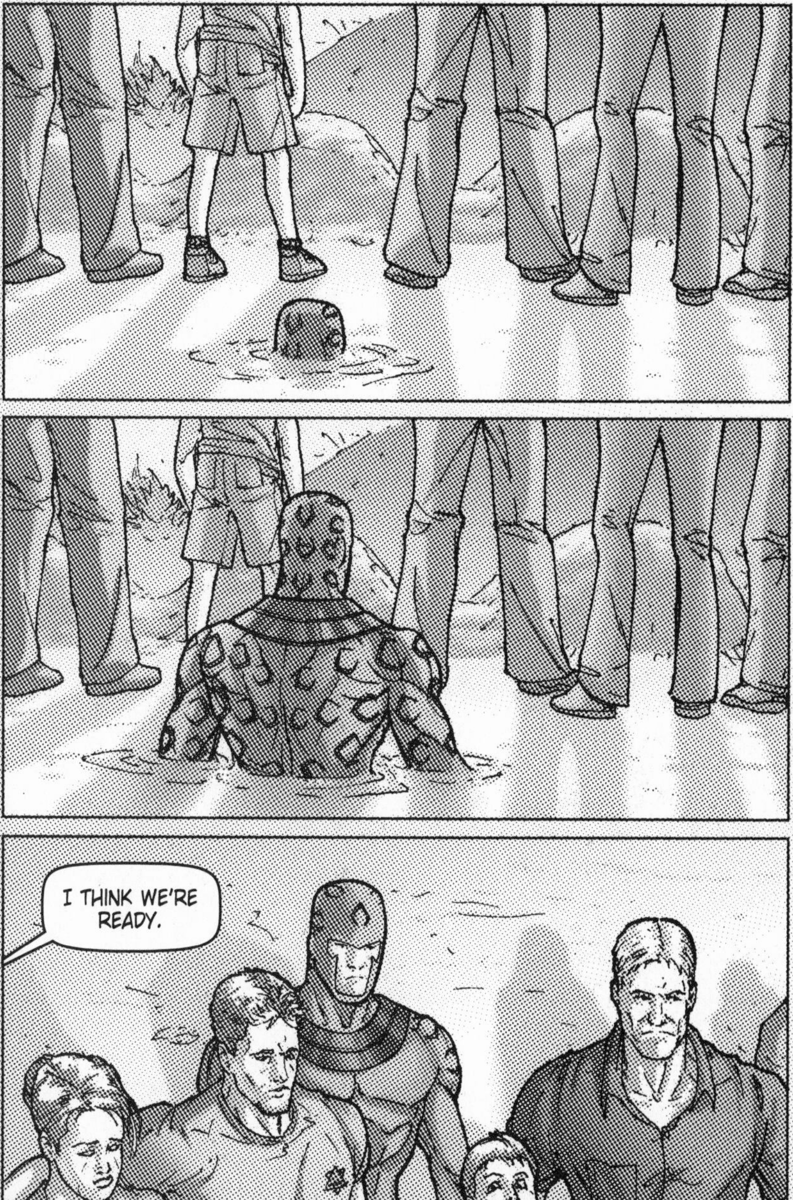
I THINK WE'RE READY.

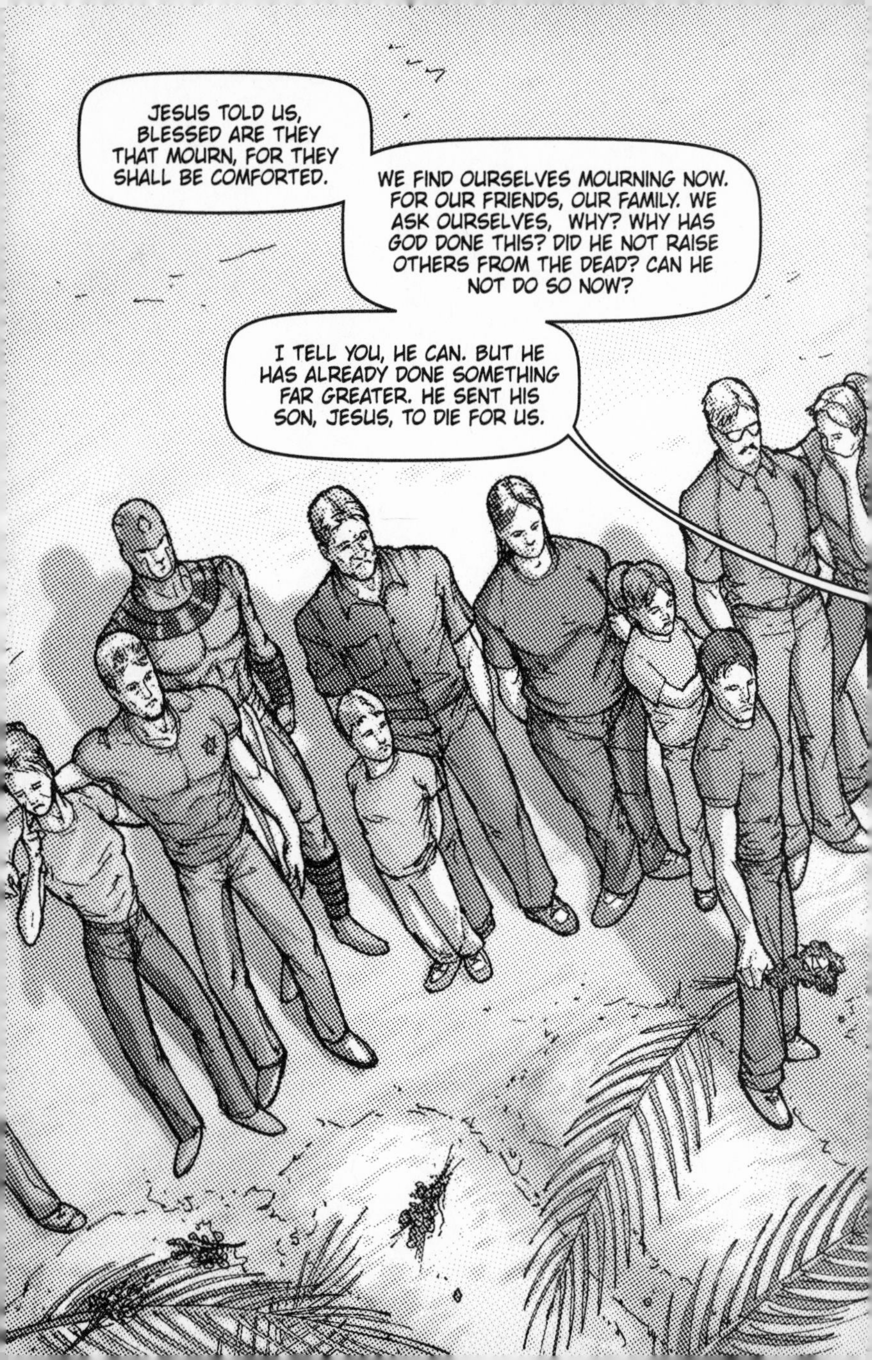
JESUS TOLD US, BLESSED ARE THEY THAT MOURN, FOR THEY SHALL BE COMFORTED.
WE FIND OURSELVES MOURNING NOW. FOR OUR FRIENDS, OUR FAMILY. WE ASK OURSELVES, WHY? WHY HAS GOD DONE THIS? DID HE NOT RAISE OTHERS FROM THE DEAD? CAN HE NOT DO SO NOW?
I TELL YOU, HE CAN. BUT HE HAS ALREADY DONE SOMETHING FAR GREATER. HE SENT HIS SON, JESUS, TO DIE FOR US.

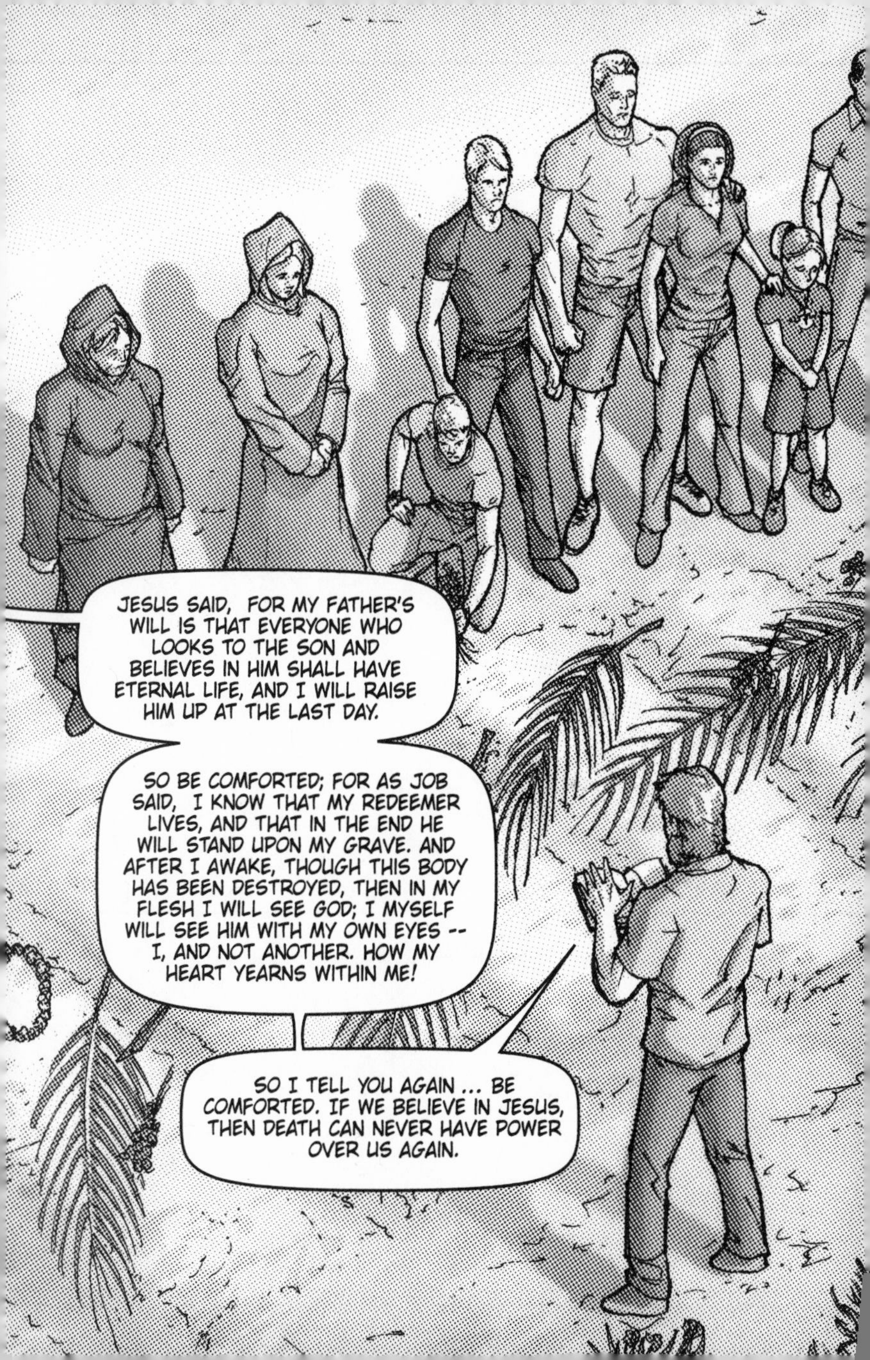
JESUS SAID, FOR MY FATHER'S WILL IS THAT EVERYONE WHO LOOKS TO THE SON AND BELIEVES IN HIM SHALL HAVE ETERNAL LIFE, AND I WILL RAISE HIM UP AT THE LAST DAY.
SO BE COMFORTED; FOR AS JOB SAID, I KNOW THAT MY REDEEMER LIVES, AND THAT IN THE END HE WILL STAND UPON MY GRAVE. AND AFTER I AWAKE, THOUGH THIS BODY HAS BEEN DESTROYED, THEN IN MY FLESH I WILL SEE GOD; I MYSELF WILL SEE HIM WITH MY OWN EYES -- I, AND NOT ANOTHER. HOW MY HEART YEARNS WITHIN ME!
SO I TELL YOU AGAIN ... BE COMFORTED. IF WE BELIEVE IN JESUS, THEN DEATH CAN NEVER HAVE POWER OVER US AGAIN.

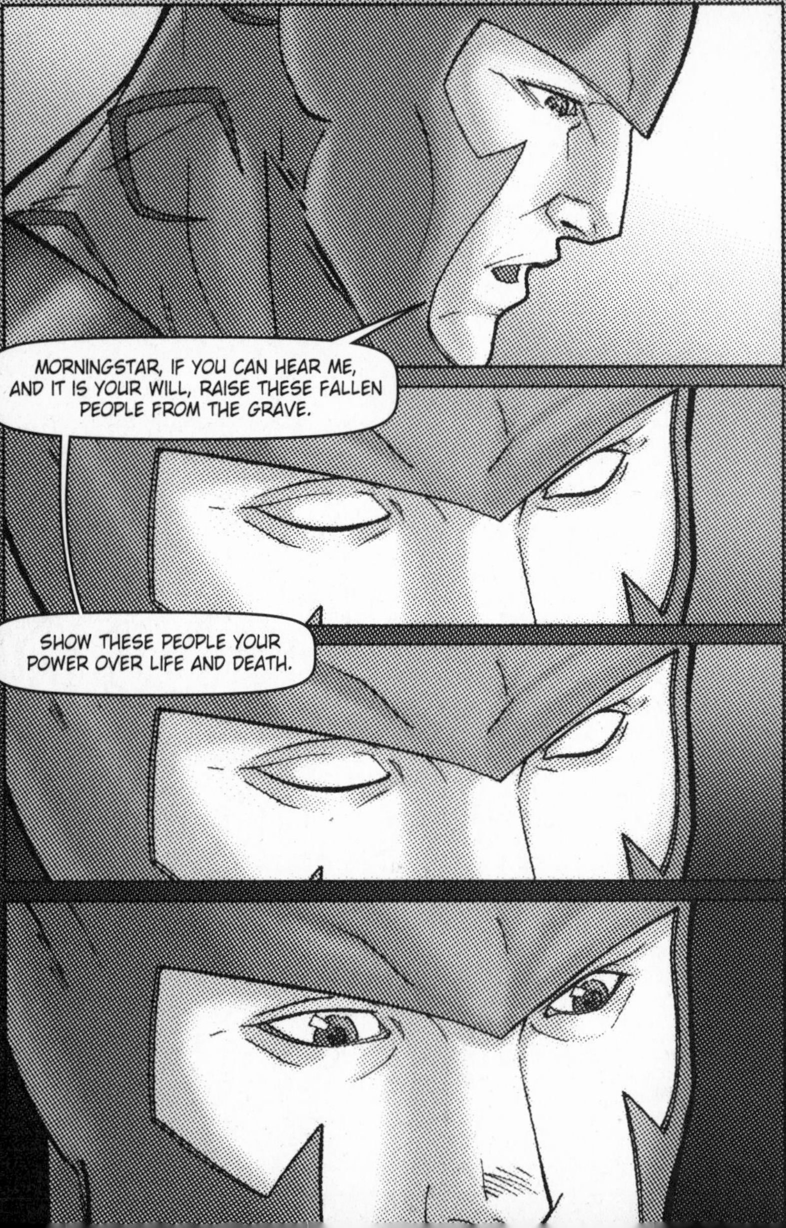
MORNINGSTAR, IF YOU CAN HEAR ME, AND IT IS YOUR WILL, RAISE THESE FALLEN PEOPLE FROM THE GRAVE.
SHOW THESE PEOPLE YOUR POWER OVER LIFE AND DEATH.

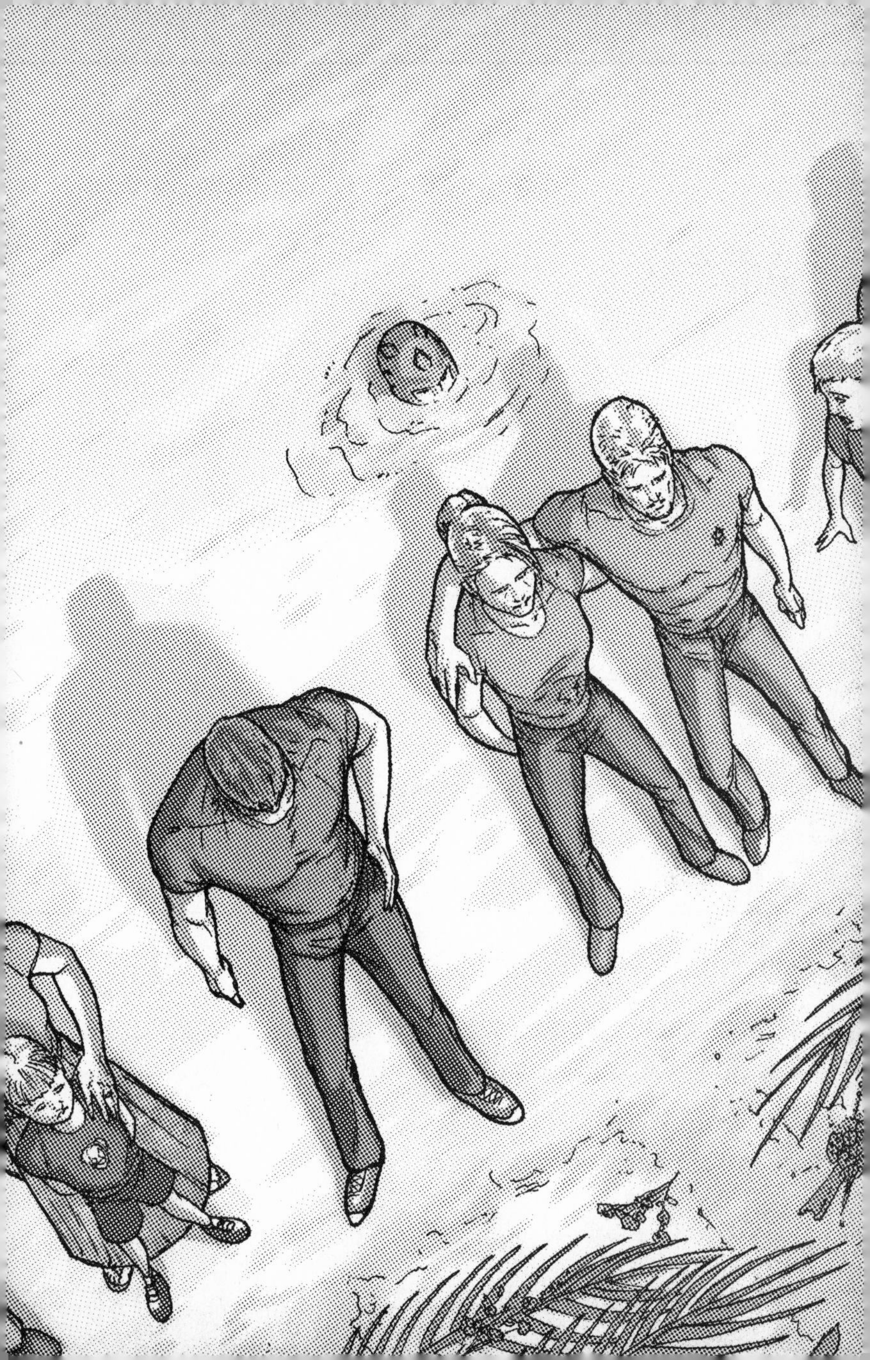

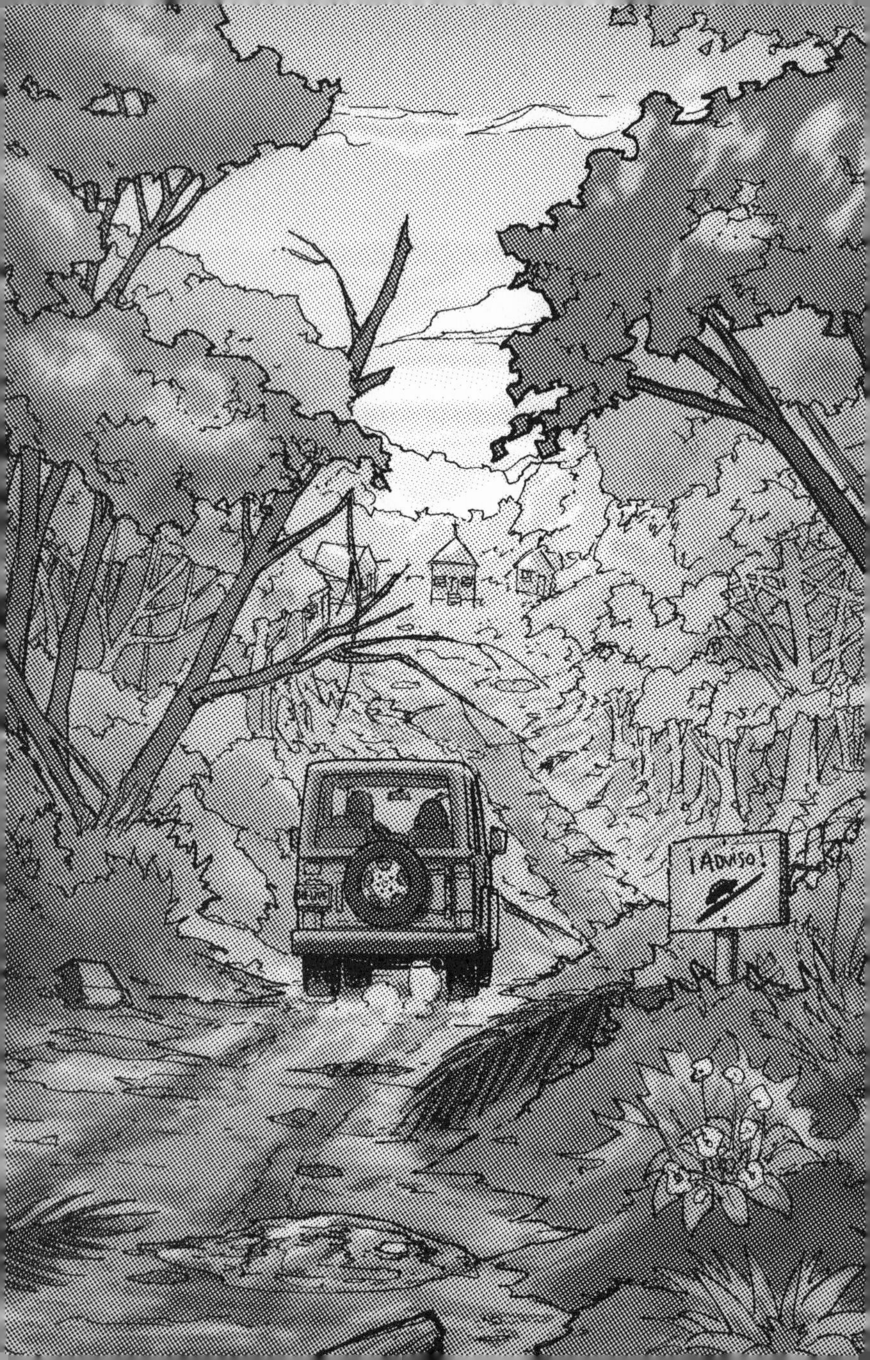
¡ADVISO!

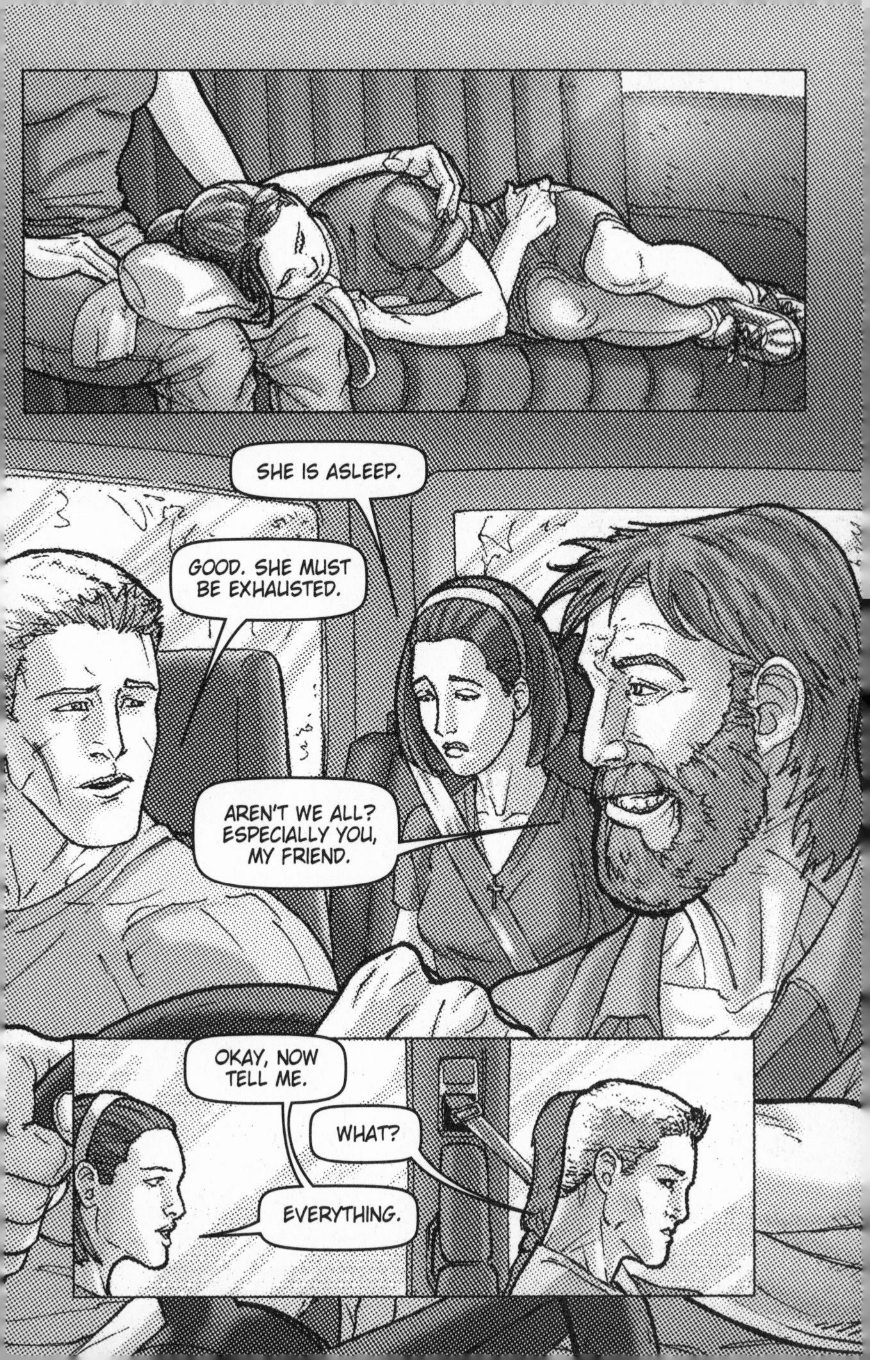
SHE IS ASLEEP.
GOOD. SHE MUST BE EXHAUSTED.
AREN'T WE ALL? ESPECIALLY YOU, MY FRIEND.
OKAY, NOW TELL ME.
WHAT?
EVERYTHING.

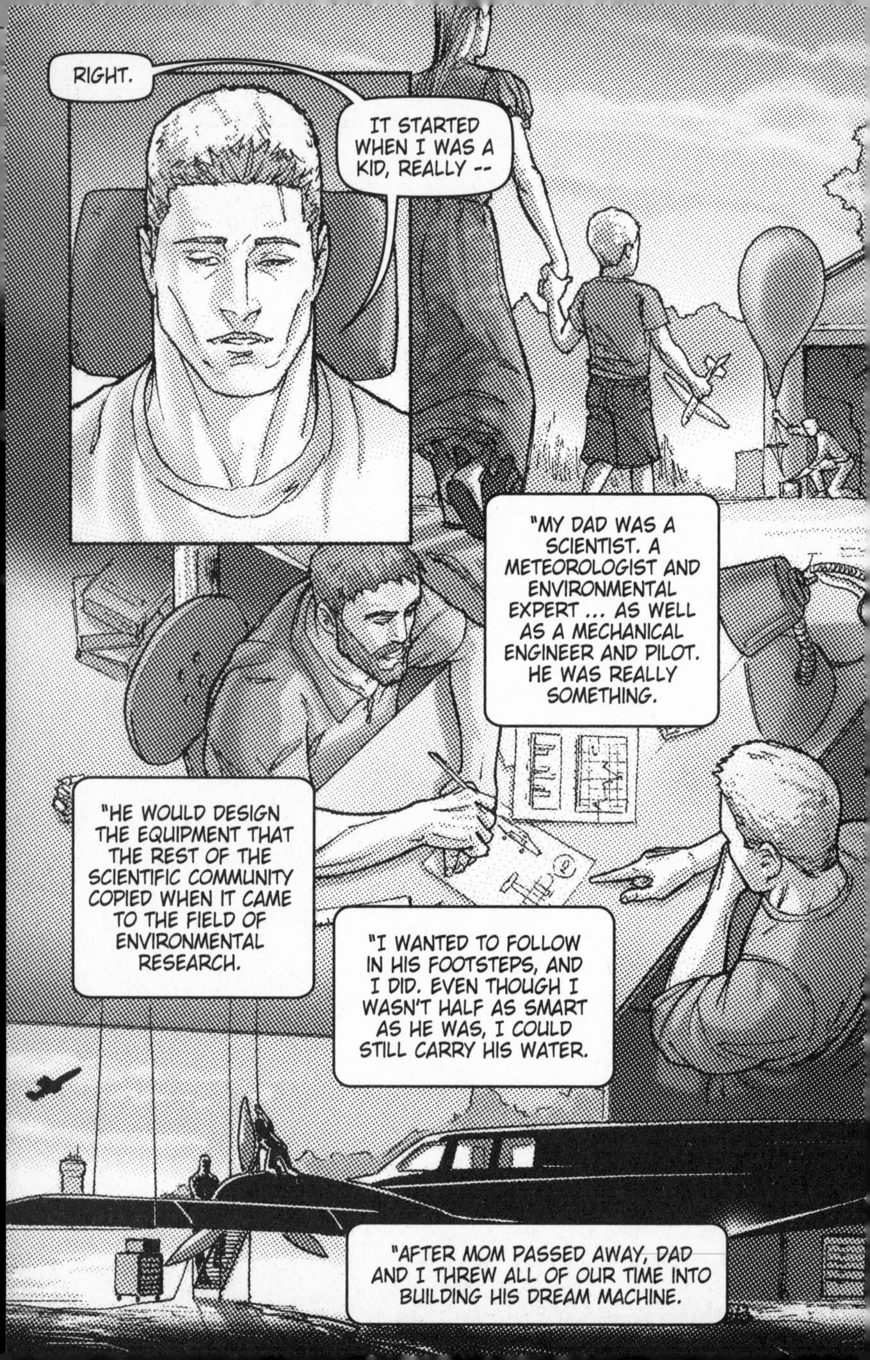
RIGHT.
IT STARTED WHEN I WAS A KID, REALLY --
"MY DAD WAS A SCIENTIST. A METEOROLOGIST AND ENVIRONMENTAL EXPERT ... AS WELL AS A MECHANICAL ENGINEER AND PILOT. HE WAS REALLY SOMETHING.
"HE WOULD DESIGN THE EQUIPMENT THAT THE REST OF THE SCIENTIFIC COMMUNITY COPIED WHEN IT CAME TO THE FIELD OF ENVIRONMENTAL RESEARCH.
"I WANTED TO FOLLOW IN HIS FOOTSTEPS, AND I DID. EVEN THOUGH I WASN'T HALF AS SMART AS HE WAS, I COULD STILL CARRY HIS WATER.
"AFTER MOM PASSED AWAY, DAD AND I THREW ALL OF OUR TIME INTO BUILDING HIS DREAM MACHINE.

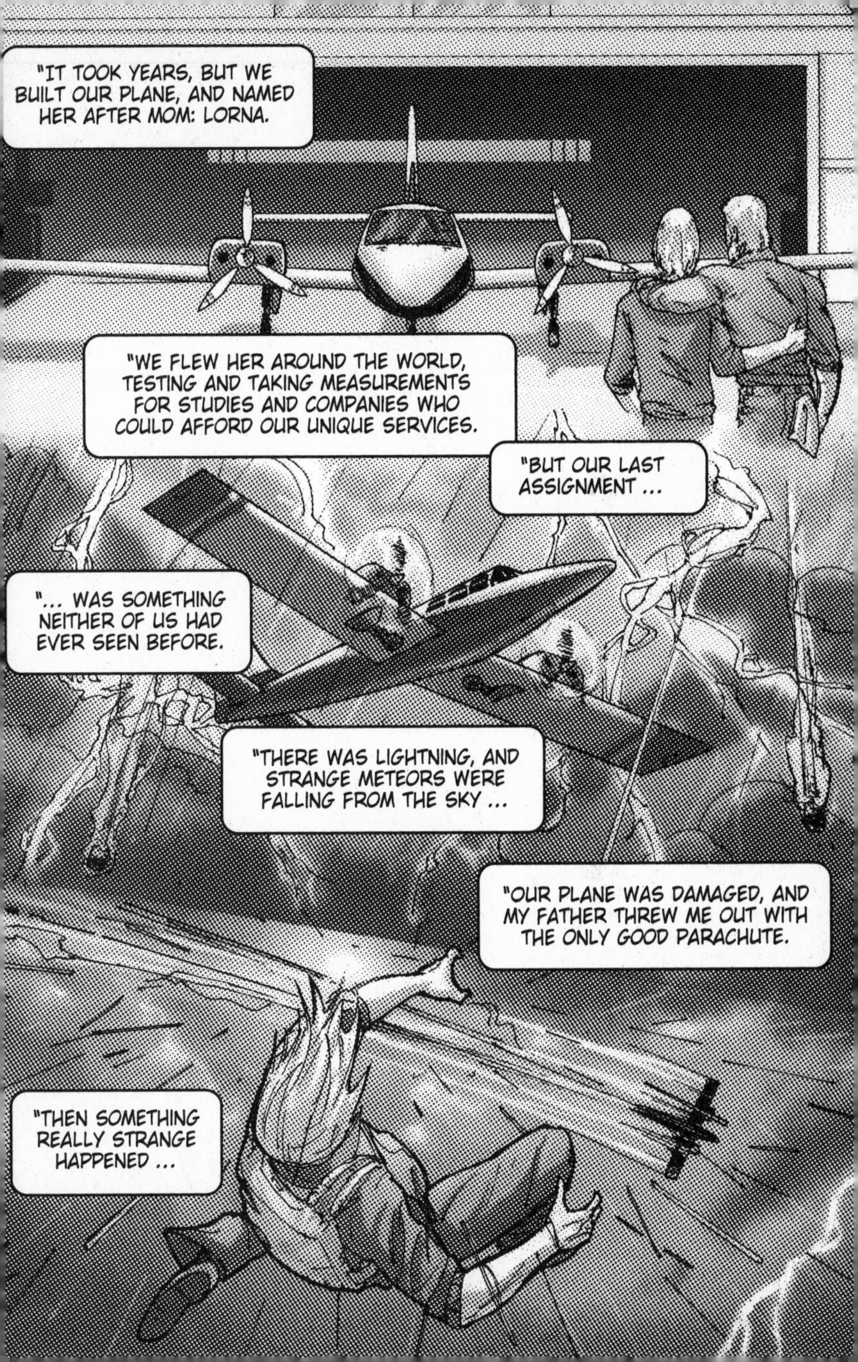
"IT TOOK YEARS, BUT WE BUILT OUR PLANE, AND NAMED HER AFTER MOM: LORNA.
"WE FLEW HER AROUND THE WORLD, TESTING AND TAKING MEASUREMENTS FOR STUDIES AND COMPANIES WHO COULD AFFORD OUR UNIQUE SERVICES.
"BUT OUR LAST ASSIGNMENT ...
"... WAS SOMETHING NEITHER OF US HAD EVER SEEN BEFORE.
"THERE WAS LIGHTNING, AND STRANGE METEORS WERE FALLING FROM THE SKY ...
"OUR PLANE WAS DAMAGED, AND MY FATHER THREW ME OUT WITH THE ONLY GOOD PARACHUTE.
"THEN SOMETHING REALLY STRANGE HAPPENED ...

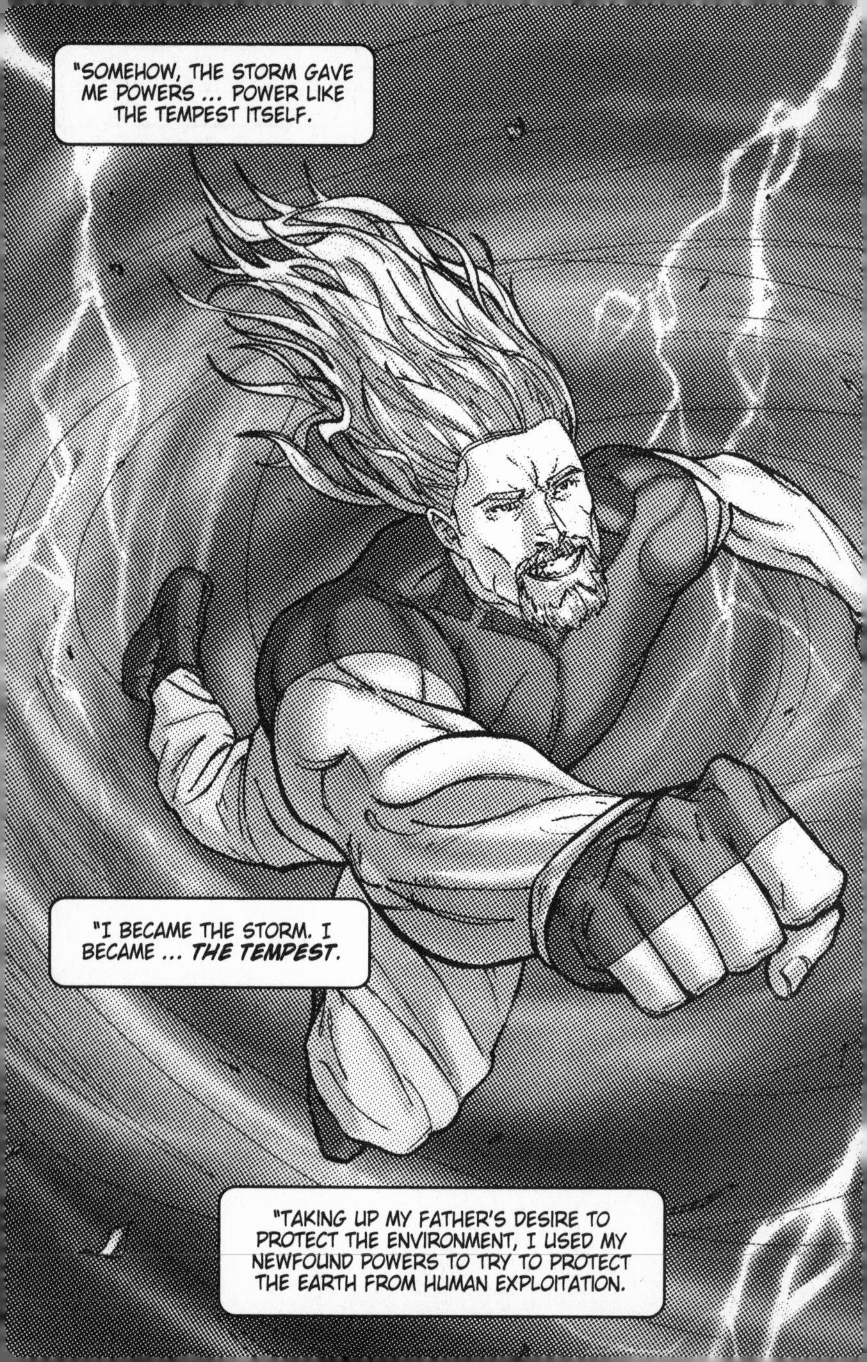
"SOMEHOW, THE STORM GAVE ME POWERS ... POWER LIKE THE TEMPEST ITSELF.
"I BECAME THE STORM. I BECAME ... ***THE TEMPEST***.
"TAKING UP MY FATHER'S DESIRE TO PROTECT THE ENVIRONMENT, I USED MY NEWFOUND POWERS TO TRY TO PROTECT THE EARTH FROM HUMAN EXPLOITATION.

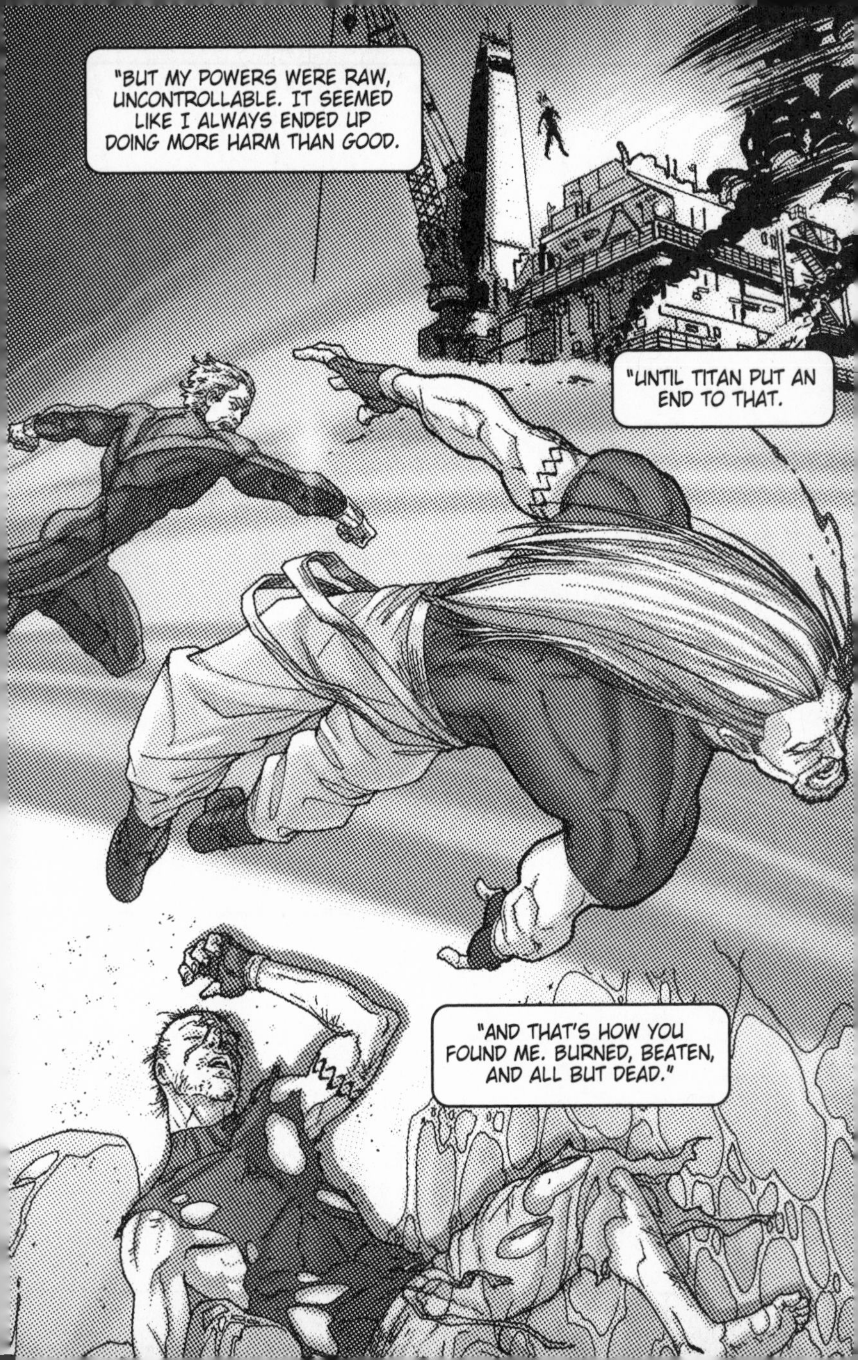
"BUT MY POWERS WERE RAW, UNCONTROLLABLE. IT SEEMED LIKE I ALWAYS ENDED UP DOING MORE HARM THAN GOOD.
"UNTIL TITAN PUT AN END TO THAT.
"AND THAT'S HOW YOU FOUND ME. BURNED, BEATEN, AND ALL BUT DEAD."

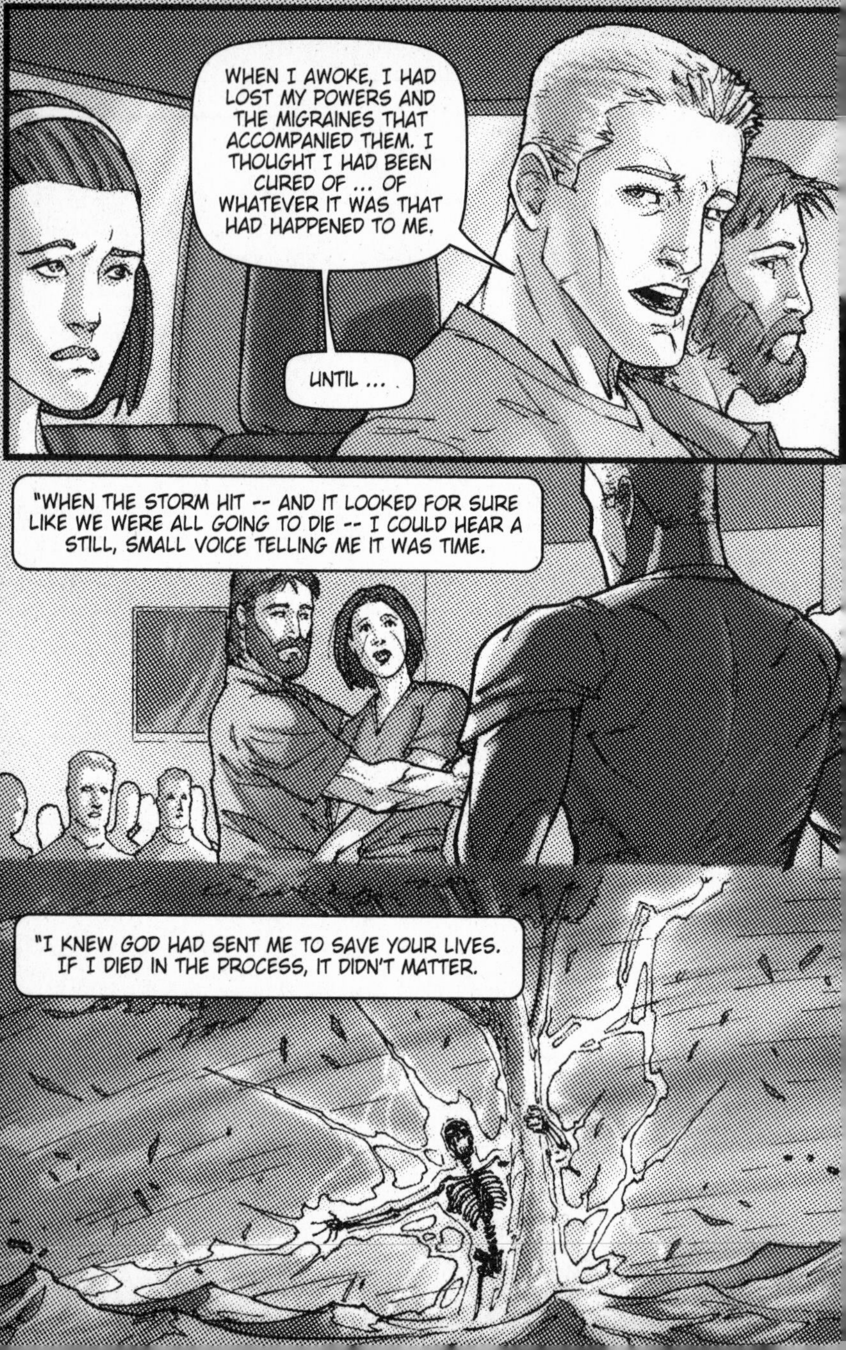
WHEN I AWOKE, I HAD LOST MY POWERS AND THE MIGRAINES THAT ACCOMPANIED THEM. I THOUGHT I HAD BEEN CURED OF ... OF WHATEVER IT WAS THAT HAD HAPPENED TO ME.
UNTIL ...
"WHEN THE STORM HIT -- AND IT LOOKED FOR SURE LIKE WE WERE ALL GOING TO DIE -- I COULD HEAR A STILL, SMALL VOICE TELLING ME IT WAS TIME.
"I KNEW GOD HAD SENT ME TO SAVE YOUR LIVES. IF I DIED IN THE PROCESS, IT DIDN'T MATTER.

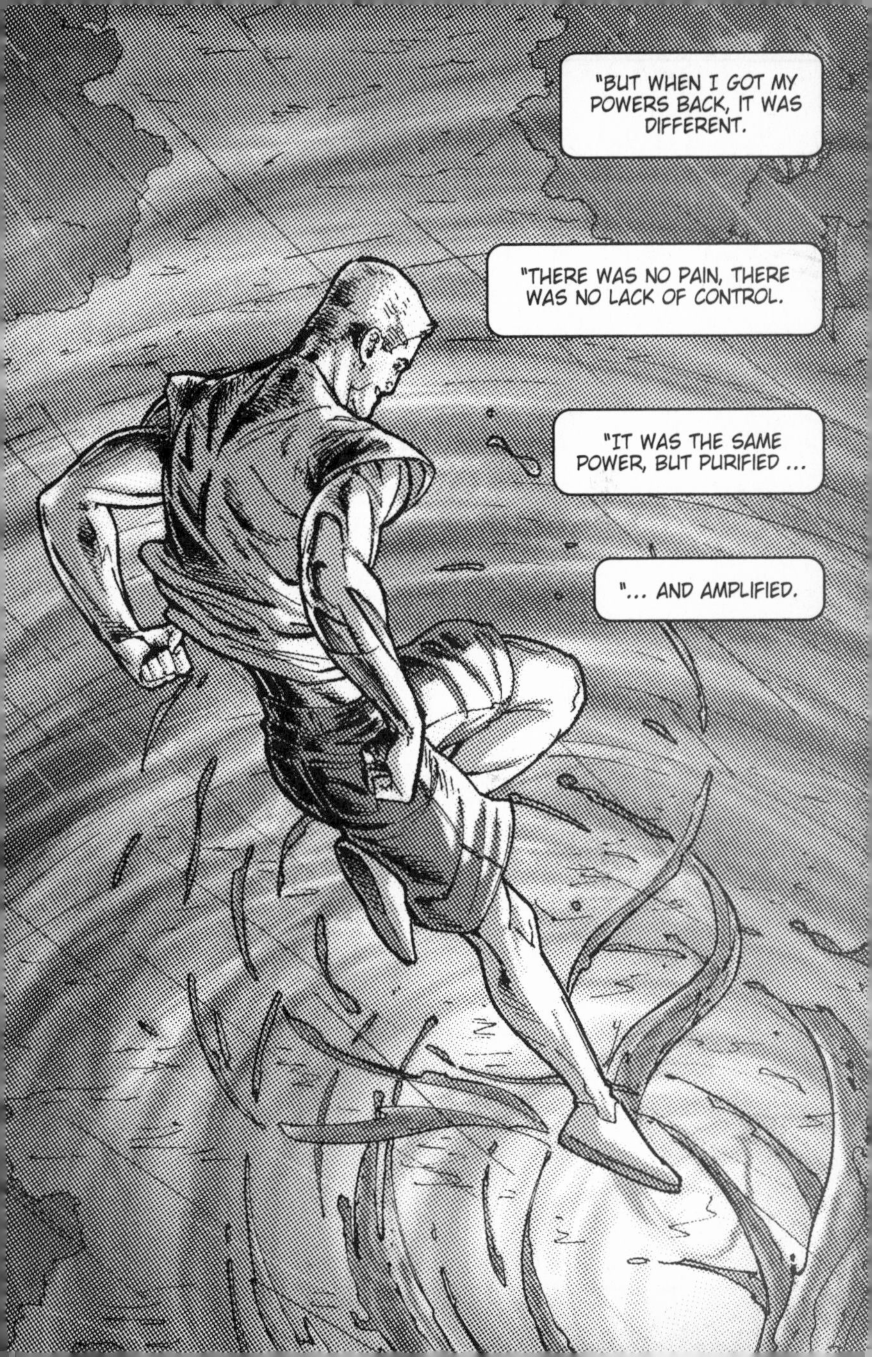
"BUT WHEN I GOT MY POWERS BACK, IT WAS DIFFERENT.
"THERE WAS NO PAIN, THERE WAS NO LACK OF CONTROL.
"IT WAS THE SAME POWER, BUT PURIFIED ...
"... AND AMPLIFIED.

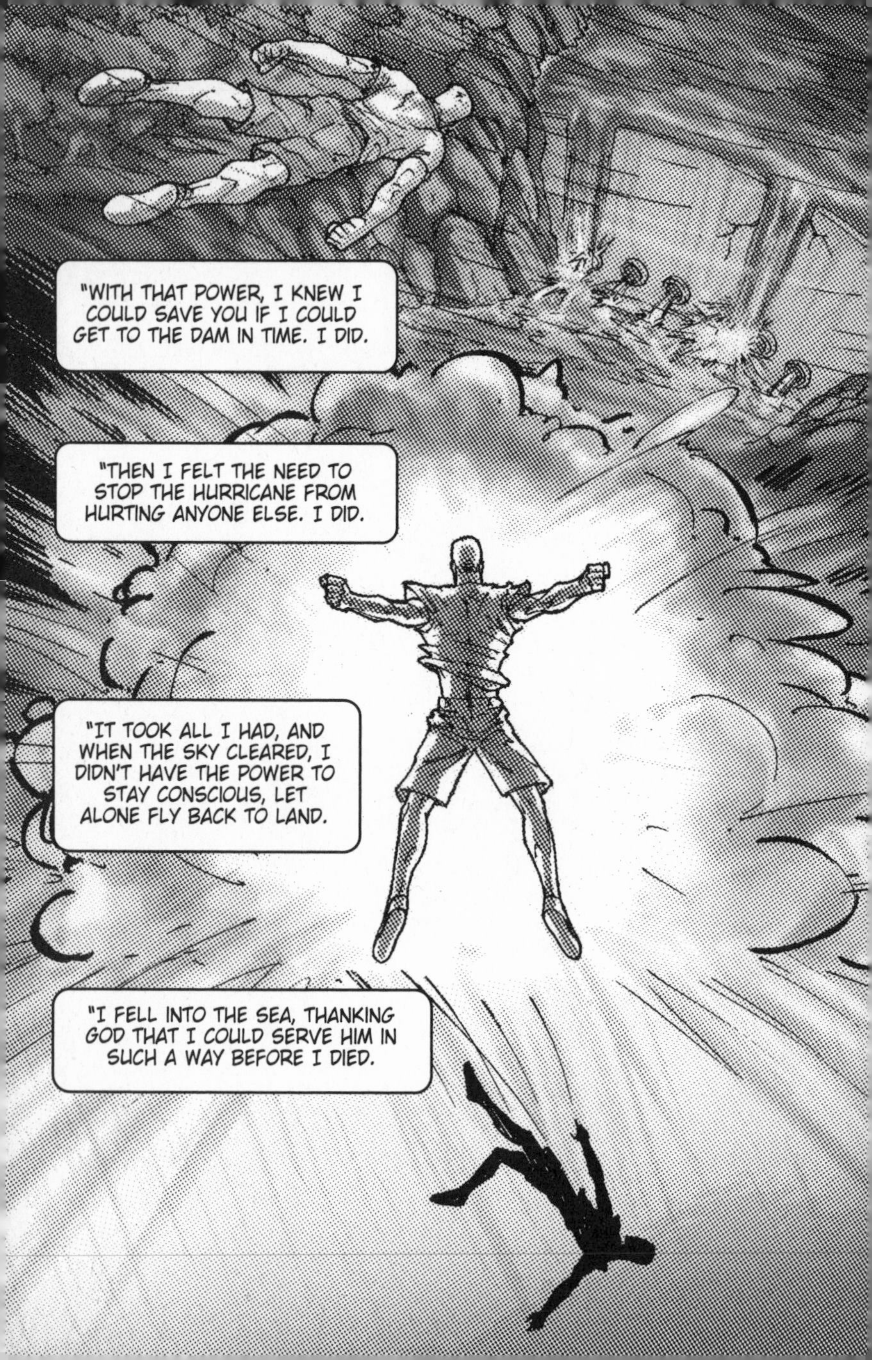
"WITH THAT POWER, I KNEW I COULD SAVE YOU IF I COULD GET TO THE DAM IN TIME. I DID.
"THEN I FELT THE NEED TO STOP THE HURRICANE FROM HURTING ANYONE ELSE. I DID.
"IT TOOK ALL I HAD, AND WHEN THE SKY CLEARED, I DIDN'T HAVE THE POWER TO STAY CONSCIOUS, LET ALONE FLY BACK TO LAND.
"I FELL INTO THE SEA, THANKING GOD THAT I COULD SERVE HIM IN SUCH A WAY BEFORE I DIED.

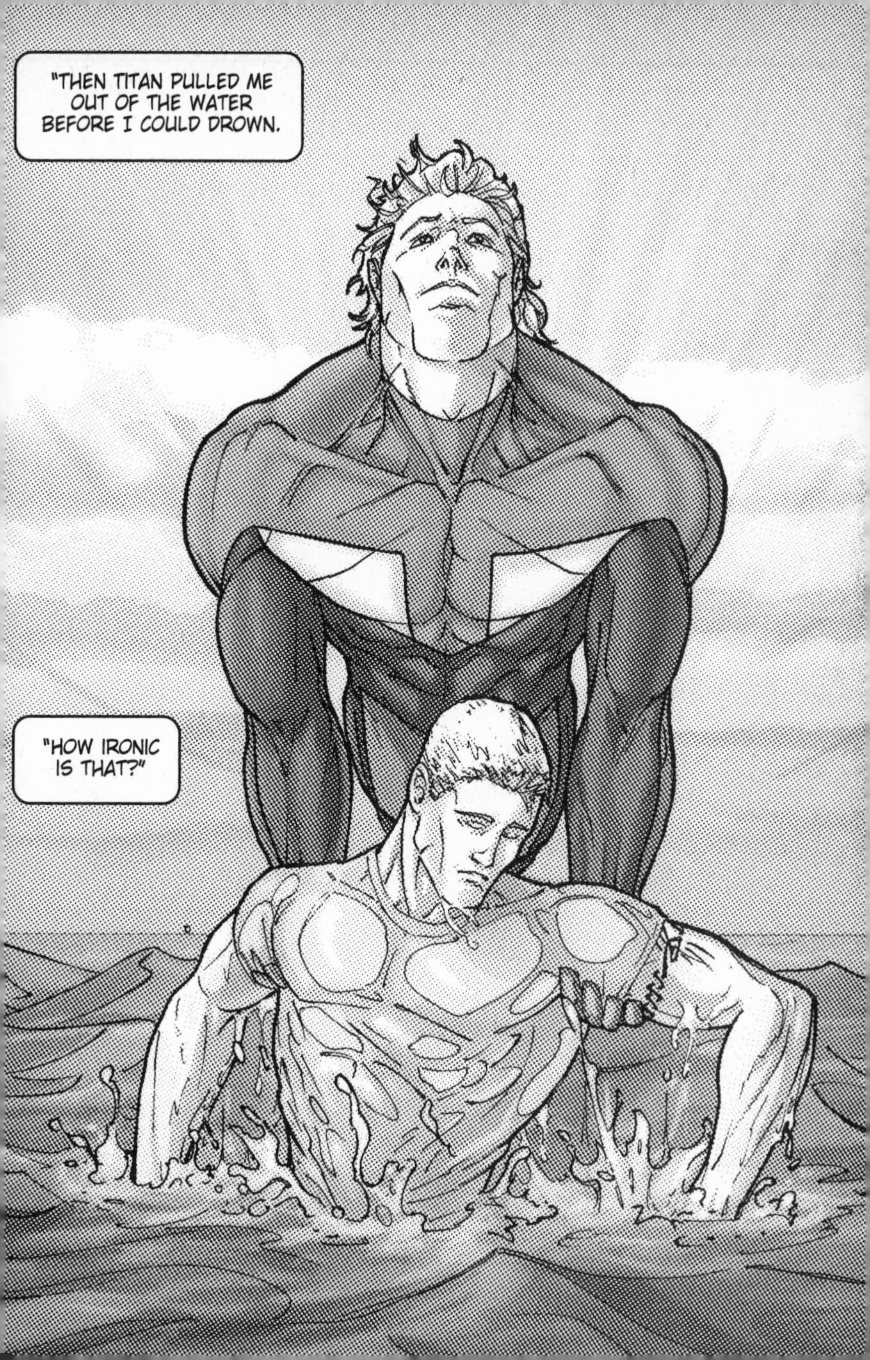
"THEN TITAN PULLED ME OUT OF THE WATER BEFORE I COULD DROWN.
"HOW IRONIC IS THAT?"

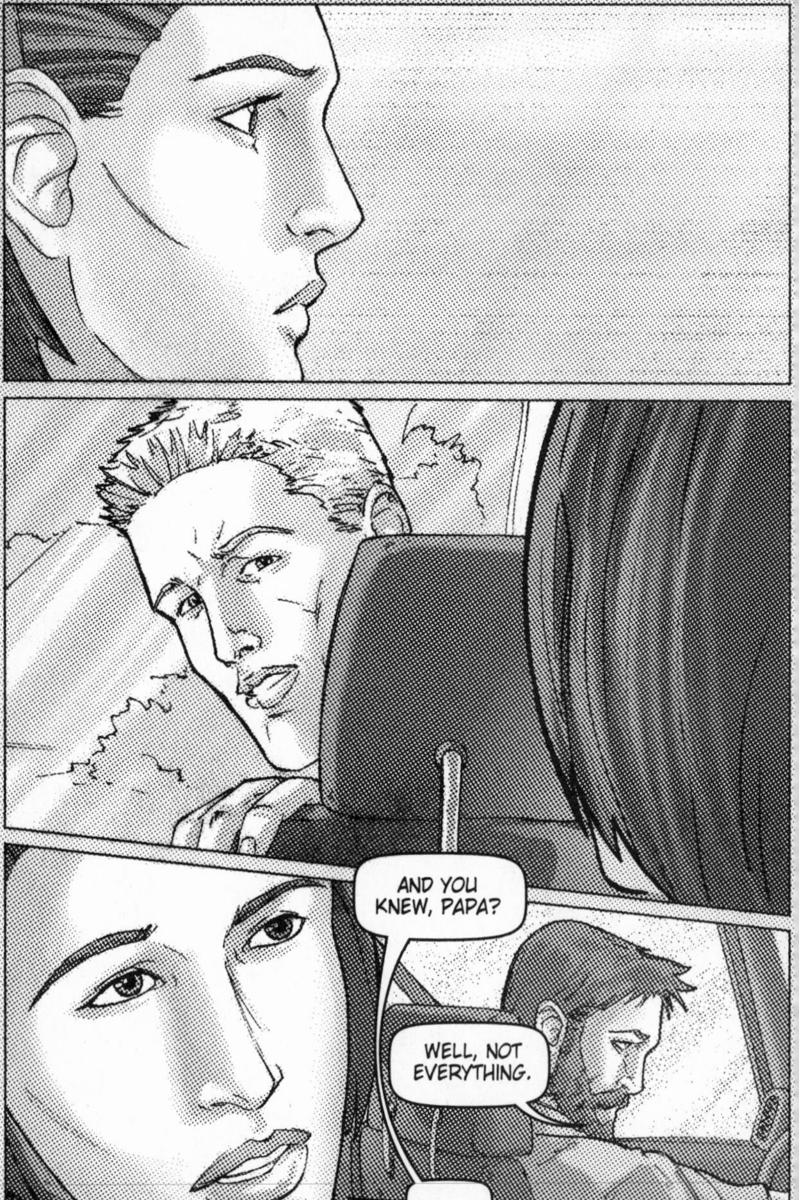
AND YOU KNEW, PAPA?
WELL, NOT EVERYTHING.
...

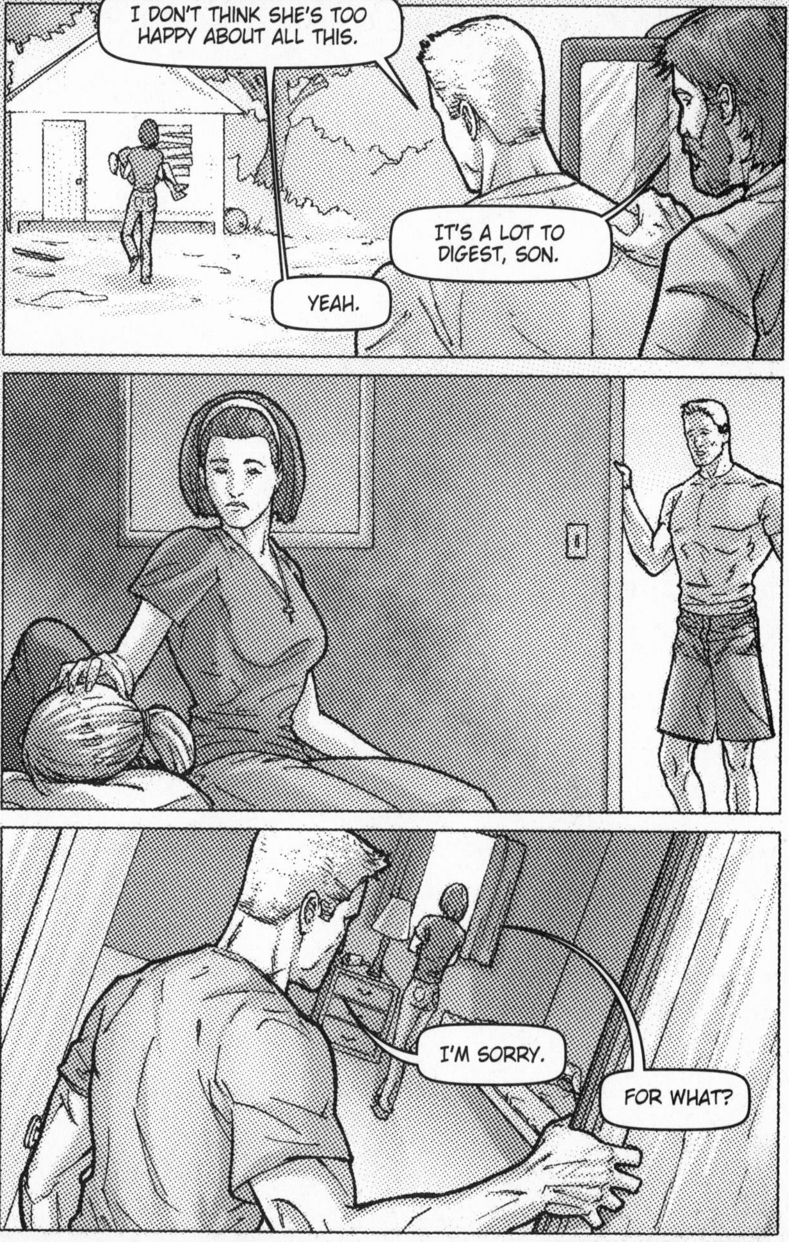
I DON'T THINK SHE'S TOO HAPPY ABOUT ALL THIS.
IT'S A LOT TO DIGEST, SON.
YEAH.
I'M SORRY.
FOR WHAT?

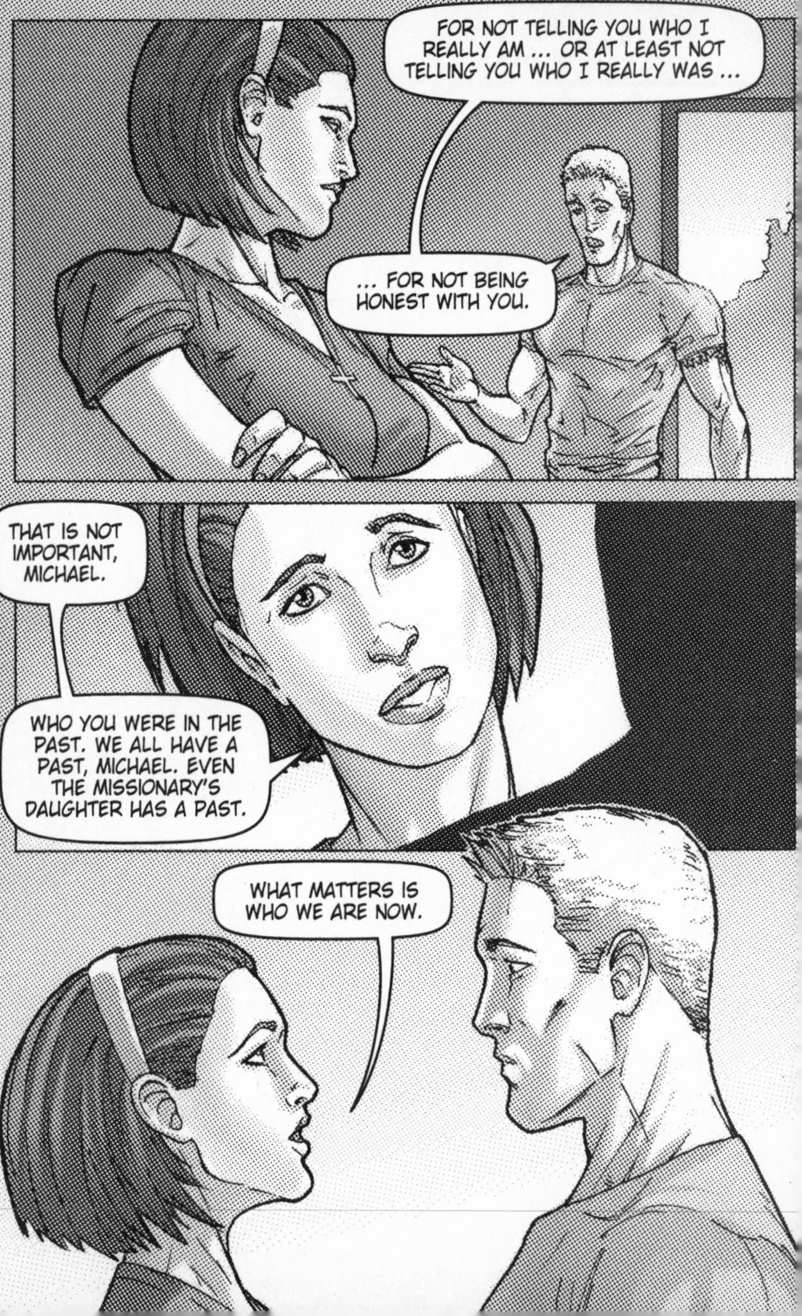
FOR NOT TELLING YOU WHO I REALLY AM ... OR AT LEAST NOT TELLING YOU WHO I REALLY WAS ...
... FOR NOT BEING HONEST WITH YOU.
THAT IS NOT IMPORTANT, MICHAEL.
WHO YOU WERE IN THE PAST. WE ALL HAVE A PAST, MICHAEL. EVEN THE MISSIONARY'S DAUGHTER HAS A PAST.
WHAT MATTERS IS WHO WE ARE NOW.

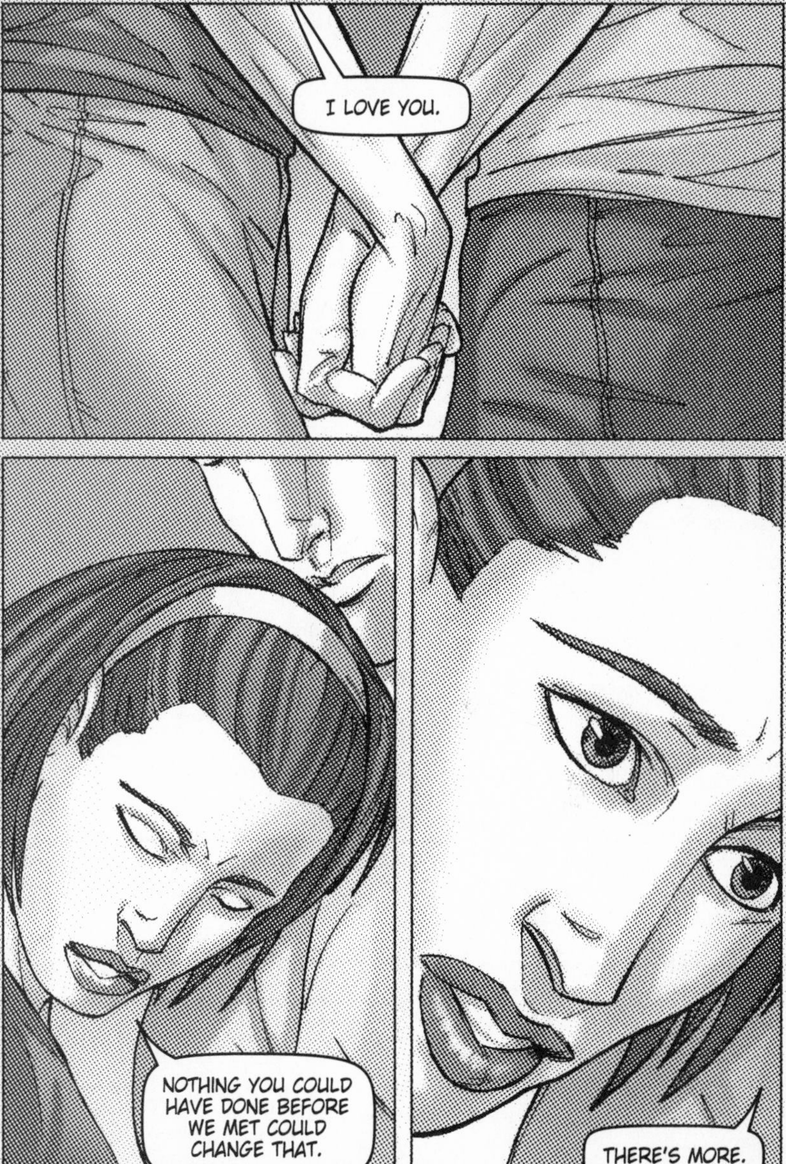
I LOVE YOU.
NOTHING YOU COULD HAVE DONE BEFORE WE MET COULD CHANGE THAT.
THERE'S MORE.

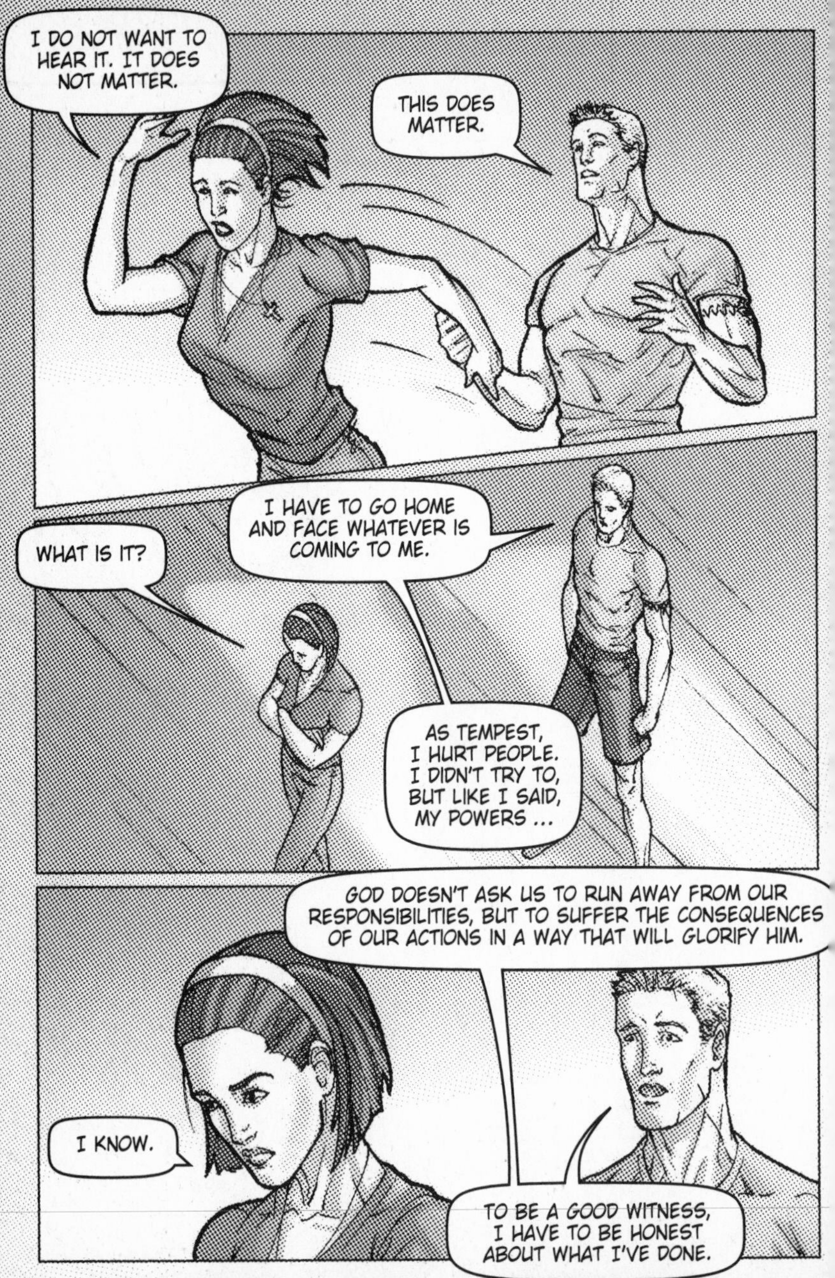
I DO NOT WANT TO HEAR IT. IT DOES NOT MATTER.
THIS DOES MATTER.
WHAT IS IT?
I HAVE TO GO HOME AND FACE WHATEVER IS COMING TO ME.
AS TEMPEST, I HURT PEOPLE. I DIDN'T TRY TO, BUT LIKE I SAID, MY POWERS ...
GOD DOESN'T ASK US TO RUN AWAY FROM OUR RESPONSIBILITIES, BUT TO SUFFER THE CONSEQUENCES OF OUR ACTIONS IN A WAY THAT WILL GLORIFY HIM.
I KNOW.
TO BE A GOOD WITNESS, I HAVE TO BE HONEST ABOUT WHAT I'VE DONE.

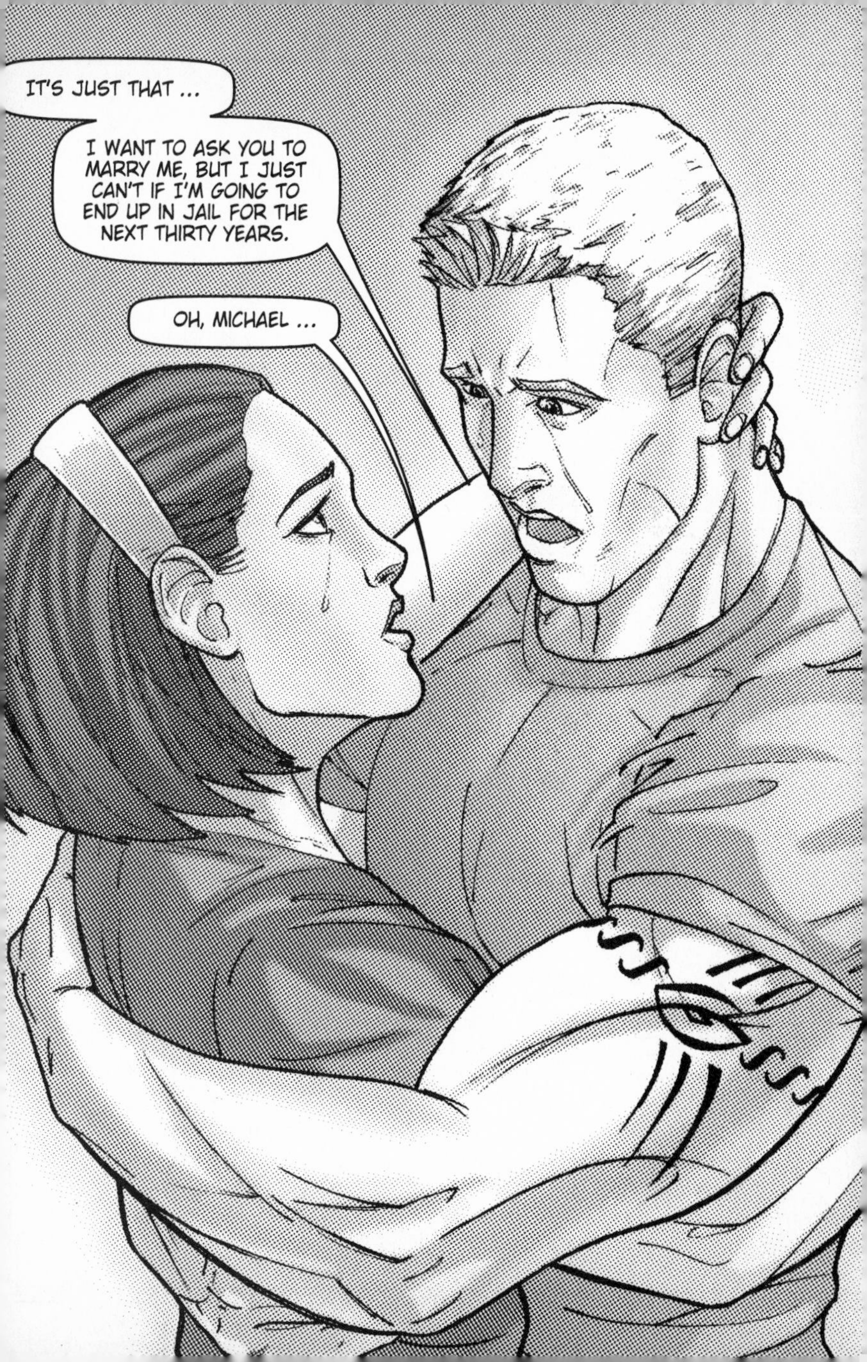
IT'S JUST THAT ...
I WANT TO ASK YOU TO MARRY ME, BUT I JUST CAN'T IF I'M GOING TO END UP IN JAIL FOR THE NEXT THIRTY YEARS.
OH, MICHAEL ...

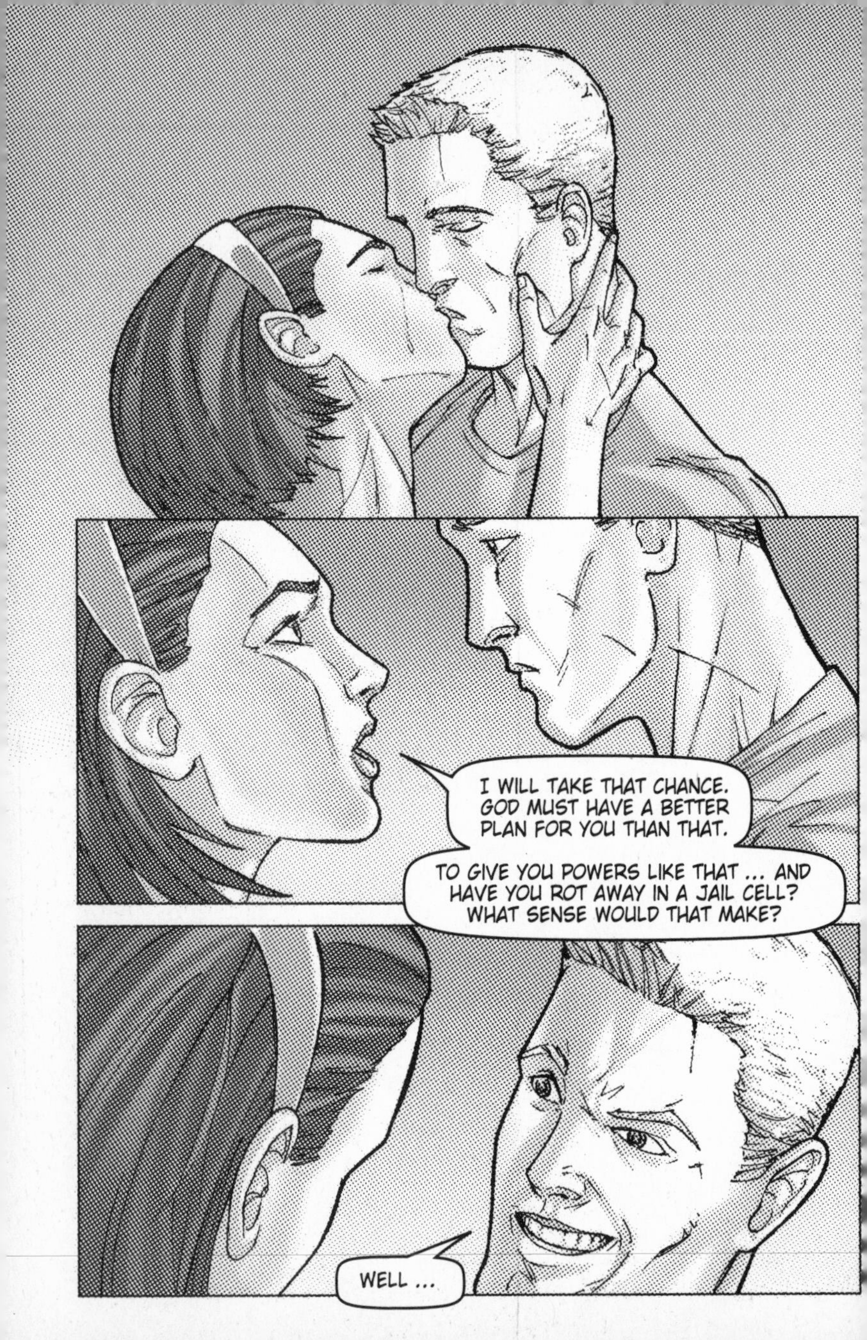
I WILL TAKE THAT CHANCE. GOD MUST HAVE A BETTER PLAN FOR YOU THAN THAT.
TO GIVE YOU POWERS LIKE THAT ... AND HAVE YOU ROT AWAY IN A JAIL CELL? WHAT SENSE WOULD THAT MAKE?
WELL ...

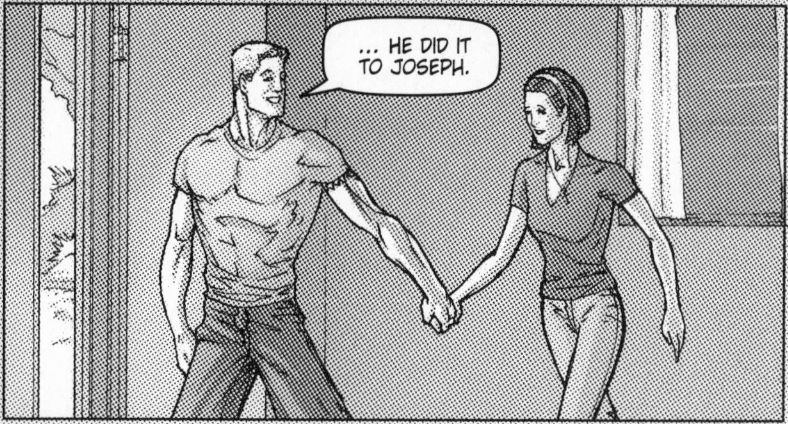
... HE DID IT TO JOSEPH.

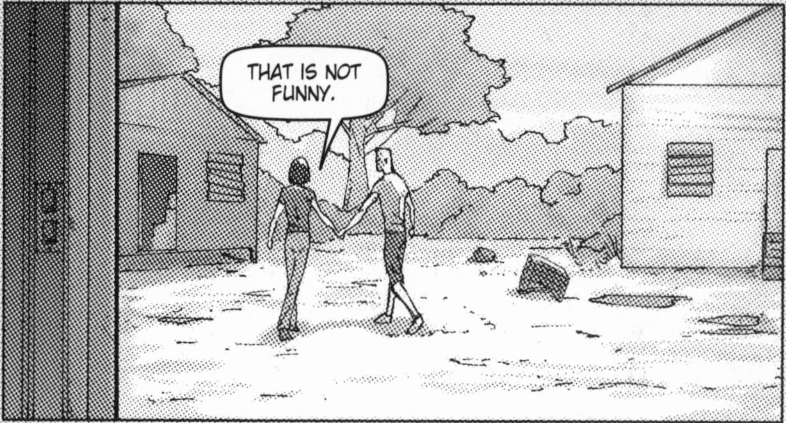
THAT IS NOT FUNNY.

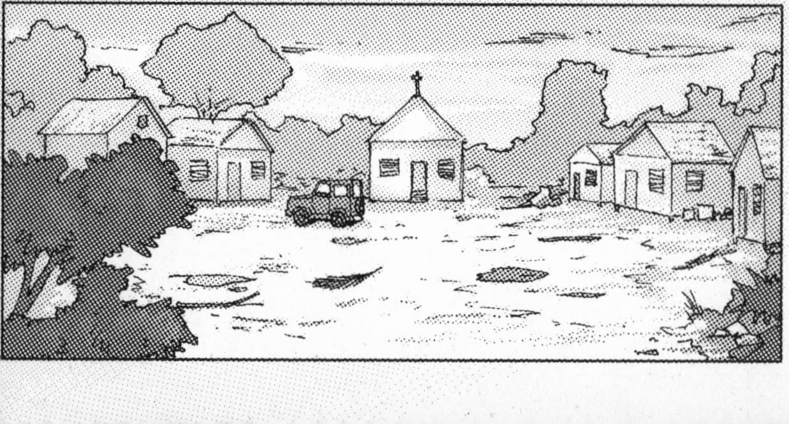

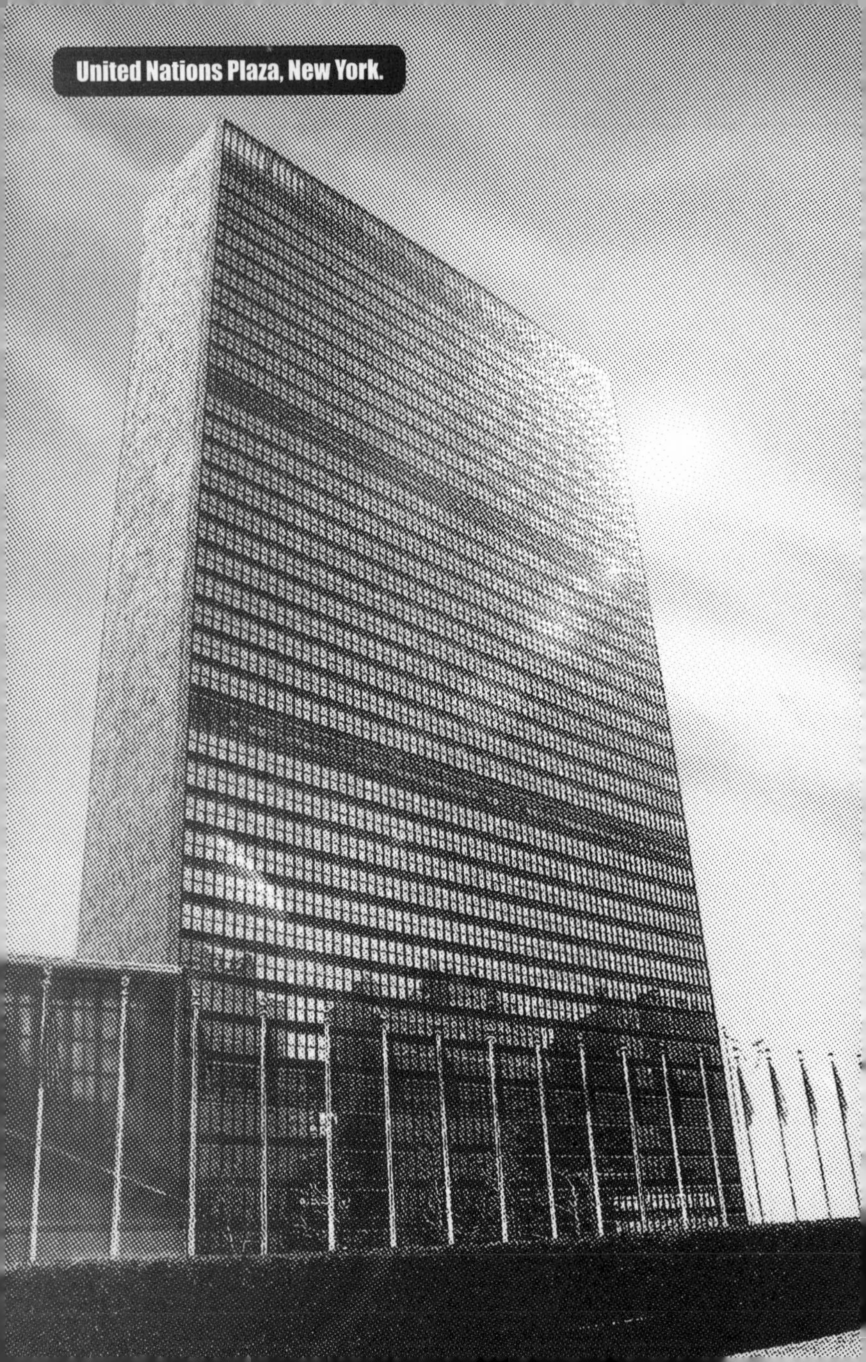

United Nations Plaza, New York.

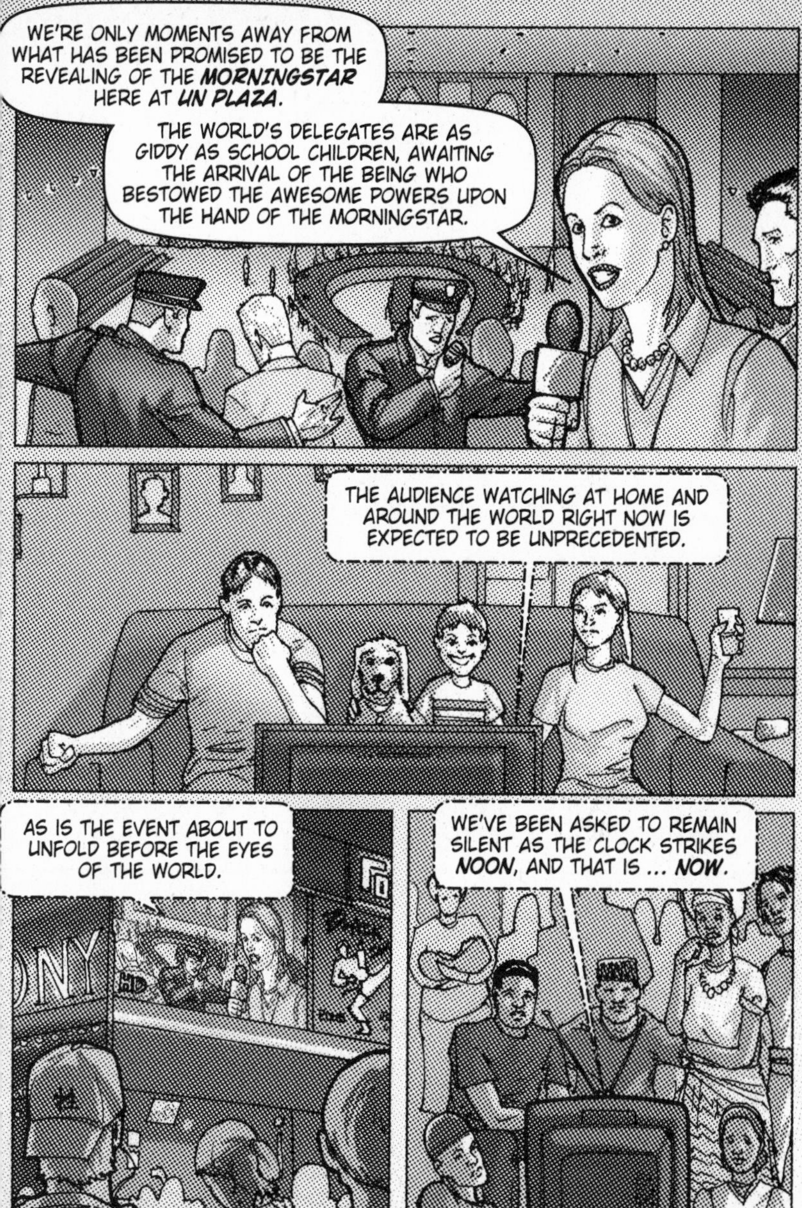
WE'RE ONLY MOMENTS AWAY FROM WHAT HAS BEEN PROMISED TO BE THE REVEALING OF THE MORNINGSTAR HERE AT UN PLAZA.
THE WORLD'S DELEGATES ARE AS GIDDY AS SCHOOL CHILDREN, AWAITING THE ARRIVAL OF THE BEING WHO BESTOWED THE AWESOME POWERS UPON THE HAND OF THE MORNINGSTAR.
THE AUDIENCE WATCHING AT HOME AND AROUND THE WORLD RIGHT NOW IS EXPECTED TO BE UNPRECEDENTED.
AS IS THE EVENT ABOUT TO UNFOLD BEFORE THE EYES OF THE WORLD.
WE'VE BEEN ASKED TO REMAIN SILENT AS THE CLOCK STRIKES NOON, AND THAT IS ... NOW.

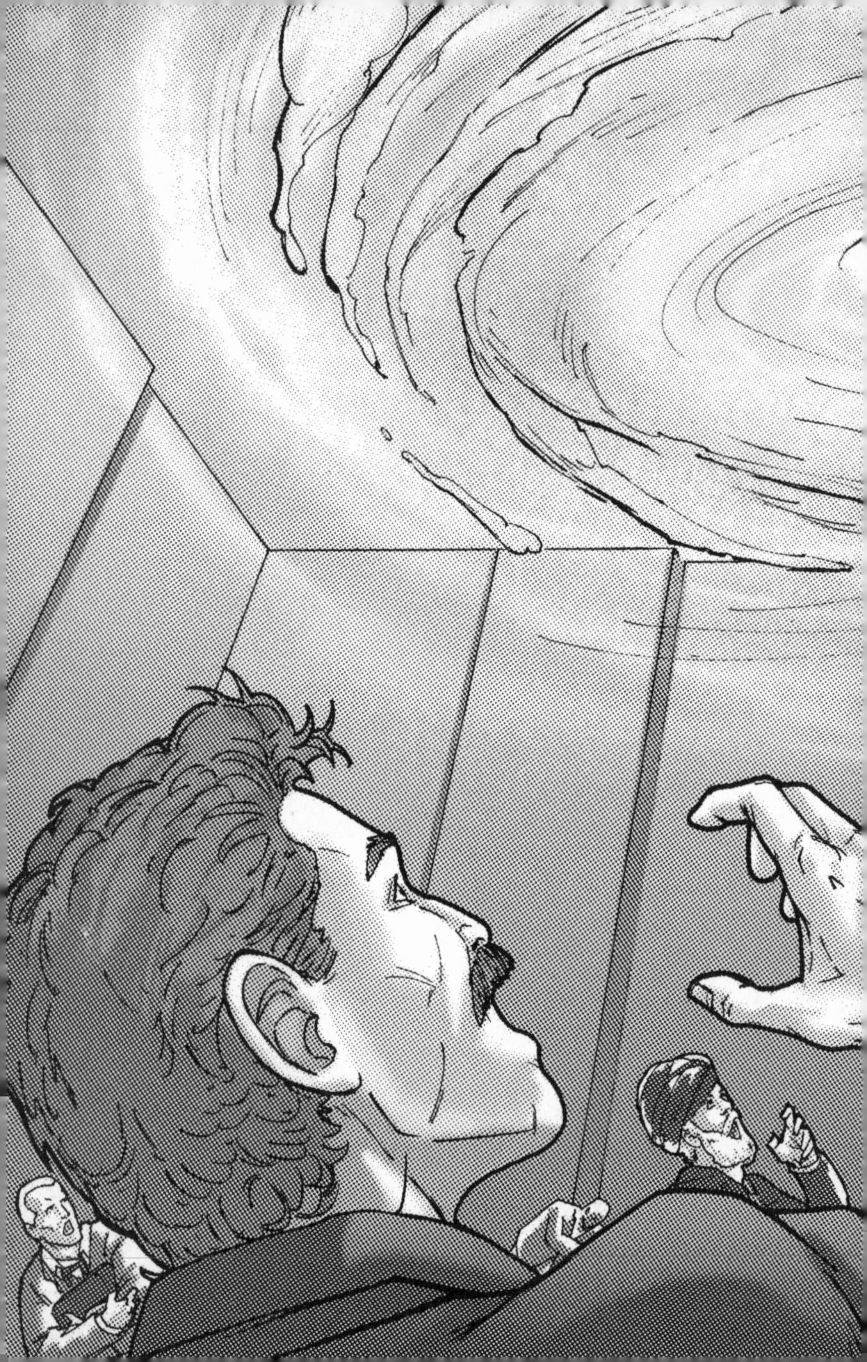

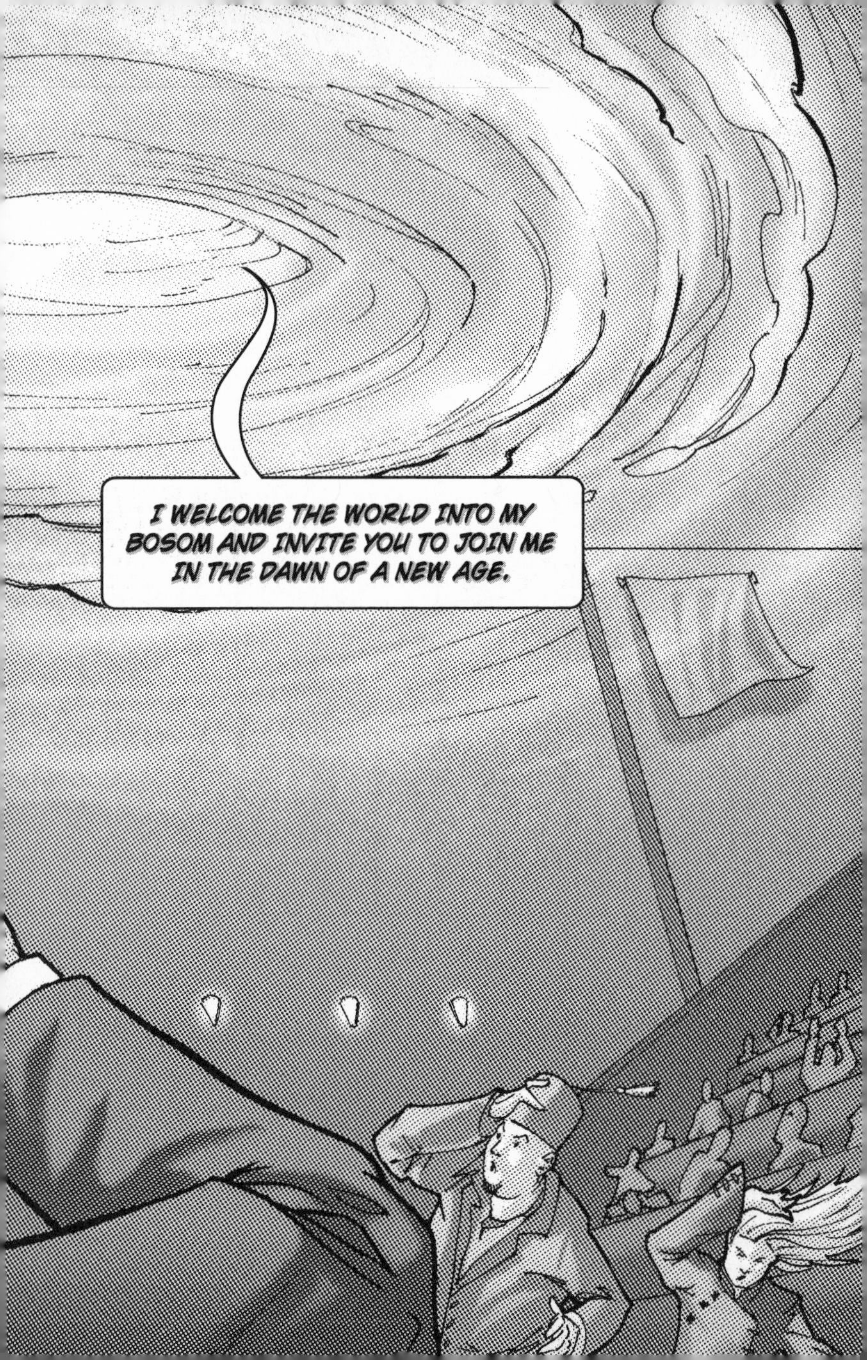
I WELCOME THE WORLD INTO MY BOSOM AND INVITE YOU TO JOIN ME IN THE DAWN OF A NEW AGE.

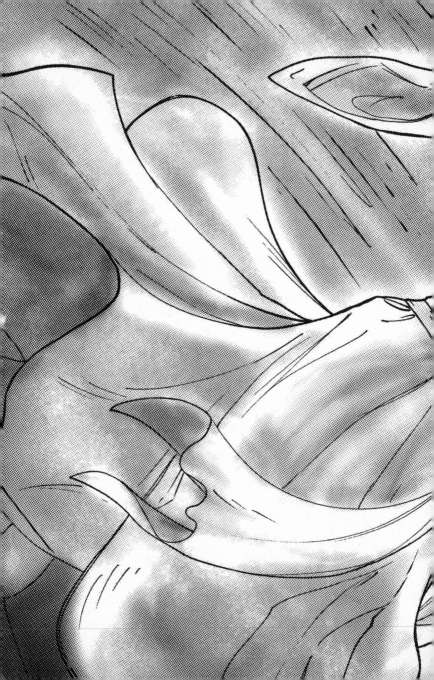

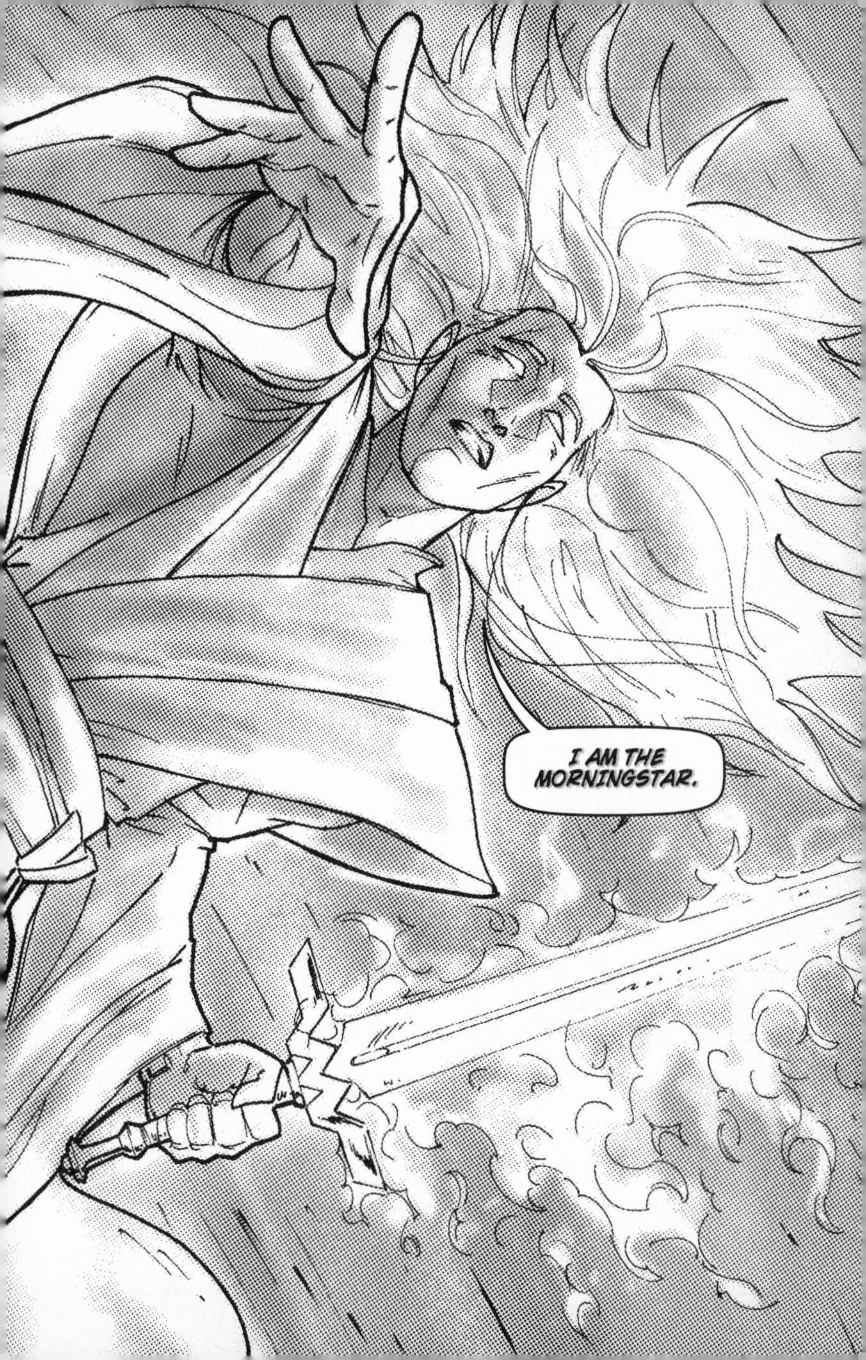
I AM THE MORNINGSTAR.

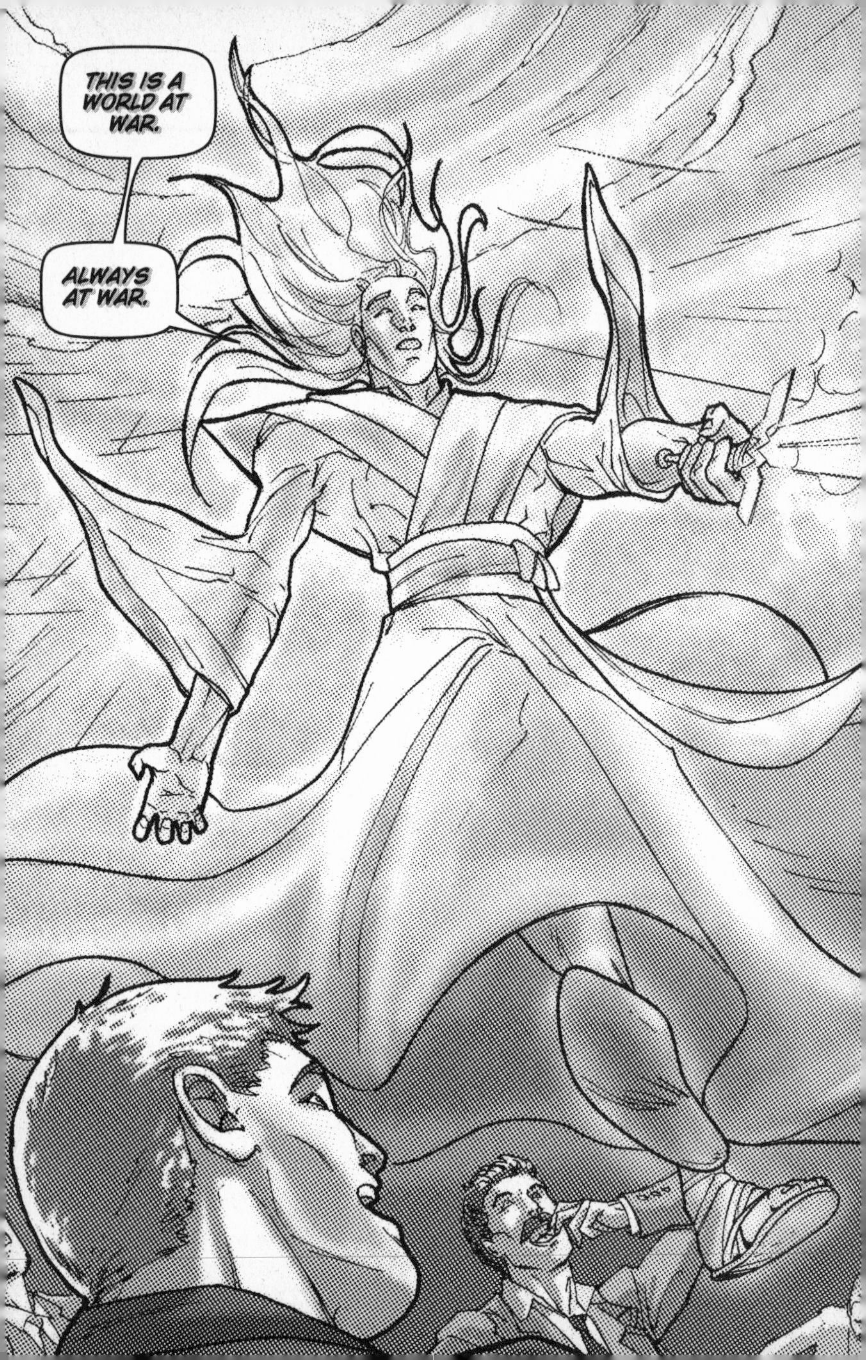
THIS IS A WORLD AT WAR.
ALWAYS AT WAR.

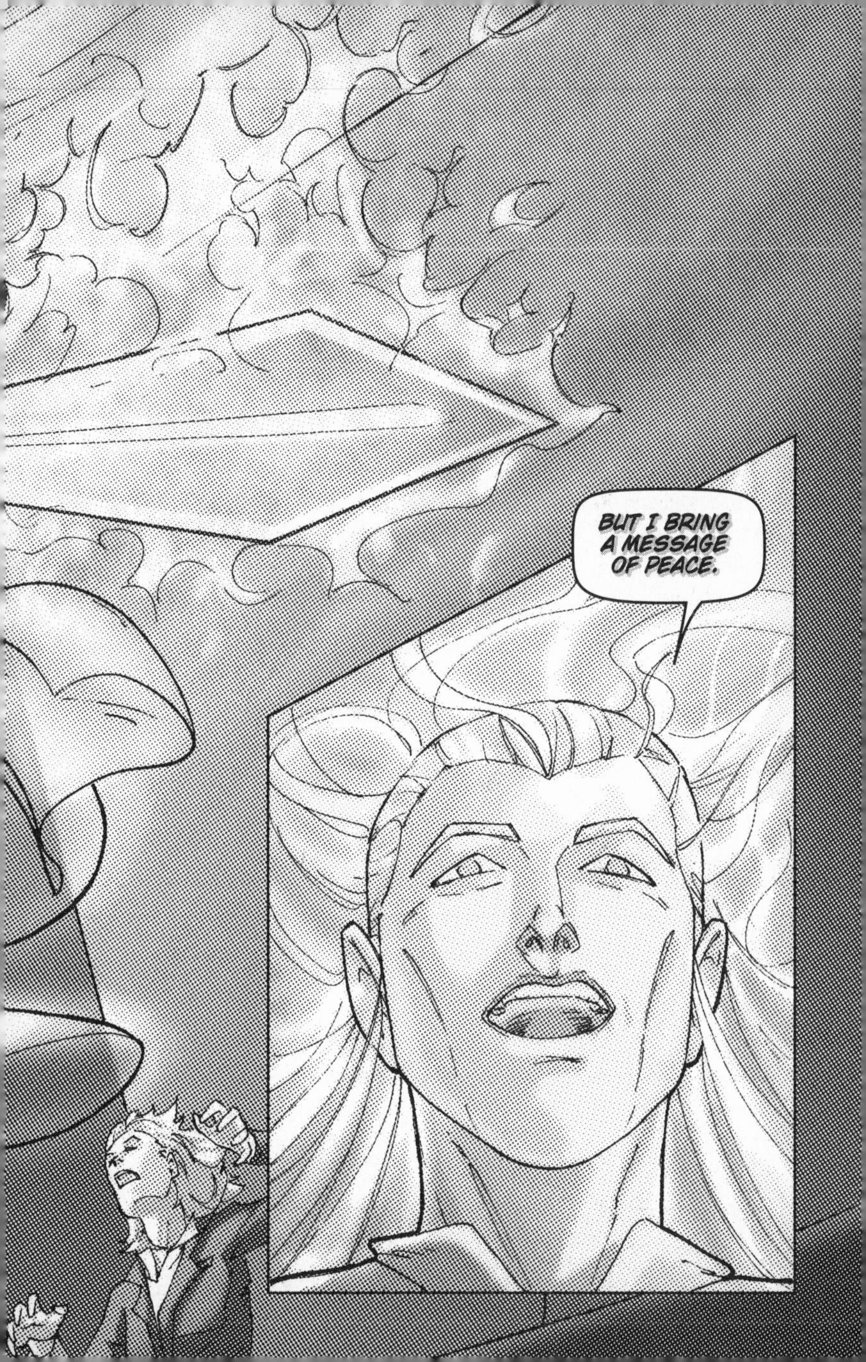
BUT I BRING A MESSAGE OF PEACE.

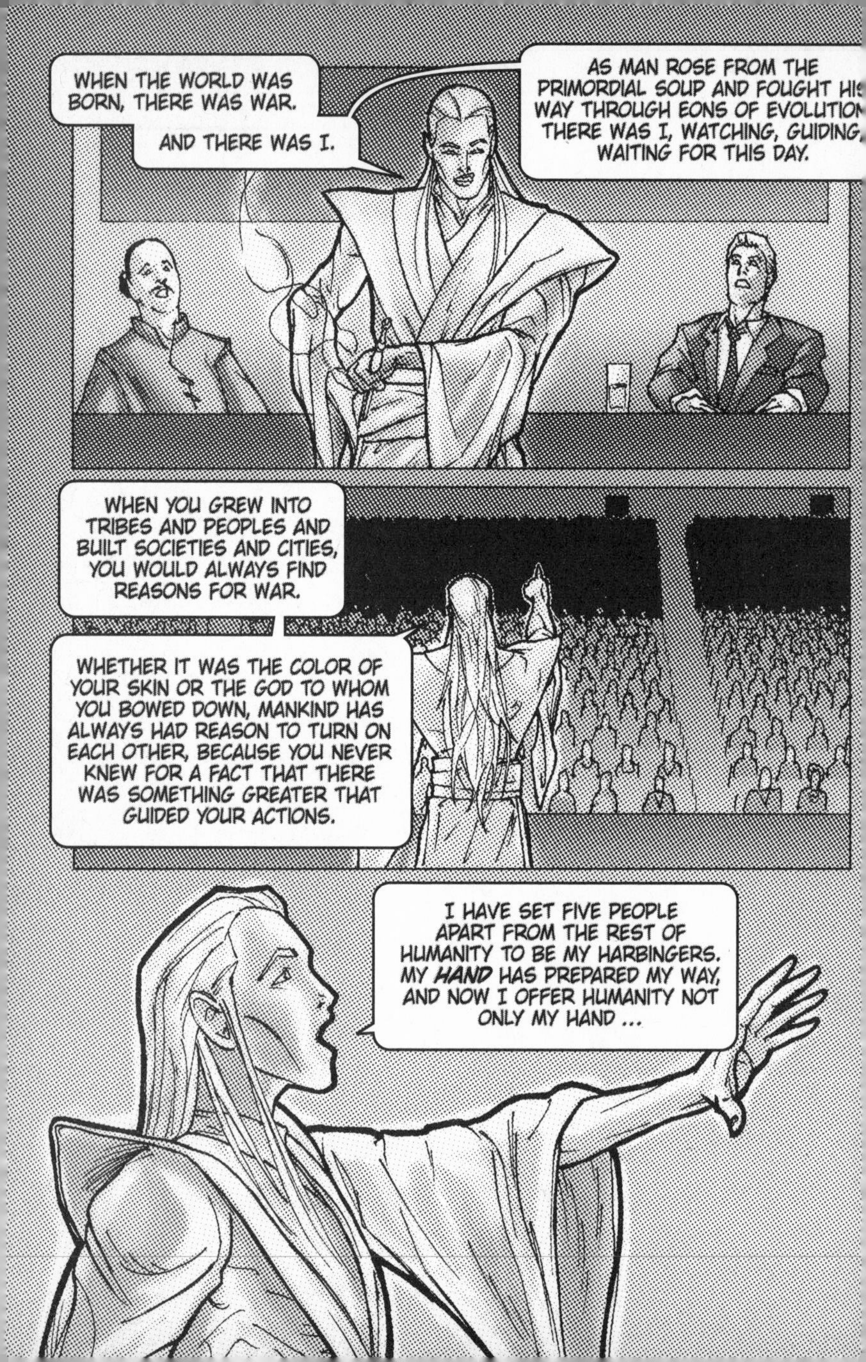
WHEN THE WORLD WAS BORN, THERE WAS WAR.
AND THERE WAS I.
AS MAN ROSE FROM THE PRIMORDIAL SOUP AND FOUGHT HIS WAY THROUGH EONS OF EVOLUTION THERE WAS I, WATCHING, GUIDING, WAITING FOR THIS DAY.
WHEN YOU GREW INTO TRIBES AND PEOPLES AND BUILT SOCIETIES AND CITIES, YOU WOULD ALWAYS FIND REASONS FOR WAR.
WHETHER IT WAS THE COLOR OF YOUR SKIN OR THE GOD TO WHOM YOU BOWED DOWN, MANKIND HAS ALWAYS HAD REASON TO TURN ON EACH OTHER, BECAUSE YOU NEVER KNEW FOR A FACT THAT THERE WAS SOMETHING GREATER THAT GUIDED YOUR ACTIONS.
I HAVE SET FIVE PEOPLE APART FROM THE REST OF HUMANITY TO BE MY HARBINGERS. MY *HAND* HAS PREPARED MY WAY, AND NOW I OFFER HUMANITY NOT ONLY MY HAND ...

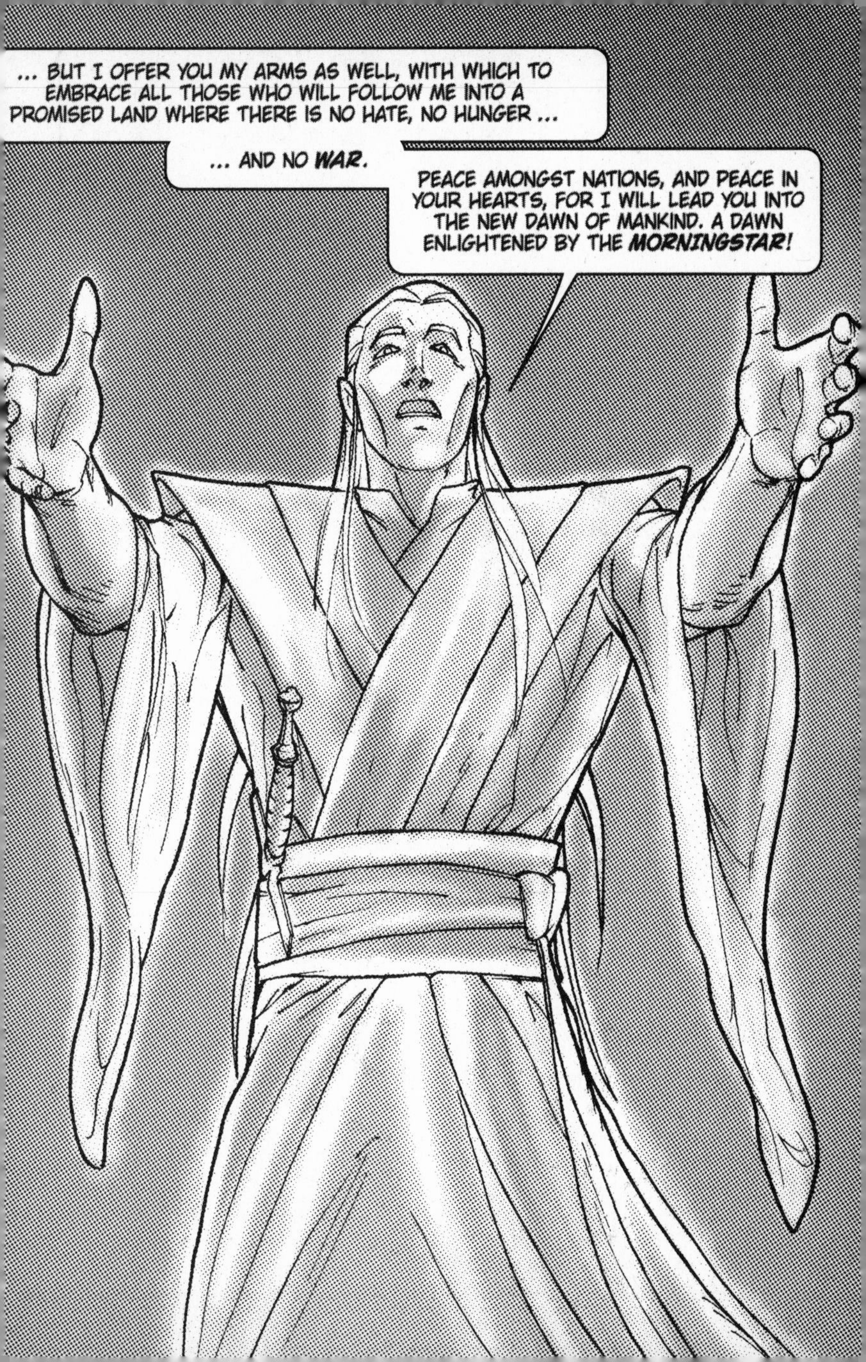
... BUT I OFFER YOU MY ARMS AS WELL, WITH WHICH TO EMBRACE ALL THOSE WHO WILL FOLLOW ME INTO A PROMISED LAND WHERE THERE IS NO HATE, NO HUNGER ...
... AND NO WAR.
PEACE AMONGST NATIONS, AND PEACE IN YOUR HEARTS, FOR I WILL LEAD YOU INTO THE NEW DAWN OF MANKIND. A DAWN ENLIGHTENED BY THE MORNINGSTAR!

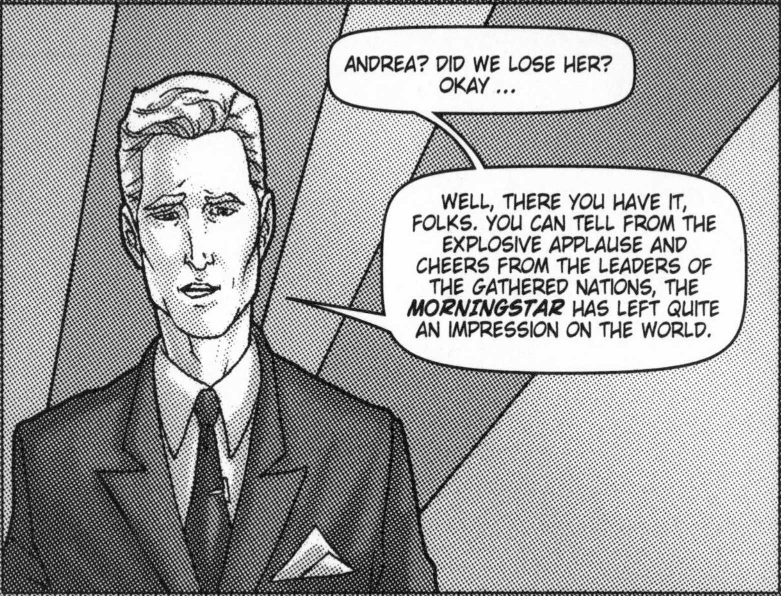
ANDREA? DID WE LOSE HER? OKAY ...
WELL, THERE YOU HAVE IT, FOLKS. YOU CAN TELL FROM THE EXPLOSIVE APPLAUSE AND CHEERS FROM THE LEADERS OF THE GATHERED NATIONS, THE *MORNINGSTAR* HAS LEFT QUITE AN IMPRESSION ON THE WORLD.

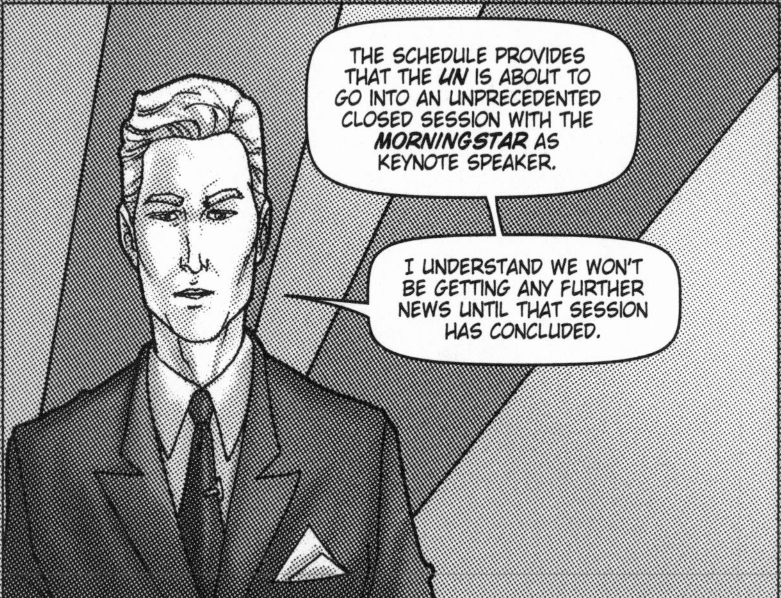
THE SCHEDULE PROVIDES THAT THE *UN* IS ABOUT TO GO INTO AN UNPRECEDENTED CLOSED SESSION WITH THE *MORNINGSTAR* AS KEYNOTE SPEAKER.
I UNDERSTAND WE WON'T BE GETTING ANY FURTHER NEWS UNTIL THAT SESSION HAS CONCLUDED.

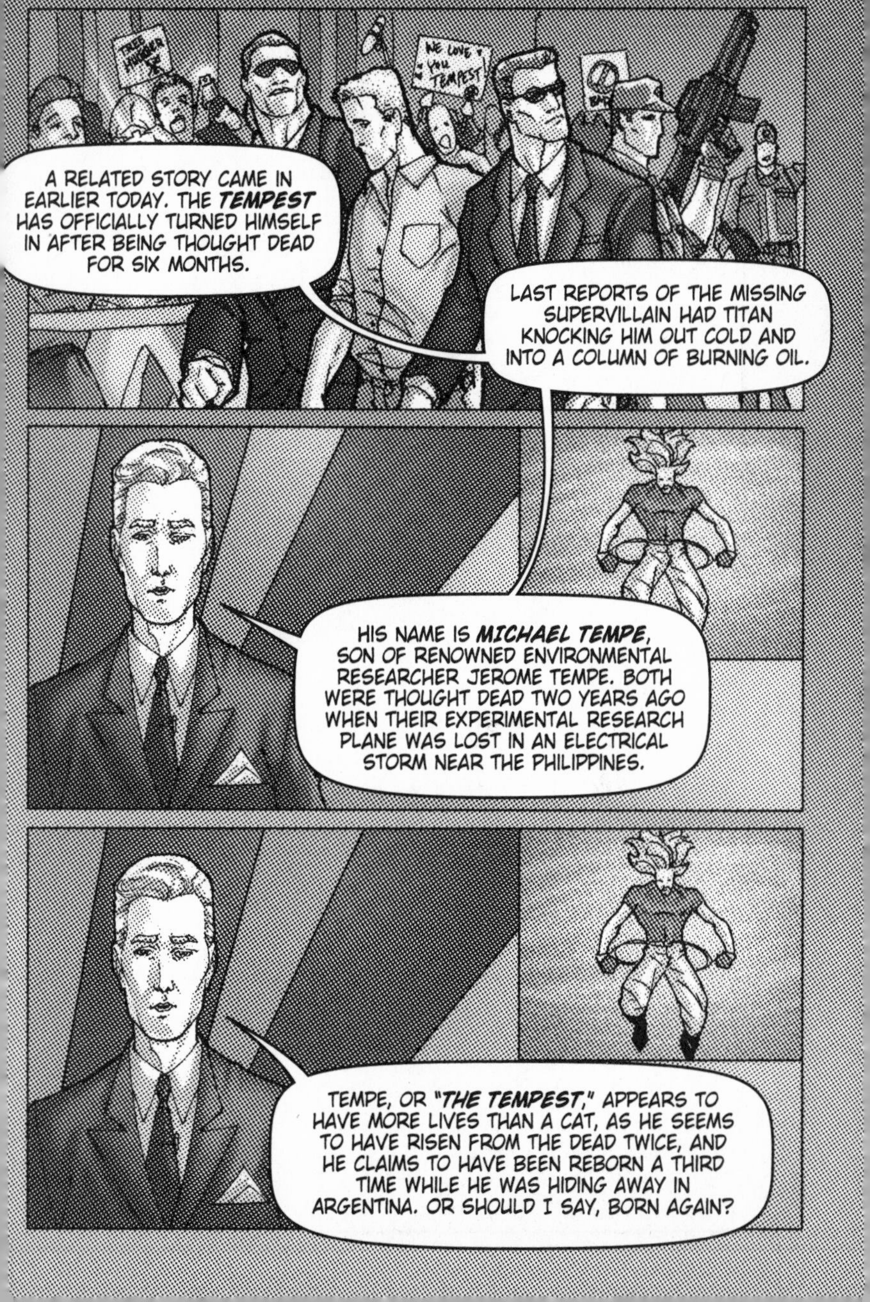
WE LOVE YOU TEMPEST
A RELATED STORY CAME IN EARLIER TODAY. THE ***TEMPEST*** HAS OFFICIALLY TURNED HIMSELF IN AFTER BEING THOUGHT DEAD FOR SIX MONTHS.
LAST REPORTS OF THE MISSING SUPERVILLAIN HAD TITAN KNOCKING HIM OUT COLD AND INTO A COLUMN OF BURNING OIL.
HIS NAME IS ***MICHAEL TEMPE***, SON OF RENOWNED ENVIRONMENTAL RESEARCHER JEROME TEMPE. BOTH WERE THOUGHT DEAD TWO YEARS AGO WHEN THEIR EXPERIMENTAL RESEARCH PLANE WAS LOST IN AN ELECTRICAL STORM NEAR THE PHILIPPINES.
TEMPE, OR "***THE TEMPEST***," APPEARS TO HAVE MORE LIVES THAN A CAT, AS HE SEEMS TO HAVE RISEN FROM THE DEAD TWICE, AND HE CLAIMS TO HAVE BEEN REBORN A THIRD TIME WHILE HE WAS HIDING AWAY IN ARGENTINA. OR SHOULD I SAY, BORN AGAIN?

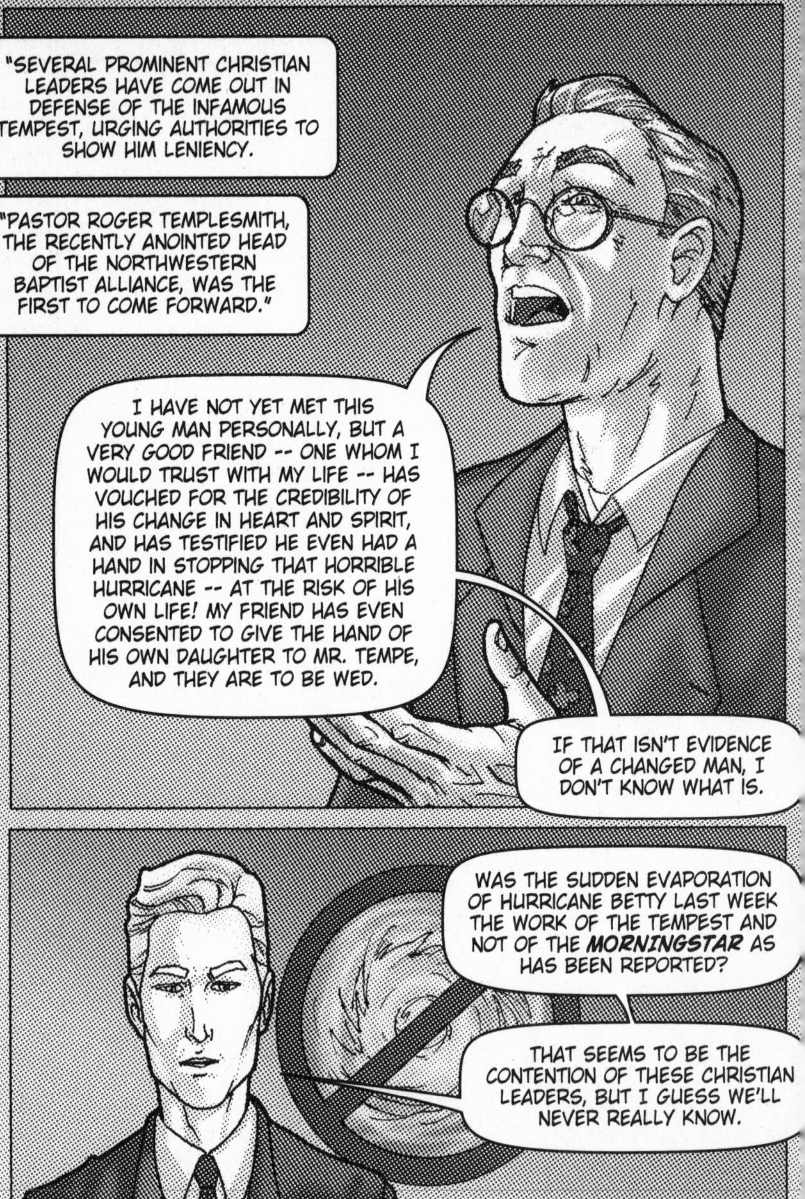
"SEVERAL PROMINENT CHRISTIAN LEADERS HAVE COME OUT IN DEFENSE OF THE INFAMOUS TEMPEST, URGING AUTHORITIES TO SHOW HIM LENIENCY.
"PASTOR ROGER TEMPLESMITH, THE RECENTLY ANOINTED HEAD OF THE NORTHWESTERN BAPTIST ALLIANCE, WAS THE FIRST TO COME FORWARD."
I HAVE NOT YET MET THIS YOUNG MAN PERSONALLY, BUT A VERY GOOD FRIEND -- ONE WHOM I WOULD TRUST WITH MY LIFE -- HAS VOUCHED FOR THE CREDIBILITY OF HIS CHANGE IN HEART AND SPIRIT, AND HAS TESTIFIED HE EVEN HAD A HAND IN STOPPING THAT HORRIBLE HURRICANE -- AT THE RISK OF HIS OWN LIFE! MY FRIEND HAS EVEN CONSENTED TO GIVE THE HAND OF HIS OWN DAUGHTER TO MR. TEMPE, AND THEY ARE TO BE WED.
IF THAT ISN'T EVIDENCE OF A CHANGED MAN, I DON'T KNOW WHAT IS.
WAS THE SUDDEN EVAPORATION OF HURRICANE BETTY LAST WEEK THE WORK OF THE TEMPEST AND NOT OF THE ***MORNINGSTAR*** AS HAS BEEN REPORTED?
THAT SEEMS TO BE THE CONTENTION OF THESE CHRISTIAN LEADERS, BUT I GUESS WE'LL NEVER REALLY KNOW.

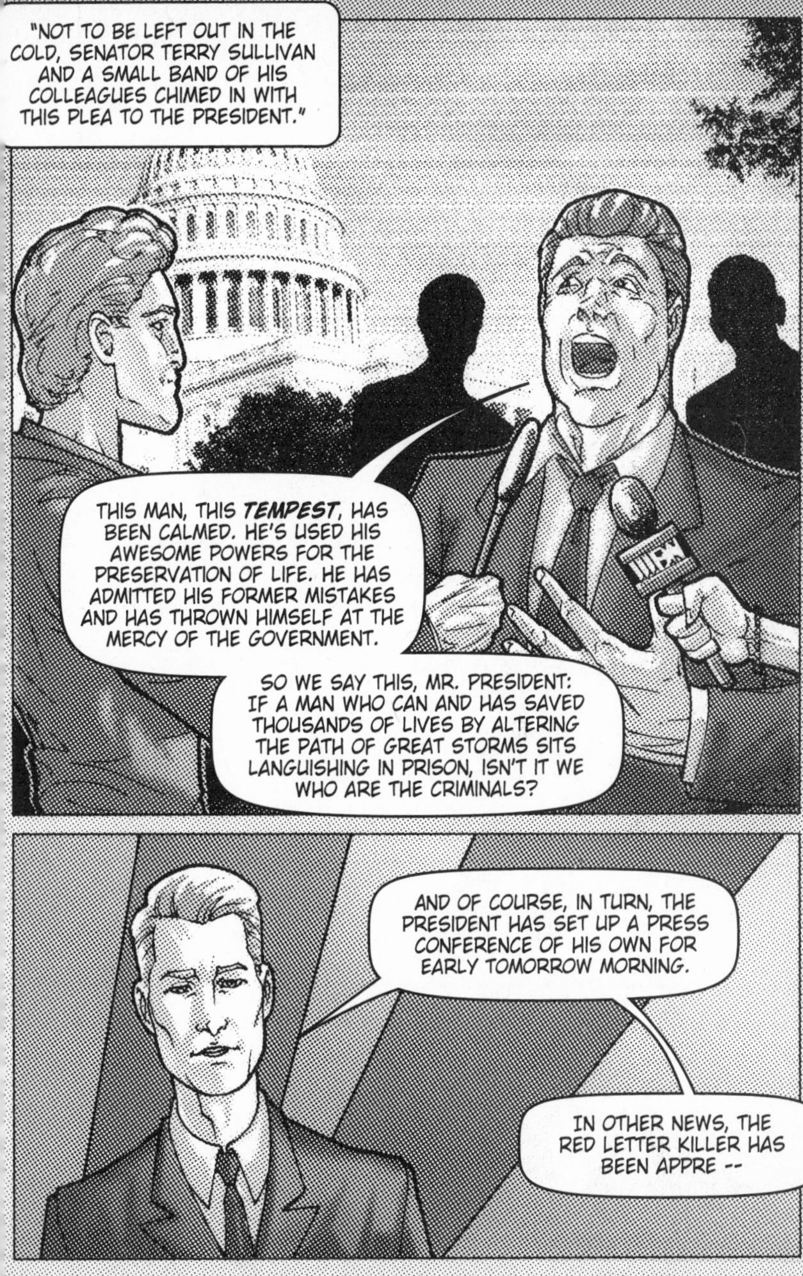
"NOT TO BE LEFT OUT IN THE COLD, SENATOR TERRY SULLIVAN AND A SMALL BAND OF HIS COLLEAGUES CHIMED IN WITH THIS PLEA TO THE PRESIDENT."
THIS MAN, THIS *TEMPEST*, HAS BEEN CALMED. HE'S USED HIS AWESOME POWERS FOR THE PRESERVATION OF LIFE. HE HAS ADMITTED HIS FORMER MISTAKES AND HAS THROWN HIMSELF AT THE MERCY OF THE GOVERNMENT.
SO WE SAY THIS, MR. PRESIDENT: IF A MAN WHO CAN AND HAS SAVED THOUSANDS OF LIVES BY ALTERING THE PATH OF GREAT STORMS SITS LANGUISHING IN PRISON, ISN'T IT WE WHO ARE THE CRIMINALS?
AND OF COURSE, IN TURN, THE PRESIDENT HAS SET UP A PRESS CONFERENCE OF HIS OWN FOR EARLY TOMORROW MORNING.
IN OTHER NEWS, THE RED LETTER KILLER HAS BEEN APPRE --

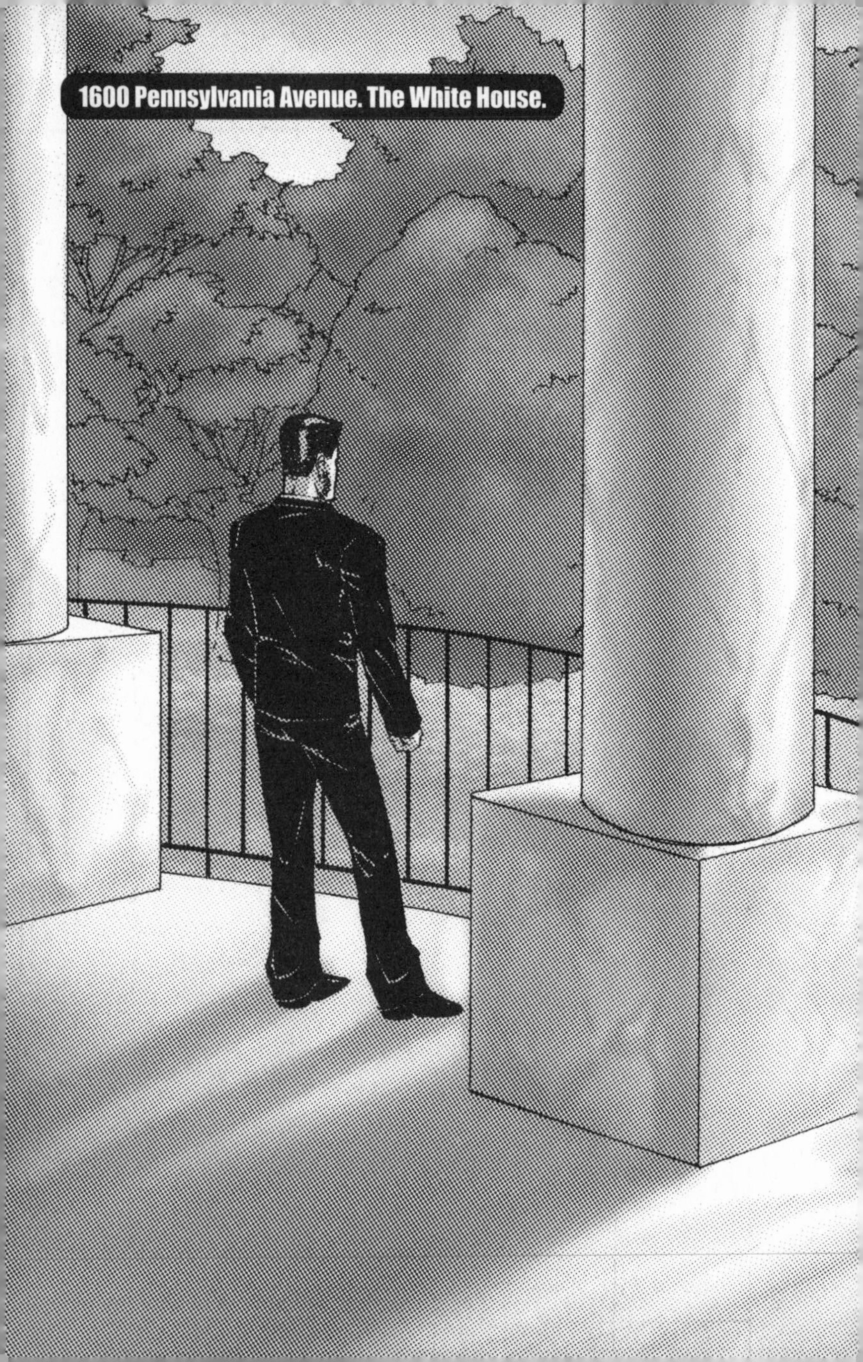
1600 Pennsylvania Avenue. The White House.

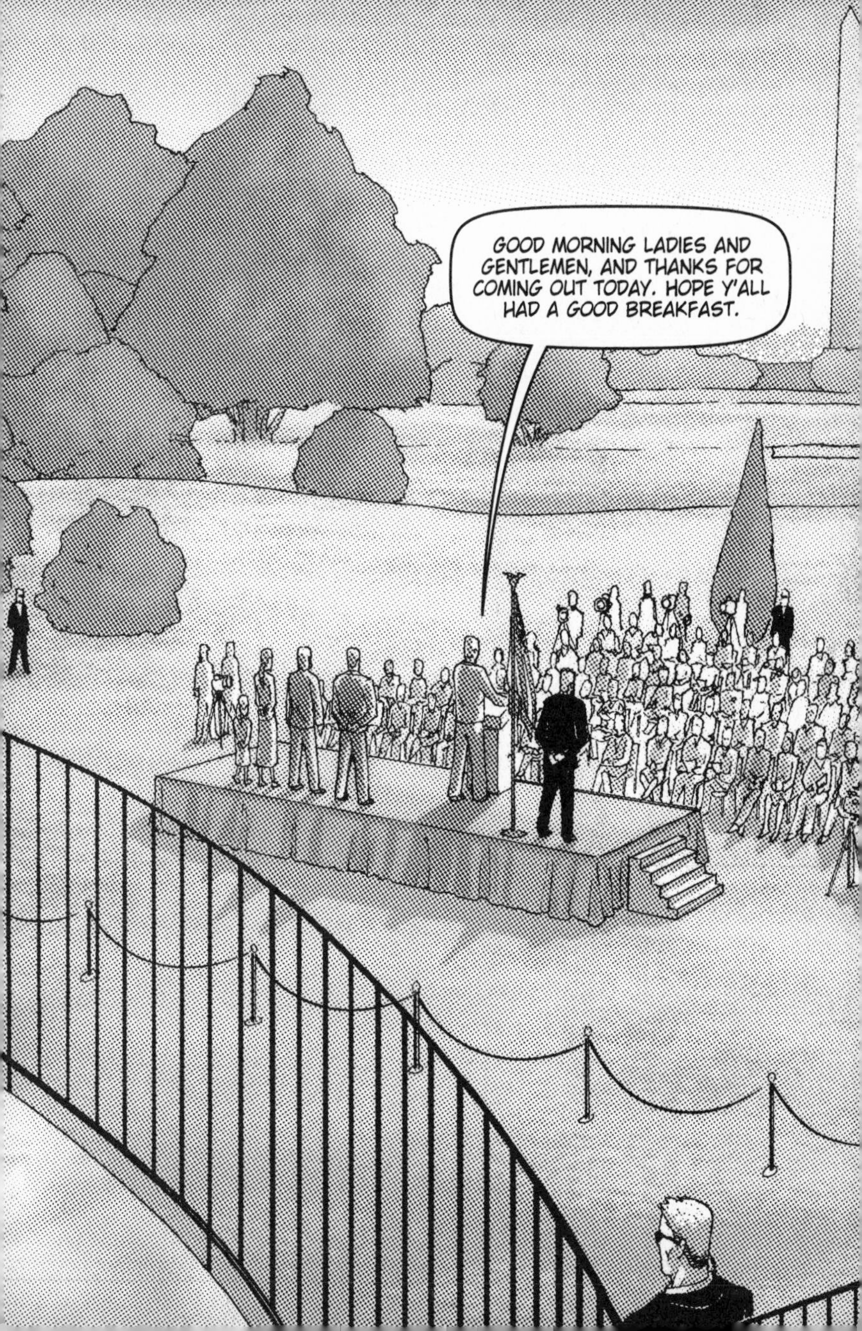
GOOD MORNING LADIES AND GENTLEMEN, AND THANKS FOR COMING OUT TODAY. HOPE Y'ALL HAD A GOOD BREAKFAST.

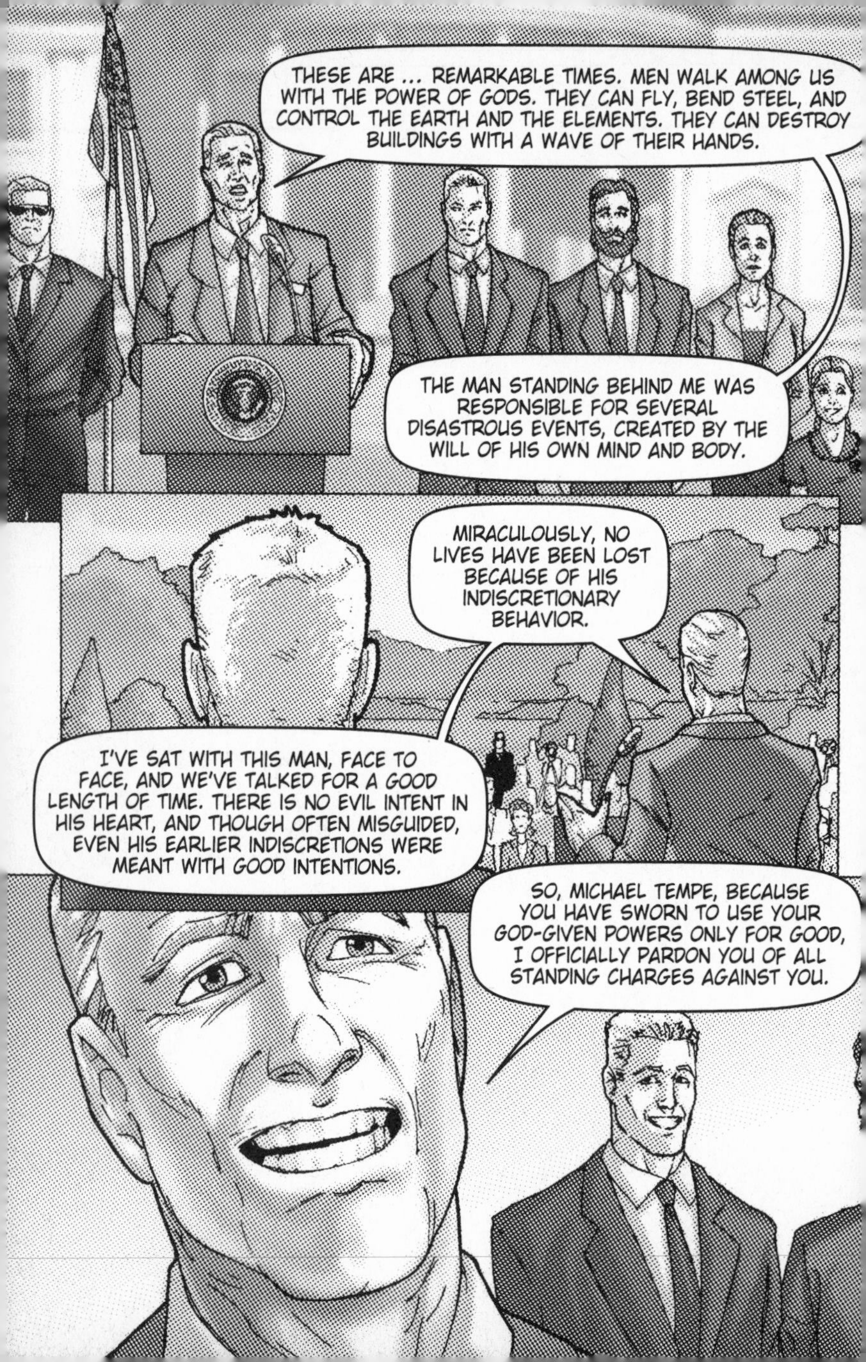
THESE ARE ... REMARKABLE TIMES. MEN WALK AMONG US WITH THE POWER OF GODS. THEY CAN FLY, BEND STEEL, AND CONTROL THE EARTH AND THE ELEMENTS. THEY CAN DESTROY BUILDINGS WITH A WAVE OF THEIR HANDS.
THE MAN STANDING BEHIND ME WAS RESPONSIBLE FOR SEVERAL DISASTROUS EVENTS, CREATED BY THE WILL OF HIS OWN MIND AND BODY.
MIRACULOUSLY, NO LIVES HAVE BEEN LOST BECAUSE OF HIS INDISCRETIONARY BEHAVIOR.
I'VE SAT WITH THIS MAN, FACE TO FACE, AND WE'VE TALKED FOR A GOOD LENGTH OF TIME. THERE IS NO EVIL INTENT IN HIS HEART, AND THOUGH OFTEN MISGUIDED, EVEN HIS EARLIER INDISCRETIONS WERE MEANT WITH GOOD INTENTIONS.
SO, MICHAEL TEMPE, BECAUSE YOU HAVE SWORN TO USE YOUR GOD-GIVEN POWERS ONLY FOR GOOD, I OFFICIALLY PARDON YOU OF ALL STANDING CHARGES AGAINST YOU.

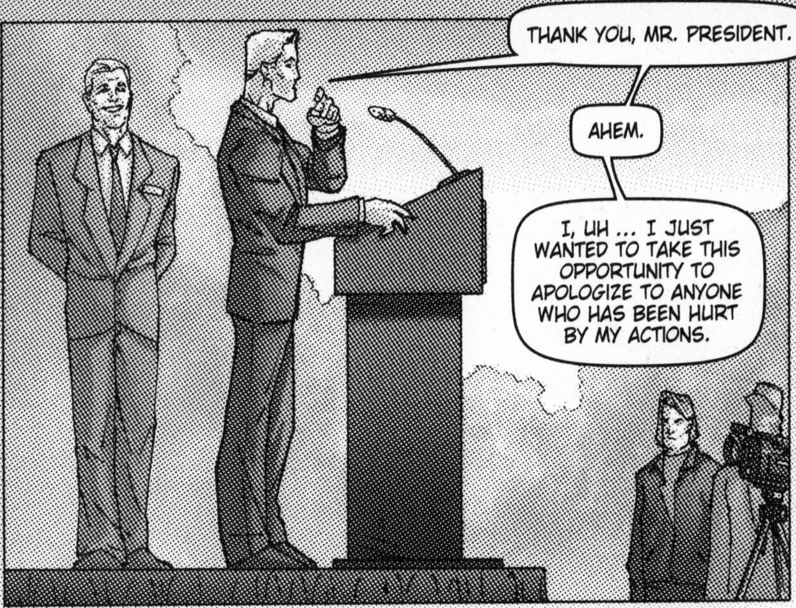
THANK YOU, MR. PRESIDENT.
AHEM.
I, UH ... I JUST WANTED TO TAKE THIS OPPORTUNITY TO APOLOGIZE TO ANYONE WHO HAS BEEN HURT BY MY ACTIONS.

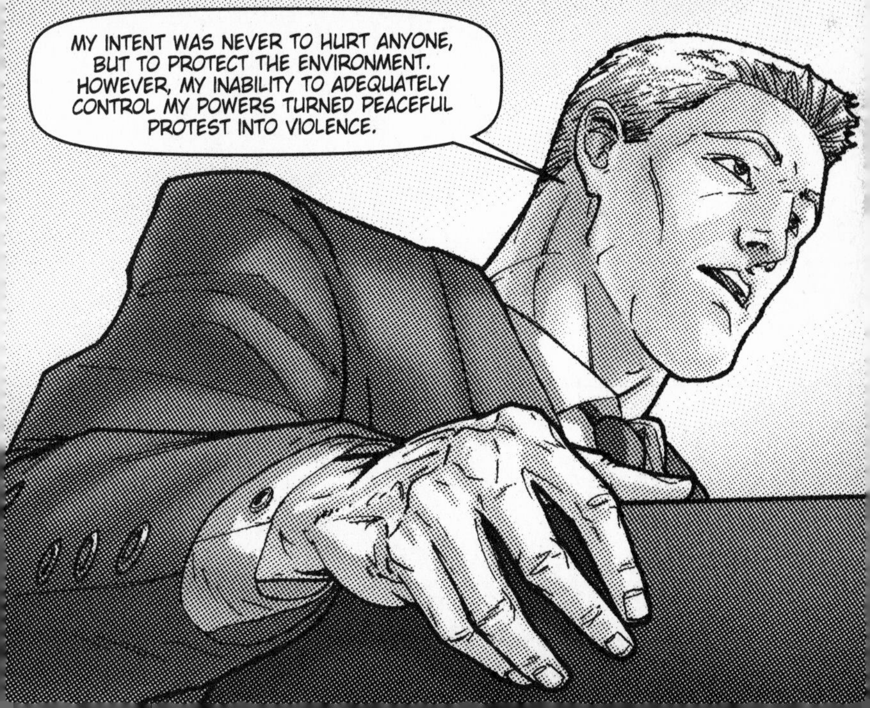
MY INTENT WAS NEVER TO HURT ANYONE, BUT TO PROTECT THE ENVIRONMENT. HOWEVER, MY INABILITY TO ADEQUATELY CONTROL MY POWERS TURNED PEACEFUL PROTEST INTO VIOLENCE.

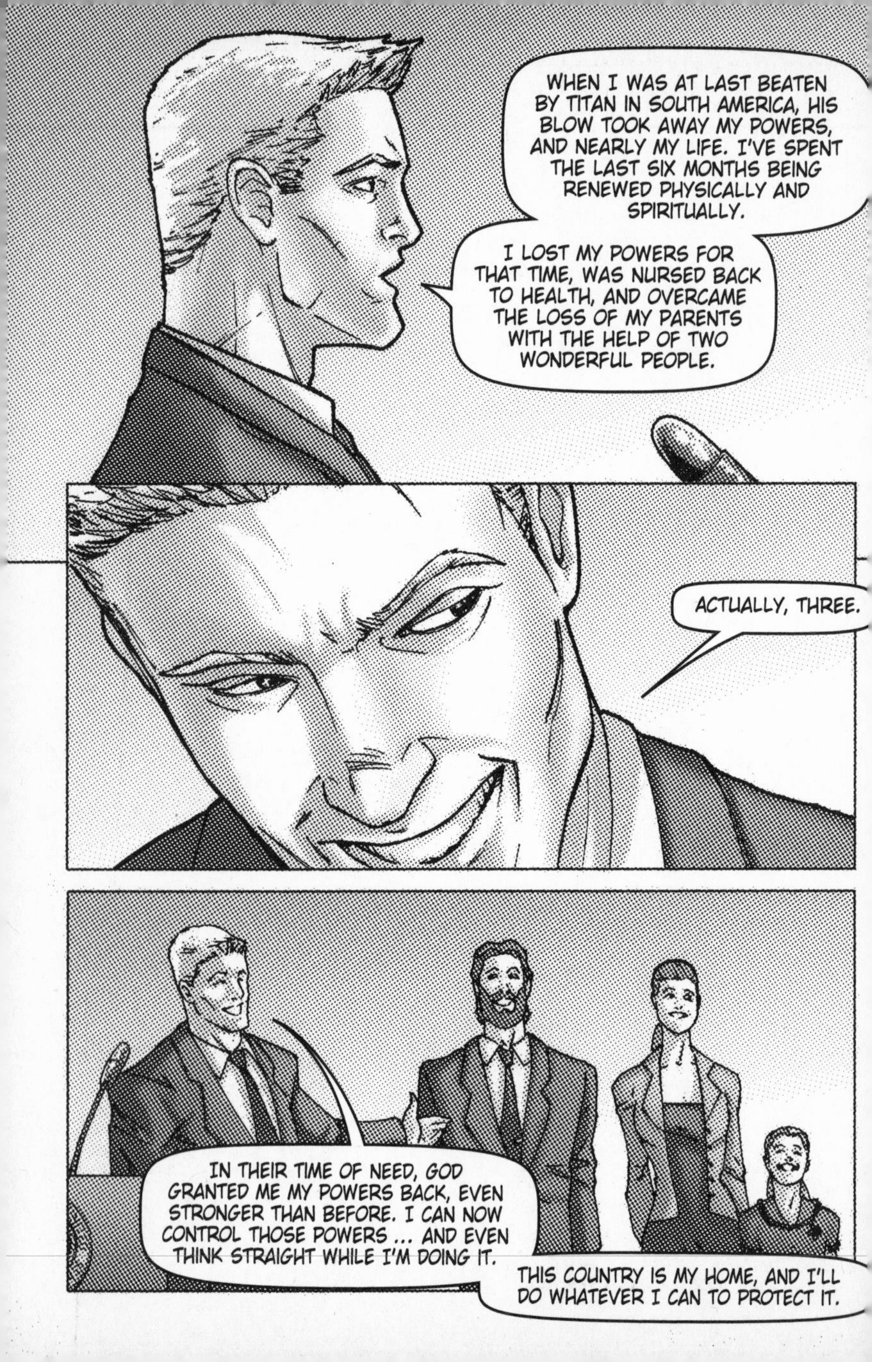
WHEN I WAS AT LAST BEATEN BY TITAN IN SOUTH AMERICA, HIS BLOW TOOK AWAY MY POWERS, AND NEARLY MY LIFE. I'VE SPENT THE LAST SIX MONTHS BEING RENEWED PHYSICALLY AND SPIRITUALLY.
I LOST MY POWERS FOR THAT TIME, WAS NURSED BACK TO HEALTH, AND OVERCAME THE LOSS OF MY PARENTS WITH THE HELP OF TWO WONDERFUL PEOPLE.
ACTUALLY, THREE.
IN THEIR TIME OF NEED, GOD GRANTED ME MY POWERS BACK, EVEN STRONGER THAN BEFORE. I CAN NOW CONTROL THOSE POWERS ... AND EVEN THINK STRAIGHT WHILE I'M DOING IT.
THIS COUNTRY IS MY HOME, AND I'LL DO WHATEVER I CAN TO PROTECT IT.

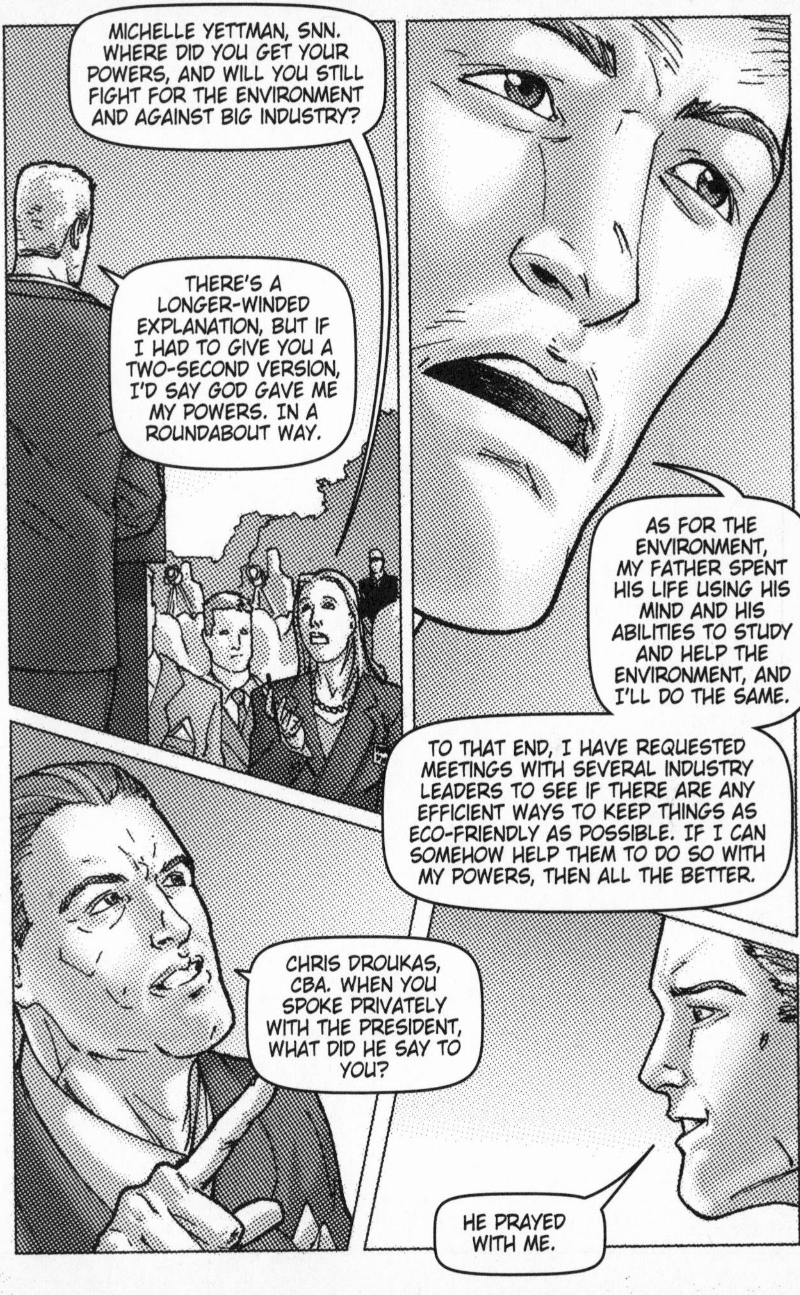
MICHELLE YETTMAN, SNN. WHERE DID YOU GET YOUR POWERS, AND WILL YOU STILL FIGHT FOR THE ENVIRONMENT AND AGAINST BIG INDUSTRY?
THERE'S A LONGER-WINDED EXPLANATION, BUT IF I HAD TO GIVE YOU A TWO-SECOND VERSION, I'D SAY GOD GAVE ME MY POWERS. IN A ROUNDABOUT WAY.
AS FOR THE ENVIRONMENT, MY FATHER SPENT HIS LIFE USING HIS MIND AND HIS ABILITIES TO STUDY AND HELP THE ENVIRONMENT, AND I'LL DO THE SAME.
TO THAT END, I HAVE REQUESTED MEETINGS WITH SEVERAL INDUSTRY LEADERS TO SEE IF THERE ARE ANY EFFICIENT WAYS TO KEEP THINGS AS ECO-FRIENDLY AS POSSIBLE. IF I CAN SOMEHOW HELP THEM TO DO SO WITH MY POWERS, THEN ALL THE BETTER.
CHRIS DROUKAS, CBA. WHEN YOU SPOKE PRIVATELY WITH THE PRESIDENT, WHAT DID HE SAY TO YOU?
HE PRAYED WITH ME.

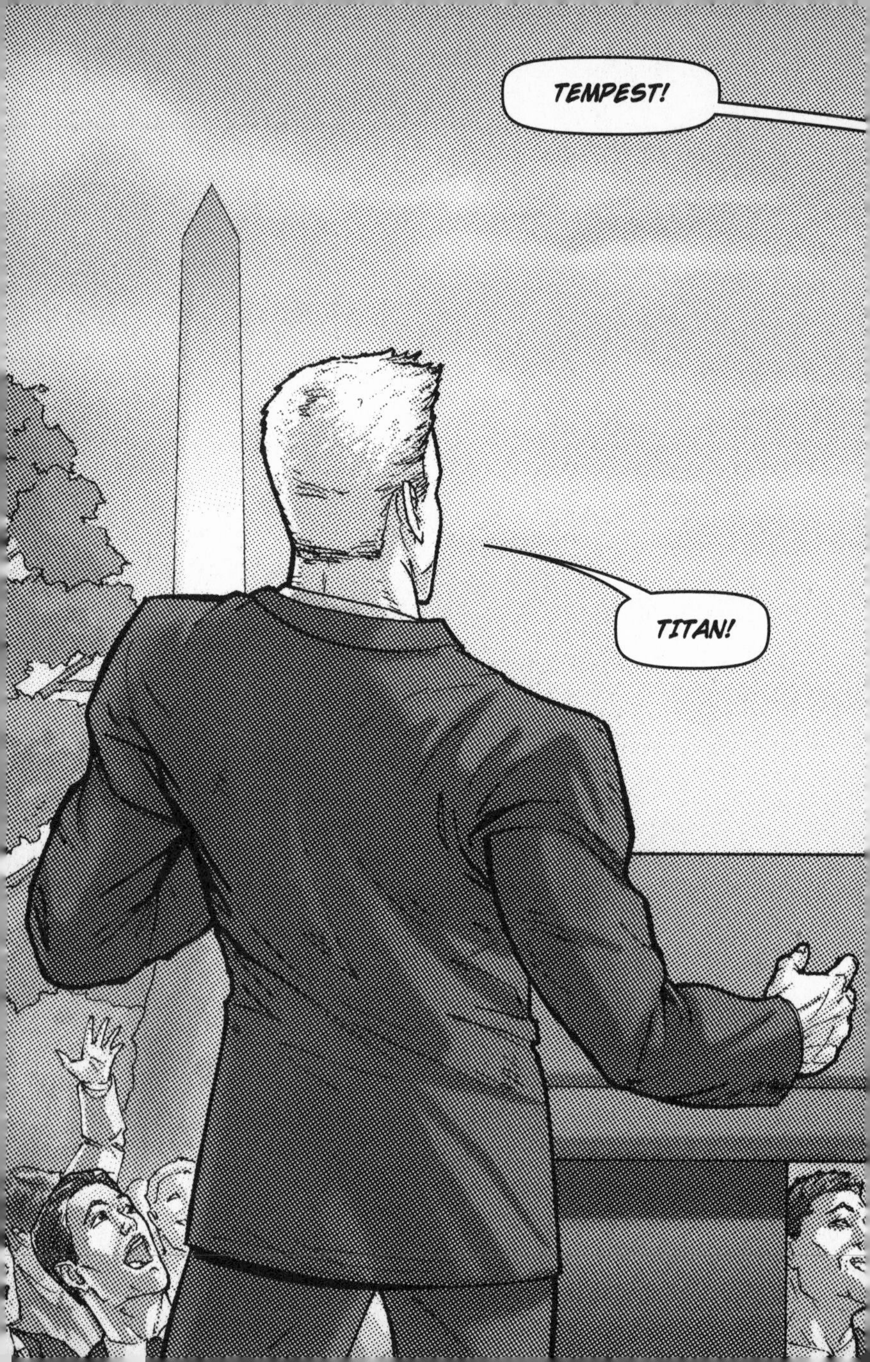
TEMPEST!
TITAN!

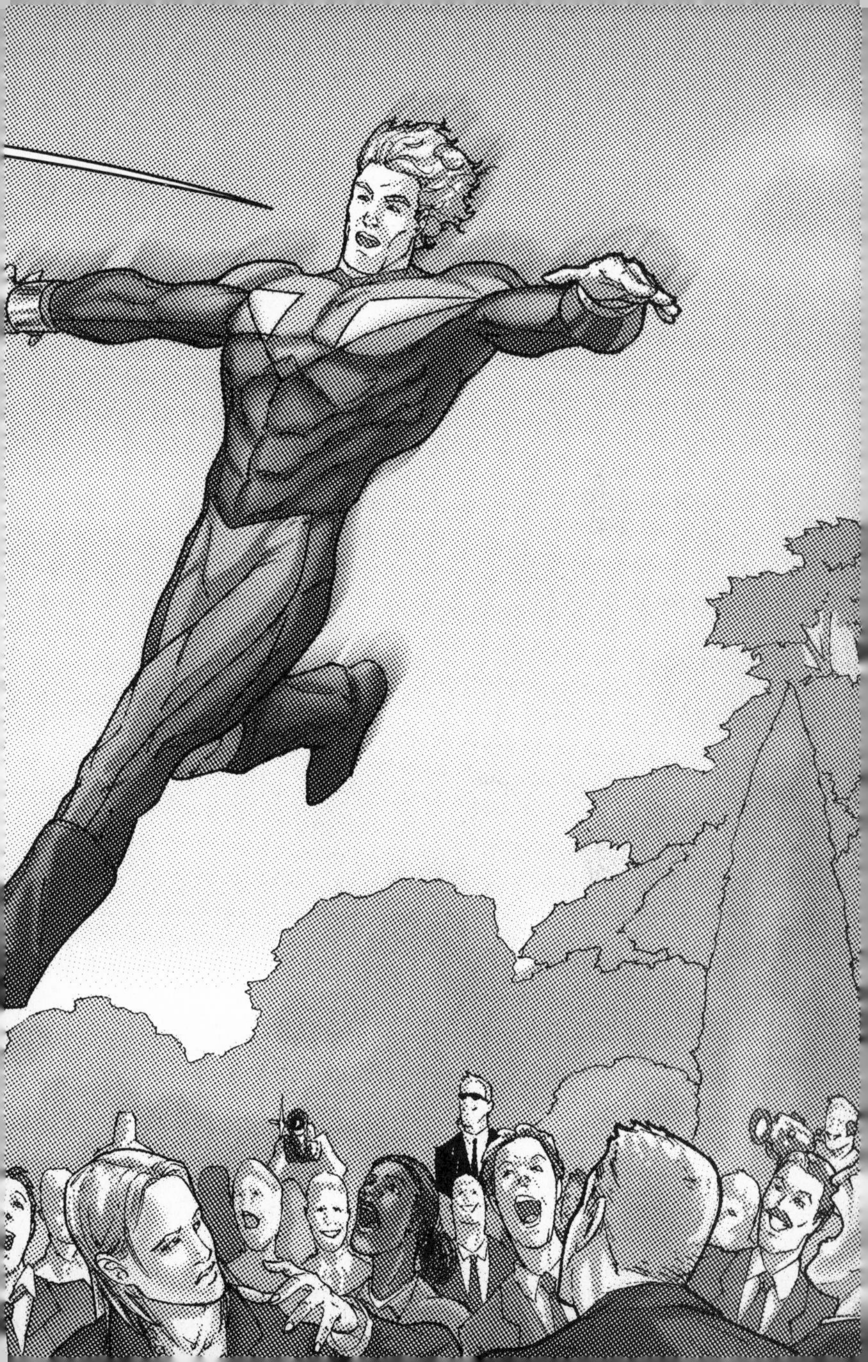

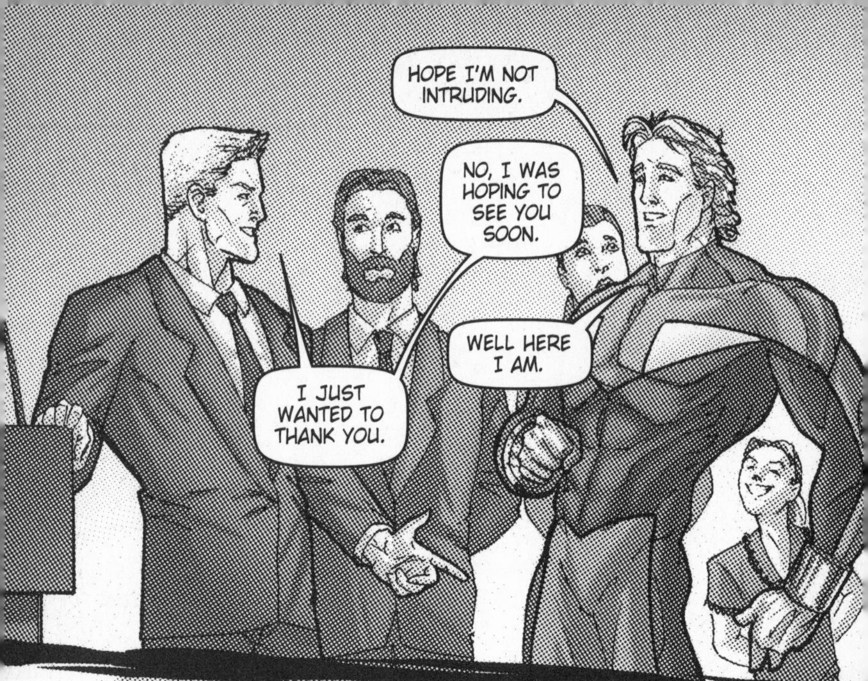
HOPE I'M NOT INTRUDING.
NO, I WAS HOPING TO SEE YOU SOON.
WELL HERE I AM.
I JUST WANTED TO THANK YOU.

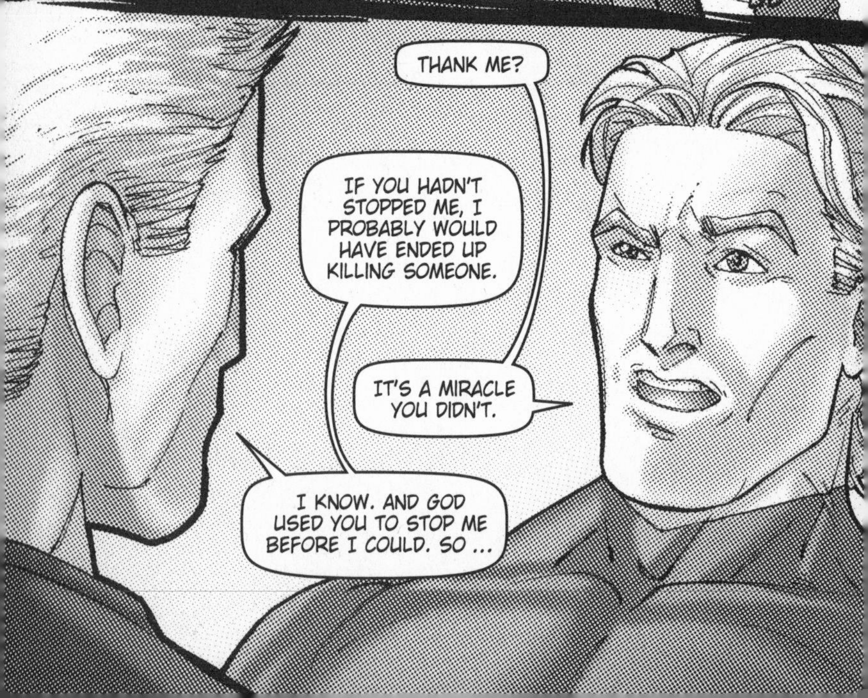
THANK ME?
IF YOU HADN'T STOPPED ME, I PROBABLY WOULD HAVE ENDED UP KILLING SOMEONE.
IT'S A MIRACLE YOU DIDN'T.
I KNOW. AND GOD USED YOU TO STOP ME BEFORE I COULD. SO ...

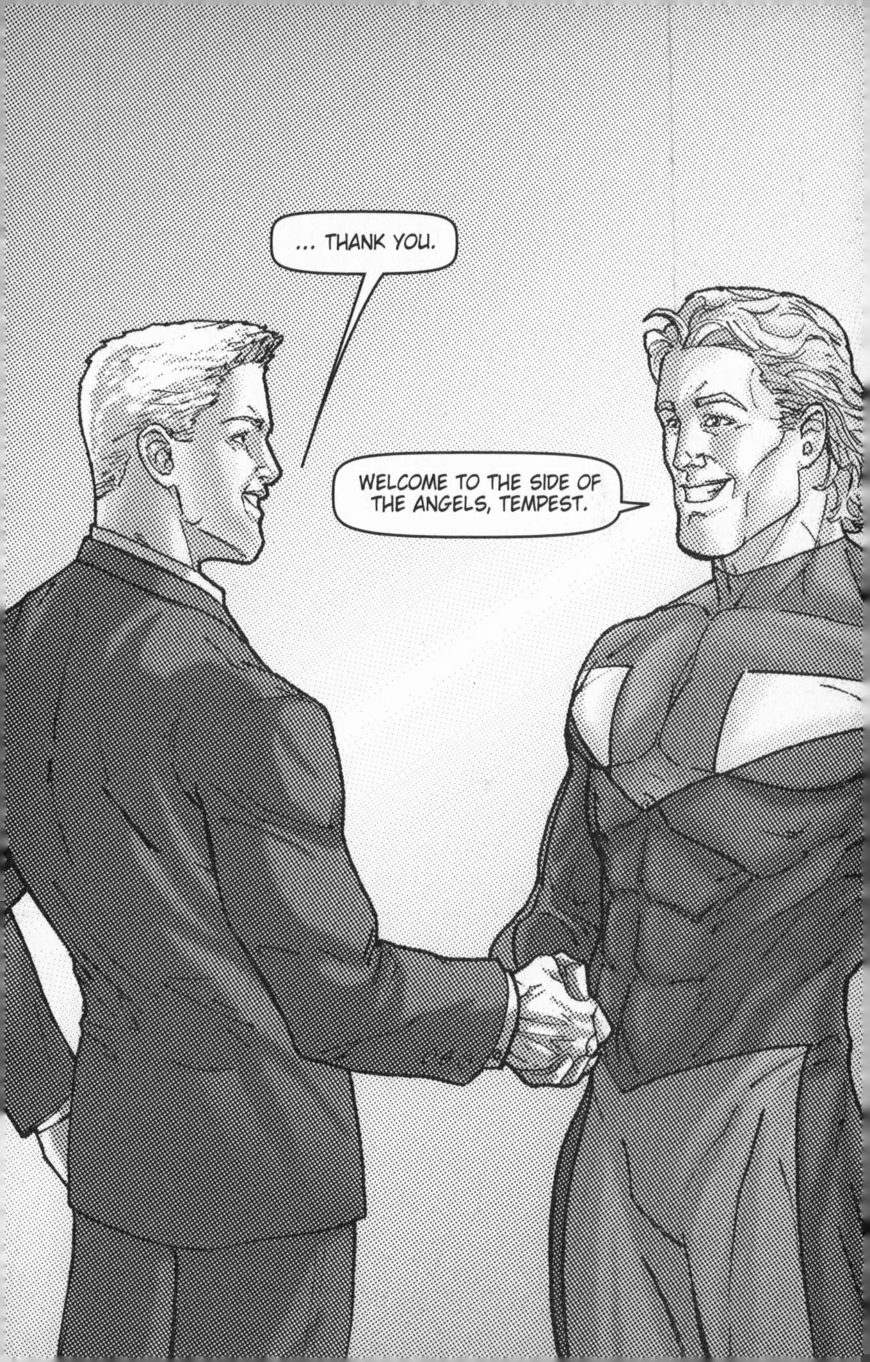
... THANK YOU.
WELCOME TO THE SIDE OF THE ANGELS, TEMPEST.

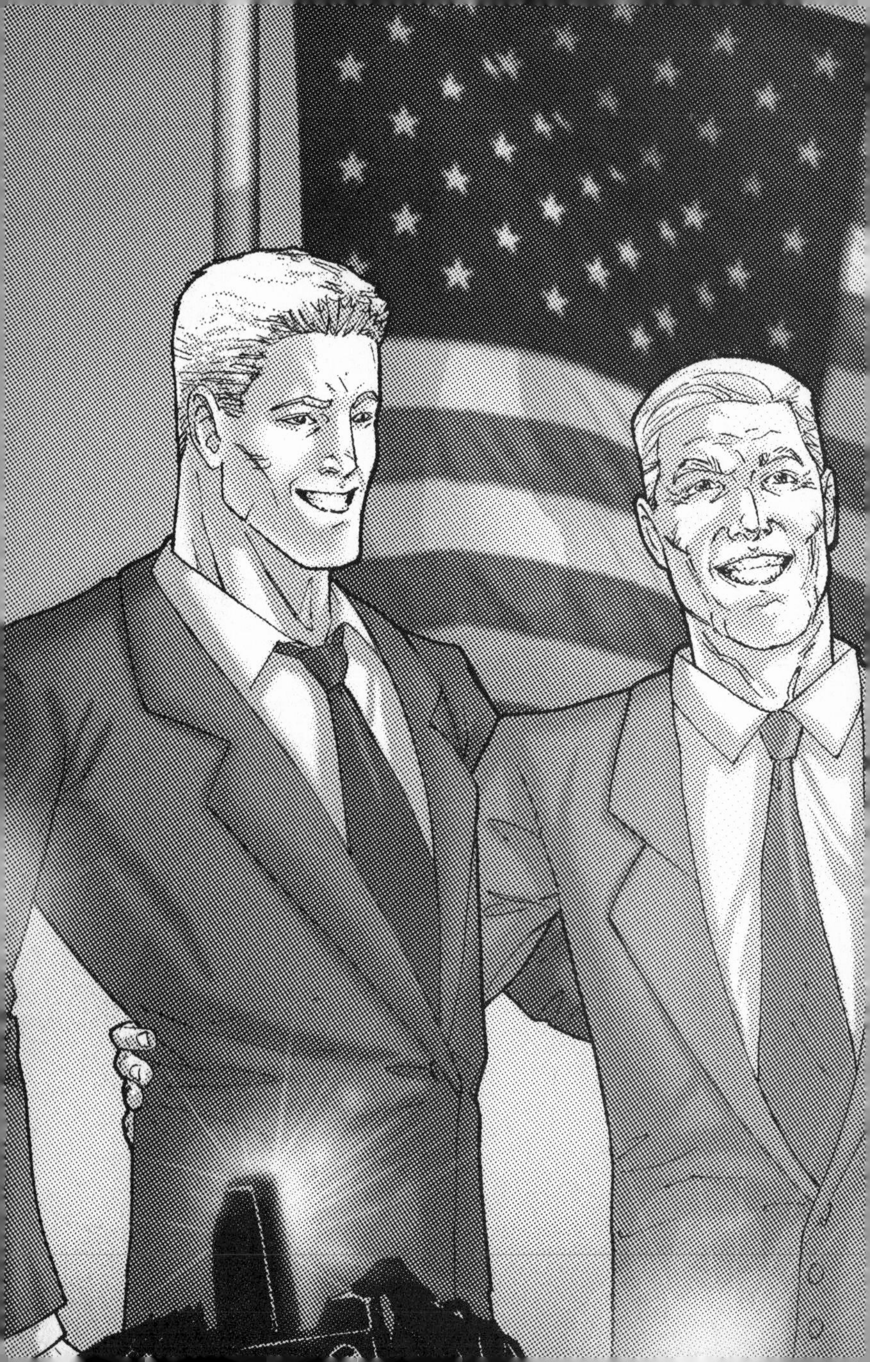

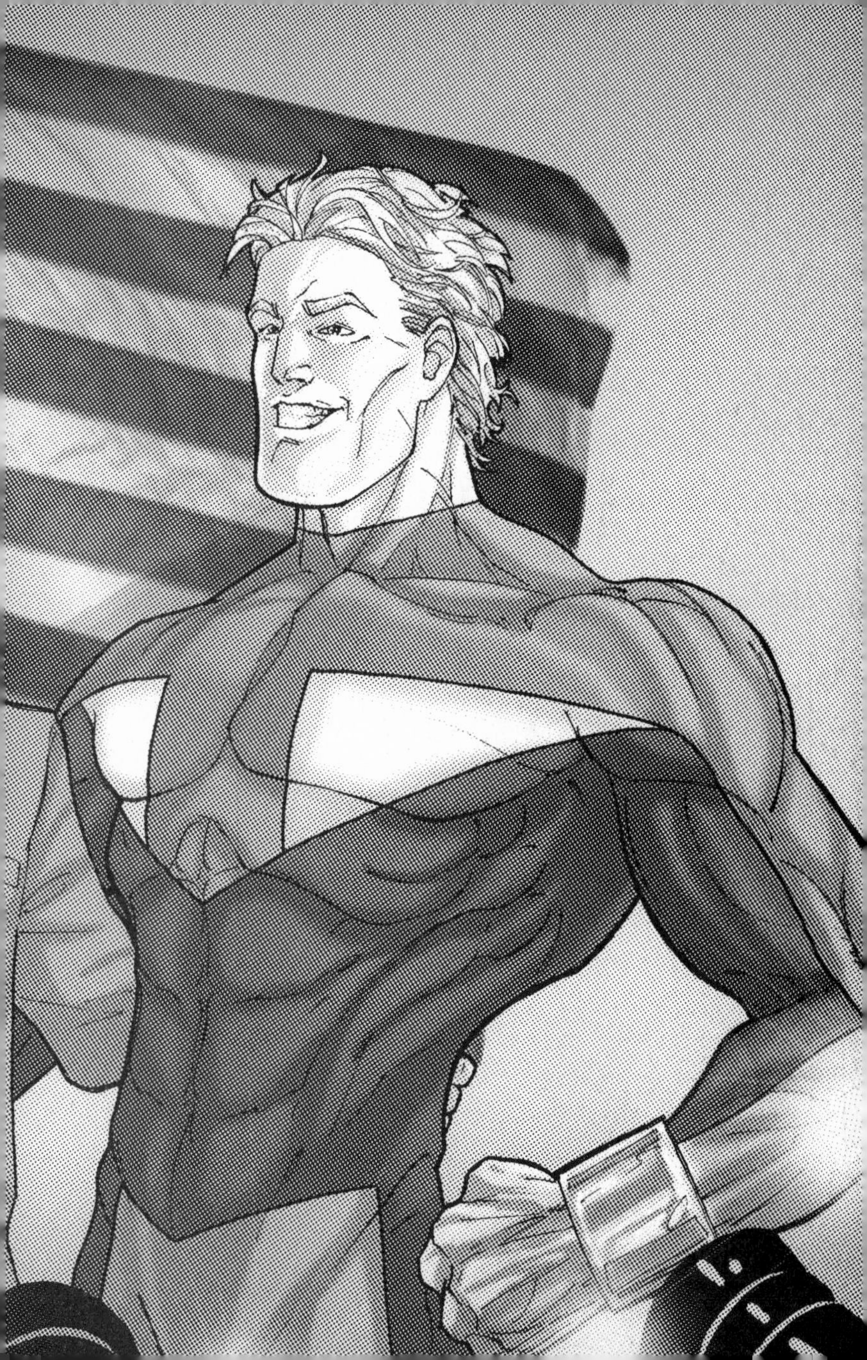

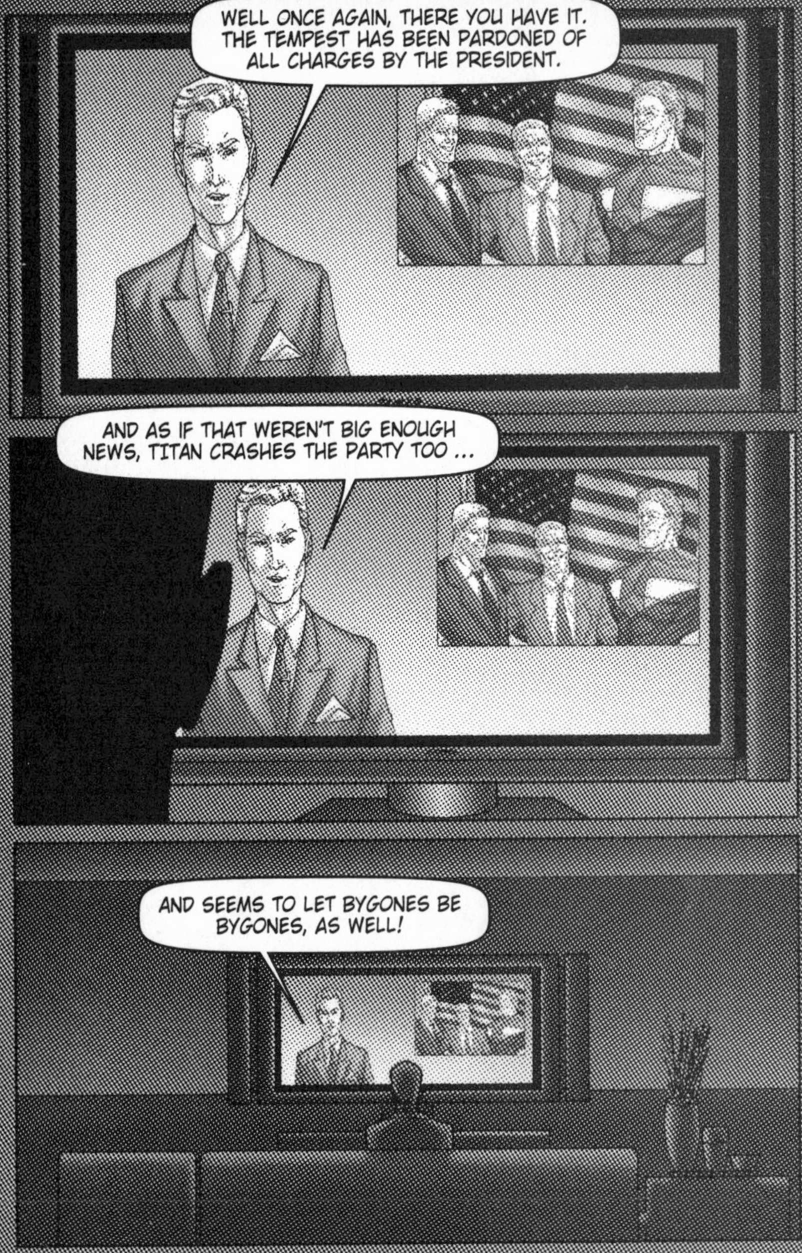
WELL ONCE AGAIN, THERE YOU HAVE IT. THE TEMPEST HAS BEEN PARDONED OF ALL CHARGES BY THE PRESIDENT.
AND AS IF THAT WEREN'T BIG ENOUGH NEWS, TITAN CRASHES THE PARTY TOO ...
AND SEEMS TO LET BYGONES BE BYGONES, AS WELL!

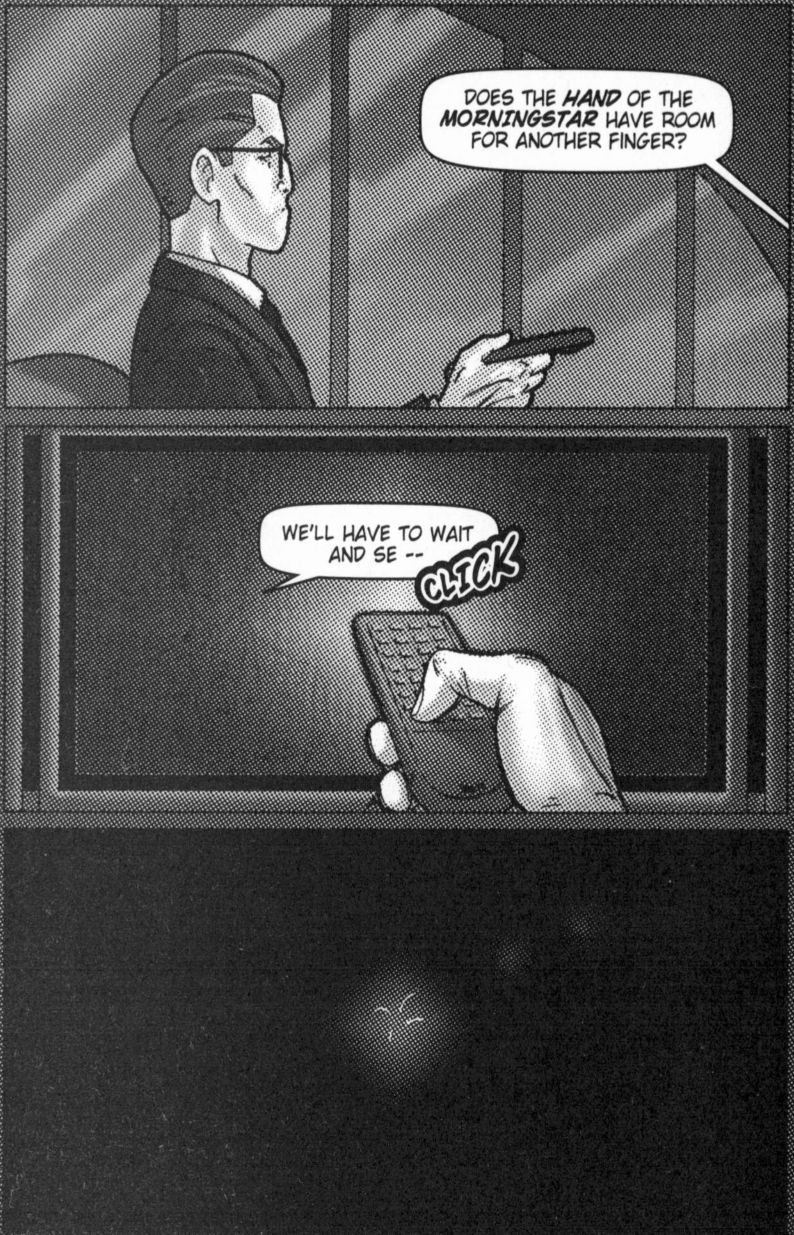
DOES THE ***HAND*** OF THE ***MORNINGSTAR*** HAVE ROOM FOR ANOTHER FINGER?
WE'LL HAVE TO WAIT AND SE --
CLICK

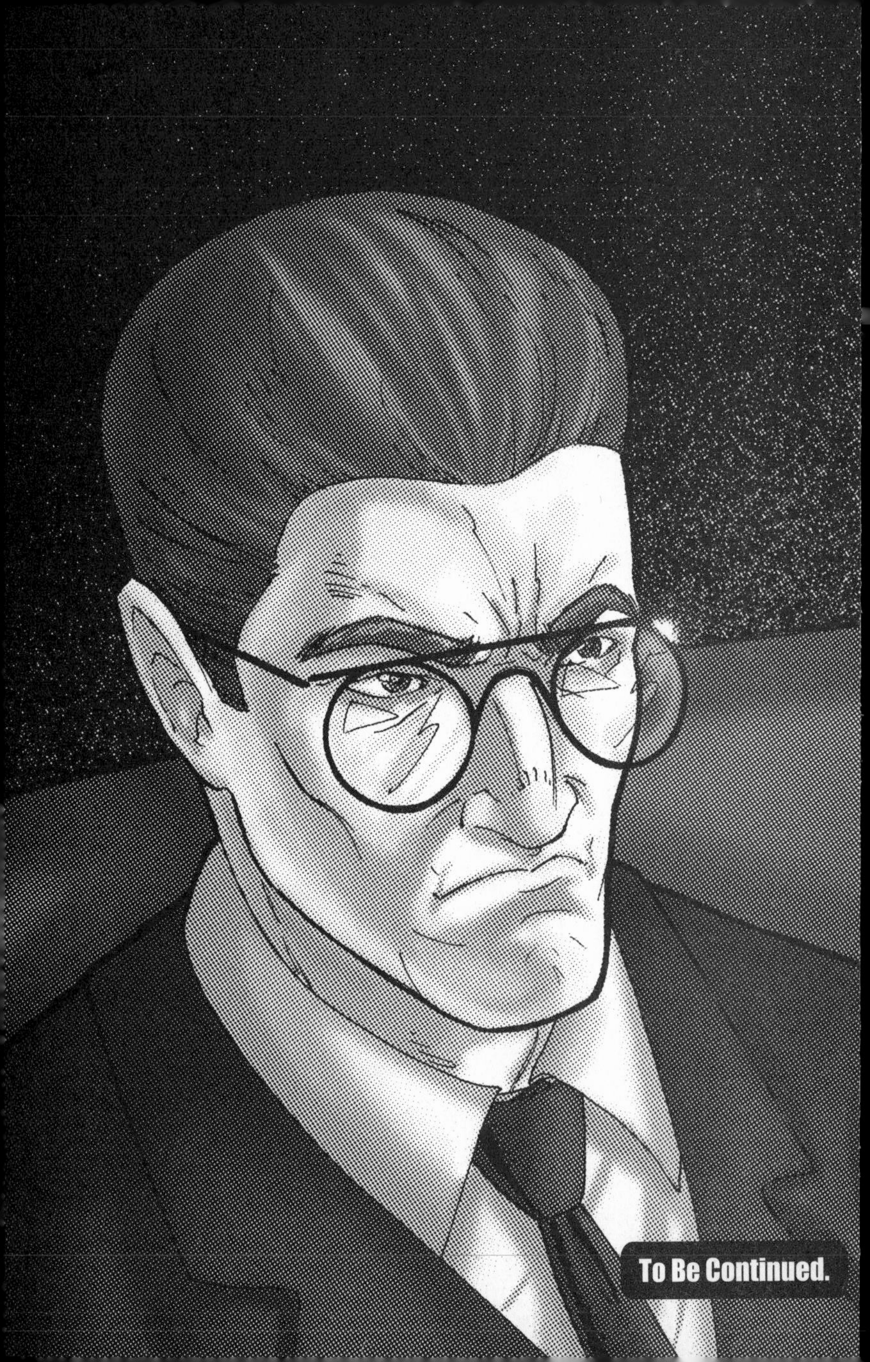
To Be Continued.

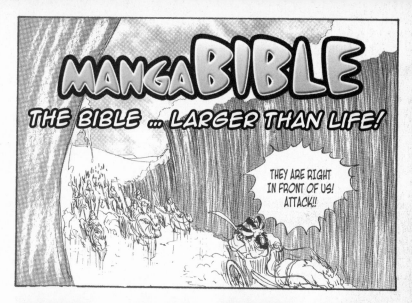

MANGA BIBLE

THE BIBLE ... LARGER THAN LIFE!

THEY ARE RIGHT IN FRONT OF US! ATTACK!!

Names, Games, and the Long Road Trip

Available Now!

Walls, Brawls, and the Great Rebellion

Available Now!

Fights, Flights, and the Chosen Ones

Available Now!

Traitors, Kings, and the Big Break

Available May 2008!

AVAILABLE AT YOUR LOCAL BOOKSTORE!

VOLUMES 5–8 COMING SOON!

GRAPHIC NOVELS

STUDENT BY DAY, NINJA AT NIGHT!

I Was an Eighth-Grade Ninja

Available Now!

My Double-Edged Life

Available Now!

Child of Destiny

Available Now!

The Argon Deception

Available May 2008!

AVAILABLE AT YOUR LOCAL BOOKSTORE!

VOLUMES 5-8 COMING SOON!

GRAPHIC NOVELS

Son of Samson

INCREDIBLE STRENGTH, HEROIC BATTLES, AND HUMOROUS ANTICS!

The Judge of God
Available Now!

The Daughter of Dagon
Available Now!

The Maiden of Thunder
Available Now!

The Raiders of Joppa
Available May 2008!

AVAILABLE AT YOUR LOCAL BOOKSTORE!

VOLUMES 5–8 COMING SOON!

ZONDERVAN®

FLYING THROUGH TIME TO SAVE THE WORLD!

Pyramid Peril
Available Now!

Turtle Trouble
Available Now!

Berlin Breakout
Available Now!

Tunnel Twist-Up
Available May
2008!

AVAILABLE AT YOUR LOCAL BOOKSTORE!

VOLUMES 5-8 COMING SOON!

Kingdoms
A Biblical Epic

THE PEOPLE OF JUDAH CAUGHT BETWEEN THE CLASH OF EMPIRES.

The Coming Storm

Available Now!

Scions of Josiah

Available Now!

The Prophet's Oracle

Available Now!

Valley of Dry Bones

Available May 2008!

AVAILABLE AT YOUR LOCAL BOOKSTORE!

VOLUMES 5–8 COMING SOON!

 ZONDERVAN®

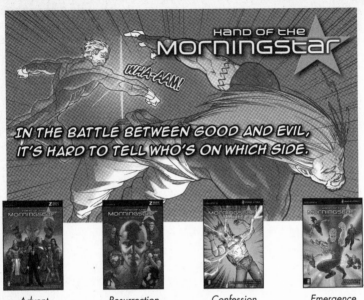

HAND OF THE MORNINGSTAR

WHA-AAM!

IN THE BATTLE BETWEEN GOOD AND EVIL,
IT'S HARD TO TELL WHO'S ON WHICH SIDE.

Advent
Available Now!

Resurrection
Available Now!

Confession
Available Now!

Emergence
Available May 2008!

AVAILABLE AT YOUR LOCAL BOOKSTORE!

VOLUMES 5-8 COMING SOON!

ZONDERVAN®

We want to hear from you. Please send your comments
about this book to us in care of zreview@zondervan.com. Thank you.

Grand Rapids, MI 49530
www.zonderkidz.com

ZONDERVAN.com/
AUTHORTRACKER
follow your favorite authors